Medicine Man I

The Chief of All Time

A novel

by

S.R. Howen

Wild Child Publishing.com
Culver City, California

Medicine Man I: The Chief Of All Time
Copyright © 2012 by S.R. Howen

Cover illustration by Tinker Productions
© 2012
For information on the cover art, please contact pookeybear291@gmail.com

All rights reserved. No part of this book may be reproduced or transmitted in any form without written permission from the publisher, except by a reviewer who may quote brief passages for review purposes. If you are reading this book and you did not buy it at one of our certified distributors, receive it as a loan from a library or a certified distributor, win it in a contest, or buy at our site, you may have a pirated copy. Please delete it from your computer and purchase it legally. Pirating hurts the entire publishing community.

This book is a work of fiction and any resemblance to any person, living or dead, any place, events or occurrences, is purely coincidental. The characters and story lines are created from the author's imagination or are used fictitiously.

Editor: Marci Baun

ISBN: 978-1-61798-065-7

If you are interested in purchasing more works of this nature, please stop by www.wildchildpublishing.com.

Wild Child Publishing.com
P.O. Box 4897
Culver City, CA 90231-4897

Printed in The United States of America

Author's Note

This is, of course, a work of fiction. Any resemblance to people living or dead is strictly coincidence. Resemblances to places, traditions, and practices by any of the American Indian tribes mentioned is intentional, and purposely fictionalized and mixed together, to protect the sanctity of those spiritual ceremonies. Although based on truth and actual practices, they do not give away any kept secrets.

I'd also like to thank the members of Group 6, you know who you are, for first reads and support during the writing of this book. S. A. Maethyn and Debi C, thank you for your help with marketing and sales.

S.R. Howen

Often in the stillness of the night, when all nature seems asleep about me, there comes a rapping at the door of my heart. I open it; and a voice inquires, "What of your People? What will their future be?" My answer is, "Mortal man has not the power to draw aside the veil of unborn time to tell the future of his race. That gift belongs of the Divine alone. But it is given to him to closely judge the future by the present, and the past."
--Simon Pokagon of the Potawatomi

What Came Before

Dangling by her leg, still wet from birth, the newborn howled along with the wind. The man grasping her thin leg looked at the silent lodges of the village. How could they still be asleep? How could they have not heard?

"Stay back," he commanded. His voice shook with his fear.

"Please, please give me my child."

He looked at the face of his wife twisted in anguish and still covered with the sweat of childbirth. She knelt in the pelting snow grasping a deerskin she had decorated for the daughter she hadn't yet held, spatters of birthing blood decorated the snow near her. He felt more fear of her blood than the evil spawned child.

"You saw her eyes; you saw them," he said.

"Husband, please, it was nothing, a trick of the light. Please, she will freeze."

The infant's wails stopped. She no longer wiggled in his grasp. A thin tendril of pain gripped his chest. He'd touched his wife's stomach, felt their child move under his hand, not an evil thing. Not a monster with glowing eyes that saw into his soul when he'd shoved the lodge cover aside not realizing his wife had gone into labor too quickly for her to get to the birthing lodge and the mid-wife. That alone added to the signs--the child was not human.

Hadn't it happened before? Certainly it had--a woman's pains came too quickly and the child's urgency to join the world too fast for the mother to leave her home. Everything inside would have to be burned that was all--burn everything and start new.

But in the dead of winter? What child would curse her parents so? He held his daughter up expecting her face to be blue and death to have taken her. In time, his wife would understand.

Large brown eyes stared back at him from a pink face. A trick of the wind made infant laughter spring from the trees around his lodge. Why had they chosen this isolated corner among the trees? At night, branches brushed the sides of the lodge, and the woods creaked and groaned with spirits. How could he have thought his child would be fine--when the very first night they'd slept in this winter camp he'd heard voices in the woods? Night after night until he believed the words of his wife and the medicine man: the wind in the trees made the sounds, no one stood in the woods tormenting him.

The child blinked her large eyes. Not green now. Not glowing. He'd been cursed on every hunt. Others landed fat deer, numerous quail, fat rabbits and even the old men came upon a lost buffalo bull. He came home with a thin half-starved squirrel, if luck favored him at all.

His wife cowered in the snow; her silent sobs made her shoulders shake. Her fault. How else could this have happened? She never wanted the others in their home. The mid-wife had never come to see them, and his wife never went into the village center. She always stayed out here, away from everyone else.

He knew what he had to do. He couldn't lose what little he had. When he started towards the circle of lodges and the bright central fire of the meeting circle, his wife scrambled to her feet and started to follow him, making noises that echoed in his head, but didn't form words. She became an annoying insect swarm of sound, and he smacked that sound away, taking step after step through the blowing snow. He'd leave the child. He couldn't kill it. No, that would only make whatever evil had spawned it angrier. If he took his wife and his belongings and left, the blizzard would hide them, no one would even miss them if they ever realized they were there to start with.

And the evil grasped in his hand would be someone else's problem.

She stood up, undid her jeans, and started lowering them as if I were not staring at her like some lusty teenager. I fled the room and shut the door on her seductive form. I stood in the hallway, leaned against the wall with my eyes shut, and tried to still the passion she invoked in me. I knew she didn't wear a bra; the absent top buttons on her shirt made it obvious. She also didn't wear any underwear. Not unless they were much lower on her hips than her partly lowered jeans. In all my adult life, I had never felt like this before.

"*You could have her. Take her,*" the elk-man's voice echoed.

"You've been too long without a wife," my grandfather said.

"Leave me alone," I said, as much to the elk-man voice as to my grandfather.

"You have been too long without a wife," my grandfather repeated. "Even I remember what it was like to be that *ready* for a woman."

I tried to yank my shirt down farther before I opened my eyes to tell him to mind his own business. I got a good view of his back as he went into the guest room. The door shut with a firm thump. The sound of the lock turning made me shake my head.

My grandfather was at his exasperating best. Later, he would wander out of there to raid the refrigerator for whatever he could find. I went into the kitchen and put the teakettle on the stove. The burner lit with a faint whoosh, and I experienced a flash of the medicine dances I'd attended in my youth. The tribal medicine man would throw fine sulfur dust into the fire to make it do the same thing. A grand show, as was everything medicine men did. None of their tricks had worked for my father.

My father, being a firm believer in the old ways, wouldn't seek out modern medicine past the point of being told he had terminal cancer. He wouldn't even consider modern healing mixed with the old beliefs. My own mother turned her back on me after he died.

The teapot shrilled, and Morning Dove's voice came from the doorway. "I am very tired."

I took a mug from the shelf above the sink. From a different cupboard, I took down the box of nighttime tea I kept there. I added water and tea to the mug and watched the steam for a moment, before I held it out to her.

"It will help you sleep," I said when she just looked at the cup.

"I have had enough white-man's medicines put into me already." Her eyes flashed with what I took for humor.

Chapter One
Chance by Design

    I parked the Jag in the usual spot, well away from the trees and the unwelcome contributions the birds always delivered to the reflective midnight-black paint. The front bumper blocked the pedestrian crossing; recognized wealth had its advantages. The police wouldn't ticket the car. From the sidewalk, I surveyed the small kiosk before me.

    For many years, it had been a concession stand serving those who frequented Lake Side Park. After undergoing major renovation, it bore the name Salaam's Kebabs. Instead of hotdogs and hamburgers, it would now sell gyros and the side items to go with them: stuffed grape leaves, Greek salads, rice, and fries. The park offered a good place to try out this new venture. On a tour of Europe, I couldn't get enough of the sandwiches the European kiosks sold and the wonderful cucumber sauce, *tzatziki*, they put on them.

    A stiff breeze came in off the lake. I pulled my hair out of my face and dug in my pocket to find the leather lace I always kept there and tied it back. My father had worn his hair in braids his entire life. My grandfather never failed to point out, as a man of *the Niitsitapii, The Real People*, my hair belonged in braids. I no longer lived among The People, much less on a reservation, so I let mine hang free all the way to my waist.

    Dried leaves, now free from a Wisconsin winter's snow, skittered across the red bricks of the patio. The benches wore fresh coats of gray paint. The tables had new matching surfaces with closed red and white striped umbrellas springing from their centers. Things looked ready for the Memorial Day weekend opening when the park would be full of holiday revelers. I glanced at my watch. It would be more than an hour before Carlos, the cook and manager of the kiosk, showed up. I hated any reference to *Indian time* so I always arrived early. In life, there might be time enough for everything, but I saw nothing wrong with *the everything* being on time.

    Black storm clouds were piling up in great angry layers on the horizon. An icy wind whisked across the surface of the lake and whipped the water into a froth of white-capped waves. The air felt charged with electrical current and smelled of freshly thawed earth. It would rain soon; most likely it would be a true thunder banger. The weekend forecast called for clear skies and sunshine, but I put little faith in those weather predictors of Television Station, WTMQ. They were wrong more than they were right.

Near the edge of the lakefront, barely out of reach of the waves crashing against the shore, a woman sat on the back of an olive-drab park bench with her bare feet on the worn seat. Many people sat the same way. Her lack of shoes struck me as odd since winter still lingered in the chill breeze. The way she sat puzzled me the most. Her arms were outstretched and her palms turned skyward. Her oversized red and black flannel shirt flapped, scarecrow-like, in the breeze. The gray watch-cap on her head, with her long black ponytail sticking out, only added to the strange picture.

The seagulls hovering around her hands dashed in to snap up whatever food she offered them. Occasionally, a bird would land on her arm and grab more than its share. She didn't move and her arm never wavered, as if the weight of the large birds meant nothing.

A rolled-up sleeping bag, a bulging backpack, and a pair of worn men's work boots, sat under the bench. *Great.* The season hadn't even started and already homeless people were waiting to raid the trash bins.

A huge wave crashed into the breaker rocks. Momentarily drowning out all other sounds, it sent a spray of water several feet into the air. One of the gulls squawked and screeched. The bench-sitter grasped a completely white gull around its legs. It beat against her arm with its wings. With an arched neck, it drove its large sharp beak against the flesh of her hand. My stomach turned at the thought of this homeless woman killing the bird and eating it raw.

I extracted my money clip from my pants pocket, unrolled the bills, and peeled off three fives from the outside. I placed the ones around the hundreds left inside before I shoved it back into my pocket. With determined steps, I made my way to the bench. I would offer the fifteen dollars in exchange for the trapped bird's life.

At the bench, despite the bird's upset screams and pecks, the woman turned to look at me. I forgot what I wanted to say. She gazed back at me with startling dark brown eyes, surrounded by a ring of green, set in a face with cheekbones as high as my own. She'd been without enough food for some time judging by the prominence of those bones.

I felt like a boy taken by his first crush. My tongue wouldn't work. I just stared at her. Cliché lines came into my head. I refused to utter any of their nonsense. With her haunting looks, she'd probably heard them a hundred times before. For a fleeting moment, a smile tugged at the corners of her sensuous lips. My ribs felt as if they were constricting the beating of my heart. She could've been some legendary sprite who wanted to steal a man's spirit away. The wind blew in from the lake in a sudden gust that gapped open her shirt to reveal the curve of a shapely breast. I tried to look away.

"Do not just stand there staring at me. Help me," she said. Her voice commanded and aroused me.

Help her? Help her kill the bird? My gaze went to the gull. Bright crimson blood streaked over her hand and yet she didn't let go. I couldn't imagine being so hungry I would ask a stranger to help me kill something. Then I saw it. The bird's feet were tangled in one of those clear plastic things used to hold a six-pack of soda. She struggled to catch the bird's wings while she continued to hold the knife in her hand.

"Drop your knife," I told her. "I have one, if you can capture its wings?"

Her knife hit the ground with a sodden thump. Without it in her hand, she held the bird tightly around its body with its wings pinned. She turned it so its black feet were in the air. I worked quickly to open my knife and slice through the offending plastic. Once the bird's feet were free, one leg dangled like a broken twig. Only a bit of flesh held the lower leg to the upper part.

"His lower leg is dead already. Slice it the rest of the way off," she instructed as if there would be no question of my compliance.

I looked at the knife in my hand and switched my attention to the bird. It watched us with its small black eyes and its yellow beak slightly open as if it knew we were helping it.

"The other birds will pick at it like a worm and damage the rest of his leg if you do not."

With a quick nod, I slid the blade of my knife through the small flap of flesh. The bird didn't move or squawk. With a radiant smile, the woman scrambled down off the bench and moved to the turbulent lake's edge. Once there, she tossed the bird into the air. It let out an indignant screech, faltered in the air, and flew out over the lake.

"It was used to flying with that thing around its legs," she said to me when she returned to the bench. After a quick rummage through her backpack, she came up with one of those water bottles everyone seemed to carry around. Only a bit of white paper still ringed the blue plastic. She must have refilled the same one repeatedly. She used her teeth to pull the black sport-cap open and began to pour water over the gouges covering her wrist and hand. I shuddered at the thought of how much bacteria lived in the water, and now occupied the wound, on top of what the bird left behind.

"Don't do that. I have a first-aid kit in my car. You don't want those to get infected."

Her gaze met mine, went to the street and to the Jag. She continued to pour water over her hand. "I am not going near your car."

I could see why she would be frightened, or at least cautious. I stood more than seven feet tall and worked hard to stay close to three hundred pounds with low body fat. She stood a bit more than five feet and looked as half-starved as a feral cat. In long strides, I covered the area to my car and came back with the first-aid kit. Taking out a bottle of iodine, I opened it and held it out to her.

"Set it down." Mistrust colored her voice.

"I'm trying to help you."

"You ever been raped?" she asked me with a cold glint in her eyes.

"What? No, of course not," I said quickly. I set the bottle down, took out a roll of gauze, and set it down as well. "Cover the whole area with the iodine. Let it dry before you roll the gauze around it. You'll need to change the bandage twice a day, so the scabs don't grow into it." I set another roll of gauze down. "It doesn't look like any of those need stitches."

"Thank you, *doctor*," she said. Her voice carried a biting edge.

I reached into my back pocket and took out my gold-plated card case. From it, I withdrew one of my business cards. I set it on the bench.

"Shannon Running Deer, trauma surgeon," she read.

"Will you let me look at your hand now?" I asked her.

"Anyone with a computer can make those things."

Her cynical tone, and obvious street sense, led me to believe she wasn't new to the life of the homeless. I couldn't even guess her age. Sixteen, maybe seventeen, and yet she seemed far older. She had to be in her twenties. The good old Fond du Lac police were hard on underage runaways and the homeless. Minors got funneled into the hospital before their parents were located. After which, social services returned the lucky kids to whatever abusive situation they'd escaped from in the first place. Justice at work.

"Will you at least let me buy you something to eat?"

Her stare cut right into me. Her gaze went to the Jag and flashed back to me.

"I am not. . ."

"Getting in my car," I finished for her. I held up my hand. "We can walk. The 101 Club is at the end of the street."

"I am certainly dressed for dinner." She laughed while she continued the struggle to wrap the gauze around her injured hand. I smiled. Her laughter sounded completely natural, almost childlike--filled with playful innocence. It gave me an idea of what she would be like if the streets weren't her home.

"The Wharf? They have a bar where the fishermen pick up sandwiches. You can walk on the other side of the street," I said with a shrug and a smile of reassurance.

She looked down the street toward the lighthouse. Just beyond it, The Wharf restaurant stood. Did she find food in their dumpsters? With a grunt, she moved around the bench and shoved her feet into the scuffed work boots. She tied their speed laces with a quick yank and tucked the frayed ends inside the top of them. They were Army surplus. I'd spent ten years in the same sort of boots. She slung her backpack over her shoulder, picked up her sleeping bag, and started for the sidewalk without a backward glance to see if I followed. I trailed behind her in silence all the way to The Wharf.

"They are not going to let me in there." We ducked under the flapping blue awning in front of the door together.

"You'll be with me. They'll let you in." I moved around her to open the door. She sprang away from me like a cat whose tail had gotten stepped on. I stared at her for a long moment. I'd expected her to smell unwashed. Instead, the scent surrounding her was musky, in a raw outdoors way--a bit of wood-smoke and clean skin, overlaid with something exotic and arousing. I swallowed hard and cleared my throat.

"I know the owners," I told her.

In one graceful motion, she sat on the sidewalk and crossed her arms over her chest.

"All right. I'll bring you something. What do you like?"

She pulled her knees up and rested her head on them. "Anything hot," she answered, her voice muffled.

When I returned with a large order of the soup of the day, a hot ham sandwich, and a huge green apple, I expected her to be gone.

She still sat in the same position.

"Glad you waited."

In one fluid movement, she got to her feet. Her tongue went over her lips. I knew she could smell the food. Her apprehensive, wide-eyed look reminded me of a caged panther. She mirrored the same seductive form, standing totally still, yet tense with the desire to bolt--watching, waiting--expecting treachery in some form. Carefully, I set the bag with the food in it on the walk in front of her and backed up a step.

She rushed forward and snatched up the bag. I almost expected her to devour the meal right there while I watched. Instead, she straightened her back and met my gaze again.

"I thank you for the food."

With the bag clasped tightly, she stepped off the walk. The thin fog rolling in off the lake entwined itself catlike around her feet and legs, making it look like she floated above the blacktop.

"Would you tell me your name?" I called after her.

"I am called Morning Dove. My People are the *Siksika* of Silver Creek."

The Blackfoot of Silver Creek? Impossible. What would someone from my ancestral tribe be doing here this far from Canadian Alberta? It seemed an odd coincidence.

"Excuse me, sir. I believe you dropped something."

I turned to look at the man behind me and down at the quarter he pointed at. With a grunt, I waved him off and turned back. I caught only a glimpse of her before she vanished as if the fog devoured her. There didn't seem to be any place she could have hidden so quickly. I shook my head. A chill of unease made its way through my insides. For a brief moment, I thought I'd seen her in a white buckskin dress with her hair in a fan across her back.

Chapter Two
Fate

Carlos eyed his watch when I came over the bridge and crossed the grass to meet him. A speculative smile pulled at his mustached mouth.

"Late today," he said.

"I needed something to eat," I answered.

Carlos and I were good friends. We'd gotten to know each other during stints in the Army. I'd served as an officer, and Carlos as lower enlisted, but we'd found enough common ground to stay in touch. He'd done a full twenty years as a cook. I'd spent my ten years assigned to Infectious Disease Control. My credentials as a trauma surgeon only earned me extra duty at the base hospital when they were understaffed.

"Everything's set to go for Friday. 'Cept the weather," he added with a glance at the gathering storm clouds. The wind gusted and grabbed at the edges of his comb-over hairstyle.

On my drive into town each day, I often saw vagrants asleep under the wooden train-trestle bridge. Most days, I tried not to think of them and their plight, but today there would be a host of them gathered to avoid the coming storm. With a shudder, I remembered the vacant stares of those who watched the cars as they passed, while others lay wrapped in tattered coats and bits of cardboard. I thought of Morning Dove among them. That unpleasant image made me groan; too many young female runaways ended up in the trauma unit--or the morgue. I should have offered her some sort of shelter. And then what? She didn't trust me enough to get into my car. Where would I take her anyway?

"Everything okay, chief?"

"I hate it when you call me chief." Carlos knew that, but it was an old tease. I usually had a comeback of some sort, but I wasn't in the mood for mild banter.

"Okay, Medicine Man," he answered with a laugh that crinkled the flesh around his brown eyes. I ignored his barbs and unlocked the door to the kiosk. Inside, everything waited, clean and set to go. The three upright rotisseries were shiny and new, ready to roast their first meat. The local bakery would deliver fresh bread Friday morning before the ten a.m. opening time. The front windows could be opened, and Carlos would serve the food from there. We didn't need an indoor seating area. Carlos went about checking the clear plastic bins under the front counter. Just like every year, he would recheck everything several times before opening day.

Outside the back door, I examined the new dumpsters provided by the city. More places were using them. They were tall, narrow affairs, bright blue plastic, with domed lids and a place for a padlock on the front.

"The bums won't be diggin' in here this season," Carlos said behind me.

I grunted what I thought he would take for agreement. An hour ago, the fact would have pleased me greatly. Now, I shuddered at the thought. It would be a useless risk to climb over the fence and find it impossible to get into the dumpster. The street-people had been faceless for me. They weren't nymphs with shining fathomless eyes a man could get lost in. They weren't people who'd risk injury to help a wild bird. And they weren't American Indians. They were odoriferous, wizened old men who drank too much and were too lazy to get a normal job.

"This year, I'd like to put the overage from the day outside the fence--in a box."

Carlos' mouth gaped when he looked at me. "What?"

"I trust you. The waste has always been incredibly low. Doesn't it make more sense for someone to use what we would throw out, rather than fill the dump with it?" Strangely enough, I thought of the gull with its feet twisted up in something tossed aside by humans.

"Somethin' up with you, chief?"

Disregarding his bait, I took out my money clip and pulled out a fifty. I held it out to him. "There's a tiny nymph of a woman; this morning, she used that bench to feed the gulls." I nodded my head in the direction of the bench where Morning Dove had caught the bird. "I'm on call all weekend, Friday through Monday, so I may not be here. She's American Indian--a cousin of some sort. You see her; you make sure she gets a good-sized sandwich. All four days, if I'm not here."

Carlos took the cash and went inside without saying a word. I could have told him to give her the sandwiches for free. I wouldn't start doing that. For several moments, I stared out at the choppy lake. The clouds swirled and tumbled over each other while bright lightning slashed across the sky before it hit the water. The distant thunder sounded like the drums that accompanied my grandfather when he performed medicinal chants. Completely absurd. The reservation existence had died a lifetime ago for me.

It hadn't ended for my grandfather. He still lived on the reservation and embraced the life of impoverishment it offered. I spoke with him about once a month. He always told me the same thing. *"The People need your medicine. The Great-Elk marked you. You will return."*

I invariably replied, *"Grandfather, I have left that life. It's something we all need to do. There's nothing on the dusty reservation, except despair and poverty. It's time we moved on."*

There would be several seconds of silence on the other end of the phone before he would say, *"You will confront the evil consuming your soul. I have seen it on a vision quest."*

I took a deep breath to dispel the memory of my grandfather's words. Why did meeting Morning Dove make me think of him? It couldn't be possible my grandfather had sent Morning Dove to try to drag me back to the godforsaken-reservation. When I walked back through the kiosk, I glanced at Carlos. He followed me all the way to the Jag. I unlocked the door, got inside, and rolled down the window.

"If there are any problems, you have my pager number. Leave a message. You can call David--he's the guy taking care of my horses right now, if it's not too important. He'll get the message to me." Carlos hated talking to voicemail.

"Maybe people'll drive slow and sober this weekend," Carlos said.

He didn't offer any words of farewell. Instead, with his hands in his pockets, he stood very still while he examined the tops of his black loafers. He needed to say more. I waited to give him time to think of how he wanted to say it. He looked off to the other side of the street and ran his fingers through his thin, salt and pepper hair before he absently patted the narrow swath back into place over his bare head. Green-uniformed park attendants stood in the dry fountain basin. It was supposed to be operational by the weekend. Last year, it hadn't worked for several months due to vandalism.

"Shane, we've known each other some twenty years now. This woman--a relative of yours--why don't you just take her in or somethin'?" Carlos kept his gaze on the park workers while he spoke.

I refused to tell him a tiny homeless woman had spooked the

daylights out of me. What explanation could I give him for not offering her more than some food?

"What did you think the first time you laid eyes on me?" I asked.

Carlos' face split in a wide grin when he looked at me. "I was thinkin' if all you Indians were as big as you, Custer would have shit his pants rather than fight." His dark eyes lit with understanding.

The Jag came to life with its usual low rumble of power. "Make it a profitable weekend," I told him and rolled the window up as the first splatters of rain hit the windshield.

My pager screeched me to wakefulness on a cold and rainy Friday morning. I didn't have time to think about it. At three a.m., a semi-truck hit a vanload of people on the Lake Butte de Mort Bridge. Mercy Medical Trauma Center in Oshkosh expected more incoming cases than they were equipped to handle from the ten-car pile-up. I lived halfway between Fond du Lac and Oshkosh, so I sped my way down Interstate 41 to my workplace. Almost twenty hours later, I found a cot in the doctor's lounge and slept until my pager shrilled and sent me off the too-small bed in a leap. I'd only gotten four hours of sleep. It was Saturday now. Even inside, the steady whoop-whoop-whoop of the Flight-for-Life helicopter filled the air. I glanced out the window where it hovered, ready to land, before I went out the door.

Doctor John Thompson, one of my colleagues, waited at the entrance to the trauma center. He and a nervous-looking surgical resident already stood in scrubs.

"Shane, you don't want this one. She isn't going to make it. Drunk driver, didn't stop when he hit her." John continued. "Went right over her--after she bounced off the car's hood."

I knew what John wanted. This unlucky woman wasn't going to live, so he would use her as an illustrative surgery for his student--even though the case technically belonged to me. Medical service was supposed to make you hard-hearted. So far, I'd gladly escaped that fate.

"She doesn't have a good start going into this. Police said she's homeless, from Fondy," John added with a slight shrug.

My heart thrashed against my ribs. Morning Dove. I fervently hoped it wasn't her.

The doors flew open ahead of the Flight-for-Life people. They wheeled the victim in right past us. John leapt into action, as did his student. Until I received another call, I would lend my hands as well. Unlike John, I never assumed a patient wasn't going to make it until the fight ended.

I pulled on clean gloves and joined them in the trauma room. To the outsider, it always appeared chaos ruled these trauma rooms. One nurse stood next to the gurney and checked the airway the Flight-for-Life people had started. Another hung a new IV bag of lactated ringers. A third nurse held a tube of blood and wrote on the label for typing so the victim would get the correct stock. The lab would run all the normal stuff as well. Triple gloves for everyone when a homeless person came in. No one wanted AIDS, or any of the other things transmitted by body fluids. Fleas were bad enough.

John worked at the side of the gurney. He moved his gloved hands over the black-haired scalp of the patient while he offered instruction to his student. One of the nurses moved, and I got a good look at the blood-covered face of the woman. For just a moment, I thought it was a child who'd been hit until recognition dawned.

"Morning Dove," I gasped.

John turned to look at me.

Time faltered.

I shoved John aside and moved forward. Morning Dove was barely recognizable. Clearly, she suffered from more than one of the dirty dozen--twelve conditions no doctor wanted to see--even one of them put a patient's life in jeopardy. In combination there was little hope of success. I barked orders to the nurses. Page surgery. I wanted the neurologist-on-call, in the surgical arena. Stat. The Flight-for-Life people always did a field assessment. I snatched the chart out of one of the nurse's hands.

"Shane, you know her?"

I barely nodded. My attention stayed focused on the assessment of her injuries. Depressed skull fracture, combined with chest, abdominal, and most likely pelvic damage. There were fractured bones in her right arm and left ankle. Peritoneal lavage showed massive internal abdominal bleeding. She should have been DOA. I could see why John thought she wasn't going to make it. I squeezed my eyes shut. She would live.

"Damn it, Shane, get the hell out of here. You know better than this. Get out of here." John's voice came to me urgent and concerned. All of us who worked trauma knew the rules. You never worked on a loved one. I didn't love Morning Dove, no matter what strange attachment I felt to her. She needed the most skilled trauma surgeon Wisconsin offered. My success record, and the fact I was at her side, made me that surgeon.

I shoved the stat sheet into John's hands and gave the nurses further orders. Moments later, they rolled Morning Dove down the hall to the surgeries. John grabbed my shoulder. I shoved his hand away.

"It's my call. I'm taking it. She deserves better than to be a heart-beating cadaver for you to teach with."

John recoiled from the anger in my voice. He shook his head and pushed through the swinging doors ahead of me. It was going to be a long fight. My lack of intervention wouldn't be the cause of Morning Dove's death.

Chapter Three
The Old and the New

The steady rhythm of the heart monitor surprised me. After ten hours of surgery, I should have been asleep, but I couldn't leave Morning Dove's side. In the ICU, the nurses came and went, with barely a glance in my direction. The duty personnel on this floor knew me well. The rumor-mill would grind, if it wasn't already, over why I felt the need to hover over this woman. If they'd asked me, I couldn't have told them. I recalled her face as she'd let the gull go and how her eyes sparkled with life when she laughed. Something in her wild, free manner had captured me. I'd known people all my life whom I didn't feel as close to as I did to her.

A man wearing a lab coat slipped into the room and picked up Morning Dove's chart from the holder at the end of the bed. He nodded, let out a disappointed sounding sigh before he put the chart back. I frowned at him.

He wore a blue lab coat with Shilfen Pharmaceuticals stitched on the left pocket. He gave me a smile and a nod.

"Just checking to see if she's one of our vaccine test cases."

I glared at him. Shilfen had a deal with the hospital. The homeless and needy didn't want to go to the Shilfen plant and their labs, so they came here to receive the vaccines Shilfen was working on. All sorts of rumors were going around about it. The most promising claimed they were working on an AIDS vaccine. Thus the reason they wanted the homeless and poor.

"How would her chart tell you if she's one of your lab rabbits?"

"All of the ones we treat here wear an ID bracelet on their ankle. Not easy to get it off, and they don't get their wine money unless they have it." He laughed.

One of Morning Dove's monitors beeped and drew my attention back to her. It was only the normal self-check alert.

"You need sleep," John told me from the doorway. The tech from Shilfen squeezed around John and left. "When was the last time you ate anything?"

I glanced again at the heart monitor and the internal cranium pressure monitor. Both showed results well within normal, *uninjured* readings. All during the surgeries to save her life, I'd expected her to go into cardiac arrest. She'd suffered a heart muscle bruise and a free-floating flail segment of ribs that put bone splinters into her lungs. The shunt to relieve the pressure from the swelling in her brain drained continually. The fluid was a pale clear color without evidence of the blood that should have been there. DOA--she should have been dead-on-arrival. Instead, she lay here doing better than victims with half her injuries.

"Shane, come on, get out of here for a bit," John said gently. He put his hand on my shoulder. "If you weren't on staff, the nurses would have ordered you out of here hours ago."

I reached out and touched the side of Morning Dove's face. My fingers went to the one spot on her cheek not discolored from injuries. I snatched my hand back. What was I doing? John watched me as if horns were suddenly growing out of my head. I did need to get out of Morning Dove's room. With a deep breath, I followed him out into the hall.

John started to speak several times on the trip to the mostly abandoned dining hall. Each time, he stopped. I could guess at his questions. Any answer I gave him would also have been conjecture. I had no idea why I couldn't get Morning Dove out of my thoughts. In the chow line, I mindlessly loaded up my tray with whatever John handed me. He led the way to a table in a secluded corner and pulled a chair out for me. We ate in silence, with only the occasional clang coming from the kitchen, until John cleared his throat.

I looked up at him.

"She's not your normal type," he said.

"What?" I shook my head. "She's not my girlfriend."

"Social services called the floor. They want to know when they can move her to County Hospital."

They took those without insurance and means to County. Shilfen should have had their deal with them. "She's staying right here."

"I don't know what your connection is to her, other than the obvious one. . ."

I gave John an annoyed look.

"I mean you're both Native Americans," John added quickly. He stopped his words with his fork part way raised. He plunked it down and dabbed at his dark face with a thin stiff napkin. "Okay, I got it, American Indian."

"Anyone born here is a Native American," I told him for maybe the fiftieth time.

John let out a sigh, wiped his mouth again. "The police say she didn't have any ID on her. Witnesses said she's been living in the park for a while."

I sat back in the chair and shoved my untouched food away from me. "She's Morning Dove of the Silver Creek People--that makes her a relative of mine." I clasped my hands behind my head and stared up at the glitter-flecked, bumpy white ceiling for a moment. "I met her in the park the other day and decided to help her out. Whether she's a runaway or someone who walked off the reservation, I don't know, but I won't leave her to County."

John shoved a fork full of limp pasta into his mouth. "Your brother called," he said in an even tone.

"And?" I asked. My thoughts were still on Morning Dove. I didn't want to deal with Sam.

"He sounded drunk."

"Great." I snorted. Sam and drunk were synonymous. He even drank when he set up his fair booths and sold his "Made by Native Americans" whatnots. Dream catchers, flutes, medicine pouches containing only sand, chokers made with plastic beads--they all hung in his booth while he played his flute and spouted slurred ancient wisdom.

"He worried me this time--kept ranting about how he had to tell you about what he needed to do."

"What he needed to do?"

John held the fork upside down between his lips for a moment. "Told me he had to listen to the spirit voices," he said. "Muttered on and on about your grandfather taking a nap or something like that. He sounded whacked."

Sam followed tradition in everything--except when it came to the bottle, and the way he drove the Jeep I'd bought for him. He hadn't told me about any visions he'd had for years, though.

"What else did he say?" I toyed with the napkin, wondering briefly why they always chose a nasty shade of brown for recycled products.

"Not much. The other line rang. The nurse wanted me to take it--admin wanting to know why we weren't moving the homeless woman."

I tossed the now balled up napkin on top of my food. "I won't sign the paperwork to move her. She. . ."

"What in the world?" John said suddenly.

A thin, old man stood in the doorway, looking out of place, but with a determined scowl on his face. The glower belonged to my grandfather's deeply creased face. He wore his traditional reservation clothes, jeans and a flannel shirt, with his long white hair in two braids, one over each shoulder. His medicine bag hung easily over one bony shoulder. Before I could stand up, he moved across the floor with an ease that should have been impossible for a man over one hundred years old. How had he gotten here?

"Where is she? I must do the correct sings for her, or she will leave before she should." My grandfather's gaze bored into me, as if he could extract the answer without consent. "Well?" he demanded.

"Who?"

"Why aren't you with her?"

"With who?" I asked in frustration.

"Are you an owl? She is one of *The Niitsitapii*. You should be with her."

"Morning Dove? How did you know she's here?" I asked.

My grandfather looked at John and pursed his lips in a way I knew meant he wouldn't tell me with John present. He would most likely not tell me at all. I shouldn't have asked such a thing in front of the *white-man*, although John didn't qualify as white.

"Come on, I'll take you to her." I got out of my chair. John moved his chair back and started to rise. I shook my head. John settled back down.

In the hallway, my grandfather moved to face me. Despite his age, he stood more than six feet tall. "I am much shamed by you. You know the cleansing that must be done after such a thing. Would you have her spirit cross to the next world, out of harmony?"

"I don't even know her well enough to decide if she believes in all the old-time-mumbo-jumbo. They will let you do the sing, but it doesn't mean I approve of it."

He studied me for a long moment before he shook his head and started down the hallway as if he didn't need directions to the ICU. Indeed he didn't. I followed *him* all the way there. He stood to one side while I explained to the duty nurse why my grandfather needed to do a traditional religious sing for Morning Dove--in case she didn't live through the night. She gave me a dubious stare, but the woman nodded. We all knew hospital policy on this. No matter the religion, they allowed the mumbo-jumbo.

Without being told which room was hers, my grandfather moved away from the front desk and opened the sliding glass door to Morning Dove's room. I turned to go with him. A strand-thin woman, wearing a visitor's badge proclaiming she was from County Social Services, blocked my way. She stood less than five feet tall and was forced to tilt her head back to look up at me; a fact I didn't think she liked much.

"Doctor Deer?"

"Running Deer," I corrected. The pall of her perfume, stronger than the antiseptic smells in the ICU, wrapped its way around me and clawed at my sinuses.

"I understand you are the primary physician for the street person who was hit last night? I don't know how she ended up here. They should've taken her straight to County. How soon before they can move her?"

"She's not being moved to County," I told her.

"Not being moved? Doctor Deer, she has no insurance. She's a Jane Doe; as far as County is concerned, she is already checked out of here."

They had passed legislation on the federal level allowing the indigent to go where they pleased for care. On the state level, it remained policy to take them to County unless they, or their relatives, requested otherwise.

"Her name is Morning Dove, of the Silver Creek People. Morning-Dove. One name. Not a first and a last name."

"And do you also know the name of the responsible party for the bill?" Her tone bled sarcasm and at the same time she seemed bored.

Mentally, I added up the expense of Morning Dove's care so far. I could foresee how much it would eventually reach. Half the amount at County, but she would also get half the care.

"Do you have the responsible party forms?" I asked her.

"Of course I do. If you know who her parents are, I should speak to them."

"Give me the forms." I held out my hand.

"Really, Doctor Deer. . ."

"Running Deer, my last name is Running Deer."

"Yes, whatever." She waved her hand in the air as if shooing flies away. Her nails were over long--a deep dark red, like old blood, and obviously fake. "As I was saying, before you interrupted me, I must speak with her parents. There are concerns she is underage and there will be charges of neglect and. . ."

"I am the responsible party," I told her louder than I wanted to.

"Are you telling me you're her father?"

I almost laughed. At forty-seven, I probably could have been. "No, I'm not her father, nor is she underage. I'm her..." I bit down on the edge of my tongue. I'd almost said I was her husband. Why would I even think such a thing, much less say it?

"You're her?" the woman prompted.

"The relationship doesn't matter. I doubt I could explain it to you without an American Indian genealogy lecture. Give me the forms. I will sign them as the responsible party, and then you're out of it."

She searched through her briefcase and presented me with the blank forms. While I filled them out, I was aware of my grandfather's chant coming from the room behind me, and of her scrutinizing stare. I put in Morning Dove's birthday as the first of May. I counted back twenty-one years and used that date. I held the forms out to the woman. She took them and carefully checked them over before she shoved them into her briefcase. She looked disappointed in her ability to save the County several hundred thousand dollars' worth of medical costs, or perhaps her disappointment came from the lack of parents to accuse of neglect.

I slid silently into Morning Dove's room so I wouldn't interrupt my grandfather. I sat in a chair, my body weighed down by the heaviness preceding sleep. With a jerk, I sat up straighter. My eyes wanted to go shut on their own. How many hours had I been awake? I couldn't fight it any longer. With the sounds of the past echoing in my ears, I let sleep swallow me. They tell you in medical school you will learn to fall asleep instantly; your body will rapidly take you to the deeper levels of sleep--once you learn to deal with sleep deprivation. I always fell asleep quickly. Sometimes, my dreams would start while I was still aware of the conscious world.

My grandfather's chant continued into my dream world, but, this time, I sang with him. I'd both dreaded and looked forward to my graduation from youth to adult. I'd just turned sixteen, ready, in my grandfather's opinion, to set out on my first solo Medicine Vision quest. This vision would determine if I were to replace my grandfather someday as tribal medicine man.

My father had silently approved. He didn't have any brothers, and my mother's brother didn't have the patience to deal with an overly precocious child. So my grandfather had assumed the job of male role model for me. A non-biological father to nurture me, because a biological father might be too hard or too soft on a growing child. It was something many non-Indians had a hard time understanding--the importance of an uncle or a grandfather over a father. I stood on the frozen mountaintop where I'd fasted for three days and nights, considering my role in life, my future as defined by my grandfather. Traditions didn't even allow me to have a small fire, and the elements kept me shivering. Bare-chested and barefoot, I sat on the ground, despairing I would never have my Medicine Vision.

And then it happened. The clouds raced away from the moon. In the clearing, a giant elk with a tremendous set of antlers appeared. He walked up to me and lowered his head. I sprang to my feet, stumbled, and fell on my back. In a flash, he reared up and ran right over me. One of his sharp hooves cut deeply into my shoulder. I would wear a scar proclaiming me as one of the elk's own.

In my dream, I scrambled to my feet, a thing I hadn't done on my vision quest, to see where the elk went. A creature stood looking at me. Its head and torso were that of an elk, but the rest of its body appeared human. His muscular arms were crossed over his chest. He raised his head and laughed with an insane inhuman voice.

"I have marked you. You are mine. Come, Medicine Elk, let me show you what can be ours."

In terror, I turned to look where he pointed. Morning Dove stood there nude trying to cover herself.

"Take her. She is yours," the elk creature commanded.

When I tried to turn away, the creature raised a blowgun to its elk mouth. Before I could duck, a dart flew through the air and smacked into my shoulder.

I jolted upright in the chair.

"Grandson?" My grandfather stood over me.

"What?" I looked around me. I swallowed and wiped a hand over my face to chase away the dream. The savage laughter still echoed in my ears.

"You have learned much about the healing of the body. But she will need the care of a medicine man for a long time to come if she is to find harmony again. Harmony she deserves."

"If she needs more of your *medicine*, I'll call you."

"You know the future I once saw for you. It seems the ancestors still believe in your Power." He glanced back at Morning Dove. "I think they're wrong--you are not the one I thought you were."

I came fully awake. I'd never heard my grandfather doubt anything he thought came from our ancestors. "Grandfather. . ." I began.

"Often a shadow of your spirit fills my visions. You face our ancestors and pass their tests--but you wouldn't know how to behave if you faced our ancestors because your spirit has become as the white-man's."

Before I could say anything in my defense, he picked up his bag and moved from the room. I refused to believe Morning Dove came with my grandfather and jumped out in front of a car just to convince me I needed to return to the old ways. I rubbed at my shoulder, at the scar left by that crazy elk all those years ago. My shirt felt sticky and wet. I pulled my hand away and stared in disbelief at the fresh blood covering it.

Chapter Four
Visions of the Past

"How the hell did you do this?" John asked. He used a thick square of gauze clasped in a hemostat to dab at the deep cut in my shoulder. He turned and opened a drawer, taking out the packages he needed to suture the injury.

"Would you believe me if I told you I didn't have a clue?"

John peered at me over the needle and gut he held before him. "Was this some part of the ceremony your grandfather did for that woman?"

The wound was in the same place the elk had stepped on me so many years before. It was also where the elk creature in my dream had shot me. Could my grandfather have struck me with something? I wouldn't have slept through it, and my shirt hadn't been torn or cut.

"Shane?"

"What?" I snapped. "I don't know how it happened," I added more calmly.

John answered with a negative sounding grunt. He started to stitch the gash shut. I barely felt the needle.

"Odd," he said.

"What now?"

"This *is* the same shoulder you have that ceremonial mark on, right?" John's voice had an odd edge to it--stressed, frightened, maybe confused.

"Yes. Why?" I asked.

"The tissue around the new wound is soft and supple, not what I would expect from a laceration of a previously scarred area."

I tried to get a look at the spot, but couldn't see it very well. The mark that long ago elk had left on me was hideous. My grandfather had packed it with herbs and some sort of coal dust so it would be an unsightly black scar. Tradition called for it to be. Once, I had worn shirts with the sleeves ripped off just so people could catch a glimpse of the nasty spot. These days, I often wore a T-shirt, even when I swam, so others wouldn't stare at it. Now, John wanted me to believe the old scar no longer existed.

John turned away from me. He put the needle in the sharps disposal box and moved over to the bio-hazard can, where he stripped off his gloves. From a drawer, he took out a hand-held mirror. He stood with it clasped between his hands for a long time before he held it up so I could see the stitches. I glanced at the reflection. I expected to see the normal lumpy black mess of the scar--made worse by the new wound. My grandfather would no doubt tell me it was some sort of spiritual stigmata, further proof the Great Spirit chose me to be a tribal medicine man.

"What the hell?" I exclaimed and grabbed the mirror out of John's hand. Everyone considered John an artist with needle and gut--under his hands scars were minimal. My wound fit the criteria, but as I stared at the pattern the sutures made, an icy snake slithered down my spine. Gone were the unsightly black knots. In their place, there were several lines of stitches--lines of stitches that now made a pattern like the antlers of an elk. One line formed the profile of the animal's head. A cold breath pressed against my neck and made me shudder.

"Okay, John, very funny. You want to take the unnecessary sutures out of there now?"

John shifted his weight from one foot to the other. He leaned back against the counter and crossed his arms over his chest.

"Shane, I'm telling you, this is the strangest thing I've ever stitched. At first, it seemed like one laceration, but when I stitched one, the skin split apart in a new place. . .until I ended up with. . ." He raised his hand as if he would touch my shoulder but didn't.

We stood with our gazes locked. Both of us wanted an answer neither of us would, nor could, give. The door bumped open. I almost dropped the mirror.

"Where's an old man empty his bladder around here?" my grandfather said into the bloated silence.

John gave me a hard stare. He waggled his hand at my shoulder. "I don't have to tell you how to take care of that." He gave my grandfather a quick glance before he went out the door.

I put my fingers to the new stitches. "What the hell is this?" I demanded when the door shut behind John.

My grandfather frowned and shrugged. He leaned towards me and cocked his head to the side. "It is the mark of the Great Elk. The same one that has always been there. What do you think it is?"

"This is not the same mess you and that damned elk left on me," I declared.

"Isn't it? Is this the first time you have seen its beauty?"

I looked in the mirror again. Suddenly, I found it hard to remember what the black scar looked like. My mind said it had been a repugnant mess. Now, as I stared at the lines sketching the elk's head, it seemed as if it had always been this way. The spot unexpectedly itched like crazy.

I gave it a fierce rub. The freshly stitched wounds should have hurt. Instead, bits of gut came off under my palm. I stared at the black specs and almost laughed. John and my grandfather had pulled a good one on me. It wasn't something I could imagine my grandfather doing, but it wasn't beyond John. How had John hidden the old scar so well? I went to the sink, pulled out a chunk of gauze, and ran water over it. When I rubbed at the spot, the iodine came off easily. That would explain how I had seen the old scar as gone. Iodine would cover and hide anything. I grinned at my grandfather and picked up the mirror.

Nothing remained of the stitches and iodine. Wriggles of anxiousness undulated through me. In place of the old black scar, a graceful line drawing of an elk's head, much like the ones found in ancient cave paintings, adorned the skin of my shoulder. I touched the smooth lines with one finger. The beat of the medicine dance drums, as they had been done for my father before he died, sounded in my ears. I heard the chant as if it were being spoken right in this cold, sterile room.

Gooseflesh rose over my body. I closed my eyes and tried to will the sounds away. I did not want to relive that day. I wouldn't be forced to wallow in the pain that came with it. Icy fingers trailed over my flesh. I rubbed my hands up and down my arms, feeling frozen to the marrow. I looked at my grandfather. In spectral form, a large gray wolf sat next to him. It vanished.

"I gotta piss," my grandfather said bluntly. He turned and left the room without another word.

The thump of the drums grew louder. My hand tightened on the mirror. I rushed to the door. With a sweat-slippery hand, I tugged on the handle--desperate to escape the room. The door wouldn't budge. Behind me, voices and laughter mixed with the sound of the bells worn by the women when they danced. The sound wouldn't go away. I jerked on the door handle again. Fear gripped my heart. I began to tremble. This couldn't be happening.

I looked again in the mirror. The elk's head turned and gazed back at me. The smell of wood smoke assaulted me. My ears filled with the inhuman laughter from the dream I'd had in Morning

Dove's room. The mirror flew from my fingertips, as if someone tore it from my grasp, and crashed against the wall. My heart pounded in a frenzy. I took in great gulps of air and sank to the floor with my hands clasped over my ears.

The calliope of sounds from my past reached an impossible level. They swirled around me, louder and louder, until they mixed together into a furious wind of noise. When I thought I would go over-the-edge mad, the sounds sorted themselves out. I opened my eyes to find the past had consumed me and drawn me in. I sat next to my grandfather on the reservation. Never before had a vision taken me with such power.

Others sat around us, all of them intent on the women as they danced around the fire. The beat of the drums pounded in my ears and echoed off my soul. The laughter now came from some of the younger women who waited their turn to dance. I knew no one except my grandfather. He sat with a carved walking stick in his hand. A sculpted wooden mouse with a small bone clasped in its mouth sat on top of his staff.

The chant changed from the Medicine Sing to the one sung at the Women's Dance. This dance welcomed the new women of the tribe. It announced their passage from childhood into adulthood.

Shadow-filled darkness surrounded me. The silhouettes of those seated around the fire flickered on the surfaces of the tepees ringing the common area like ghostly support dancers. Hide covered lodges, as The People had once lived in.

What was going on? A man leaned over my shoulder.

"It is good you are here, my brother," he told me. It had been many years since I'd spoken the Blackfoot tongue, but I understood his words.

Another man spoke, "It is said Morning Dove will choose her husband this night." He wore a mostly white feather in his hair adorned with a single black dot. He'd killed someone in his last battle.

I watched the women as they stepped around the circle. I didn't see Morning Dove among them. All the women wore a medicine feather that marked them suitable wives for medicine men, proof the Great Spirit had touched them. Some wore the tanned and softened leather of the plains' tribes, while others wore woven grass cloth; one woman wore cloth I recognized as Cherokee. Each wore the style of their tribe in its most grand state--marriage clothes.

"Why is it...," I began.

A harsh silencing sound came from my grandfather. The mouse chattered at me from around its bone prize--a live mouse, not a carving. An incarnation of Mouse from the story of the choosing of the chief of all time? A moment later, it appeared wooden again.

Without turning, my grandfather said, "Morning Dove will not choose a husband from among those young bucks who cannot remain silent as they should be."

"She hasn't chosen a husband at any of these ceremonies," the man behind me whispered.

"None have the Power to be her husband," another said.

"She will only choose one who is equal to her," a different man said.

"We have all traveled here from afar. This year, she will choose," another man asserted.

"She has to choose this year. Next summer, she will be seventeen summers, too old to be part of this dance."

I turned to look at this man. On his shoulder, he had the elk mark as well. A much smaller one and the animal only boasted a single antler. I studied the others; each of them bore a tattoo symbol on the same shoulder I had my elk scar. Some were of lesser animals than the Great Elk. I frowned. In this vision, it appeared I was privy to the strength of each man's "Power" based on the scar he bore. In life, I had never seen anyone with a tattoo to identify their "Power." Not even myself, until recently. Perhaps what happened at the hospital was just part of this seeing? Could I have gone through surgery in the fog of a vision? It didn't seem likely. And I was the only one dressed in modern clothes. That had to mean something.

Even my grandfather wore tanned hides, with a woven blanket over his shoulder and across his lap. Everyone wore finery of some sort. My jeans and blood stained T-shirt couldn't have been considered elegant in any way. So, I was set apart from the rest, yet accepted by them.

Those around me ceased their low talking. The women stopped their dance, and their bells went silent. The steady beat of the drum and the rhythmic chant continued. The wind stopped in a slow motion whirlpool, in which I became aware of the very dust particles in the air. I hadn't even noticed the sound of a swift river in the background until it too faded away into stillness.

From out of the darkness, a woman came.

My breath caught at the sight of Morning Dove. A thin band of braided leather with a medicine feather dangling from it encircled her forehead. The fringes of her white buckskin dress swayed around her calves and gave sensual glimpses of her legs. Small intricate shell work covered the bodice with feather-decorated fringes in a V down the front. White moccasins with complex quill work encased her feet. Around her shoulders, her thigh-length, black hair swirled like an ebony cape. I imagined her nude, her hands on my shoulders, while she straddled me with her hair falling over my chest.

Yes. You can have her and all will be yours. We will have her.

Terror hooked into my heart with the inhuman voice from my dream. The words embraced me, whispered around me, and caressed me like an unwelcome lover. The words became louder and more insistent, until they drowned out the drums and the chants. I had to force myself to stay seated. The voice began to sound like my own. I began to contemplate what it would be like to take Morning Dove without her permission. The laughter from my dream sounded triumphantly in my head. With it, an arctic wind of dread blew through my soul.

Morning Dove's gaze met mine. How could I consider rape? I would take the time to get to know her. I would offer her a chaste place in my home, no matter how long her recovery took, and I would pay for anything she needed.

The elk-man's voice came to an abrupt halt. The sounds of the forest returned. Morning Dove moved into the circle. The other women left the ring around the fire and vanished into the darkness.

Morning Dove stepped around the circle in a shuffling dance that caused the bells around her ankle to tinkle provocatively. Her small, simple movements were subtle teases more powerful than any dance I had ever witnessed. The men around me leaned forward. Some shifted their positions as if they would move out of their places to attract her attention. Any man who did such a thing would forfeit his chances of winning the woman.

"It is true," the other Medicine Elk gasped from behind me.

Murmurs rippled through the medicine men seated around me. A few moved back out of the choosing place. I strained to see what they saw. Two rectangles of metal dangled from a thin chain Morning Dove wore around her neck. Two rectangles of metal I knew instinctively didn't belong in this time and place where my spirit had flown. They were a set of military dog tags.

She stopped in front of me. With graceful movements, she took the tags from around her neck and dropped the chain over my head. I glanced down only long enough to see they were mine.

"Shannon Running Deer, trauma surgeon," she said in clear English, "I have chosen you."

Everything stopped at the sound of her voice. I sensed every person's gaze upon me. What did they expect me to do?

She said my name again, turned, and raced across the camp into the darkness. There was a brief flash of light as she went into one of the lodges.

"Her words, boy? Did you understand them?" my grandfather asked me.

I nodded, unable to speak. Many years ago, I had experienced visions regularly. This Medicine Vision baffled me more than any of them ever had. It felt real. I had never been an active participant in one before. I always stood on the outside and observed the events as they played out. I heard and I saw. I felt impressed by them.

This time, I could smell the fire and feel the heat of it. The breeze ruffling my hair carried a tingle of mountain ice. The sound of the rushing river, along with wilderness night sounds, sang around me. Something fluttered over my head--a bat maybe.

Visions always had fuzzy edges, an absence of clarity that existed in real life. This one offered startling clearness, and there didn't seem to be a message I was to take out of it.

"Will you insult her by refusing?" my grandfather said.

Morning Dove called my name again. Reluctantly, I stood. The answer to this vision, I knew, waited in the lodge with her.

Chapter Five
Improbability

I moved across the camp. The closer I moved to the lodge, the stronger and more insistent her voice became. I stood outside the door flap, almost afraid to go in. She called to me again, her voice loud and assertive--too loud to be her actual voice. What did this vision want to show me? I pulled the flap aside. Lilting laughter came from where she lay. I glanced around, afraid the elk-man would show up and tell me what to do.

She lay nude, with her back to me, on what looked like a great white bear skin. I admired the way her flesh shone as if she had applied oil to it. The gentle curve of her waist and her hip, where she rested her hand, aroused me in a way that made me want to fall on her and have her no matter how old she was.

"Running Deer?" This time her voice was soft, barely a whisper, as it beckoned me to her side.

I took the few steps across the dirt floor of the lodge and knelt down behind her. The entire lodge faded from my sight. Only she remained. I'd once asked my grandfather what it meant if your vision included a naked woman. My grandfather, in his blunt manner, told me I had been too long without a wife. Gently, I put my hand on her shoulder.

At my touch, she let out an appalling groan of agony and turned on her back. I sprang away from her. In front of me was not the beautiful woman I followed from the dance. Morning Dove lay as she had on the gurney in the trauma unit. Blood covered her face. Her body lay twisted.

What did this vision expect from me? Was I supposed to try to save her with only the things available to me in this ancient time? Impossible. A shiver of horror struck me. If my vision showed her death from her injuries. . . she would die. I tried to shake that off. I no longer believed in the metaphysical garbage my grandfather spouted.

The elk-man appeared out of the darkness. He watched me for a few moments. His lips parted to reveal small, sharp teeth. "You can save her. All you need to do is embrace me. Come." He held his arms open. "Come, and I will save her. All it will take is the touch of my hand."

The creature reached toward me. I raised my hand as if I would take his.

"*No.*" I didn't recognize the voice commanding me. Somewhere, a wolf howled. I clasped my hand into a fist, turned to escape the lodge, stumbled, and collapsed--on a hard tile floor.

"Doctor Running Deer, to the ICU, stat."

My palms stung from their contact with the floor. I looked around the cold sterile treatment room and blinked in the bright light.

"Doctor Running Deer, to the ICU, stat."

I scrambled to my feet, grabbed my shirt, and pulled it over my head as I went out the door. With horror twisting my guts, as it always did when I lost a patient, I ran to the ICU expecting Morning Dove to be in cardiac arrest.

Instead, two nurses and a male orderly stood around Morning Dove attempting to keep her struggling form on the bed. Convulsions were not a good sign either. The respirator's alarm blurted in a shrill tattoo. The heart monitor bleeped in a panicked frenzy. I heard Morning Dove scream and use words I recognized as Blackfoot, but I'd lost my ability to understand them. When she called my name, I shoved aside a nurse and moved to the bed's side.

"Who removed the respiration catheter?" I demanded. Despite her injuries and casts, Morning Dove managed to strike me. I caught her wrist and held her arm down.

"Near as I can tell," the duty nurse started, "she yanked it out herself--same with the IV."

"Morning Dove, can you hear me?" I doubted she would know my voice. Her only response came in Blackfoot. I looked up at the orderly. "Out in the waiting area, there's a thin, old Indian man. Get him in here. He'll understand what she's saying."

Morning Dove ceased her fight with us. She lay on the sweat soaked bed with her chest heaving. With her injuries, I imagined she was in a horrific amount of pain.

"Morning Dove," I said quietly. Her eyes were wide when she looked at me, and, in them, I didn't see any recognition. She began to speak rapidly in Blackfoot again. Hell, why was it total gibberish?

My grandfather moved into the room and went straight to her side. "Ask her if she knows her name and where she is," I instructed.

He said some words, and Morning Dove grabbed his shoulder. She spoke rapidly, using my name several times. After a few moments of speech from my grandfather she relaxed on the pillow and shut her eyes. The orderly, and the extra nurse, left at my nod. The nurse in charge of Morning Dove gave me a leery look. No doubt she thought I would berate her for not watching her charge close enough.

"I went in to check on number three. This one's alarms started going off. I raced right in here. She had the airway yanked already and the IV as well. Her hand was on the shunt tube. I think she intended to pull it."

I used my stethoscope to listen to Morning Dove's heart. The monitor feed looked like she had a regular rhythm, but I had no way of knowing if she'd disrupted the leads. Her heart beat strong and regular; her respirations evened out. She moved her undamaged arm. Her hand landed over mine. She grasped me so tightly it almost hurt. How could she be so strong? Never in my twenty-odd years of medical practice had I seen anything like what she had just done. Airways were ripped out, and patients yanked out IV's all the time, but not the day after a car pulverized them.

"Hurts," she told me, using English in a whisper.

Hospitals used pain scales to decide how much medication a patient needed to be comfortable. Personally, I thought they were silly. A number ten for one person was often only a number five for someone else. I leaned over her and asked her how bad the pain was.

"When the gull chewed its leg," she said, with her eyes tight shut.

The nurse scowled. "I don't think she understood what you asked her."

With my hand still clasped in Morning Dove's, I stood up straight. I understood how much pain she was in. "I put in a morphine order for when she woke up, see if you can restart the IV--after you give her an injection."

The nurse gave me a curt nod and left the room.

"When she comes back, you have to let her put the IV back in your arm."

"No," she said clearly. "I want this out of my head." Her hand jerked out of mine.

I caught it before she could yank on the shunt tube. "Listen to me. A car hit you; it ran over you. You have some serious injuries. You need to let us help you. The IV has to go in, and the shunt stays where it is. I also want to get some X-rays, to see if you tore anything apart I put together."

"X. . . X what?" she stammered as if she had never heard of an X-ray. Maybe in her condition she'd forgotten what they were.

"The car crushed your ribs. That's why your chest hurts."

"My head hurts," she spat at me, "because of the thing in it."

I stood next to the bed, completely baffled. People came out of comas in a variety of ways, but I'd never witnessed anyone so cognitive after what she'd been through. Her hand tightly clasped mine again. I expected her hands to be smooth, soft, and maybe delicate; instead her palm and fingers were strong, calloused, and rough in places. That's when I noticed the gouges from the gull were gone. I glanced at her other hand, covered by the cast--it had to be the one the bird injured. I was sure, though--it wasn't important.

"I need to see if you tore apart the bone repairs I did on your ribs. It's only an X-ray, so I can see what. . ."

"See? A picture? You have done this already?" Her heart rate elevated. I realized my mistake. Some Indians had reverted to the belief a picture hurt your spirit, because you were no longer unique. She let go of my hand and swung at me. Trying to push me away from the bed, she reverted to shouting at me in Blackfoot. My grandfather moved quickly to her side.

His rapid speech in the same language did nothing to calm her this time--it only seemed to enrage her more. I went to the call button and ordered the nurse to bring a sedative with the pain med. My grandfather had his hands full with her. I moved in to help him get her under control. He let go of Morning Dove and grabbed the collar of my T-shirt. With a good hard yank, he ripped it so the elk mark on my shoulder showed. I didn't understand what he said next, but Morning Dove stopped her struggles and regarded me with mistrust. Her gaze went to my shoulder, to my face, and back again.

"You *can* trust him," my grandfather said in English.

Morning Dove reached up and gently touched the lines of the elk. Goose bumps rose over my flesh.

She whispered, "I will do as you say."

The nurse came in. I continued to hold Morning Dove's hand. I no longer cared what they would spread around the lounge later. "You're going to let her put the IV back in."

"Yes," Morning Dove said.

"When they come to do the X-rays, you're going to let them."

"Yes," she said. Her gaze stayed on my grandfather.

"You're not going to attempt to pull the tube out of your head."

"I do not like it there." Her hand went down her side until she found the chest tube keeping her lungs clear. "I do not like this one, either... or the other one."

I didn't blame her. No one liked a catheter. "They need to be there. In time, they will come out, but not before I have X-rays to help me know when they can."

"I trust you," she said and pulled her cast-covered hand out of mine.

The nurse held up the two syringes. I nodded. The sedative wouldn't hurt when the X-ray tech showed up.

"I have to leave for a bit, but I will be back later tonight. Don't fight them."

"I give my word. I will not fight them." She gave me a hard stare before she turned away. No one liked to have their freedom of choice taken away from them. It had to be even harder for someone who lived as she did. I couldn't do much about it. I needed the tests.

In the waiting room, my grandfather stood in the thin light coming in the window cast by the gray day outside. I walked up behind him. The rain fell in a steady pace that left pools of water below the eaves and along the Life-Flight veranda.

Lightning lit up the black clouds only moments before the roar of close thunder rattled the windows. I frowned. The accident had left Morning Dove covered in blood, but I didn't think her clothes had been wet. I needed to get some sleep. My perceptions were blurring.

"What did she say to you?" I asked him.

"She told me of a vision she had while her spirit wandered."

"And this made her decide to try to kill herself by..."

"So, you have decided you are again worthy of the name Medicine Elk, and I can tell you of another's vision?" My grandfather didn't look at me, but it felt as if his gaze were cutting a swath through my soul.

"I'm too tired for this tonight." I turned away from him and started across the room.

"She told me of the summer dance. In her vision, she chose a husband. He rejected her. The Medicine Elk of her vision refused her based on what one sees on the surface." He took a deep breath. "She said she saw the form of the evil one."

I drew in a startled breath. How could my grandfather know my vision was essentially the same as Morning Dove's? My hand went back to the elk mark. No blood this time, but something had happened, and I wasn't sure what. Could my grandfather be responsible for the oddities of the past two days?

"Grandfather, I. . ." I let my voice trail off. What was I going to ask him? Why did I suddenly have a vision? Why did Morning Dove stir enough lust in me to make my pants fit uncomfortably with just a thought of her? I knew what he would tell me. He would accuse me of abandoning my spirit helpers. He would reprimand me and remind me of all I'd left behind. I snorted.

I knew just what I'd left behind. Unemployment, failed families, men turned abusive--by the lack of income and dignity--and, most of all, the drink and the lure of the casinos. The new lifeblood of the American Indian––the slow destruction of my brother, Sam.

I glanced at my grandfather, tempted to tell him I had experienced the same vision. So often, in my younger years, I came to this man and shared what I "saw." He lifted his chin and pulled his shoulders back, as if he knew of my inner struggle.

"I hate rain," I said instead.

His shoulders bent, and he shook his head before he belched. "They have food in this place?"

"First day you were here, you interrupted my lunch," I replied.

"Humph. I said food, not stuff so full of chemicals your body lives in the grave after you."

I pulled out a twenty and held it out to him. "They have an organic salad bar." He looked at the twenty, but didn't take it. It wouldn't be a good idea to leave him wandering around the medical center. I retrieved my lab coat from the rack outside the ICU and put it on over my torn shirt. "Come on, I'll show you where it is."

Even as I led him from the room, I saw Morning Dove as she had been in my vision. Had she seen the same thing I had? How could that be? If it were true, what the hell did it mean? I glanced back at the doors leading into the ICU. My grandfather ran into me when I stopped abruptly.

"Step in glue?" he snapped.

"No," I whispered.

My grandfather turned to look at the doors. "Her spirit watches you," he said, and then stalked ahead of me to the elevators. "You coming?"

I only glanced away from the image I saw in front of those doors for a moment, but when I looked back, Morning Dove wasn't there.

She couldn't have been there in the first place, not dressed in a buckskin dress, or even as I had last seen her. The gray wolf couldn't have been at her side. Spirit watching me indeed. I earnestly needed more than four hours of sleep. Medicine men worked by depriving you of sleep and food. And then they used the power of suggestion and you could see anything.

Chapter Six
Seeing is believing

My grandfather filled his third plate of food from the salad bar. I pushed the same pile of croutons and lettuce in circles around mine. He sat in the chair across from me and began shoving the food into his mouth. It amazed me that he still possessed all his teeth. He never celebrated a birthday. He always said he didn't remember his coming into the world, so what did it matter? Tribal records contained no information of his birth either. He'd been old ever since I could remember and if you caught him in the right mood--he would amuse you with his extensive memories.

"How did you convince her to step in front of a car?" I asked in a harsh whisper so those in the chow hall couldn't hear me.

He didn't stop eating.

"Damn it. I'm talking to you."

"You're interrupting my meal," he said with his mouth full.

I yanked his plate away. "It's your turn to listen to me."

He reached across the table, stabbed his fork into his food, and shoved it in his mouth while watching me. "My turn to listen? Doesn't that imply you've been listening to me?"

I slouched back in the too small plastic chair and let out an exaggerated sigh. I hated it when he showed up. Normally, it meant trouble and all sorts of weird stuff happened to me, but this time--every time--he expected me to believe the Great Spirit made the things happen in an effort to put me back on the right path.

I opened my mouth to speak and forgot what I wanted to ask him. Something danced on the edges of my mind, but wouldn't solidify. The old scar from the elk itched. I rubbed at it.

I could say one thing for my medicine vision: it did leave me with a very unusual scar. People often thought it a tattoo of some sort. When I looked at my grandfather, it made me wish I had kept the faith he retained in the old ways and a belief in the spirits. His life appeared so much simpler than mine. I shook my head and sat up straight.

Where in the world had those thoughts come from? No one ever admired the scar left by the elk. They cringed when they saw it and the ridiculous Sun Dance scars I had--and his faith--as foolish as every one of The People who stayed on the reservations. They stayed in the past, with no desire to move forward. By choice, they destroyed themselves and their families, with their hope of resurrecting something better off gone.

Three nurses, two female and one male, helped themselves to the salad bar.

"You hear what happened in the ICU?" the male nurse said.

"The Indian woman?" the female nurse in the blue scrub top asked.

"Uh-huh," the male nurse said with his mouth full of something he took off the salad bar.

"Weird--you know," the second female nurse added.

"Yeah, but that's not all. Ice cube *I-don't-believe-in-love*--Doc Running. . ." The nurse in the blue scrub top turned and saw me. She elbowed the male nurse.

"Shit," he said, and all three of them hurried to seats far away from my grandfather and me.

"I looked for you in the lounge, thought you'd be asleep by now."

I jerked upright in the chair. Dave, from radiology, stood near the table. I hadn't even heard him come up to us. "I should be."

"I hate to bother you, but I think you should come down to radiology. I did the stat X-rays on the ICU hit and run." Dave looked at the tops of his brown loafers, and then back at me. "You need to see them."

Inwardly, I groaned over the thought of Morning Dove having to go back into surgery. I was too tired. Yet, the prospect of allowing anyone else do it daunted me in a way that made me feel like a first year surgical resident. The first thing you had to learn as a surgeon, or a doctor, was you were not responsible for the outcome of every case. Twenty plus years of surgeries and I still felt accountable for every case who came across my operating table.

"Grandfather, please stay out of trouble." He wouldn't listen to my words, but I needed to say them. After I dumped my food in the nearest trashcan, I followed Dave from the room. The three nurses sat with their heads close together.

In Dave's office, he moved to the other side of the room and hit a wall switch illuminating the bank of lighted X-ray view boxes. A large brown envelope lay on his desk. From it, he took out the X-rays done on the night Morning Dove came in. Silently, Dave anchored them under the clips at the top of the light boxes. He left enough space between them for the new films to be put up for comparison.

"I've only seen films like this on a cadaver," he commented.

In the surgical arena, I'd been intent upon one thing at a time--fix and move on. Now, I silently agreed with him. The skull fracture alone should have killed her. When you added in the massive hemothorax and the flail chest--why she wasn't dead fell into the realm of the miraculous.

"Heard your grandfather did some sort of In--Native American religious ceremony for this one." Dave stood with his hands submerged in the pockets of his lab coat. He rocked back and forth on his heels. He tilted his feet outward, as if he had stepped in something sticky, so some of the crepe soles showed. He repeated the motions. I wanted to grab him and lift him off the floor to stop the repeated squish squelch squeak.

"He did." What was Dave getting at? Everyone I worked with walked on glass shards around me when it came to anything ethnic. I was obviously Indian. At first, people openly made comments and asked questions. And then they learned. Shannon Running Deer did not like those questions at all.

"Think I'm about to convert to whatever you call your beliefs."

"What?"

Dave didn't answer. In order, he jabbed the new films under the retaining clips--the chest series, the skull series, and then--

"They're not--" I started to tell him they were not my beliefs, but the new films took my voice away.

"If I hadn't done these myself, I'd say they weren't from the same person."

Morning Dove's skull appeared as whole as my own. Several thin lines of scar tissue on the cranium showed where the accident fractured her skull. On the series of chest X-rays, the plates and screws I'd used to put her ribs back together remained, but thin lines of scar tissue replaced the fractures and splits. The bones of her arm, once crushed from the car's tires, were whole with barely any scar traces. Her ankle, not yet in a cast, appeared to no longer need one.

I looked at Dave. What could I say that wouldn't sound ridiculous? Of course they were her X-rays. Dave was a careful and observant man.

"What the fuck?" I finally said.

"My opinion exactly," Dave answered. After a deep breath, he added, "She told me the shunt tube hurts. She wants it out."

Ceremonial drums sounded--a dog or a wolf howled. I jerked

my head around, trying to see where they were coming from. Dave watched me carefully. Did he hear them? No, his reaction was the result of my behavior. Voices echoed with the drums, and I had to concentrate on Dave's words.

"I've been in this business a long time, seen all sorts of things. Once saw a guy already pronounced DOA get up and walk away. He wasn't this busted up, but the mind can do wondrous things. If she could hear your grandfather and believed strongly enough. . ." Dave shrugged dramatically. "Who knows?"

"I should be home sleeping off too many days of hell. Instead, I have this to deal with."

Dave took the new films out of their clips. I turned and stopped. The elk-man stood in the doorway with his muscular arms crossed over his furred chest.

Dave walked around me and stopped. "Something wrong?"

"Get away from me."

"Jesus, Shane. Get some sleep," Dave muttered before he moved quickly into the hall.

The elk-man faded, but his laughter echoed after me all the way to the ICU. I hurried past the desk on my way to Morning Dove's room. The hospital administrator's wheezing voice stopped me.

"Shane, just the man I was looking for."

I closed my eyes, willing Pete Charles to go away.

"Shane?"

I turned to face him. The administrator grew more rotund every time I saw him. I doubted he had seen his feet in the last ten years, and now his stomach arrived before he did. His double chins and reddish complexion made me wonder why he hadn't had a coronary already. Today, perspiration dotted his receding hairline and soaked his shirt collar.

"What can I do for you, Pete?" I asked with false pleasantry. I wanted nothing to do with him or whatever he wanted of me.

Pete scowled. He hated when someone called him by his first name. I disliked him calling me Shane, only those close to me did so. A smile crossed his lips--it didn't shine in his eyes.

"I need you to talk to the Shilfen people," he said.

"What?" I couldn't deal with them today. Didn't want to contend with them at all.

"Shilfen wants someone familiar with infections disease protocols. They know you. So you're it. They're in lab five." He turned as fast as a man his size could and waddled away from me. He stopped before he got to the hallway junction and took out a handkerchief and wiped his forehead with it before he vanished around the corner.

After I informed the duty nurse I would be in lab five, I took the stairs into the basement. Shilfen had claimed an entire hallway on this lower level. One of their guards sat in a metal chair with his head against the wall. His mouth hung open and a bit of drool ran down his chin. His black hair stood up in a quasi-military burr cut. I'd noticed many of the guards Shilfen hired were Indian. Mostly Menominee.

He jerked awake and almost fell out of his chair when I cleared my throat. His eyes went wide, and he stared at me.

"I'm Doctor Running Deer," I told him. "I'm supposed to speak to someone down here." Why hadn't Pete told me who wanted to talk with me? Maybe it was the cotton that seemed to be in place of my brain--Pete had told me, but I didn't remember him doing so.

The guard made a swipe at his face and stood, hitching his gun belt up as he did so. "You scared the shi--sheep outa me," he said and shook his head. "I must have been dreaming. When I first saw you, I could have sworn you were dressed for a Pow Wow."

Automatically, I glanced down at my scrub shirt, seeing only the greenish fabric that hid blood stains so well.

The guard checked a logbook hanging from a hook on the back of his chair. He glanced at my hospital ID badge and pulled his own Shilfen ID and pass card from his shirt pocket. He slid the card into a slot in the pad next to the door. The doors clicked and the pressure difference made the left-hand one open a bit.

"Thanks," I muttered.

"Funny, these doors. The ones at the plant--you have to push the door with your foot while you swipe the card. Otherwise you could stand there all night, and they'd just keep re-locking."

"What room am I looking for?"

He checked his log book again.

"Doctor Martins. She's in lab six," he supplied and resumed his seat.

I headed into the Shilfen hallway. Why had Pete told me lab five? I had no idea. My footsteps echoed despite my walking shoes. All hospital basements seemed to follow one designer's idea. In areas the public rarely saw, gray became the color palette. Concrete floors covered in thick gray paint. Walls joined to the floor with rounded base edges in the same shade. Overhead ducts, pipes, and conduits all painted in a lighter hue of the same gray. Sounds echoed, and pipes made noises--a horror movie director's dreamscape.

Although the lights down here were not as bright as upstairs, they felt too bright. My head started to hurt. I needed sleep. I needed to get my grandfather out of the hospital. I needed to look in on Morning Dove and verify what the X-rays had shown.

The door to lab six stood open. Inside, a tall blond woman stood over a microscope. Her short bob haircut curtained off her face and the top of the scope.

"If you're in here, you better be the IFDP doc Pete said he would send me," she said without looking up.

Ex-military. She had to be, no other industry used acronyms like the Armed Services did.

"Actually, I'm a trauma surgeon." Her head came up. "But I've worked Infectious Disease Protocols."

Her shining blue eyes narrowed, and she raked an appraising gaze over me. I almost asked her if she wanted me to pirouette.

"Pete didn't tell me his IFDP was Indian."

My eyebrows drew together. "You have a problem with that?"

"I need someone who can look at these slides and confirm my findings. Someone with the experience and education to do it with credibility. No offense, but some reservation scholarship doc isn't going to cut it."

"John Hopkins good enough for you? Ten years of Air Force IFDP, Desert Storm, Bosnia. . ." I let my voice trail off. I didn't need to justify myself to this race stereotyping woman.

She crossed her arms over her chest, making her blue lab coat pull tight over her muscular arms. The woman worked out.

"You ever talk in front of a crowd? A judge? The AMA, the FDA?" she demanded.

"I can go back to Pete and tell him you had no interest in an uncivilized savage doing whatever it is you needed me for." I turned as if I would walk out. I had every intention of walking out. I needed outside air.

"For God's sake," she spat. "Your credentials better hold up." As if I had already agreed to help her, she said, "Take a look at these."

With no choice, I moved to the microscope. I looked into it. "What am I looking at?"

She let out a sigh. "Smallpox."

"What?" I said and stepped back. What was Shilfen working on? What were they doing with live *vaccina* samples here? Did Pete know they were breeding smallpox in the basement?

"We have all the right permits." Regardless--this lab wasn't the place for it. She stared back at me.

Very carefully, I looked again, recognizing the disease ravaging the blood cells on the slide.

"Now," she said and removed the slide I had been looking at. "Look at this one."

On the new slide, the blood cells appeared shielded against the invaders. "And?" I said, standing up straight. "So you vaccinated this person."

"Not vaccinated in the normal sense--this vaccine is edible. We could put it in a water source, in food, heck in Jell-O for that matter." She opened a brief case and took out a vial. "We're working on a combo of things for third world countries, war ravaged places, and, of course, protection against bio-terrorism. A whole plethora of drugs. And this one small vial can treat. . ."

My pager screeched. I glanced down at the number, now annoyed at the interruption. "If I may," I asked and nodded my head toward the nearby phone. I didn't wait for her answer. I picked up the phone and hit the three number speed dial for the ICU. The nurse who answered sounded frantic.

Morning Dove had shoved a nurse when they tried to move her gown to look at her incisions. Could I come down and see if I could talk to her? I gave her an affirmative answer before I hung up.

"Doctor Martins, I have a trauma patient in need of me. What is it you want from me?"

She shoved a thick packet of documents across the table. I glanced down at it. Clinical trials were listed in index form. I paged through quickly, stopping when I got to the endorsements page. Five doctors had signed the paper. Five names I knew as credible and competent people. The sixth line remained blank.

"You want me to sign something that says I know this ingested vaccine of yours works?" I shook my head. "I can't do it. I would have to go over your trials and certainly see more than this one slide."

"All I need is the endorsement, if you have the credentials you claim, it will be enough with the other signers to get the stuff into

FDA trials."

The woman must have thought I was an idiot. I glanced around the lab. Tables stood empty with the microscopes covered. It didn't look like any work was being done here at all.

"Backed up by our research, of course," she added.

I shoved the document back across the table, filled with unease. "Not without firsthand knowledge," I said. I turned my back on her and stalked out of the Shilfen lab area. All the way to the ICU, I puzzled over what Pete thought I would do and why.

In the ICU, the duty nurse shook her head when she saw me. "I had to let your grandfather in here to calm her down."

"Who'd she go after?"

"Brian," she said.

Maybe Morning Dove didn't like male nurses. And Brian was an abrupt caregiver. He did things without letting the patient know what his intentions were.

"I'll see what I can do," I said.

My grandfather slept in the chair next to Morning Dove's bed. Morning Dove lay staring up at the ceiling. When she noticed me, she sat up.

"I did as you said. Now will you take this out of my head?"

"You can't hit the nurses."

"I woke up, and he had ahold of my clothes--was I supposed to let him do whatever he wanted?" Her gaze locked with mine as if I would tell her that she had to submit to rude behavior.

"I'm sorry he did that. The nurses need to keep your chart updated so I know what's going on."

"I want this thing out of my head."

"I need to look at you before I can decide."

"You are looking at me." With those words, the corner of her mouth twitched, and I found myself smiling at her. The tension between us flew away.

My grandfather snorted in his sleep and broke wind.

"I don't know why the nurse let him in here again," I said by way of apology. I knew why, but I didn't want to dwell on something that would make her fight me.

"He is an elder. They have earned the right to disregard what manners they wish to." Her eyes lit with humor. I wanted to gaze back and get lost in them. A whisper of the drums from my vision brushed across my mind.

I used the call button to summon a female nurse before I shook my grandfather awake.

"Why aren't you gone? Not much time left, you know," he said when I touched him.

"Gone where? I have to check her injuries. You need to get out of here. After this, I'm going home, and you're coming with me."

He looked me square in the face. "I am, am I? Well, yes, I suppose I am. Anyone ever tell you that you're a damned fool?"

"You just did. Please, don't make this an issue." Normally, my pleas fell on conveniently deaf ears. This time, he grunted his way out of the chair and left the room without argument.

Morning Dove watched me warily as I washed my hands and pulled on gloves. Her chart told me she didn't have any kind of disease, but rules were rules. Most patients would have been insulted and indignant if I didn't wear them, not to mention the possibility of a lawsuit.

"Your head first," I told her when I reached to touch her head.

She leaned a bit forward and tilted her head toward me. I ran my hands over her scalp, feeling bones that were whole and strong. In places, her hair was stiff from dried blood. Around the shunt tube, her flesh felt swollen. She flinched when I touched the area. The monitor told me that her internal cranium pressure was normal, now and for the last ten readings. Twenty-four hours was standard operating procedure for a shunt tube, even if the readings were normal. However, with the X-rays and the swelling, I thought the tube needed to come out, or she would be risking infection.

"Your ribs next." The nurse leaned over the bed and tugged up her hospital gown, so I got a good view of her rib cage and her well-formed breasts. I'd never seen a woman as thin as her, who wasn't all but flat-chested. I thought I'd gotten over being stirred by nude human bodies under my care long ago. In this case, I hadn't.

I ran my hand over her ribs applying gentle pressure. A bit of discoloration remained around the incision areas, but nothing like the bruises there should have been. The area around the drainage tube looked more like a several week's old site, rather than days old. When I ran my hand back up her rib cage, I could feel the plates under her thin flesh. I stopped with my hand just below her right breast. Why did she tempt me so much?

"Does any of this hurt?"

"The tube does. Please...."

"Hang on for a bit." I pulled open a drawer on her care-cart and took out a stitch remover. I held it up for her to see. "This is just to remove stitches. I won't cut you with it."

The nurse met my gaze with alarm in her own.

"If you would assist me?" I said to her.

She moved to my side of the bed and put a drape over Morning Dove's breasts for which I felt grateful. Exercising caution, I removed one stitch at a time. Her flesh was healed completely. The nurse gasped, started to say something but didn't.

"Have you helped pull a chest tube?" I asked the nurse.

"Yes, Doctor," she said and went to the care-cart to get the necessary supplies.

"Morning Dove, I'm going to pull the chest tube." My words sounded insane. She should have been in need of the tube for a week at least. "It shouldn't hurt, a sharp tug, and you might cough and feel like you can't breathe for a few seconds."

Her eyes were wide, but she nodded her compliance.

The tube came out easily, and Morning Dove only gasped.

"Call someone from anesthesia," I told the nurse. She gave me a tight nod and left the room.

I leaned over Morning Dove and spoke quietly. "I need to take you down to a treatment room to remove the shunt. Someone from anesthesia is going to come and put you out for a bit."

She gave me a tight shake of her head.

"It's the only way to get the shunt out."

With a small nod, she gave her consent.

Finished, I stood at the sink washing my hands and giving the nurse orders to have Morning Dove moved to a post-ICU room. According to her X-rays, her arm needed to come out of the cast as well. It would have to wait until morning. Dave came in and stood against the doorframe.

"Shane? Look. I'm sorry about the religion thing. I didn't mean to offend you."

"Forget it," I said, without turning. What was I supposed to tell him, that I felt caught in the process of losing my mind? If I told him I saw weird creatures who spoke to me it would amount to the same thing. I needed to take some time off.

"Oh, I forgot to give you this."

I shook my hands free of water before I turned to face him.

"Don't know how they missed them, or if the nurses gave them back to her."

He tossed something at me.

I snatched it out of the air. My military dog tags rested in my hand.

Chapter Seven
Without Explanation

"You have been away for a long time. When was the last time you greeted the dawn with respect? When did you last fast and cleanse your body in the proper manner?" my grandfather asked. He picked up a magazine from the table and began to page through it as if I didn't exist.

Irritation with my grandfather made me want to grab the magazine away from him and rip it in two.

"Being away for thirty years and unexpectedly seeing nightmare creatures has nothing to do with getting up with the sun and taking a sweat bath," I growled.

One of the night nurses gave me a startled look. I glared at her. She hurried out of the lounge. The door shut behind her with a bang.

My grandfather put the magazine down with a smack. He studied me for a long moment. "I cannot help you if you refuse to believe what the spirits say to you."

I sat staring at his face. He stared back. His dark eyes always seemed to find a path directly into my soul. I looked away.

"Damn it. You know what's going on. Tell me." My voice rose with my frustration.

He cocked his head to one side as if I were speaking in a language he didn't know and said, "It's raining outside. Your home is a long way from here. Shouldn't we be going? I am too old to go without sleep."

"There is a rational explanation for this," I said.

He sat back in his chair and yawned. "I am an old man. By custom, you are an elder as well, even if you are acting like some foolish, battle-hungry youth." He yawned again, this time, he stretched his arms above his head until his spine popped and cracked into alignment. "You will not find the answer in this manmade, white-world."

"I certainly won't find the answer back on the rez." He followed me out of the lounge. I needed sleep. In the morning, things would be clear again, and the effects of sleep deprivation would amuse me.

On the way home, rain came down in sheets against the windshield. I could barely make out the road. Other cars popped out of the miasma as small red taillight eyes in front of me. I shifted into a lower gear and slowed the Jag to a crawl. The windshield wipers rapped back and forth at their top speed, but the rain continued to be a shimmering sleek wall across the glass. My grandfather slouched in the back seat, asleep by the sound of his snores.

Irritated, I hit the button on the CD player. The car instantly filled with beating drums and the echoing voices of an American Indian chant. The language wasn't Blackfoot. The car swerved when I jabbed at the screen to shut it off. With my heart lodged in the back of my mouth, I managed to hit the eject button. The music died.

My grandfather snorted. He grumbled about a kink in his neck and about the car being too stuffy.

"Did you put this in there?" I asked him.

"Put what, where?"

Grabbing the CD, I tossed it behind me into the back seat.

"Never did understand these things," he said.

In the rearview mirror, I could see him holding up the CD as he peered at it. As a child, I used to think every picture I saw of an old Indian in the white-school textbooks was my grandfather.

"Make a good mirror," he said, "but how light can make sound. . . Since when did you decide you were *Niitsitapii* again? Thought you'd listen to white-man's stuff, all cussing and swearing."

"What the hell," I interrupted. Through the sheets of rain, I saw a person walking down the side of the road. I slowed the car almost to a stop and recognized Morning Dove. I pulled onto the shoulder in front of her, wrenched the parking brake up, and reached over to open the front passenger's door.

"Morning Dove," I called, "get in here. Right now."

My grandfather leaned forward and shoved a blanket onto the passenger seat. Now where had that come from? My grandfather, no doubt. It was mostly red. The design of our tribe--his tribe.

Morning Dove stopped at the open door and leaned over, so she could look into the car.

"Get in here out of the rain," I repeated.

"I will not. . ."

"Come, young one, he is a fool, but worthy of your trust," my grandfather said from the back. He pushed open the back door. I expected her to sit next to him.

Morning Dove slung her backpack and sleeping-bag onto the floor in the back before she sat in the front. I leaned over her and yanked the door shut.

"What are you doing out here?" I demanded.

"I did not like it there. How can a person heal with everything so impersonal?"

"Whether you liked it or not, you needed to stay there. How did you get out?"

"I asked the nurse where my things were. When she left the room, I got dressed and walked out. It was not hard."

In the dim light of the dash, I studied the set of her jaw. She trembled in a way that made me think she wasn't only cold, but in pain. I turned up the heat on her side of the car and tugged at the edge of the blanket.

"Put this around you. When we get to my house, I'll find you something warm and dry to wear." I drummed my fingers on the steering wheel. Visibility wasn't improving. The downpour got worse, forcing me to shift into first and creep along the shoulder of the road. I hoped I wouldn't hit another car with its lights out.

"I don't see how you walked out of there. Someone should have stopped you, or seen you. You should know better than to be out here in this storm. In the damned dark, no less. Were you trying to get hit again? One miracle not enough for. . . ."

"Forgive my grandson. Living among the white-man, he no longer realizes sometimes the best conversations happen in silence."

My jaw snapped shut. I glared at my grandfather's reflection in the rearview mirror. I was rambling. Not because I wanted to fill the silence with useless chatter, but to try to calm my nerves. Nothing in all my medical training could explain how she could be in my car, curled up on the leather seat, wrapped in my grandfather's blanket, as if I had plucked her out of the rain without her ever being hurt.

"I am afraid my time of travel will end . . . fruitlessly," Morning Dove whispered.

"Where did you travel from?" I asked, mentally daring my grandfather to accuse me of speaking small words.

"Medicine Elk, you know the answer," Morning Dove said. "All you have to do is look inside yourself to see the way."

I scowled. She sounded like my grandfather. Maybe he'd slipped me some peyote, and his suggestions were creating all of this. It would wear off, and I would be at home with a titan-sized headache.

She watched me intently as if I would spout some form of spiritual advice that would lead everyone on the path to metaphysical harmony. *Medicine Elk*? She had called me by my title of respect; come to think of it, she'd used my title in the hospital as well. True, she had seen the scar, but it didn't equate to knowing my title. With a start, I realized the cast on her arm was gone. Yet another oddity in one long string of peculiarities.

"I don't have any idea how you simply walked out of the hospital or how it is one day you're almost dead and tonight you're out here getting soaked in a downpour, but. . . "

"Will you use rude words now as well?" my grandfather asked.

The commanding force of my grandfather's words cut off my debate. Morning Dove was a guest in my car and would be in my home. I didn't have the right to demand answers of any sort from her. In time, she would tell me what she wanted me to know. I didn't know how I would survive two traditionalists in my home for an undetermined amount of time.

Morning Dove favored me with a slight smile. "I do not know why I heal this way. It has always been so. You have the Power to heal with the touch of your hands. I have the Power to heal myself. Both are gifts from the Great Spirit--Napi made us so we could receive them. A person should not question Power given by our creator."

"You should have stayed at the hospital," I said, scoffing at the idea of Napi, the supposed creator of everything the Blackfoot People had, having anything to do with my talent as a surgeon or her ability to heal miraculously.

"I told you, I did not like it there," she said in a firm tone. "They would not even give me any food."

I'd forgotten to put in an order for her to have food. I'd assumed she wouldn't be eating for some time.

"I'm sorry. You can have whatever you want at my home." The roaring engine of the Jag prompted me to shift up a gear. It had let up enough so I could pull back onto the road. Someone who healed as she did would be the subject of controversy. Perhaps that's why she'd left the hospital. Morning Dove took a deep breath and jerked the blanket tightly around her.

"I thank you, for healing me, for the offer of shelter, and for the offer of food." She pulled the blanket over her head. I assumed she went to sleep.

My grandfather sat in the backseat humming to himself.

"Why is it every time you drop on my doorstep, I fall right back under the brainwashing you're so good at?"

"I didn't drop on your doorstep. I took a bus. It took me to the place where you work." I looked at him in the rear-view mirror. He stared straight ahead with a glassy look. "If I could wash your brain of the dirt the white-man has put into it--I would. I'm afraid you have opened yourself to. . . "

A truck passed me. It rocked the car and sprayed it with so much water I couldn't see for several seconds. By the time my heart stopped thrashing in my chest, my grandfather's snores filled the car. He went to sleep in the same way he heard things. Selectively.

The gates at the entry to my driveway opened slowly. I drove between them, watching in the rearview mirror as they swung back shut. Once they were closed, I hit the arming switch for the alarm system and pushed the button to open the garage door. I shut off the car, flexing my stiff fingers, relieved to be out of the torrential rainfall. When the garage door clunked shut, Morning Dove jolted awake.

She looked out of the windshield with her eyes wide. Maybe she was homeless because she suffered from some form of severe claustrophobia. There were those who couldn't tolerate being indoors at all without meds. After getting out of the car, I went around to her side and opened the door. My grandfather climbed out and stood by the door leading into the house.

"Come on, the ceilings are higher inside," I told her before I reached for her backpack.

Her arm hit mine in a solid crack. I jerked back. "You may not touch those," she told me forcefully. I met her glare, seeing almost wild panic. There were dark circles under her eyes, and her complexion was sallow. It didn't matter; breathtakingly beautiful didn't begin to describe her.

Her gaze never left me when she reached back and pulled her backpack and sleeping bag out of the car. Both were still wrapped in the plastic bags the hospital put patients' things into. Hers were in the large blue bags the homeless got their possessions sealed in to keep lice, bed bugs, and other pests out of the hospital rooms. All but the protruding straps of her backpack should be dry.

I moved back so she could walk to the door without feeling threatened. Over the top of the car, I tossed the keys to my grandfather who deftly snatched them out of the air. I hoped I would be as spry as he was when I reached the centennial mark. Morning Dove ambled across the garage to stand next to him.

With a grunt, I retrieved the blanket. I tried not to think of how wet the car's seat was or of the water soaking the carpet. A slight noise made me look at the dash. Part of a CD stuck out from the door of the player. I snatched it out. How had a CD gotten back in there? The title was *Sacred Spirits*. I almost snapped it in two. One glance at Morning Dove and my grandfather changed my mind. I dropped it on the car's floor and shoved it under the seat.

My grandfather fumbled with the keys as if he had never opened a lock in his life.

"Let me." I took the keys and jammed them into the lock.

"Makes no sense to me why you'd want to live where you have to keep everything locked," my grandfather grumbled. He rudely pushed past Morning Dove to be first into the house. Once inside, he acted like we didn't exist. He went straight past the kitchen and through the great-room to the door into the guest suite.

"Young one," he said to Morning Dove with his hand on the doorknob, "even the white-man understands some form of honor when a child is concerned."

Fury rose in me. Did he think I would seduce her when he left the room? I knew damned well she might be underage. I took a step to cross the room and stop him from taking a room he should have offered Morning Dove.

"Honored Elder, it will not happen. Even if it did, it is too late; by next summer I will be seventeen summers. Too old to join the dance, too old to travel any longer--I will not have a daughter to follow me. I have failed you and Sister Mouse."

Morning Dove wore a look of pure misery. In my soul, I knew it had nothing to do with the fact she stood in my house soaked to the skin or that she had recently been so grievously injured. Her look was one only the most profound of horrors could have brought. What did she think she had failed at? It didn't matter. Traditionalists subscribed to some foolish beliefs. More than likely, her feelings arose from them.

"Morning Dove?" She gave me a sharp look. I realized my offense. When face to face with a person, to speak their name was rude. "You are free of the reservation now. I don't know what my grandfather has been up to, but, even at his best, he can make anyone feel like a failure."

"My lack of success is not the fault of your grandfather. It is my own doing."

She gave me a hard look with her shoulders pulled back and her chin raised. I doubted I would get any more explanation out of her than I ever got from my grandfather.

"All of us are born for a purpose. Napi made me so I could journey where his spirit helper cannot," she said, startling me. She possessed the same knack, as my grandfather seemed to, for answering me as if she read my thoughts. "If I did not succeed in the tasks they set me to, before I reached the age of exclusion from the new women's marriage dances, I needed a daughter to replace me. Many of the spirit paths close once a woman is no longer a youth." She shook her head. "There is not enough time, even if I conceived a child this night."

I swallowed hard. It could have been considered an invitation. The smile she gave me went straight to the core of my soul and stirred a strong male reaction.

"Women of all ages participate in the single's dance. You're still young," I said.

"The traditions have changed. There was once a dance for those still young enough to be new women. It is a separate dance for those less than seventeen summers. I speak of that dance."

I hadn't been away from the reservation long enough for something like that to have changed. I ransacked my brain--I still had no idea what dance she talked about. The laws would not allow a girl under the age of seventeen to marry, and having a child at less than age eighteen was considered bad form, on and off the reservation.

"You know the answers; they are in all of us who are born one with the spirits of the earth. We must simply seek them out and listen. Surely, it has not been so long since you had a medicine vision? Not if your hands and Power healed me so easily."

I answered with a negative grunt. My mind instantly went back to the vision I had been drawn into at the hospital. When my shoulder tingled, I brushed at it. "There is nothing in a drug-induced vision except the ambiguity of your own mind, or the foolishness of the one interpreting the vision."

Without giving her a chance to respond, I turned, took a few steps down the hall, and opened the door to the extra bathroom. Inside, I switched on the heat lamps before I opened the linen closet and took out a huge towel and a white terry robe. I turned on the shower before I hung the towel over the shower bar. Morning Dove lingered in the doorway, watching me.

"Get out of those clothes and warm up. The shower will help.

Take as long as you need." I pointed to the robe. "It'll be big, but it's better than the wet clothes."

She went past me into the room, sat on the toilet seat, and tugged at the laces of her boots. Her hands shook as she tried to undo the wet strands. I knelt down in front of her and undid them for her. I yanked the laces loose. She must have been barefoot when she'd gotten hit. Otherwise, they would have cut off her boots on her way to the trauma center. I pulled the tongue out as far as it would go and pulled on the right boot first. They came off with difficulty, most likely because she didn't wear socks.

Her feet were stained bluish black from the wet leather. The chill material of her boots had left her flesh colder than the floor tiles. I vigorously rubbed her feet to improve her circulation. They were tiny and delicate, but calloused on the bottom. Her toenails were clean and clipped--again not what I expected given my experience with the indigent who came into Mercy.

"How did you get the cast off your arm?"

She smiled and rubbed at her previously broken arm. "A large rock was kind enough to hold still for me."

In the soaking rain, I didn't doubt the cast would have been easy to smash. Morning Dove wiggled her toes. I let go of her foot when I realized I was simply holding it between my hands.

She stood up, undid her jeans, and started lowering them as if I were not staring at her like some lusty teenager. I fled the room and shut the door on her seductive form. I stood in the hallway, leaned against the wall with my eyes shut, and tried to still the passion she invoked in me. I knew she didn't wear a bra; the absent top buttons on her shirt made it obvious. She also didn't wear any underwear. Not unless they were much lower on her hips than her partly lowered jeans. In all my adult life, I had never felt like this before.

"*You could have her. Take her,*" the elk-man's voice echoed.

"You've been too long without a wife," my grandfather said.

"Leave me alone," I said, as much to the elk-man voice as to my grandfather.

"You have been too long without a wife," my grandfather repeated. "Even I remember what it was like to be that *ready* for a woman."

I tried to yank my shirt down farther before I opened my eyes to tell him to mind his own business. I got a good view of his back as he went into the guest room. The door shut with a firm thump. The sound of the lock turning made me shake my head.

My grandfather was at his exasperating best. Later, he would wander out of there to raid the refrigerator for whatever he could find. I went into the kitchen and put the teakettle on the stove. The burner lit with a faint whoosh, and I experienced a flash of the medicine dances I'd attended in my youth. The tribal medicine man would throw fine sulfur dust into the fire to make it do the same thing. A grand show, as was everything medicine men did. None of their tricks had worked for my father.

My father, being a firm believer in the old ways, wouldn't seek out modern medicine past the point of being told he had terminal cancer. He wouldn't even consider modern healing mixed with the old beliefs. My own mother turned her back on me after he died.

The teapot shrilled, and Morning Dove's voice came from the doorway. "I am very tired."

I took a mug from the shelf above the sink. From a different cupboard, I took down the box of nighttime tea I kept there. I added water and tea to the mug and watched the steam for a moment, before I held it out to her.

"It will help you sleep," I said when she just looked at the cup.

"I have had enough white-man's medicines put into me already." Her eyes flashed with what I took for humor.

"This is a mixture of natural herbs, no preservatives, no artificial colorings, no caffeine. . . "

With a smile, she took the cup. Her fingers brushed against mine, sending an electric chill along my nerves. I led the way to my study and turned on the gas fireplace. Morning Dove went to the thick sheepskin rug in front of it and sat down. While she sipped the tea, I went to the closet and retrieved a pillow and some blankets. I paused with them in hand to watch her. She sat in the terry robe and held the mug in both hands. She took a small sip and stared into the fire.

Her hair hung down over the robes back in a glimmering wet curtain. One corner of the robe slipped down to reveal her shoulder. I wanted to sink to the floor and wrap myself around her. With a grunt, I pulled myself away from thoughts of intimacy with her. I covered the couch with a sheet and punched the pillow a few times--to fluff it.

The gate buzzer sounded loudly in the silent room. What nut would be out on a night like this unless they had to be? I pulled the door to the study shut and went to answer the gate intercom.

No one answered. When I turned away from it, thinking the storm had made it go off, it buzzed again. Loud and insistent. I jabbed the button.

"Who's there?"

I heard nothing in return except the thunder rumbling overhead. I pulled open the front door. Down the drive, through the sheets of rain, it looked like a set of round headlights on the other side of the gate. My brother's Jeep?

I reached back inside and pushed the button to open the gate.

Lightening cracked so bright I couldn't see for a moment. I blinked back the brightness, tried to blink it away again.

It didn't help. The deer filling my driveway didn't go away. They ran past the house in a steady stream, an entire herd. Where had they come from? The drums sounded behind me.

Chapter Eight
Broken Reality

I spun around, refusing to get caught up in another vision. I slammed the door shut. Those deer couldn't be in my yard. A chill came over me. The drums pounded in my head. My medicine mark tingled. I touched the scar. How was it the lines of it made up an artful design? Whirling at the edges of memory, I seemed to remember it hadn't always been so. The harder I thought about it, the louder the drums echoed--a howling wolf sung harmony.

The doorbell sounded. I jerked the door open. My brother, Sam, stood on the other side. It so surprised me I couldn't say anything. He stared back at me with manic-looking eyes.

"You're not going to help me," he shouted, washing me with the foul smell of consumed beer and whisky. He turned and stepped off the porch.

"Sam, wait. You can't drive like this." I grabbed for his arm, and he vanished. He hadn't been there in the first place.

"Medicine Elk?"

Morning Dove stood in the doorway of the den dressed in a long, tan buckskin tunic with very few fringes, over matching pants. On her feet, she wore well-used moccasins without design. She carried a rough cloth satchel over her shoulder. How in the world did all of it fit in her backpack?

Reality seemed to have slipped away from me. Maybe a car had hit me. Who truly knew what a person went through while they were in a coma? The mind could imagine anything. The only choice I had was to believe this reality, to make my way through it and come out the other side sane and alive. It took both the mind and body to heal a person from severe trauma. The spirit needed to be treated as well. I slammed the door shut. The drums died away.

My grandfather needed to go home, and Morning Dove needed to go with him. I wanted her to stay--traditionalist or not.

"Look at her. Look at her, Running Deer. She stands in your home. No one will stop you. Have her. The reward will be all she possesses. The Power of the Great Spirit will be yours to command. You will be as timeless as she is. Take her."

I pressed my eyes shut and compelled the voice of the elk-man to go away. What in the name of the spirits was wrong with me?

Insanity. It seemed the only answer. Madness had sucked my

mind into its wake. Too many hours in the trauma unit could do that. Everyone knew the risk of burnout. I should have recognized it when I believed Morning Dove could heal miraculously.

When did I lose touch with reality? Before the Life Flight brought Morning Dove in? Or had it been earlier, at Lake Side Park, when I first saw her? Could I be in the psychiatric ward right now and not aware of it?

On the other side of the room, the patio door slid open. The twittering of birds filled the room. Amazed, I looked outside. Sunlight shone in bright rays through trees that shouldn't have been in my back yard. Sunshine? It was only half past twelve a.m. A dog barked. Another answered it. On the patio two mangy dogs, about the size of small huskies, wagged tails and panted. Each dog wore a harness attached to a loaded travois.

Morning Dove moved out of the house to stand in the brilliant light. The dogs wiggled with contentment at her touch. Shaking my head didn't dispel this newest twist to my derangement.

"We will be late. Hurry."

Filled with mischief, Morning Dove's voice teased me as if I were always tardy, or perhaps she knew how much I hated being late.

"Come, boy, she's not your bride yet. They won't choose you if you arrive after the council has met." My grandfather walked past me, leaning heavily on a thick walking stick. The carved mouse from my vision perched on top of it. He wore the same sort of travel clothing as Morning Dove. A single black and white feather adorned his hair. Years of applying dark ashes to the moccasins he often wore explained his darkly stained feet.

I stumbled to the front door and jerked it open. Thunder crashed while the sky lit with lightening. Rain still pelted the ground. Behind me, I could hear the birds and the dogs panting. I started to gasp for breath. I was soaked to the skin--so it was raining. The sunshine couldn't be. Instantly, I felt warmer, and dry.

My feet itched. I looked down. My shoes and socks had disappeared. I started to tremble. My heart sounded in my ears. My eardrums felt as though they would burst from the beat. I hugged myself, and then jerked my arms out in front of me. How had I ended up dressed in leather as well? Over my shoulder, a pair of new moccasins hung by their laces. Was I supposed to put them on? It didn't matter. This couldn't be real. Filled with apprehension, despite the unreality I felt, I moved toward the patio doors. Just deciding to go with Morning Dove eased my panic.

"Have you lost your senses this morning?" my grandfather asked me.

He jabbed his walking stick at a man's pack with a shoulder bag and a rolled up fur resting on the edge of the patio. I assumed he meant I should carry them, so I slung the pack over my shoulder, along with the fur and the bag. The smell of herbs coming from the bag brought swift recognition. How had either of them found my medicine pouch?

Morning Dove smiled at me. I would have gladly stayed insane just to have her do it again. With a cluck to the dogs, she started down the beaten trail through the woods now residing in my back yard, along with bright sunshine, in the middle of the night. The gray wolf stood off to the side watching us through slitted yellow eyes.

Chapter Nine
Kills Many

Rays of sunlight filtered down through the trees and illuminated the path in front of me. Morning Dove walked with her head held high and one hand on the dog nearest her. My grandfather walked just in front of me, grumbling about everything. The trail was too sodden. The leaves were too slippery. The squirrels were too noisy. What a thing for an animal to do . . . use the trail for a toilet. His walking stick gave him slivers. Morning Dove turned and looked at me with a smile and a slight shrug. How could she find his constant complaints amusing? They always irritated me.

"Grandfather, when we get to the camp, I will find one of the warriors to smooth the roughness from your stick," Morning Dove said to my grandfather in a lilting tone.

"I'm sure Kills Many will be glad to do it." My grandfather glanced at me before looked back at Morning Dove. "Just so he can sit across the fire from you. Mind you, he likes blackberry tea with a bit of mint." Each step he took got punctuated with the hard thump of his walking stick into the soil. "Now Kills Many would be a good provider. Fed his whole tribe one winter when the lung sickness struck them. Saw him burning with fever, and he still hunted. I imagine many girls would like to share his blankets."

"Grandfather, please."

He turned and speared me with a sharp look. His walking stick smacked into the ground so hard it stood on its own.

"Kills Many has spoken to the council three times already. They are pleased with what he plans. You have not spoken once. Not that it matters, your words are all foolishness anyway."

I didn't have an answer to give him. I didn't know what council or what plan he spoke of. When I saw Morning Dove well ahead of us, and it looked as if my grandfather had no intention of moving, I went around him. It took only moments before I heard the steady thump-thump of his stick. We followed the trail around a sharp curve.

Out of the corner of my eye, I saw a man move quickly through the trees. He stood on the trail ahead of us. In one hand, he held a spear almost as long as my grandfather's walking stick. A huge stone war axe hung from his belt. He wore red paint in rectangles across both cheekbones. His bare feet were darkened almost black;

many years of walking in wet moccasins would do that. The most striking thing about him was his height. He stood only a bit shorter than me. A smile split his fierce countenance, and he stepped up to Morning Dove.

"It is good to see you." His gaze went to me. He looked me up and down much the same way I did him. "So another has come to speak. Are you a man or a woman? The one to save us cannot be a woman."

Anger made my face burn. I wasn't foolish enough to try to assault him. I wasn't the sort of man to attack someone anyway. I didn't have any idea where and when my mind had taken me to, but this man's words echoed my father's.

"Why do you wear your hair like a woman's?" The words were my father's, but the voice saying them was the elk-man's. The elk-man continued, *"Are you a woman? A man would already possess her, wouldn't he?"*

"I'm as much a man as you are," I said, surprised by the confrontational tone of my voice. I hadn't meant my words to come out that way at all. The elk-man laughed at me. I ground my teeth together.

The big warrior sneered. "A warrior who carries no weapons?" He glanced at my grandfather and Morning Dove. "Why is he here?"

Morning Dove reached out and touched his shoulder. I wanted to knock her hand off him, and shove her behind me, before I ripped the man's throat out.

"Kills Many," she said with her fingers still on his shoulder.

Was she deliberately insulting him?

"He is a medicine man from far away. Not every tribe's traditions are the same as ours. You must remember that." Morning Dove talked to this warrior as a mother would instruct a child. She pulled her hand back and lifted her chin. "Kills Many? I spoke to you."

Kills Many. I would remember his name and his face. The look in his eyes said the same thing. There was also recognition. He saw I was of *The Niitsitapii*, just as he was.

"It will be some time before they allow you to speak, perhaps not until after the *first* frost." With those words, Kills Many turned and walked away from us. My grandfather walked past me, giving me a hard shove, as if I were in his way.

Morning Dove smiled at me. "He thought you a warrior. He does not like competition, but it is good for him to have some. It is foolish to assume you have the quarry you seek before it is in your hands. Come, the camp is just ahead. You will put your things in my lodge."

Great. Kills Many would like that. If I got beaten to death in a dream, would I be dead? Popular belief held I would be. At the same time, I would've gladly fought the man for her attention.

Her lodge turned out to be a large one, covered with painted symbols only half of which I recognized. My grandfather didn't stop at her doorway. He went past her to a smaller tepee, where he disappeared inside. Morning Dove gathered up the numerous packs from the dogs' travois. Free of their burden, the dogs ran out to mix with the others from the camp.

Inside, she indicated I should put my things along the left wall where the head of the household would sleep. She should have offered me the guest's place at the rear. When I started for the guest spot, she stepped in front of me and pointed again at the left-hand place.

"Put your things there." She didn't move until I put the pack and fur down--where she wanted them.

I imagined her smiling at how uncomfortable I felt. By giving me the husband's place, she was granting me permission to have marriage like relations with her. Now what? I didn't know what to say to her.

With a mischievous lift of her brows, and a slight smile, she turned and took a bag down from a hook. It appeared to be the stomach or bladder of an animal. I didn't want to think on that any more than I wanted to think of her apparent teasing. Both gave me physical reactions I had little control over. When she ducked out the door, I let out a breath of relief and looked around her home.

I knew I was back quite far in time. Everything was either stone or animal in nature--no steel at all. Near the central fire pit, a flat stone rested next to the scapula of a deer. There were several utensils, also made from the bones of animals, placed in tightly woven reed baskets. Suspended from the lodge poles were several rolled up furs and more bags made from stomachs, bladders, and pieces of hide. A hatchet hung near the door along with several snare lines. I remembered well learning to set those with my father. Tradition required that we learn everything without modern intervention. I never understood why Natives couldn't combine the better of the two.

Medicine Man: Book 1: The Chief of All Time

I sat on the floor near the left dewdrop. Made from a smooth white hide, Morning Dove had anchored it to the lodge poles about five feet from the floor. A good wall height for her. She'd constructed her tepee from thirteen poles, so the dewdrop gave her a thirteen-sided home.

How much food did she have hidden behind it already stored for the winter? What sort of containers did she use to keep out rodents and bugs? I found myself more than curious about what sort of other possessions she might have. It would have been more than rude to look.

She'd covered four of the dew cloth walls in small pictographs and bits of neat script--both modern and hieroglyph. They were notes of some sort, perhaps painted on with a fine brush, and arranged in rows of blue outlined boxes. As I looked closer, I saw it could be some sort of calendar. Each square contained a name and several small line drawings, possibly to tell something of the person or date specified. I recognized one name written in English script. Kills Many. His square contained a stick figure holding a spear. I assumed it indicated a warrior. There were several others that contained the same figure. For some reason, the block with Kills Many's name in it had a smear of bright red across it. I located three more with smears across them. Two were disfigured with a black line. In heavy black lines, they also contained a small picture of a burial platform. This I understood. These people were dead.

The other with a red smeared across it was so blurred I couldn't read the name. Over the red in heavy dark lines, this one featured a burial platform as well. Not a normal one, though. This one showed a chilling depiction of a person set to look upon the sky--without their head. His head rested against one of the platform legs with a hatchet imbedded in his skull.

I stood up and stepped back. Why did the block about Kills Many have the red smear? Did Morning Dove think he would die a violent death soon? Or did she think he should be dead? I didn't have any idea. Perhaps Morning Dove was some sort of historian.

There were three rows of empty boxes near the bottom. In the last box to have a notation, Morning Dove had drawn a figure with the medicine symbol over its head. Near that motif, she had drawn a female figure with an upward pointing arrow above it and a diamond shaped pattern under it. Morning Dove and myself? I frowned and looked closer at the tiny drawings. A depiction of a wolf graced the left corner of the square. I thought the small round design in the right corner was a sundial. The paint appeared smeared giving the picture a stretched out effect. That didn't make sense. All the other drawings were neat and precise, except those deliberately marred.

Raised voices came from outside. More than five people, it seemed, argued about something. When I opened the flap to see what was going on, Morning Dove stepped through it. She hung the water bag on a lodge pole hook and turned to face me.

"It's cold. There must already be ice high in the mountains." From a woven basket, she took out a hollowed bone cup that appeared to be the skull of a small animal. After filling it with water from the stomach skin, she drank deeply. She refilled it before she held it out to me.

Revulsion gripped my insides. Once, I wouldn't have hesitated, but now. . . Morning Dove's gaze locked with mine. I took the cup and drank the fresh clear water.

I glanced at her decorated walls. "Are you keeping some sort of record?"

She smiled and took the cup out of my hands. "It is what I do," she said.

Careful not to actually touch the designs, I pointed to the last box. "Me?"

"Yes," she answered carefully.

"The other figure? You?"

"Our paths have crossed, have they not?"

"I guess they have." I studied the drawing a bit longer. "What do the symbols mean?"

"You are a medicine man," she told me. Humor danced in her eyes.

"These," I said, indicating the arrow and diamond symbols near the female figure.

"There are those who say I am a true daughter of the Great Spirit, formed from clay by Napi."

I thought about her words. Every religion claimed the believers were children of whatever god they worshiped, but something about the way she said it disturbed me.

"Because of how you heal?" I guessed.

She shrugged.

The voices outside rose in pitch.

"They should not argue," Morning Dove said.

"What are they arguing about?" I asked, accepting her reluctance to talk about herself.

"You will want to join them. Come and sit, I will help you with your hair."

At first I wanted to refuse. Kills Many's words rang in my ears-- *"Are you a man or a woman?"* I gladly sat down to let her braid my hair, hoping she wouldn't want to twist part of it into what I considered a ridiculous looking horn at the front of my head.

Outside, with my hair in two braids, and a small part of it gathered into a standing horn shape well back on the top of my head, I joined the group of men who sat in a circle near the center of the camp. Off to one side, my grandfather sat with four other elders, watching the circle of younger men. One man stood in the center of the ring and waved his arms as he spoke. His clothes were old and roughly put together, with no adornment.

"I have had the same vision, or I wouldn't be here," he said. His voice sounded as if he were barely a man. "These white-skinned men will come, not those who have come before in peace and understanding, but those who will make war on us. We must make war in return."

Another jumped to his feet. "And what of the fire-sticks they will carry? Has this part of the vision escaped you? We must run. I have seen many routes in my travels. We can escape them."

"And you would have us abandon our ancestral homes because these unnatural creatures come?" This man wore woven cloth and sandals of a sort I recognized. He was Cherokee. This made me look around. There were people from almost every nation I knew of. Tribes who shouldn't have been together--in a time before steel.

"And what would you do?" the roughly dressed youth spoke again. "Run from the sickness they will bring? I have seen it as it rides the wind. All who come near these men will get it and die." His frustrated agitation rang apparent in his voice.

"It eats the flesh and burns the body," another said.

"I have seen great piles of belongings, and the bodies of the dead--burned so nothing remains. This sickness is an evil thing that leaves a person with no way to enter the next life. It will fill our world with the ghosts of the dead who will torment the living with their desire to go on." The young man who said this wore a medicine feather in his hair. His wide eyes and pale complexion told me the vision he had seen truly frightened him.

There were nods all around. Warriors could fight men, but evil spirits who caused great sickness were much harder to fight. Was this vision trying to tell me we should have united against the Europeans? If we had done so, would we have survived as a nation of Native Americans? How could that have happened? Perhaps all this vision wanted of me was to feel guilty for abandoning the ways of The People.

Kills Many stood and waited until the others around him were silent before he spoke. "I have seen these white-men. I have seen the great canoes they will come in. I am not afraid of any beast or any warrior, yet this vision of our lands in the wake of these white-men filled me with terror. Whole villages burned. The buffalo gone. Whole tribes dead of hunger. Many young men and women dead. All of it because of this white-man." He held up his hand when arguments started again. "It is not only the white-man. I see some of our own joining them. I know this is true. For many generations we have fought each other. If not for our wise elders, and the return of Napi, we would be fighting now, instead of united to find a way to survive the onslaught of these evil men. We must find a way to hold together and fight against them. It is the only way to survive."

Others nodded. Clearly, Kills Many was popular, if not some sort of sub-chief. I glanced at my grandfather and even he stared at Kills Many and tilted his head in agreement with his words.

I got to my feet. Kills Many looked at me before his gaze went to Morning Dove's lodge. Yes, he knew where my packs were. "I have seen these men. They will use lies to confuse us," I said.

A collective gasp went up from those in the circle. Many turned to look at a blackened circle of earth in the camp. A ragged lean-to stood nearby where a woman and a small child sat. They had received the punishment for lying. Their tribe had burned all their worldly goods. I didn't know if it was the woman's fault or her mate's, but I couldn't allow my pity for them to show on my face.

The men around me started arguing the validity of what I said. Kills Many watched me thoughtfully. His loud voice stopped the others from arguing. "I have not seen this. Tell us of their lies."

Great, the man wanted me to make a fool of myself. I moved into a dry and packed area of the circle. The smell of many campfires rose with every step I took. With a stick, I scratched in the dirt, *We the people, in order to form a more perfect union.* Many faces turned toward me in surprised puzzlement.

"They will lie with their words. Because they think we can't read them, they'll tell us what they say. Those who meet with them will believe them because," I looked toward the punished family, "who would lie and suffer the loss of all they own? But their words won't be true. They'll think because, in their minds, we are savages that they don't have to keep their word."

Arguments started again. The Cherokee man got to his feet. "It's true," he shouted. Many turned to look at him. This time should be before the Cherokee had written language, but he wrote in the dirt near my writing.

"What does it say?" he asked.

Many men shook their heads. An Apache trader entered the circle. "'Napi said to us, I will one day return when your need is greatest.'"

The Cherokee man continued. "I could have told you anything, and if Jumper didn't know how to read my marks, you would have believed me. Written words lie easily because you don't hear them said."

Further debates broke out, but these were more along the lines of who would learn the white-man's words. How long would it take? Did all men have the Power to have this knowledge? Nightfall came, and I found myself almost too tired to keep my eyes open. How long had it been since my mind believed I'd slept?

Kills Many shouted over the top of their arguments. Once he had their attention, though, his voice dropped. He spoke with clarity and calm. A politician sure of his popularity.

"Knowing their words is a good thing." He glanced at me with fire in his eyes. "But this will not stop them. We have all seen in our visions that they won't talk, and if they lie when they do--talk with them is useless." He straightened his shoulders, and his hand went artfully to his axe. A gesture not missed by those around him. They murmured and nodded.

"All here know I have led many men into battle and returned with all those men victorious. When I lead you against these men, all those who follow me will return."

There were shouts from the younger men around the outside of the circle. Those in the inner circle paused to consider his words, and even they smiled and began talking of following Kills Many and his war plans.

Kills Many tossed me a triumphant look before he turned to the crowd expanding further on his war plans.

"Come," Morning Dove said to me with her hand on my shoulder.

I started. I'd been so focused on Kills Many I hadn't even been aware of her behind me. I got to my feet aware of Kills Many's caustic gaze eating into my back as I made my way to Morning Dove's lodge. A small victory on my part. He may have had the power to sway people's admiration towards him, but I had Morning Dove.

Chapter Ten
Before Written Time

Inside Morning Dove's lodge, tantalizing smells greeted me along with Morning Dove's smile. She moved to the fire and brought me a plate filled with strips of meat and what looked like a mixture of wild rice and bits of fruit. I took the plate out of her hands. It surprised me to find both the top and the bottom smooth to the touch. An expert craftsman could only have done the muted red paint, with vivid black zigzags, who knew how to properly fire clay. The plain's tribes didn't fire pottery, so she must have traded for it.

I looked up at Morning Dove, who wore a troubled expression. "I didn't expect you to have anything like this," I quickly stammered out. I didn't want her to think something was wrong with the food.

"Jumper brought me several pieces of it--as a gift," she said.

"Jumper? The Apache trader?" I sat near the fire on a woven grass mat. Using my fingers, I tried a bit of the thinly sliced meat. Thick juices ran over the back of my hand, and, in my mouth, the meat needed little chewing. I hadn't tasted buffalo in years. Morning Dove had richly seasoned it with what I thought were mushrooms, onions, and perhaps sage.

I tried a bit of the rice next. It exploded on my tongue with a wild nutty flavor. The bits of fruit were cranberries and some other tangy berry I didn't recognize. Why had I thought my ancestors lived on a diet of stringy dry meat and bland side dishes, if they had them at all?

Morning Dove handed me a red clay cup decorated with a design matching the plate. Jumper traded with tribes from much farther south than he should have traveled. Jumper himself was out of place here. Very slowly, I touched the designs on the cup. Anasazi perhaps? The designs were right, but I had never seen a piece that wasn't old and worn from spending time in the ground. I held the cup in both hands letting the tea inside warm me.

A Christian friend had once told me a trip to the Middle East had reaffirmed his faith. I felt both chilled and warmed, but could I call any of this a reaffirmation in the *red way*? This cup was a connection with the history of a Nation that no longer existed--well, they existed, but that was part of the problem. As I saw it, we Indians existed on the reservations, but too many of us didn't really live life.

While I savored the lush food, I thought of the men around the fire. The Cherokee who knew the written language of his People--out of place among people who used weapons from the Stone Age. The faces around the fire tugged at me as I tried to place them. With a laugh, I realized one man wore wire rim glasses. Glasses didn't seem out of place to me, so I hadn't thought of it before. Another man wore his hair in a flattop crew cut and sat with a glassy-eyed look speaking of fear and disbelief. I knew how he felt.

They did share one thing in common.

All of the men expressed more than interest in Morning Dove. Kills Many certainly did. Jumper brought her very expensive gifts, both in terms of trade value and of work to carry them a great distance. If I believed this a dream of some sort, then my grandfather was right. I had been too long without a wife and my subconscious was trying to make Morning Dove the most attractive woman I knew.

Here inside her lodge, she wore a short, thin sleeveless tunic made from woven cloth. I doubted she wore anything under it as it fell over her breasts in a way that made me want to sigh with the pleasure of looking at her. I reminded myself of her age and tried to concentrate on my food. That's when I realized she wasn't eating. She wasn't going to stand on some ridiculous ancient tradition where I got served first, and she ate the leftovers.

"Have you already eaten?" I asked her.

"I am not very hungry. Tired."

I stood up and took my plate over to her. "You should eat."

She shook her head and sat down on the pile of furs and blankets behind her. The fur I'd carried lay among them. Two choices met me. Either the fur belonged to her, and I'd carried it, or it was an invitation. I wondered if I could refuse.

I sat back down and looked at my plate of food, anywhere, but at her. She sat on the furs and blankets, undoing her hair. She pulled a carved bone comb through it before re-braiding it.

"What year is it?" I asked her. I needed to think of something besides her sitting there as if we were husband and wife, and she expected me to act as a mate.

"Finish your food. It is late. They will start their debates at sunrise."

The need to press her on a date buzzed in my brain. Her careful avoidance made me realize I wouldn't get an answer--if she even knew. Maybe in non-reality, it didn't matter.

"Tell me about Kills Many," I said.

She glanced at her history wall. "There is little to tell, and at the same time there is too little time to tell it."

More avoidance. "He doesn't like that I'm in here with you."

Anger flashed in her eyes. She made a rude sound, drew in a deep breath, and let it out slowly. "He is angry at the council this night because the others favored your idea over his talk of war. He is sure he will be chosen as The Chief of All Time. Any interruption of his fantasy, however briefly, makes him behave like a wounded bear."

With those words, she lay down and pulled a blanket over her shoulder, leaving a clear amount of room between her body and the dewdrop behind her.

I sat for a long time after I finished my food, staring into the tiny flames of the central fire. How could this be a dream, or a vision? The taste of the food was alien to me. Yes, I knew the ingredients, but it was prepared in a way I had never tasted. The inside of her lodge smelled pleasant enough, but I had never experienced it before: an odd mix of spices, overlain with a tanned leather smell. Lodges, at the Pow Wows I'd once attended, were made from canvas and were much larger than this because of lightweight modern materials, the advent of horses, and in modern times, trucks to carry poles and coverings. I moved aside one edge of the nearest dew-cloth. Morning Dove had filled the storage area behind it with baskets. In my time, they would have brought a small fortune. The weaving perfect--the designs true works of art.

I studied her pictograph-covered walls. On the bottom of the third panel, she'd added my name--Medicine Elk--in precise small letters. Next to my name, she'd drawn a stick figure holding a rattle and a feather fan: the symbol for a medicine man. In the corner of my square, she'd added the figure of an elk. The added pictographs reaffirmed my idea that she kept some sort of historical record.

Things here were too clear for fantasy and dreams. I didn't understand Morning Dove's attitude at all. First, she wouldn't go near my car, afraid I would rape her, and now she wanted me to sleep in the same bed with her. Kills Many wouldn't like it if he knew of her offer. I smiled to myself. His jealous look and protective behavior toward Morning Dove provoked something in me. I wanted Morning Dove, and I would fight for her if I had to, and enjoy doing it. Even if Morning Dove thought the man's only concern was to be this Chief of All Time, I knew his look--he wanted it all. Morning Dove and the Power of being a chief.

Admiring her as she lay on her back, with her arm above her head and her body barely concealed by the blanket, made desire burn through me in a trail of agony. Telling myself what I saw in her was more than physical didn't work. She frustrated me, angered me, and came from something I'd left behind on the reservation. I never dated Indian women. I never dated anyone who looked remotely as if they could be even a fraction Indian.

Once, I had thought I was in love. I remembered clearly the wild desire I had felt and the way I had wanted to protect and care for her.

My former wife. A selfish, self-centered woman without an ounce of compassion in her. Tall, blond, blue-eyed, with model caliber looks--and a complete bitch. Our union lasted only two years. At the end of our time together, I gladly signed the divorce papers.

Morning Dove lived as an independent young woman who had a mind of her own and didn't pretend otherwise. It pained her to follow anyone's advice. I had to admit, although my physical desire for her astounded me, deep down, I knew what I felt for her would bloom into love.

I stood and pulled off my shirt. I sat down to take off my moccasins and stopped when I remembered in this era I should wear them to bed. As Morning Dove did. If an enemy attacked the village, a person didn't want to be searching for shoes before running to fight or get away. Why the others walked about barefoot in the camp I had no idea.

I crawled into the bed next to her. She reached over and pulled the blanket back. It felt like two parts of me were fighting. By the laws of this time and of our heritage, she was of age. Even in my time, some countries gave the age of consent as sixteen, some younger. She measured her life by summers, so she could be past seventeen.

With a groan, I flopped on my back. I would not touch her. I couldn't. No matter how much I rationalized it, I'd lived among the white-man and in the modern world too long. Morning Dove moved so she lay half over my chest. Her hand brushed down my face. Women always seemed small in my arms, but Morning Dove belonged there. We fit together like old friends, as if we had lain this way a thousand times before. Her body felt so very warm against me, and, within moments, I realized she slept.

With my arm tight around her, I tried to rationalize the way I felt toward her. Until a few days before, I knew nothing about her. Now, I lay somewhere in the past, with her lying in my arms, as if we had known each other for a lifetime.

I touched her smooth soft hair and closed both my arms around her in a possessive hug. My heart rate sped up. I had wanted women before, but not like this. I didn't just want Morning Dove; I needed her to feel whole. I pressed my lips to her forehead and drew back. I wouldn't do anything I would later regret, or that would destroy what chance I had to have more with her. My jaw cracked when I yawned. Stifling another yawn, I was glad I was so exhausted. With Morning Dove held close to me, I shut my eyes and let sleep have me.

I awoke to what I thought were branches hitting the side of the lodge. The night had left me rested, but I felt disoriented, and, for a few moments, I didn't even know where I was. The tap-tap-tap came again. I pulled the blankets over Morning Dove's shoulder against the chill dawn. All night, she had lain asleep over my arm and against my chest. Life before this had never granted me so much contentment. I'd slept soundly without waking once.

When the tapping came again, I croaked out the proper entrance greeting to whoever wanted to come in, without thought to whether Morning Dove wanted them in her home or not. I wanted every soul alive to know she chose me, even if her choice might not be consummated any time soon.

Immediately, I regretted my decision. Kills Many stood just inside the door flap. A dead rabbit dangled from his hand by its rear legs. A look of shocked surprise contorted his face. His other hand grasped the handle of his war axe. I leapt to my feet, expecting Morning Dove to wake up and do something to soothe him. She would tell him she had invited me to her blankets.

Instead, Morning Dove flopped away from me. She lay on the packed dirt floor like a tossed aside rag-doll. Without thinking of Kills Many, I fell to my knees at her side. The warmth of her flesh came to me in a flash along with the realization my arm felt sticky where her head had rested against me. My hands went to her skull, my fingers seeking out the incision where the shunt tube had been. I didn't get very far in my examination of her. With a roar, Kills Many knocked me into the wall.

"What did you do to her?" he demanded. He didn't wait for an answer. He picked her up and kicked dirt at me. I scrabbled to my feet, reassured he couldn't attack me while he held her, but desperate to help Morning Dove.

"Let me look at her." I failed to sound calm. Infection, or worse, inter-cranial swelling had happened to her. She needed help now. All thoughts of this being some sort of wild dream left me in an instant. What existed in this time to help her?

"You have done enough," Kills Many told me with a snarl. He turned and went out the flap taking Morning Dove with him.

Outside, people rushed to follow Kills Many as he made his way across the camp. Jumper ran up beside me. He looked at Morning Dove in Kills Many's arms, and he scrambled away. On the far side of the camp, a huge double-tepee stood. I recognized its designs even before my grandfather came out the door flap of the Medicine Lodge. Kills Many stood with Morning Dove held close to him before my grandfather.

"Honored elder, the newcomer has wounded her." A chill came over me. Kills Many sounded hurt and concerned, but something in his tone rang false. He was acting. I was sure of it. I pushed my way to the front of the gathered crowd. Those nearest Kills Many parted for me as if I were the white-man's plague already among them.

"Grandfather," I began.

With a shout of rage, Kills Many put Morning Dove on the ground and spun to face me with his war axe in hand.

"Kills Many, I'm not a warrior. I don't want to fight you." Not when he held a war axe, and all I had were my bare hands, and not before I helped Morning Dove.

"You should have considered that before you harmed her," he barked at me.

"I didn't do anything to her," I asserted.

"You thought to silence her. You are no better than the other who journeyed from your place." He rushed forward.

Chapter Eleven
Kills Many's Rage

Kills Many raised his axe. I dodged out of the way of his swing. His foot shot out and caught me in the back of the knee. I hit the ground. He landed on me, driving the air out of my lungs. I held his arm in both hands. My muscles screamed with effort as I tried to keep him from bashing me with his weapon. Despite years of weight training, I struggled for breath as I battled this hardened warrior. Through fatigue-darkened vision, I saw my grandfather and three other elders kneeling near Morning Dove. Kills Many applied greater pressure. My arms started to shake with the effort of keeping him at bay.

"Warrior, let him up."

I didn't recognize the stern voice trying to help me.

"Kills Many, listen."

Kills Many roared and applied greater pressure against my arms. No longer able to hold him at bay, the muscles of my arms failed me. With his weight on my hips, I couldn't even roll out of the way. His axe hit the ground right next to my head. How could he have missed? Then I saw how. Three men held Kills Many back from me. I scrambled to my feet and kicked his axe away from us.

"He will die," Kills Many bellowed. He struggled with the men who held him. Adrenaline surged through my veins when I thought of him getting away from them. Hand to hand, I would strangle him. What was I thinking of? I didn't want to fight this man.

"Ah, but you will. You will if you are to have Morning Dove. You should have taken her last night--now, this one will have her." I took a step towards Kills Many before I realized the elk-man was after me again. He wanted me to attack Kills Many. His voice whispered in my head, repeating his words. Determined to ignore the creature's commands, I stepped back from Kills Many.

"Kills Many, you are an honored warrior. Do not stain your hands with the blood of an innocent man."

Kills Many stopped his struggles long enough to meet my grandfather's gaze. "He is no more innocent than the other from his place. He. . ."

"Saved Morning Dove's life. And he must see to her now, if she will live through this," my grandfather told Kills Many in a tone that offered no room for argument.

When my grandfather tilted his staff, the men let Kills Many go. I braced myself for his attack. Instead, he snatched up his axe, stalked off across the camp, and disappeared into the trees. My grandfather held the flap of the Medicine Lodge open for me. I ducked inside. Morning Dove lay on a woven mat near the central fire. A woman, as old as my grandfather, washed her face in a way that made me think Morning Dove was already dead and they were preparing her to meet the Great Spirit.

My mind raced over the lessons my grandfather had given me all those years ago about the things the Great Spirit had given us to heal and help. I gently turned Morning Dove on her side and moved her hair to find the shaved place where I had inserted the shunt. The flesh appeared swollen and red-streaked. I looked at my grandfather. He added herbs to the fire in preparation for his healing chants.

Squatting next to me, he blew sacred smoke over Morning Dove and me. I didn't have the time to go through a proper cleansing, so the smoke would have to do. I longed for all the modern trappings of medicine I didn't have. My insides contorted into a loop. Here in this place and time, I only had the old way. All accepted a person might die. The purpose of the sing was to purify the person's soul, so they were ready to travel to the next world.

I wouldn't give in to the idea Morning Dove would die. She had survived a car running her over. Nothing in this world would keep me from using everything I knew to save her.

"Grandfather, please start." I got to my feet and went to the many baskets lining the edges of the Medicine lodge. My teen years returned as I looked them over. They sat here in the same order they had been in when he taught me herbal medicines. I selected with careful thought, putting together a combination of things to help draw the infection out--willow bark shavings, and *chuchupate*--a natural occurring antibiotic, went into a ceramic bowl that already held steaming water. In a basket hung far from the floor, I found his surgical tools--pieces of sharpened flint, and his prized flake of obsidian. When he'd first shown me the flake, it had amazed me that the piece of volcanic rock could be as sharp as the steel scalpels I used in medical school.

"You will come home again. There will be much you will do to help our Nations." I glanced at my grandfather. On the day he had shown me this blade for the first time, he had used those words.

I hadn't questioned that I would return to the reservation. Even when I served my first residencies, I hadn't doubted I would return--until the phone call from my mother. Too many years of scientific training had influenced my thinking. I lacked confidence in the old ways. When my father lay dying--I completely lost all faith in them. I couldn't afford to do so now. I had to believe, or I wouldn't be of any help to Morning Dove.

The old woman put sage branches in the fire. The lodge quickly filled with their fragrant scent. My grandfather started his low singing chant as I ran my fingers over Morning Dove's head. I'd never done anything surgical with my bare hands. It didn't do any good to long for something to cleanse them in.

Using the obsidian blade, I cautiously lanced the infected area. I applied pressure to the area with a heated bit of thin wet hide. In a clay bowl, my grandfather kept a paste mixture of witch hazel, *chuchupate*, and milk thistle. I spread it in a thin layer over the infected area and covered the entire area with the heated bit of hide.

A thin young man slipped into the lodge and sat against the wall. He held a small drum in his hands, and, at my look, he started to beat out a rhythm. I recognized him as the fear-haunted youth from the night before. My grandfather's chant picked up speed and urgency in time to the drum. Very slowly, I got to my feet. There, lying on a bit of white hide, were the implements of what I once thought would be my life's work--feather fans and gourd rattles. I would be a medicine man, as my grandfather was. I would be a healer and a medicine man to my People. I would commune with the Great Spirit through induced visions--after which, I would relate them to those who needed the wisdom.

"Shannon, it is as it should be. I am at peace." Looking down at Morning Dove, I heard the echo of my father's last words to me. He was at peace. My mother was a different story. She'd taken her anger out on me and blamed me for my father's death. If only I had sung for my father. I needn't have carried the full burden. If only I had taken turns with my grandfather and sung the joint parts with him, instead of leaving them to the young singer who had never called a soul back from the spirit land before. I'd left the reservation for good shortly after. No sing would have saved my father any more than it would have saved my mother when she chose to starve herself, still cursing me on her deathbed.

"You could have saved him." My mother's voice faded and be-

came the elk-man's. *"You can save her now. Come to me."* Why would this creature not leave me alone? I wouldn't turn to see if he stood behind me. Somewhere in my mind, I had created the thing, and every time I doubted myself, it came to remind me of my weaknesses. I focused on my grandfather's words, forced away the past, and concentrated on this time and place.

My grandfather came to a part of the sing requiring two voices. The drummer stopped, and the young man looked at me with eager question in his fear-haunted eyes. My fingers tingled when I picked up my feather fan and rattles. First, I offered a pinch of tobacco to the fire, and then offered some to each of the six directions: north, south, east, west, up, and down. I did the same with corn pollen. The sharp smell made me think of my medicine bundle--ignored for all these years. Would it still guide me after my neglect? Did I even remember how to do this after so many years?

When the drumming started again, I added my voice to my grandfather's. I felt as though I were doing my very first sing. My voice cracked, and I was unsure of where my feet should go. The walls of the Medicine Lodge wavered. I danced in a circle, half bent over, turning when the guidance of the spirits called for it. Dust began to rise around my feet. Before long, the dust blurred all evidence I danced inside a lodge. I turned, shook the rattle to the beat of the drum, and lost sight of the lodge completely. Now, I found myself dancing alone in a fog-filled place where drums echoed and voices called.

"This way," a beckoning, shadowy figure whispered. The figure retreated into the mists. I followed. Everywhere I looked, I saw death. First, it was just a body here and there, lying along the misty trail. A man with a crushed skull; another with most of his face and upper body torn away--perhaps attacked by a bear--an old woman sitting in the snow, her eyes shut, her face composed in the frozen-death she had most likely chosen; all around me death waited. My insides turned to molten steel and snaked away from me. This was the land between the spirit place of afterlife and life on the earth.

These people lay as they were, or as their relatives had prepared them, waiting for the Great Spirit to call their name and send them to the afterlife. There were other singers in this transitional place. Another man moved in a slow shuffling step, chanting until he got to the old woman who sat in the snow. He stood looking at her and said, "Grandmother, you have chosen the frozen death. It is honorable you have given your life so those younger than you can survive the starving moon. Those of the spirit-world welcome you."

The grandmother's hair darkened, and the wrinkles smoothed from her skin. Her gaunt face filled with the robust look of someone who has never known hunger. With a smile, she got to her feet. She and the singer vanished into the fog.

I refused to accept what seemed to be my role here. It wouldn't be me singing Morning Dove's spirit across. I concentrated on the healing chant I used and raised my voice, despite how hoarse and tired I felt. I would find Morning Dove. I would make her come back with me--it could be no other way.

My march along the trail of death soon took me to whole villages lying in the fog like ghost towns forgotten. In this village, corpses lay unburied and uncared for. I recognized the sores marring the faces of the dead. Smallpox. What should I do? There wasn't a medicine man here or anyone else who would do anything for them.

I raised my arms and danced around the communal fire pit. I called to the Great Spirit, asking it to take the dead into the next life. Near where I danced, their medicine man sat up and looked around him. The rot and open sores fell away. He got to his feet and stood for a moment with his head bent. Very slowly, he moved to make a fire. I continued my chant while I helped him build up the fire. He added sage and cedar branches. When I moved to dance around the first body, he gently touched my arm and shook his head. It wasn't my place to sing those of his village across.

I moved on and didn't look back. The path I followed led to an open prairie. The sun beat down on me and rose in waves of scorched heat. Tall buffalo grass swept one way, and then the other, golden in the slanted rays of sunlight. The mists kept me company even here. Across this plain, I went, until I saw the blackened and bloated carcasses of buffalo--heaps of rotting flesh in an endless sea across the fog-shrouded plain ahead of me. Each of them was minus its hide, some without their heads, but all of them wasted by greedy buffalo hunters. The reality of it swam around me in a sea of flies and acidic stench, so strong I almost gagged. I couldn't stop my dance or my chants.

This dream place seemed to want me to travel forward in time. The wrong direction, or the right one? I had no way of knowing. The time where Morning Dove lived had to be before the coming of the Europeans. The things I saw now happened after their coming.

My legs were turning to mush. I could no longer feel my feet. I couldn't stop to call to Morning Dove for fear if I did, the spirits would yank me from this place, and I'd lose any chance of finding her. In a stab of fear I recognized where I was. I stood in Morning Dove's lodge. The same one I had seen in my vision at the hospital when she had turned to look at me still mangled by the car. A slender form lay on her bed completely covered with a blanket.

With fear making my limbs rubbery, I pulled the blanket back to find Morning Dove. I touched her neck and didn't find a pulse. Her chest didn't move with breath. I bolted to my feet. My chant died away.

"I will not let you take her," I screamed at the fog around me. I screamed the words repeatedly. Her lodge no longer existed. If nothing had a form, this was it. Endless darkness, that felt as if I would fall away and slip forth into eternity, surrounded me. This was the place you got to just before you fell asleep and thought you were falling. I stood center-stage with a solitary tendril of light twining itself around my feet and slithering over Morning Dove's corpse. Eyes watched me. Judged me.

"I will not let you take her," I said. My own whisper felt as if it would shatter the fragile dark. Finally, I lay down next to Morning Dove and wrapped my arms around her cold limp body. I pressed my face into her hair. My angry tears fell on her. I could not lose this woman.

"I will not let you take her," I said again. I wouldn't let go of her. If the Great Spirit wanted Morning Dove, he would have to fight me for her.

Chapter Twelve
Returned Spirits

Awareness came slowly, and, with it, the realization that someone held onto my hand. I hurt from one end of my body to the other, as if I'd stood in the surgeries for thirty hours straight. I opened my eyes. Miraculously, I was in the Medicine Lodge. Morning Dove lay in my arms with her chest rising and falling in regular rhythm, and her small hand grasping mine. When I moved, she opened her eyes and looked at me. My hand shook when I touched the back of her neck; her skin felt cool and soft. I let the tips of my fingers brush across her face. We were alive and together.

"Medicine Elk, go. I will sit with her." I looked up at my grandfather in surprise. While others sometimes called me by the honorary title of Medicine Elk, my grandfather never did--sarcasm aside.

"How do you feel?" I asked Morning Dove.

"Not as bad as when the buffalo ran over me," she answered with a slight smile.

I frowned. She had been hit by a car in my time and run over by a buffalo sometime in her era?

"I can't imagine a buffalo stomping on me," I told her.

"Both the car and the buffalo ran over me," she whispered, "together."

Questions wanted to escape me, but I wasn't sure what I wanted to ask first. Instead of asking her to explain things she could clarify later, I slipped my arms around her and pressed her close to me. Tears wanted to escape me. Did others mean this total sense of oneness with another person when they spoke of their *soul* mate?

"I am glad you live," I whispered to her.

"Your Power is strong," she said back. Traditional words were the last thing I wanted to say to her, but tradition was the only thing I could use in the Medicine Lodge.

Reluctantly, I got to my feet. In the ceramic pot near the fire, I found the tea I'd brewed, now boiled down to a thick paste in the bottom. I added water, stirred it together, and poured the mixture into a wooden cup. Morning Dove accepted it, made a face at the taste, but drank the infusion down. My grandfather watched me as if I were a man he didn't know. I didn't want to leave her side, but nature didn't give me much of a choice.

"I won't be gone long," I told Morning Dove and went out the flap into the misty sunset.

After I left the men's toilet area, I made my way back to the Medicine Lodge. I stood outside it, taking in deep cleansing breaths of the dusk air. The air held a crisp cool edge to it, suggesting autumn. Birds twittered and went silent before starting again. People moved about making sure things were ready for the night. Mothers sang softly to their children, with nature as their accompaniment. Wood smoke rose from the tops of lodges, and I thought I smelled popcorn.

Kills Many sat on a large rock at the edge of the camp overlooking a meadow. With a determined step, I turned away from him and stopped. I needed to speak to him if for no other reason than his apparent concern for Morning Dove, even if I thought it false.

"They say you fought the Great Spirit to bring Morning Dove back to us," Kills Many said when I approached. He didn't look at me.

Had I fought the Great Spirit for her? If so, I didn't remember doing it--a brush with deity would be something a person wouldn't forget--unless the deity in question wanted me to forget. It seemed the only explanation for her once again coming back from the brink of death.

"I didn't hurt her. She got run over by a car . . . a machine, a beast that lives in the place I come from."

He gave me a wry look. "I know what a car is."

I stared at him for a long moment. Was he also displaced in time?

"Napi told me what happened to her. I don't know why she went back to your," he looked directly at me, "time."

Astonishment seized my voice. My grandfather had to be the one who told him what had happened to Morning Dove. Why had Kills Many called him Napi? Surely they didn't think my grandfather was our creator.

"You won't rule The People any more than you will have Morning Dove," Kills Many said into the silence between us.

"Is she your--was she your wife?" I stammered out. Divorce could be simple. The couple decided to split, or the man threw his wife away. A woman could throw her husband away as well, but it happened less often. I wasn't sure what customs this strange mix of people followed.

"No. She will be the wife of the one The Elders choose to lead us against the white-man." His voice held a cold edge. Although he spoke civil words to me, it seemed he still wanted to jump on me and smash my head. "But--she shared my lodge for three summers."

Good lord. Could Morning Dove have thrown him away and then invited me to share her bed? I shook my head. It didn't seem like something she would do. Anything I thought to say would sound like a lame platitude. Silence stretched out. The sun began to dip below the horizon. I noticed the scars on Kills Many's shoulders and on the thick biceps of his arms. I'd gotten a glimpse of the ones on the pectorals of his chest as well. Kills Many had participated in the Sun Dance more than a few times. My own scars from my once participation in the ritual were not as prominent as any of his.

"I followed her once," Kills Many said. "When Napi came back to us, he said if the tribes could affect peace for twelve summers, we would be saved from the coming of the white-man." Kills Many didn't look at me. His words sounded rehearsed, flat, and he said them in the same cadence as the elk-man. "At only twelve summers, Morning Dove had been a woman for three already, all who saw her said she communed with the spirits--and it had nothing to do with her appearance just when Napi returned to us. She didn't speak, and she lived as a wild thing. She slept where she pleased and ate at anyone's fire. No one wished her harm in any way. Once the twelve summers passed, she wandered into the united tribal council and took a seat right next to One Feather."

"One Feather?" I asked.

He glared at me, but answered. "Our Headman at the time. She shocked us all by speaking, first in Blackfoot, followed by Cherokee and Apache, on and on she went--using languages none of us present knew. She told of the coming of the white-man and what it would mean. She announced that at sunrise of the next day she would leave to bring those of the true visions to us."

He glanced at me. I looked back at him, staying silent.

"Napi brought us his council of honored Elders. They were to be our temporary leadership until The Chief of All Time could be chosen. Morning Dove would be the Chief of All Time's wife--she would travel time to find those suitable to lead for eternity."

Silence stretched out again. He sat there on the rock with his legs crossed and his axe in his lap. His fingers went over the handle and to the stone head again and again, as if it were a favorite pet. It wasn't my place to speak. The time belonged to him. He would tell me what he thought I should hear . . . and then maybe he would kill me.

"With each trip she took," he began again, "she became more frightened by things around her. Where once she roamed free at night and all around the camps, she kept to the line of lodges and often didn't move about in the dark at all. She never went to anyone's fire, and she became very thin. I started to hunt for her. Each time she came back, I made sure she had good food and enough of it. I even cooked it for her," he admitted. "One night, she returned without anyone, she had been gone for many moons, long enough we thought perhaps she wouldn't return."

"Was this when the other one from my time hurt her?" I asked and immediately wished I hadn't. I shouldn't have spoken.

"No. She said she'd gotten lost. She didn't know how to find food or anything else in the time the spirits led her to. She hadn't even known how to get home. She told me an Elder found her and sang over her to bring the spirits to guide her. It was the only way she found her way back."

"What time are you from?" I asked him. I really wanted to know what era Morning Dove came from, and it seemed they were from the same one.

He looked at me as if he wouldn't answer. With a deep breath, he said, "I was born in this time, this time before the white-man who will come in his big canoes and think we are savage animals." His hand tightened around his axe. His shoulder tensed. I flinched.

"And Morning Dove, do you know when she was born?"

"Midwinter, at least, that's when we found her, on a day when the air crackled with cold. The snow crust broke under people's feet with every step--and there she lay, covered in blood, in the village gathering place. She didn't belong to any of our women."

He shook his head and rubbed at the handle of his axe. How in the world had a woman, who didn't belong to Kills Many's tribe, give birth and leave her child behind in the dead of winter, without anyone knowing about it?

"Morning Dove didn't even cry. I was only thirteen summers, but I remember well looking down at her, wondering why she just lay there in the snow, staring at the sky and not crying. No one wanted to touch her. There were those who said an evil spirit left her and it would infect any who went near her."

He seemed to be deliberately leaving out the fact that the entire gathering place would have been considered contaminated. Had they immediately relocated?

"An old man hobbled into the square. He walked right up to her. Without regard to the blood, he picked her up. Those gathered murmured he was insane or perhaps the witch who had left her. He indicated an old woman. Night Girl, who many said was more than a hundred summers old and as frail as a woman could get. He pointed his staff at her and said, *'I am Napi and you, woman, will feed this child.'*"

I almost laughed, imagining my grandfather doing just that. My grandfather was Napi. The Napi. Someone whom they believed was the Old-Man of our creation myth. If I accepted I was here in this time, then I had to accept my grandfather was Napi.

"All around me, people laughed until Night Girl screamed. She grabbed at her chest and fell on the ground. All of us thought her heart had given out at the shock of this bent old man holding the newly born girl. She threw off her robes and pulled her shirt over her head so all could see her shrunken breasts were young again and full of milk. None doubted any longer. The Old-Man had returned. He demanded we care for the child, and we did. After that, they said the Great Spirit had given birth to Morning Dove. They said she had dropped from the womb of the sky--a perfect human without the flaws we other humans must endure."

The sun vanished, only a flare of pinkish light remained along the horizon. I worried about Morning Dove. Her life had started out surrounded by bizarre events. No wonder they treated her with respect and awe. I didn't know what to think or believe. I no longer considered myself insane or gravely injured. This was reality. The reality my grandfather believed in, and I had closed off my spirit to. My spirit had even been closed to it when I openly studied with my grandfather.

"Kills Many," I began, forgetting the taboo against saying a person's name to their face, "in my time, people marry because they are in love. I wouldn't want a wife who wanted another man. She would be unhappy, and I would. . . "

"Morning Dove does not love me." His statement came out flat and abrupt. Pain and hate were evident in his voice. "And I do not love her--I will lead The People. To do that, I must have Morning Dove."

I stood staring at the boulder. He thought of Morning Dove as a tool to gain the power he wanted. I couldn't imagine what such a marriage would be like for Morning Dove. Was that why she sought out strong men--those who could compete with Kills Many and offer her the chance for a marriage of love?

"And the one who hurt her before? Did he love her?" I asked.

"When she brought the one from your time," he said, "at first, he acted as if he had lost his wits. He got up and proclaimed he had the cure for the horrible sickness the whites will bring. He promised he would bring the proof by the next night. His mind was not right. He spoke of small beings that lived in the blood and caused illness. He said he knew how to kill them."

The sound of crickets and frogs from the nearby river punctuated the silence. An owl screeched. A flock of birds lifted and settled back down. Along the edge of the moonlit meadow, a fox trotted across the tree line, followed a short time later by another fox leading a couple of kits.

"I watched as Morning Dove set out towards the burial place where she let the spirits take her to different times. This, medicine man--Stands Tall, went with her."

I caught my breath. I knew the name Stands Tall. Impossible he was the same surgeon who had worked with me at Mercy for three years.

"I followed." He fondled the axe in his lap again. "I found Morning Dove standing across the trail those cars use. One of them stopped. She got inside it. It was not so hard to follow the car. It stopped often. I had already figured out when its strange light blinked it meant that it would turn. It went into an area filled with trees. I lost it for a time. I heard Morning Dove scream."

I closed my eyes for a moment, remembering her reluctance to go anywhere near my car and how she had mistrusted me. What changed her mind?

"The Great Spirit told her in your time she would find one who held many truths. She needed to trust him. She believed this evil one was the one they spoke of. I came upon them in a small area hidden from view. He hit her with his fist. Morning Dove sunk her teeth into his arm, and I heard her jawbone snap with the force of his next blow. I split his skull in two and escaped with Morning Dove before anyone else came to find us. We had to live in your time for three moons because the evil one had frightened Morning Dove's spirit helper. I didn't know how to return on my own."

I leaned against the large boulder with a shudder. The man who attacked Morning Dove was the same Stands Tall I had worked with. He had been found with his skull split apart, with the blood and skin of his supposed attacker under his nails and imbedded in the horrendous wounds to his fists. The police came to the conclusion that he'd fought hard against whoever killed him--with a sharp rock of some sort. With a stone war axe. Later, the rumor mill turned out the word: he'd been a pedophile. In his home, there had been stacks of child pornography--all of the children had been about eleven or twelve years of age.

Vividly, I saw the red smeared square on Morning Dove's wall. Did the square contain the name Stands Tall? Did Kills Many's square have a red smear because he had killed Stands Tall? My mind wanted to believe it was the reason, but my soul tried to put it down. I wasn't seeing something I should have.

"Morning Dove cursed the spirits afterwards and refused to serve them. She reverted to the way she had been before the first time she spoke. Many members of the tribe whispered that she conversed with the spirits--quarreled with them. She forgot to eat and wandered from place to place as she had as a child. I took her in and cared for her when her spirit helper abandoned her--she had to stay in our time." He turned to look directly at me with fire in his eyes. He raised his arm and struck the air with his fist. "I have led The People since Napi brought the peace. Now she brings you. All the others, none of them think to take the leadership from me--none of them think to keep me from my right to be selected as Chief of All Time. None of them think they will have the Power Morning Dove offers."

"I don't want to take leadership away from you." I didn't even know what he was talking about. I knew the story of the Mouse and Napi, when they chose the Chief of All Time, but I saw the tale as something in our past: a story, a myth, a legend--a way to explain why my mother never killed mice. It struck me suddenly--I was in the past.

"You want Morning Dove, so you want to be chosen. You will not be. I am the best choice to lead. I will kill these invaders. It is the only way," Kills Many said.

Chapter Thirteen
Choices and Challenges

"Medicine Elk?" Morning Dove's voice rescued me.

"You shouldn't be up," I said and stepped towards her.

"I am well. I would rather sleep in my own bed than with the spirits who reside in the Medicine Lodge."

Kills Many got down off his perch. He shoved his axe into the loop on his belt before he moved towards her. I paced away from them to give Kills Many some sort of privacy with her. I didn't stray far, though, and stood in the shadow of a tree watching the way the moonlight shone off Morning Dove's hair. Morning Dove pulled her shoulders back and sent a hard look his way before she turned and went back into the camp. I followed her with my gaze, wishing she would have stayed near me. I truly hated Kills Many. Just being near him made the hair on the back of my neck raise, and I wanted to lash out at him. I had an unreasonable desire to do away with him. It frightened me because I didn't have any true explanation for feeling that way.

"There's no reason for us to fight," I told him. He was right, I wanted Morning Dove, but I didn't see how that equated to being chosen as The Chief of All Time.

"Words solve nothing," he said.

"Neither does fighting over Morning Dove. It's her choice."

He laughed at me. The sound of it loud and echoing as if his voice came from inside and out. "Her choice? What do you know about her choices? It does not matter who she wants--the one they choose will have her, and she will be wife to that man."

I opened my mouth and shut it. Words of protest came to me, but I held them in. In this time, I was sure the Elders could tell Morning Dove who her husband had to be. I thought of her time travel--what that would do for a chief--yes, it would be considered a great Power and a great gift. The one who possessed Morning Dove would possess her powerful gift as well.

"Women now, they have too much say in the ways of men. A man should not allow a wife to toss him out."

"Even if the marriage is not a good one?" I asked.

"If a man hunts and provides--the marriage is a good one," he asserted.

"There is more to a marriage than simply providing for physical needs," I told him. "If a woman's husband does. . . "

"Do you know what she did to me?" he interrupted in a hard tone. "I came back from a hunt and found my things piled outside the doorway to her lodge. I understood what it meant. The Hopi are too peace loving. I wanted to shout at her, but I would have gained nothing by doing so--many have adopted the Hopi custom of putting a man's things out. Men have done the same."

With his back straight, he was only a slight bit shorter than me. "She does not want a husband," he told me as if he were the expert in all things about Morning Dove. "She only wants a man so she can have a lodge full of children."

I almost told him I hadn't been with Morning Dove like he thought. I stopped myself because the admission might only serve to give him hope, and I had to admit I liked the fact he burned with jealousy over the relationship he thought Morning Dove and I had. What did Morning Dove feel for this warrior? For that matter, what did she feel for me? I found it odd that when I thought of her, I wanted to run to her side. I loved her, even if I hadn't known her long enough.

"Can you, *medicine man*, provide for her and her many children?" he snarled.

"At least I can give her children," I snapped out, not knowing if I were perhaps as infertile as he seemed to be saying he was. If Morning Dove was barren, then anyone she chose would disappoint her.

With an angry grunt, Kills Many shoved me. I refused to stagger and gave him a hard shove in return. He instantly stepped back, shaking his head and taking quick breaths.

I held up my hands, indicating I didn't want to fight with him, even though I wanted to pound him into corpse powder.

"It isn't our choice," I reminded him. It should have been Morning Dove's choice. I didn't like the idea that the Elders would give her to whoever they chose as the Chief of All Time.

He took a deep breath before he scanned the woods around us. No one had seen our little shoving match.

"They will choose me to lead, but if they don't--you won't have her either." He left the threat hanging in the air between us and stalked off into the night.

A shadow moved out of the trees and followed him. It was the elk-man. Did the creature follow Kills Many now because I hated the man and would have liked nothing better than an excuse to stalk after him and continue our arguments? I considered warning Kills Many, but brushed it aside. He would have to deal with the inhuman creature just as I had done.

I crossed the camp and spent a moment at the low burning central fire. I ached with exhaustion and the desire for a cigarette, although I'd quit several years before. My grandfather sat on the other side of the fire, wrapped in a blanket. His intense stare stayed fixed on me, but he said nothing.

"Kills Many thinks you are Napi. Are you?"

"Do you think I am?"

I gazed at him. He hadn't changed since I'd first met him--forty-four years before. I'd been four, given a quarter by my father. I'd raced down to the local trading post to get as much candy as twenty-five cents could buy. I'd already been in the second grade, awing the white teachers with my unusual intelligence--for an "Indian."

I'd dropped the quarter and had to crawl under the porch to get it. Sitting on the step when I crawled out had been this wrinkled old man. I'd expected him to smell of booze. Instead, he'd told me candy would rot my teeth, but if I was going to get some anyway to make it chocolate. I'd gotten a Hershey's bar, sat on the step, and shared it with him. Rudely, I'd asked him his name. He'd told me he was my grandfather.

"When you followed me home all those years ago--my dad, he didn't even blink when you asked to live with us." How could I believe I was sitting across from, well, a god?

"Didn't your dad, and you at the time, believe Napi made all of you?"

I stifled a laugh. "Yes, yes, I did."

"So then you are my grandchild, aren't you, or just stupid?"

That would be it. He wouldn't tell me anything more. I either accepted he was Napi, or that he'd convinced everyone here he was. Easy for him to do. He'd just badger them until they relented.

"When do they expect me to speak?" I asked him.

"You will know when it is time. The Elders thought to end the time of talk on this day, but you fought the Great Spirit. So, they will wait until you are ready to speak."

"How often has Kills Many spoken?" I failed to keep the agitation out of my voice.

"Kills Many does not lie, but he omits." In this time, my grandfather seemed just as bent on not answering my questions.

"Omits?"

"Morning Dove made him very angry. Mad. Crazy. She was desperate to have a child, so she returned to honoring the Great Spirit. In her vision--the spirits told her she should lay with a different man. She sought out Jumper and followed her vision."

Anger and envy rose in me. I fought it down. This happened before I met her. It didn't matter, but I also wondered how I would deal with her infidelity, if I were chosen.

"A moon later, she knew she carried Jumper's child. Kills Many had been gone the entire moon. He returned to find his things outside her door in the Hopi way of divorce, though he wasn't her husband."

"Where is her child?" I asked--demanded.

"Kills Many became enraged when he found out she carried Jumper's child. He confronted Jumper and attacked him. Morning Dove got between them. Kills Many hit her instead of Jumper, and, with much pain, she lost her child."

Heat rose to the top of my head and made my arms ache with my desire to hurt Kills Many in some non-repairable way. I had a good reason to hate him now.

"Kills Many swore to protect and provide for her for the rest of her life for what he did. Morning Dove has refused his request, but she honors his devotion to it." My grandfather got to his feet and walked away.

I thought of what I would have felt had I been Kills Many. Anger beyond words and to have hurt Morning Dove would have sealed my fate. I would have taken my own life. I understood why Kills Many regularly participated in the Sun Dance. I could see him with an eagle bone whistle clinched between his teeth. He would watch Morning Dove, while the medicine man skewered his flesh, to see if she had forgiven him yet.

While he hung from the central pole by those skewers, waiting for his flesh to tear, did he blow through the whistle to take away Morning Dove's pain? Or was it simply a way to endure the pain of the Sun Dance ritual and gain what he wanted?

I'd tried to blow away my pain over my father's death through the same sort of whistle. It hadn't worked.

I sat on the ground near the fire. The last few days blurred together. I didn't understand how I had ended up in this time any more than I understood how I had lost my soul to Morning Dove.

The events happening around me, and the time I had already spent here, led me to accept this time travel, or whatever, was real. I could still feel the way Morning Dove felt laying in my arms. The joy I experienced at her being alive went beyond description.

Medicine visions were real enough, but the images they held were often surreal and would have made no sense in the real world. There were things here that made no sense: people from different times mixed together, tribes who should have been at war--cooperating, and the way they simply accepted this was what should be--the metaphysical accepted as part of everyday life, and the Sun Dance--obviously being done in a time before modern history claimed, but all this had a solid real world feel to it.

Picking up a stick, I made lines in the dirt until I had drawn a pyramid. Around the pyramid, I made designs like those in the ceramic dishes Morning Dove owned. Most likely they had come from Mexico or farther south, gifts from Jumper. I erased the lines.

Thinking of Jumper made me angry. I thought of Kills Many as well. Morning Dove had chosen me, it seemed, but how long would it be until she cast me aside, as she had them? With a grunt, I realized Morning Dove had no choice. Why would she want a permanent relationship, one she gave herself freely to, when the Elders would choose for her in a short time?

If they let Kills Many keep the power of leadership, he would be her husband. If they chose Jumper to replace Kills Many, Jumper would be her mate. I didn't understand why it was so important Morning Dove be the Chief of All Time's mate. But if that's what it took--I would find a way to take that from Kills Many.

Somewhere in the dark, a laugh rang out, a short burst of an infant's cry came to me. The sound cut off sharply when the mother most likely pinched the child's nose shut. It wasn't a cruel thing to do, children had to be quiet or they could put the whole band in danger. Even if the child had to learn to be silent by having his jaw held shut as well. A raised voice came from somewhere, and it too went silent quickly. I wondered if someone's things would be set outside in the morning. Here in this camp, customs had turned into a hodge-podge mixture of whatever worked.

I got to my feet and dusted off my hands. Morning Dove would be asleep by now. I would sneak into her lodge and curl up on the guest bed. I would try to sleep, though I doubted it would come easily with her right there near me.

The door flap rattled only a small amount when I went into her lodge. The fire burned brighter than the one outside. A lit stone lamp hung from a center pole. Morning Dove sat up quickly.

"It's just me," I said, chiding myself for thinking I could sneak in on her. The blanket Morning Dove wore around her shoulders slipped down to reveal one of her breasts. I wanted to go to her and tug the blanket back up, simultaneously I wanted to yank it away from her. With a sigh, I turned away from her and moved to make my bed ready.

"Have you taken a vow of celibacy?"

I straightened my back. Some medicine men did. Even when I'd been dedicated to the ideals of the past, I'd never seen the reason for it. What was I supposed to say to her? She wasn't some innocent child. I thought of Kills Many and Jumper, I doubted they were her only lovers. In this time, she had been a woman almost half her life. I tried to tell myself she was only sixteen, maybe only fifteen--a good reason to stay away from her and refuse her offer. But she had been pregnant with a child she wanted and lost it. She lived alone and traveled the time stream on her own. With slow movements, I pulled off my shirt and sat behind her.

She leaned back into me. I wrapped my arms around her. A pleasant chill ran along my nerves. "How old are you?" I asked her, dreading the *modern man* in me who wouldn't let go of the issue of a number age.

Her laughter filled me with longing. I hugged her tighter. "By the way those from your time count age, I am nineteen."

Would she lie to me? I saw no reason why she would. "You told my grandfather you were going to be seventeen." Why didn't I just leave this alone and make love to her? She obviously wanted me.

She clasped my hand and brought it to her face. "When your grandfather gave me to Night Girl, all thought I would die. I did not grow and had many illnesses during the first year of my life. At my first birthday, they did not accept me as a person yet, so I did not receive a name."

"My grandfather just let them do this?" I demanded. If he could use some form of mystic Power to bring milk to Night Girl, I didn't see why he would let them treat Morning Dove as a non-person.

"What could he do? He could not come and change all overnight. I went through my second year just as ill, so they did not name me then either. I was no bigger than a nine moon old child at my third birthday. Napi, your grandfather, proposed I be left in the woods overnight. If I were found alive in the morning, I would be considered a person and given a name. There were many who thought I should have been left to die long before that." She kissed the palm of my hand, and fire shot through my veins. I no longer cared how old she was or how many lovers she'd had before me.

"Obviously, you lived." At the moment, I couldn't remember ever feeling so alive.

"When dawn came, I walked into camp with a flock of doves following me. They landed in the trees all around the central circle, and a lone wolf stood at the edge of camp. Throughout the night, the wolf had watched me. I thought I would be his food. Off in the forest, an elk stood watching over me as well. On this morning, all who saw them wondered at the Power I held. So I was one, when I should have been three, and they started counting that day as if I had just come from my mother's womb." She twisted around to look at me with a slight smile. "I will be twenty soon, not jail bait by any means."

I laughed, remembering to keep it low. Without another word, I touched my lips to her forehead and brushed them against her eyelids. I kissed each of her cheeks, before I pushed my lips against hers. She answered me with surprising hunger. Moving my hand up and down her bare back, I let the strands of her hair fall through my fingers like liquid silk. Her hands found me, and her fingers encircled me. Her touch explored me as an experienced woman would.

"I will be gentle," I said more to myself than to her. I felt on fire from too long a period of abstinence, with the passion she stirred in me, and with the love I had discovered for her. I wasn't going to be able to control myself very well.

She pulled back from me and held my face in her hands. She looked into my eyes as if she saw my spirit laid bare. Her hands went over my chest, her fingers stopping at my Sun Dance scars, before she went on to touch my medicine mark. She put her fingers to my lips as if she knew I wanted to speak.

"I do not want your gentleness. I want to feel the flame of the passion our spirits have found in each other."

I needed no more encouragement. I understood what she wasn't saying. We should share now, because soon the Elders would choose a husband for her. And I damned well would do everything I could to make sure it would be me. I closed my arms around her small form. Her firm breasts against me were warm and inviting. I cupped my hand around one of them and let the feel of her stiff nipple stir me to greater excitement. I locked my mouth over hers and pulled her down to the blankets.

Chapter Fourteen
Past Perfect

Dawn came too early. Lying with Morning Dove clasped in my arms, I kept my eyes shut against the sunlight pressing against my eyelids. When my pager went off, I leapt out of the bed. Standing, with the beeping sound loud in the room, I stared around me in dread and amazement. I was in my room--in my own house. I grabbed up the pager. What a dream and I couldn't remember having gone to bed.

Morning Dove stood on the other side of the bed, watching me warily. The pager shrilled again. The number on it meant the Flight-for-Life people were bringing someone into Mercy. I looked back at Morning Dove.

What had I done? Could Sam have brought something I had decided to indulge in? I'd seduced Morning Dove, and it had gotten lost in some drug-induced hallucination? No, I didn't think so. The scent of wood smoke and tallow lamps filled my room and surrounded me. But time travel . . . how could that be?

"You must gather what you need. We have to return. Now." The urgent edge to her voice brought my attention fully to her. Shame made my face burn. In the past, I'd dismissed the idea of returning. I didn't know how to get back. Morning Dove lived there, and that was all I wanted, at that moment, in the past. Now, I was here and she was here--and someone needed me, I had to go. I went around the bed and drew Morning Dove against me. She had bruises on her hips and thighs. I'd covered her shoulder and the upper curve of one of her breasts with suck-marks and not a few marks from my teeth.

"We'll talk when I get back. I have to go." Reluctantly, I pulled back from her. Whenever someone told me they had found their soul mate--I'd scoffed. Love at first sight got the same treatment. I wasn't even sure love, as a thing of the heart, existed. Love resulted from a balance of chemicals that ensured the species would propagate and survive. With Morning Dove, I found love to be a real thing, an emotion so strong my chest grew tight at the thought of leaving her for even a few moments. She'd scratched and bitten me as well. I would have liked nothing better than to fall back into bed with her and forget the world.

"No, we must go now. I am. . . ."

"It's the Flight-for-Life people," I cut her off. "They could be bringing someone in, like they brought you in. If I don't go, they might die."

"So you choose one life over the life of The People?" Her words were bitter. With an angry movement, she jerked a blanket off the bed and wrapped it around her. I sat on the edge of the bed and dialed up the hospital to report in. Behind me, I could hear Morning Dove moving around the room. The short sharp breaths she took tugged at me. I didn't want her to cry or to be unhappy. I jerked on a pair of pants and grabbed a sweatshirt out of a drawer. Morning Dove had on her flannel shirt and was pulling up the zipper on her pants when I turned to look at her again.

"Morning Dove, we *will* talk when I get back. We'll decide together where we should be." Frankly, I didn't see how any of my plans, or anyone else's, were going to make much difference when the Europeans came and wanted the land. It didn't matter if we banded together--disease would wipe us out. Outsiders would still kill and do away with us, in the name of kings, religion, and greed. Kills Many had The Peoples' support. I was an unknown. Why would I risk losing her to him?

With Morning Dove here in my time, I had her. Given enough time, she would come to enjoy all the modern conveniences just as I did.

"Morning Dove," I began.

"Do not use my name anymore, Shannon Running Deer--Trauma Surgeon. You may be one of The People by blood and you may look like one of us, but you are as the white-man inside. You are one man and do not see others around you."

"I've worked to save others every day for the last twenty-two years," I snapped out at her.

"One *other* at a time. You do not care for the fate of the group as a whole. You care for the fate of those who made your life possible even less. Go, great white-man, and do what you must."

After I shoved my feet into running shoes, I moved to intercept her path out the door. She turned away from my gesture when I tried to touch her face.

"Wait until I get back. We'll speak then. I promise. We can't leave things like this."

She pushed at my hands on her arms. When I let go, she took a few steps back into the room and sat in a chair. With her arms crossed over her chest, she glared at me.

"There's plenty of food in the kitchen--if my grandfather hasn't eaten it all. I'll call you as soon as I can."

Going out the door, with my keys in hand, I felt I was making a great mistake. What would I do if she wasn't there when I got back? No, she would be. It could be no other way. I would make her see all the modern world had to offer.

The helicopter touched down as I pulled up to the hospital. I would have just enough time to get into scrubs. In the locker room, John sat on a bench and tied his shoes.

"Couldn't get a hold of you all day yesterday or the day before," he said.

"I was busy." I pulled off the sweatshirt and snatched a T-shirt out on my locker.

"Looks like it," he said behind me. "Don't think I've seen you quite so scratched up--not since that stallion of yours threw you into the thorn bushes."

I twisted my head to the side. Morning Dove had scratched my back worse than I'd thought. I moved to pull a second shirt out. If any of those scratches opened up, and I bled through my shirt and scrubs, I'd be kicked out of surgery. I would have to give someone an explanation.

John went to a cabinet on the other side of the room. He came back with some antiseptic spray. He stood behind me, coating my back with it, before he applied bandages to cover the scratches. I let him, waiting for his questions.

"Guess you made someone happy," he said before going back to his shoes.

"Last night, this morning, she's pissed as hell I'm here."

"That tiny Indian woman?"

"Don't start again how she isn't my type." With a yank, I pulled the last tie on the gown shut and went to the sink. I tugged on a surgical-cap. I had to yank the ties off the small bent and twisted hair-horn on the top of my head and force my braids up under the cap. John watched me with a bemused expression.

"She spooked the heck out of me and everyone else," John said.

With good reason, I thought.

John went out of the room before me. I scrubbed in the sink, waiting for the timer to go off to tell me I'd done it long enough. The face staring back out of the mirror surprised me. Had I fooled myself so long I'd started seeing myself as white? I looked like I'd recently walked off a reservation. The timer dinged. I shook water from my hands and gave my reflection one more glance. It was my eyes. In them, I saw the same far off look my grandfather's always held. I heard the echoing solitary screech of an eagle and one solid drum beat as if a door slammed shut. In the mirror, I actually saw the mystic look leave my eyes. A cube of ice bumped down my spine. I felt as if I'd lost something I hadn't even known I'd possessed.

In the ER, John repeated orders given by the on-call pediatrician who stood at his side. I shuddered. I hated it when children came in. So many things happened to them.

"That's what the Life-Flight people said. She spilled her daddy's soda pop. He grabbed her by the ankles, swung her around, and let her fly into a wall." This came from a duty nurse.

I joined the circle of people around the small body of a child who looked no more than three. The trauma to her small body had horribly colored her face and left it sticky with blood. The collar around her neck and the backboard spoke of spinal injuries. The heart machine shrilled. The auto voice started screeching we had a code-blue. No one in the room needed the machinery to tell them she'd gone into cardiac arrest. I think everyone knew, even as we fought to restart her heart, she was already gone.

John looked at the clock when he stepped back. "Time, oh six hundred–June third." He went to the sink area and jerked off his gloves with angry movements. "I'd like to do the same to her father."

I followed him out into the waiting area where the EMTs still lingered. Adults had indulged Indian children in the past. They disciplined them only when an action would put the whole tribe in danger. Otherwise, children were left to discover many dangers on their own, but I never heard an adult raise their voice to them. Grandparents, uncles, and others helped care for the young as a community. No stigma got attached to letting others care for your child, so no adult needed to feel pushed to the point of abuse. Once a child was past a week old anyway, but it seemed a better set up.

I shook my head at the EMT's and saw them both deflate.

"The mother was DOA at the scene," one of them told me. "The police think she tried to stop him from doing it. She got her head caved in with a lamp for her effort. The caring father says his wife beat the baby, so he killed her."

The other EMT scrubbed a hand over her face. "The guy'll get a good lawyer and walk away." With those sardonic words, they left the room.

I didn't have much time to think on it. The screech of sirens sounded and an ambulance, followed by two more, rushed in under the awning. This day wasn't going to go well at all.

They were gang members. The head scarves and rolled up single pant legs were not only bad fashion statements, but the gang affiliation it advertised had cost four of them their lives. Out of the nine involved, three went straight to surgery. Two, from rival gangs, sat in the waiting area with the police when I came out of the O.R.--they'd received only minor injuries--so they were low on the triage list.

Normally, I changed or put on a lab coat to hide the blood spatters covering me. Today, I didn't. I walked out and stood looking at the two young men. The boy I had worked on would never walk again. His life was all but over, as far as the physical side of things went. These two sat on opposite sides of the room, glaring at each other as if they would pull guns and finish what they'd started.

I studied them and concluded, although they were young, they were over eighteen. How long had gangs been their only family? Cast-offs was what they were. No aunts, uncles, or grandparents to watch out for them. Parents overworked and unsupported by the system, and the approach of the tough teen years, equaled a recipe for ruined lives.

"Hey, look," one of them shouted and pointed at me, "it's Sitting Bull." He laughed and his enemy laughed as well.

The policeman shook his head. I didn't look anything like Sitting Bull, but I'd heard it before. It still failed to amuse me in any way.

"There were nine of you to start with. Four of your buddies are dead. One is now a paraplegic. One will be a slobbering vegetable--if he makes it. And the other has lost an arm." Rage boiled inside me. "What the fucking hell was worth doing this over?"

One of the boys leaned back with his arms clasped around his ribs and stared at the ceiling. The other glared at me.

"We ain't had nothing to do the fuck with it. Besides, injun-man, you should understand defend'n territory. Them spics asked for it--was on our turf."

"The hell we were, nigger," the other yelled. At this point, both jumped to their feet. The police rushed in to keep them apart.

"What a waste," I spat.

"Injun-man, maybe you should take lessons--you know, dumb injuns lost their land. Boo whooo."

The other boy sank back on his chosen couch and spat a stream of tobacco juice on the floor. "Not our fuckin' fault, them gay crackheads was on our fuckin' turf. They asked for it."

"It's ghetto, man," the other said, almost starting a fight again. At least he could admit the whole thing was a waste.

In all the arguments I'd heard about the various ways to save us in the past, the young had been equally hotheaded. When an Elder spoke, though, they became silent. Even if they were sullen, they had respect. When had people lost that respect? The young on present-day reservations no longer valued their elders as they should have either. In the past, youth died. It was easy to get mauled on a hunt. And before they had reached the peace, many died in battles over petty quarrels. But it paled when compared to the disputes of modern times.

I escaped the room. My heart pounded in my chest as if it wanted to be free of me at the cost of blasting through my ribs. Sweat made a trail down my back. Everyone was a victim, and they saw nothing wrong with lying, child beating, and killing each other--over a patch of cement. It only counted if you got caught. Why had I never felt like this before? It was all part of modern life. *Time enough for everything*. There should have been time enough for everything, but there wasn't. Time got eaten up with stinking shit that didn't matter, or shouldn't have been.

I leaned back against the cold, froth green tiles of the wall. The sterile smell of the trauma unit made my sinuses burn. I rubbed at the bridge of my nose and tried to clear my throat. I felt as if I were suffocating. I needed some outdoor air.

My pager went off. The trauma center was filled to capacity. There would be no time for a breath of fresh air now. I moved to the back, changed my scrubs, and disinfected without thought. My brain felt filled with frozen slush, numb--my thoughts sloppy. In the treatment room, I found a pale-faced girl on the gurney. A tech slipped a needle into the vein in her arm to get a blood sample. The girl continued to stare at the ceiling as if he hadn't done it.

The duty nurse handed me her chart. At least this one appeared routine. The girl had a history of seizures. She'd had one. The parents called when she'd failed to recognize them afterwards.

"Sandy? Can you hear me?" I asked, with my hand on her shoulder. Her gaze never left the ceiling.

John moved to her feet and pulled off one of her worn athletic shoes. He used the handle of a reflex hammer to test for responsiveness by running it along the bottom of her foot. She didn't move.

As I ordered neural scans and tests, the subtle beat of a medicine drum filled my ears. The chemical smells around me suddenly stank horribly. Why hadn't I ever noticed the sticky sweet smell of old blood overlaying it before?

My sense of smell heightened until I could pick out each chemical. The room jumped into sudden clarity as if I had been fasting. My temples throbbed in unison with the soft beat of the drum. I jerked around towards the hallway when I thought I heard the click of a dog's nails on the tiles. A passing nurse gave me an odd look before hurrying away. I grabbed a tissue and moved off to the side and blew my nose clear of the odors assaulting me. I refused to let the drums draw me in. This girl needed my help.

Once she was on her way to the nuclear medicine wing, I made my way to my office where her parents waited for me.

Inside the room, a tall gruff-looking man stood examining the diplomas hanging on the paneled wall behind my desk. His dingy jeans and denim shirt, with his crop of red hair, made me think of lumberjacks. A dark-haired woman sat perched on the edge of a wing chair as if she wanted to take flight. Her kaftan hung on her slim frame, a pink crystal dangled from a chain around her neck. She wore three tiny silver hoops in her left eyebrow and a pink stud in her nose. They didn't make a likely couple.

They turned as one to look at me when I shut the door. My shoes whispered across the thick blue carpet. I cleared my throat and waited for the man to move so I could sit behind my desk. He stood with his shoulders pulled back, and his angry gaze locked with mine.

I held out my hand. "I'm Doctor Shannon Running Deer. I've seen your daughter. I'd like to talk about her."

He glanced down at my hand, but didn't grasp it. I looked at my hand, thinking I had blood or something on it.

"Her regular doc? Where's he at?" the man asked.

I lowered my hand and sat on the edge of my desk, setting her file next to me. Under normal circumstances when I reduced my considerable height, it put people at ease. It did nothing to make this man relax his hostile stance.

"As I understand it, Doctor Stevens is out of the country. The staff neurologist is seeing Sandy right now. EMS brought her into trauma, so that makes me her primary at the moment."

"You really go to John Hopkins?"

I always wanted to snap out at people--no. I hadn't--I'd copied my diplomas from someone else. "Yes."

"How is my daughter?" the woman asked.

Giving the man a pointed look, I stood. Reluctantly, he moved away from my desk and sat on the couch--away from his wife and away from me. I sat in my desk chair and opened the file on Sandy Brozman.

"Mister and Misses Brozman. . ."

"He's Mister Brozman. I'm Lisa Sheridan. We're divorced."

That explained some of the ice hanging in the room's air. "At this point, we are waiting on the neurological scans to be done and the results looked at."

"In other words you don't know squat," Mister Brozman informed me.

"For Christ's sake, Tom. Can't you be civil?"

"Civil? You have custody and next thing I know they're calling me at the site and telling me Sandy's on the way to the hospital. Her regular doc's off playing somewhere and we have. . ." He glanced at me and stopped, perhaps changing his mind on what he wanted to call me. Teens I could take calling me names, but had this man come out with a racial slur--my reaction would not have been a calm one.

"I understand this is a trying situation. Perhaps there is someone I can call for you? The hospital has a nondenominational clergyman, if you would like me to call him?"

"There isn't any god. If there was, Sandy wouldn't be this way," he snapped back at me as if I would argue with him. Once, I may have agreed with him. No longer.

"We're atheists," Lisa Sheridan informed me. "It's the only thing we ever agreed on. How soon before we know what's wrong with Sandy?"

"When the test results are back, I'll have more to tell you. She's currently breathing on her own and the lack of response could be a result of the seizure she experienced."

"Temporary?" Lisa asked me.

Before I spoke, I gave Tom Brozman a chance to speak over what his ex-wife asked. When he stayed silent, I looked at Lisa Sheridan. "From what I saw in the trauma center, there is the possibility of permanent brain damage."

Tom Brozman smacked his fist into the wall. Lisa wrapped her arms around her ribs. I called the hospital social worker before I got to my feet. "Please don't hit the wall again. It won't do you any good to have a broken hand."

"This wouldn't have happened..."

"Mister Brozman, it won't help anyone to assign blame here. Your daughter's condition is a serious one and has been since her birth. Please control yourself." I sat next to his wife. "Lisa?"

She shook her head, holding back sobs. "Damn it, damn it," she said again and again.

I sat with my hand on her shoulder, enduring Brozman's glares until the social worker came. Genuine relief washed over me when they left with her. I sat in my chair, leaned back, and rubbed at my temples. The three rating of the Glasgow Coma Scale on Sandy's records haunted me. With a number so low, chances were she would never wake up.

I pressed the phone to my ear and dialed my home number. It rang and rang. My grandfather should have answered it even if Morning Dove didn't want to. Was my grandfather even there? Why had I so easily decided everything had been a dream? I knew damned well it hadn't been.

"Come on, Morning Dove, answer," I muttered and re-dialed when the phone cut out, letting me know I had let it ring too long. Still, no answer. I shouldn't have left her. My perspective had changed. I still didn't accept the modern Indian had to live in self-inflicted poverty, adhering to ways that didn't work anymore, but in Morning Dove's time those ways did work.

As if in answer to my thoughts, the drums came up louder. I heard the soft sound of a spirit-healing chant. I shut Sandy Brozman's records. With determined steps, I went to the cabinet where I kept a few things that had once adorned my office. A feather fan, a rattle, a tin of tobacco and another of corn pollen, along with a small medicine pouch, sat on the lowest shelf.

Moving out of my office, I made my way to the ICU where Sandy lay. The nurses had covered her eyes so they wouldn't dry out. From the waiting room, the raised voices of her parents, as they argued about who would stay in her room, came to me.

I shut the curtain over the closed glass doors and turned to the girl. Very softly, I sang along with the chant echoing in my head. I moved back and forth next to her bed, letting the hospital fade out. I marched around her in the medicine lodge of Morning Dove's village with the young medicine man beating the drum. My grandfather chanted the harmony parts with me.

"It is time," my grandfather stated.

I found myself alone in a small cave with Sandy Brozman. She lay in her hospital gown on the rocky ground. A hole opened up near her, and a badger crawled out of it. The drummer continued. I kept up my chant while I watched the badger.

"What you seek is here," Badger told me.

I looked at the corner of the cave where Badger now sat. From the top of a pile of bones, a human skull grinned at me.

"Free the trapped spirit of this one and free the trapped spirit of the pale girl." Badger vanished back down his hole and pulled the dirt in behind him.

I picked up the skull and looked inside it. There was a considerable amount of bone growth on the inside of the cranium. Whoever it had belonged to had suffered a great deal of pain in their life. At my feet, a large flat rock and a rounded grinding stone rested on the packed reddish ground. I understood what Badger meant.

I crushed the skull.

Then I pounded it into a fine powder. I gathered the powder and started my chant again. I knelt next to Sandy and blew the powder over her.

"What in the hell are you doing?"

Tom Brozman's angry voice snapped me back to Sandy's room.

"I'll have your license for this," he shouted at me next. My hand felt grit covered. John stood near the station desk behind Brozman, looking at me with wide eyes and a shocked expression. The neurologist standing next to Mr. Brozman wore an expression I'd seen before. More than likely he was here to tell us Sandy Brozman's brain no longer functioned on the higher levels.

"Daddy?"

Everyone turned to look at Sandy. The neurologist pushed past Sandy's father. "This is impossible," he said.

Brozman shook his finger in my face. "You are through." He shoved past me to go to his daughter.

I moved out into the hall. I could barely see. Why were the lights so damned bright?

John's hand went to my shoulder. "Shane, what the hell's wrong with you?"

The Power is in you, Running Deer. I chose you. Do not disappoint me again.

I shook my head and looked around the hallway, expecting to see my grandfather. Instead, I saw the wary looks of every person on the ICU floor. The hospital smelled awful. The lights kept getting brighter. Every beep and ding made me jump. This was the unreal dream. Reality lay with Morning Dove and the ways born in my blood.

I tore off my cap and shoved John out of the way. As I stumbled out of the ICU, I pulled off my scrubs and dropped them where I ran. In the locker room, I snatched up my keys and ducked out of the building.

Chapter Fifteen
Perhaps Too Late

The back bumper of the Jag hit a post. Metal crunched, and the shattery sound of a busted taillight filled the car. I jammed it into first and took off out of the parking lot. Morning Dove would understand why I left her. She had once abandoned all she believed in. I refused to think I'd used up my one chance when I left her in my bedroom. I passed a car on the right, churning up gravel on the back-road shortcut to my house. The driver of the car flipped me off and blew his horn. I didn't care.

Morning Dove and I had shared each other repeatedly the night before. I'd felt like a man starved. She'd answered every need I had. When we finally lay tangled together, with the fire dancing before us, she had taken my hand and put it on her stomach. *"Perhaps I already carry your child."*

That worried me. What if she did? With a laugh, she'd told me it would be a connection between us no one could break, even if they chose another to be her husband. I understood I would support her child. I'd held her in my arms as she'd slept, determined she would be mine even if I had to take her away from her People. Had my wish somehow brought us back to my time? It was very unlikely she became pregnant after only one night together, but the chance did exist.

Impatiently, I hit the button to open the gates. Moments crept like hours before they were wide enough for the Jag to go through. I bumped the front of the car up on the walk, ramming the underskirt into the brick retaining wall--antifreeze began to leak out in a sickly-sweet curl of steam. I no longer cared.

The keys didn't want to go into the lock. I dropped them twice before I succeeded in getting the front door open. Inside the house, I went to the closet and dug out two leather backpacks I stored in there for my brief visits to the reservation. I tossed them on the couch.

"Morning Dove," I shouted as I passed the steps. It was dark outside. I had been at the hospital for almost eighteen hours. Morning Dove was most likely asleep. In my den, I scanned the shelves looking for books I wanted to bring. The entire *Foxfire* survival series was a must. I owned a set of books containing all the treaties the US government would offer the different Indian nations, those

I would bring. As I grabbed several of my *Mother Earth News* survival-in-the-wilderness books, I thought of what I would say to the council. I imagined the white-men coming and discovering what they thought was witchcraft. Solar power and natives who had electricity--I couldn't guess at the era Morning Dove had taken me to. Before the coming of the Europeans, but not so far away they would forget the visions of the medicine men.

We, as a nation, would have plenty of time to advance beyond the scope of the white-man. And if we spoke their languages and had an organized government, at least on the surface that they understood and recognized--we might still have to fight. However, I believed we would win. Win and keep at least part of our lands.

I rolled up the sheepskin rug and tossed it on the couch along with the books in the great-room. With my hand on the stair-rail leading to the attic, I hesitated. I needed my medicine bundle and the things I had set aside for the white-man's life. The thought of touching the Bundle after I had so long neglected it chilled me through and through.

I would get the whole footlocker. How would I atone to the spirits for my neglect? Perhaps Morning Dove would know what I should offer after such an offense. I touched my Sun Dance scars. I didn't need to ask Morning Dove. I knew what I had to do.

Once I had the trunk downstairs, I realized the growing pile of what I wanted to bring would be impossible for Morning Dove's dogs to pull. My horses. Either I took them with me, or I called David--and told him what? He'd been caring for the horses for two years already--he'd know I was gone, and if the horses were too? Everyone I knew would be left with a mystery.

I glanced out the sliding door to the patio. The stables were only a bright spot where an outdoor light glowed. Would one stallion and twelve mares be a large enough base to start a herd? It had to be.

I possessed the poles for making travois for four of them. The poles and the canvases were enough to make a small lodge with enough room for a single man. A single man. I wouldn't be a single man. I would convince the council I was the best choice and have Morning Dove.

With a grunt, I got to my feet and retrieved a lidded wicker trunk from the bathroom. I dumped out the towels and began packing what I wanted to bring. I ended up going into the kitchen and getting another basket to put more stuff in. It amounted to a lot of things, but I could load all of it on one or two travois. If Morning Dove wasn't frightened of the horses, she could help me lead them. I hoped she could bring the horses through with us.

I stood staring at my reflection in the glass of the patio doors. Kills Many had said Morning Dove's spirit helpers had abandoned her. Were those helpers the ones letting her come and go in time? What if they weren't happy with my actions? I wouldn't consider the possibility of being left in my time now that I no longer wanted to be in the modern world.

I hesitated at the steps leading to my bedroom. How would I explain to Morning Dove why I'd doubted everything? Would she believe I'd decided and now truly accepted the old ways? If I had the horses packed and ready to go, she would know of my choice and there would be little discussion of it. Perhaps she would even forget her anger at me.

I turned on the lights in the stables and stood by Wolf's stall. For a stallion, he was a calm animal--a good-tempered, checkered Appaloosa. I rubbed him between the ears and let him nuzzle my hand. Summer whickered at me from the next stall. I almost considered only taking the two of them. It would make things easier. Wolf, though, had never dragged anything. He'd spook. I took the poles down from a rack in the tack room and laid them out on the sandy floor between the two rows of stalls. Summer banged at her stall door and let out a long whinny. She snorted and pranced around her stall.

"It has been awhile," I said to her, "but you still remember, don't you, girl?" As if in answer to my words, she reared up a bit and nodded her head up and down.

I led her out and backed her up between the poles. She stood calmly until I tossed the harness over her back. She danced to the side and shook them off. I went back to the tack room and got out one of my saddles. She stood well for saddling and didn't even flinch when I lashed the harness over it. I backed her between the poles and strapped two poles on each side of her. I tied two shorter poles, parts of the door flap, crossways over them. Over the framework, I laid out a truck-box cargo net and anchored it down. I loaded brushes, hoof clippers and picks, saddle blankets, and as much tack as I could into a lightweight plastic foot locker. It got anchored to the cargo net with bungee cords.

"I guess if they accept those of us from the future without question, they will accept my strange belongings as well." Summer blew air out through her nostrils and pawed the ground. I selected Sherri to carry the other four poles and the canvas coverings for the lodge. By the time I loaded all the stuff from the house and secured it, several hours had gone by. The horses had once been used to this, but it had been a long time since I'd participated in a Pow Wow. Wolf pranced in his pen, snorting and upset because I had two mares out of the stables. I would ride Wolf and lead these two, letting the others follow on a stringer. It wasn't the best arrangement. If Morning Dove would ride by herself and lead one string, we would be fine. My only concern would be convincing those of her time that they were more useful as a travel tool than as food. When the white-men landed and saw the natives already had horses--would they think us more civilized from that alone?

With that thought, I changed into buckskins and traveling clothes. My own clothes this time, saved from twenty years before, with properly blackened moccasins, and the decorated and fringed clothes of a wealthy medicine man. Why had I even saved them? The answer--my grandfather was right--I was returning to The People. From the hall closet, I dug out two blankets with the tribe design on them. I kept them there so my grandfather wouldn't complain too much when he came to visit about proper hand woven blankets. One fur and two blankets--I would be very cold in the winter.

No, I wouldn't be. People would pay me for my sings and for my skill as a healer, which would astound those from Morning Dove's time. I already knew they were leery of me because I had fought the Great Spirit to bring Morning Dove back--even if I couldn't remember doing so.

I climbed the steps two at a time and pushed open the bedroom door. Morning Dove had made the bed. The room stood empty. I checked the bathroom with my heart battering my ribs. What if she'd left? What if my chance had come and gone? In a panic, I searched the entire house and couldn't find any trace of her or my grandfather.

I sat outside on the damp grass with my head on my upraised knees. I kept hoping she would come and lead me to her time. She couldn't have abandoned me--like she thought I'd abandoned her.

I stood up and scanned the edges of my yard, no trees where they shouldn't have been, no shafts of sunlight at night, marking the path to her time. Very slowly, I removed my medicine things from the packs.

Forcefully, I began to recite the words my grandfather had taught me long ago. They were words I should have said each day at sunrise and sunset. Would the Great Spirit forgive me? I sang, chanted, and offered sacred tobacco. I promised to hang in the very next Sun Dance with skewers through thick layers of flesh. A single low whistle came to me like the first bird of the morning would make.

While still chanting, I opened my eyes and saw a single dim slant of sunlight piercing the darkness. The gray wolf I'd seen before stood in the shaft of light. Would I end up in the right place and time? It was the only chance I had. I leapt on my stallion's back, checked the knots on the other lead lines, kicked his flanks, and trotted the horses toward the shaft of light.

As soon as trees surrounded me, I knew something was odd. The trees were showing signs of autumn. They didn't have many colored leaves, but the tips of the oaks were turning bright red. The birch had a mix of green and yellow leaves. I didn't have any idea where I'd ended up, and Wolf danced around--spooked by the sudden change in surroundings.

Kills Many melted out of the trees and stood on the trail before me. He held his bow, and, even before I shouted at him, he let out an astounded gasp at seeing me mounted on the horse's back, I thought. He'd followed Morning Dove, but it didn't mean he'd seen horses before.

I swung down off Wolf as Jumper and a few others emerged from the woods. All of them talked and pointed excitedly.

"They are not good to eat," Jumper said over them.

"Look, they carry packs like a great dog," another man put in.

"Dogs are good in the winter, when there is nothing else," someone else added.

"Stop this," Kills Many commanded.

My soul curled in on itself. Every person around me stilled. I knew the council of Elders was to make its choice after the first frost. Judging by the trees, the first frost could have come already.

The horses started to stomp their feet and tug at the line. I feared losing control of them. I sought out Jumper in the crowd.

He'd known the horses weren't food and didn't have any apparent fear of them.

"Can you ride?" I asked Jumper.

Jumper gave me a grin and took a leaping step that landed him on one of the mare's backs. I quickly undid her halter from the string and looped the rope through her mouth before I handed Jumper the reins. Grabbing up the stringer, I handed the rope to Jumper. I held Wolf and the two mares with the travois.

"I think the meadow at the lower south side of the camp would be a good place to hobble them."

"At least until we find some youth willing to ride and keep track of them." He let out a soft chuckle. "I never thought to see a horse again. Nor you," he added. With a triumphant shout, he took off down the trail at a full gallop, ducking branches as he went.

I leapt up onto Wolf's back, glad Jumper knew about horses. I assumed there would be others as well. The man with the glasses, I was sure would. It didn't mean he could ride, but he would understand them.

As we made our way to the meadow, a great crowd began to follow us. Some of them followed right on the trail, unafraid, while others kept their distance. I heard a mixture of talk centered on my horses. For each who saw them as food, there was someone who pointed out how they dragged the lodge poles and of what other uses they exhibited far outnumbering their value as food.

At the clearing, Jumper shouted for the youth to gather. Once those nine years old and up had assembled, they stood in a solemn line and watched the horses warily. Whispers were still going on among the adults gathered. I couldn't help overhearing mention of my strong medicine. I didn't feel strong. I'd made a choice, too many in my lifetime, I could see were so very wrong.

"They are called horses," I said, addressing the youth. "The best way to keep the great gift of the horse safe is to build a fence, hobbling works, but a fence is better." They met this with dubious stares. I doubted they knew what a fence or hobbles were.

Jumper joined in with explanations. "A fence is a great lodge to hold them, with no walls and no roof. We need only a framework."

Kills Many stepped forward dragging two strong logs. He set them upright in an X shape. I quickly gathered some rope and tied the center of the X. Another longer pole was dragged forward. We leaned the X against it, made another, and put the pole across the two, sawhorse style. Kills Many may not have seen horses, but he understood fencing.

An elderly man moved forward and watched this operation, after which he raised his hand and moved to stand facing the gathered people. I scanned the crowd, looking for Morning Dove and didn't see her.

"This day, we should announce the one who will lead us against the white-man. We cannot do so. This man has shown us his Power once again. He can steal the Power of the white-man. Who has not seen in his visions this great-dog? We were not to have this powerful animal until we took it from the white-man--we have it now."

Another bent old man hobbled forward. With a start, I realized it was my grandfather. Was he ill? "The spirits have brought us a late frost. We have enjoyed a long summer with more than enough time to choose the one to lead us--the frost is the spirit's sign that we are to choose our leader."

I took a step towards my grandfather. I had known for a long time he thought me a fool--but I was here now. Something inside me rolled into a quivering ball at the thought of my grandfather disliking me so much he wouldn't support my chance to speak. When I thought of him as Napi, I wanted to slink away--under the dirt.

"Honored Elder," another elderly man said. He stepped forward. "Clearly all can see the advantage in having these animals. I believe..."

My grandfather held up his hand. "Yes, we have discussed this. Having the Power of the horse before the coming of the white-man is a great advantage. Medicine Elk has brought us..."

"So surely he has earned the right to speak," this came from an elderly woman. All these Elders carried a staff much like the one my grandfather held, minus the carved mouse. Was this the council of Elders Kills Many had spoken of?

My grandfather thumped his stick against the ground. The others took a step back from him. "I am Napi," he said. "Does that give me the right to finish speaking . . . before you interrupt me?" He waited until only the sounds of nature could be heard before he said, "When I am done, you may argue all you wish."

Wolf nudged me. I stumbled. My grandfather gave me a cross look. I stared at the ground. I felt betrayed by him. He would speak and as the leader, as the Old-Man, as Napi--no one would argue with his words once he said them.

"The spirits of winter waited a long time before bringing the frost," he started, "all can see the time of choice is here. But with last night's frost, the spirits returned Medicine Elk to us, along with his horses. This old man thinks the spirits wished to wait for Medicine Elk's return. All know if the spirits of winter don't get their chance to live in the land of men, there wouldn't be any spring--no continuation of life--the frost had to come. Do any of you doubt the spirits brought Medicine Elk back to us? Do any of you doubt the spirits wish him to speak?"

Only Kills Many took a step forward. As one, those gathered looked at him. He moved back into the crowd. When weighing his popularity, I was sure he realized they wouldn't want a leader who opposed Napi--who opposed our creator.

"It is done. Medicine Elk will speak. We will make the choice at the first snow." My grandfather left the center of the circle with his Elders around him.

I still didn't have any idea when they would permit me to speak or even how often they would let me do so. With the cold edge to the air, it could snow any day. At least they were granting me the time to speak. I had to be happy with that.

Chapter Sixteen
Kindred Spirits

By midday, the fence stretched more than half way around the meadow. More than one hundred people worked to help build it. Many others came to gawk at the horses. My body ached, and I longed for sleep. I still hadn't seen Morning Dove, and no one had offered me any information about her. Most of the morning, I'd worked alone.

With a final swing, I chopped off the last bit of a branch. I now had two supports the same length. Another man held them in their upright position while I lashed them together.

"Thank you," I told him, expecting him to walk away as others had when I spoke to them.

"The others," this man said, with a nod in the direction of those working on the fence, "they are undecided who they want to lead them. Kills Many has always had the favor of the spirits, his Power has always been strong--even stronger than some of the medicine men who have come. Now, you are here. Many think the spirits favor you. And these horses--taken from the white-man before his arrival--it is something Kills Many couldn't do. Last summer, he brought us one of the white-man's fire sticks."

I glanced at Kills Many. He strutted around and offered instruction on how to build the fence. He helped as well, but his arrogant posture said he had little patience for someone who couldn't grasp such a simple concept. Again, as I watched him, I felt as if he were acting out a role he had no love for. He had brought them a gun--how had he gotten his hands on one?

"This fire-stick made a terrible noise. The darts it threw made the rabbit he killed taste very bad. It riddled the meat with tiny stones that chipped people's teeth. It was not a good thing. And the Power he held over it," the man shook his head, "it did not last very long. It soon would not make any noise at all, and it no longer shot the hard bits of stone."

"It needed bullets," I said.

He frowned.

I held up my steel axe. "The fire-sticks are called guns. They are made from the same," I searched for a word for steel, "hard stuff as this is, called steel. A powder goes in them, along with small bits of steel. Like blow darts, once you have used them, you must put more inside the gun for it to work."

"Ah," the man said with a nod. I didn't think he understood what I'd said. "Kills Many said an evil spirit made it stop working. I see he didn't understand the Power he'd stolen. I wonder if such a man should lead us."

Before I could say anything else, he walked away from me. He stood in the shade, talking to several others who were eating their midday meal.

I set aside the support and started on the next one. Kills Many could have maimed someone with a gun--or killed them. Would he have cared?

"Horses are a much more impressive choice over what I brought." A beefy man stood near me holding two uneven support poles.

"I didn't bring them to make an impression on anyone here. I had in mind how they would impress the white-men," I told him. He held the poles in an X shape; I lashed.

"I'm a blacksmith. What good's that in this place?"

I looked at my axe. "I couldn't make an axe, but you can."

"No forge here. Though I could build one--I don't have the materials to do it."

I retrieved two more poles and held them while he lashed. "Shannon Running Deer--Blackfoot," I told him.

"They have been calling me Falls Down. I busted up my glasses right after I got here, so I trip over stuff sometimes. I'm Dineh--Navajo--1920," he added.

I glanced up at him, momentarily stopping my work. "I'm a good century after you," I said.

He stood looking at me gap-mouthed for a moment. He glanced back at the horses. "The motor car, it didn't last?"

"Oh, it lasted all right. Newer and better versions. But the horse is still around, mostly for pleasure now."

He made a throat clearing sound and shook his head. "My forge burned down. My son died in the fire." He stood very still for a moment. "My wife, she'd died the year before. I went to the medicine man looking for a cure for the bad luck following me. I met Morning Dove in the spirit place the medicine man led me to. Turns out it wasn't a spirit place--backwards in time--H. G. Wells and his time machine, except this is real. I didn't have anything left in my time, so I stayed. I turned down the chance to speak. I'm not a leader and don't want to be."

I didn't know if he wanted me to tell him how I had met Morning Dove or if he wanted sympathy. He must have stood out in his time--an educated "red-man."

"I was a surgeon," I said lamely.

"You have Power," he said and walked away.

I picked up the next two pieces of wood and balanced them against a tree. I might have Power, but my Power didn't seem to extend to keeping any help. I felt lost here. I'd decided to come back--to be with Morning Dove--yet, I hadn't seen her all day. Was she still angry with me?

Someone coughed behind me. I turned around to see a short man with a crew cut and wire rim glasses. He pushed the glasses up on his nose and mopped sweat off his brow. After he shoved his red bandana into his pocket, and wiped his hands down his jeans, he held out his hand.

"Jack Crow Dog, Lakota–1975," he said when I grasped his palm.

I told him my name, tribe, and year. He stuck around for a bit, helping me with the support pieces. He was a geologist. When Morning Dove had come for him, he'd been in the Army. He didn't leave behind any close family either, nor did he have an interest in being the leader of these people.

As the day wore on, people came and went. I gathered a good amount of information just from the snippets they each told me. There was a broad range of time covered; the closest to my own was the man from 1975. None of us had close family, or if we did, they played a minor role in us arriving here. Very few of the men were interested in leadership. But all of them possessed some skill I could foresee a use for.

Morning Dove and my grandfather had not chosen randomly. The spirits had sent her to gather many men, not just because they would have a good plan, but because they had the skills to put The People far ahead of the white-man before he set foot on our soil. It gave me much to think on and consider.

The longest anyone had been here was five years. I put together what Morning Dove and Kills Many had already told me. Twelve years of peace and at least five years after that for Morning Dove to travel. Morning Dove was almost twenty. Peace had reigned since she'd arrived among them. That meant two decades of mixing time for tribes who had been made aware of each other and brought together with a common vision among their medicine men. Had history actually happened this way? It couldn't have, or the white-man would have found a much different people just from the ideas introduced to them.

I watched everyone moving together. Those from more modern times simply blended in. They were the ones who had never left reservations or were from times before the white-man. It surprised me to find I felt as if I belonged here as well. I could have simply fallen in with these people and disregarded all of modern time. It shocked me. I didn't understand how primitive people easily accepted all of this with no fear of witches or magic. Could I be so far back they simply thought this was the result of spirit Power bestowed on some and not others?

The false, stilted sound of Kills Many's laughter carried across the meadow. He worked bare-chested with his shiny Sun Dance scars exposed. He belonged in this era, yet he accepted time travel and that all this should be happening. The modern mind, I concluded, with its knowledge of science and so forth, made things like this seem unable to happen.

Near the hide bag containing water for those working, my grandfather sat under a tree, chewing a bit of jerked meat. I hadn't taken a break all day. And I needed to talk to my grandfather. I shouldn't have doubted his support of me. I drew water from the bag. He smacked his lips together and used a twig to pick a string of meat out of his teeth.

"Chocolate," he said.

"What?"

"Chocolate. I am going to miss *Hershey's* chocolate."

I laughed suddenly. Of all the things the modern world offered--he would miss chocolate.

"And toilet paper. Leaves are all right, I guess, but they are hard on an old rump."

With my hand on the tree the bag hung from, I laughed until tears came to my eyes. "Grandfather, I'm sorry, but I didn't think to bring you any T. P. Eventually, I am sure we will have chocolate, and you will be the first to get some."

"You do that. But it won't be me indulging. I have places to go once the choice is made."

I watched the progress on the fence for a bit. The thought of my grandfather leaving me, whether in death or otherwise, hurt to the core of my spirit. There was so much I wanted to learn from him yet. I'd wasted so much time. Expecting he would not answer, I asked, "It would help me to know what year it is."

"It is the year of the decision," he answered.

"In modern terms," I said with an exasperated grunt.

"The white-man's god, he will not be born for many years yet."

I turned a shocked look on him, unable to answer. The Christians' Christ wouldn't be born for "many years yet?" From the information I'd gathered so far, I thought the one chosen would lead The People against the white-man. There had been a bit of talk about others who had already come. I'd assumed they were the Vikings who came to the North American continent long before Columbus. Two-thousand and some odd years, if I believed the Christians. I wondered how anything made sense to me. Had we lived the same way for so long? There had been archaeological finds suggesting isolated pockets of innovation. They always died out, vanished. Why?

The conclusion I drew was the tribes were too far from each other. If one group discovered metalworking, and another went to war with them and wiped them out, the technology got lost. This time, they were all in communication with each other. I had at least fifteen hundred years before the white-man came. It was more than enough time for an industrial revolution of sorts to take hold. If I had anything to do with it, the white-man would come face to face with a nation much advanced over them in terms of technology and spiritual enlightenment. The enlightenment the natives already had, it was the technology holding them back.

My grandfather farted. I let out a frustrated gasp. I thought of this time and the acceptance of natural function these people had. It really didn't matter.

"They're going to think you're lazy," he stated.

I didn't wait for him to tell me again before I went back to work.

At sunset, we turned the horses loose inside their new home. There wasn't any shortage of exuberant and honored youth to get water for them and stand watch. I sat near my pile of belongings, exhausted and emotionally drained. I dreaded the time it would take to set up my lodge after a long day of hard work. Why hadn't Morning Dove come out to speak with me? I'd hoped she would let me know I was still welcome in her lodge. Jumper came and started to lash lodge poles together without asking me.

"Has Morning Dove spoken to you?" I asked him carefully. I felt leery of his help because of the link he had once shared with Morning Dove. I expected him to be as angry with me as Kills Many.

"She has not spoken to anyone, but the honored Elders," he answered just as carefully.

I let out a breath of frustration. He helped me raise the three blanched and bark-free main poles. I kicked dirt in the holes around them to help hold and balance them before we added the other six and began to stretch the canvas over the framework. I'd have to gather dried leaves and grass to insulate the space between the dewcloth and the outer walls.

"Your lodge is a nice one," he commented. He touched the fabric nearest him.

"It's small. Enough for me." I hated the forlorn sound of my words.

"We all thought you would not return." He took a deep breath. "Kills Many would have been glad if you had stayed away. An entire moon is a long time to be gone and reappear. I think all can see the horses took your time. I didn't expect Morning Dove to go back for you at all."

A day for me and a month for Morning Dove. Could she still be angry with me after that much time? The amount of time I'd missed with her most likely added to her ire. Did I dare tell Jumper she hadn't come back for me? At least, I thought she hadn't.

We worked in silence until my lodge stood complete. Jumper looked up at the sky. I followed his gaze. The moon shone behind the clouds--a bright silver disk of light. A breeze whispered through the trees, bringing with it a few splatters of cold rain.

"I don't mind the rain in the summer, or even the spring, but when fall comes--wet and cold," Jumper said. He started across the camp to a small lean-to. Next to it, a modest pile of wood peeked out from under a protective covering. On the other side, several packs leaned against the shelter. The wind grabbed the covering over them and beat it against the side of the lean-to. Jumper's home? It had to be. I followed after him. He didn't seem to hold any animosity toward me.

"There's enough room for another to be out of the elements in my lodge."

He gave me an apprehensive look. Maybe he didn't want to stay in the home of a medicine man. Who knew what spirits lurked around me? I also thought of my medicine bundle. I needed to honor it. It was well past sunset. I didn't want its spirit to think I had no intention of keeping the promise I had made to honor the old and true ways.

For an answer, Jumper picked up his bedroll and started toward my lodge. I grabbed a bundle of his things and followed. Inside, it was dark and not much warmer. I needed to dig a fire pit and gather sand and stones to line it with--dig an underground chimney pit to give it air in the winter. I'd have to line it with a hollowed out log--until we had some sort of tile.

To start the fire, I would transfer an ember from the central fire to mine. Jumper went back to his lean-to and returned with an already lit stone lamp.

The crowded interior appeared to shift about in the flicker of the tallow lamp. Soft drumbeats that evened out into the gentle thudding of a heartbeat came from the trunk containing my Bundle. I'd brought a lot with me. Enough to leave me crowded. With two of us sleeping in here, we would be jammed in.

"If you tell me what I may touch, I will see about hanging some of this," Jumper said with a keen edge to his voice. His eyes were wide, and I suspected he was aware of the Power in my medicine bundle as it called to me. The soft heartbeat serenaded me and filled the entire interior of my lodge. The air felt rife with static electricity.

I went to the wicker trunk. "Don't touch anything in here. All the rest doesn't matter." The trunk held all my books. It also held my bundle. The plastic truck-box could sit outside as well.

Jumper nodded. "When the rain stops, I'll move my lean-to. We can use it for storage." He turned and escaped outside. "I will get the rest of my possessions first," he said in a voice muffled by the canvas cover of the lodge.

I sought out my medicine bundle, handling it with care. Each item in it would have to be unwrapped and honored. A good night's sleep didn't seem to be anywhere in sight--it could take up to three days to even start to atone for my negligence. Thunder shook the trees, and, a moment later, lightening flashed bright against the canvas. Rain began to fall into the lodge through the open smoke flap.

Ducking outside with my bundle, I jerked the flap shut over the smoke hole and secured the pole holding it, leaving only a sliver open to let the smoke out. I headed for my grandfather's lodge. The light of Morning Dove's fire seeped around the edges of her lodge door. How I wanted to stop and talk to her. She had to know I'd come back.

I clutched my bundle tighter. I knew what I had to do. The Great Spirit had let me return. There would be time enough for me to speak to her later.

Chapter Seventeen
New Understanding

I tapped gently on the door flap of my grandfather's lodge and stood in the drizzling cold rain, waiting for him to answer. A branch snapped in the woods. I couldn't see anything out there. The hair on the back of my neck rose. Someone or something had to be in the trees. A moment later, a gray wolf melted out of the swarthy night. He sat looking at me with his red tongue lolling out to one side. His yellow eyes never left my face. I tapped at my grandfather's door again. I didn't even have a knife with me to defend against the animal if it decided to attack me. What was it doing in the middle of the camp? It looked like the same spirit-animal I'd seen each time I got pulled into the threads of the past--but this wolf was clearly a live animal.

The wolf looked back into the woods where more twigs snapped and rustled. Great. Maybe there were a bunch of them waiting to have a foolish person for dinner. The wolf yelped once, bounded off across the camp, and into the darkness. I expected more to follow it. Instead, someone stood just inside the ring of trees.

Kills Many. My legs turned to stone. He stood with his arms crossed over his chest and watched me with a showing of bright white teeth in the darkness. I stared back at him. With a quick movement, I tapped again on the door.

"Give an old man a chance," my grandfather growled from inside.

I glanced away from Kills Many. "Grandfather, I need to speak with you." The door-flap bumped into my legs when my grandfather pushed it open. I looked back at Kills Many. Kills Many no longer stood there. In his place, the elk-man watched me.

"Are you going to stand there all night--the heat is getting out?"

I blinked rain water out of my eyes. The elk-man vanished. Maybe he had never been there in the first place. Self-doubt had to be the catalyst that brought the creature out. How did a person get rid of all self-doubt? My grandfather had done it. Morning Dove certainly had. And I had to admit Kills Many seemed unwavering in his idea that he would lead.

I ducked inside my grandfather's lodge.

"What do you need at this hour?"

Very carefully, I held out my bundle. My grandfather gave me an affirmative sounding grunt and pulled the fur around his shoulders a bit tighter.

"Wife?" he said.

A slight movement came from the pile of furs on the right side of his lodge. The woman who sat up blinking in the firelight was the same one who had helped with Morning Dove. She looked at me, and at the bundle in my hands, before she crawled out of the furs and added wood to the central fire. From a basket, she brought out a long object wrapped in deerskin. She enfolded herself in some furs and picked up a different basket before she went to stand by the door.

"I will go see if Morning Dove wishes my company this night." She ducked out the flap before I could say anything about the wolf.

"Night Girl knows her way in the darkness. No harm will come to her," my grandfather said.

He indicated I should sit with my back to the west--the direction of introspection, of looking into one's spirit. My grandfather sat with his back to the east--the direction representative of quiet reflection and meditative thought, where the old ones passed on their knowledge. From a basket near the fire, he added red willow bark shavings to the flames. He unwrapped a simple pipe and put the three pieces together before he set it on the woven mat in front of him. He took out a woven twist of sweet-grass, lit the twist in the fire, and fanned it with an eagle feather to keep it going. He stood and passed the braid over me, using the eagle feather clasped in his right hand to fan the smoke four times--from my head downward, in the four main directions.

Once finished, he sat in his place again and filled the pipe with tobacco. He lit the pipe and offered it to each of the sacred directions. First to the west, the direction the spirits of the dead go. Next to the east, the direction of renewal, guidance, and enlightenment. Then to the south, the dwelling place of the guardian spirit of growth. Lastly to the north, where the spirits of healing and purification lived.

He sat back down and took a long draw of smoke from the pipe. He handed it to me so I could do the same.

"Everything in our world goes in a circle," he said.

I nodded.

"It is good you remember that much. You see what the circle has done for you. It has brought you back to us."

"Grandfather," I began and held up my bundle. My hands trembled. "I ask for your help in returning my bundle to sacredness."

My grandfather nodded. He wouldn't touch my bundle, but he would help and guide me on what I should do. I set it down in front of me and cautiously unwrapped the cracked ancient hide covering the things inside. There was a chunk of a blue coffee cup--the piece still had the handle attached. It had been my mother's favorite cup. I ran my fingers over the smooth paint.

"Now, you be careful with my cup," my mother said to my nine-year-old self.

"I will," I answered. I'd opened the juice can and poured myself a cupful. Sitting near the fire, I'd drunk from it, feeling like a grown-up because I could use my mother's ceramic cup.

"Damn you, Shane," my mother's voice screeched.

I jumped to my feet. The cup now lay on the floor, shattered amidst the contents of my mother's neglected dinner tray. Soup ran over the bread and snaked a trail through the rosy-red applesauce that had been her favorite. Steam rose from the puddle of tea the cup had contained. I was twenty-four. Two weeks before, my father had died. While I'd gone into the mountains to camp and to figure out who I was, and what I believed--she'd stopped eating.

"You killed him," she accused.

"I had nothing to do with his getting cancer," I'd said back. In frustration, I'd swept everything into the dustpan and dumped it out the back door.

"The Power is in you. Why wouldn't you use it to help your father?"

"The Power would have been in the proper treatments." I sat in a hard, straight-backed chair near her bed. "Mother, please." I took her hand in mine. "You have to eat."

She'd jerked her hand away from me and turned to look out her bedroom window at the setting sun. "You didn't have to carry the full burden. All you had to do was sing with the others. That's all."

A week later, she died. She'd given up fluids entirely.

The piece of cup I held came back into focus, blotting out the memories. I'd sat on the back porch the day of her death, holding this fragment of her life. I'd left and never turned back. When I'd packed away the trappings of my former life, I'd put this shard with the other things I left behind.

"So, you have come back."

I raised my head. My mother sat across the fire from me.

"Can you forgive me?" I asked her.

She looked at me for a long time. The fire crackled, and outside the rain tapped an irregular pattern on my grandfather's lodge. In the distance, a wolf howled.

"I cannot forgive you," she said. "You must find the forgiveness in yourself." She vanished, and I was looking at my grandfather.

"It is always good to make peace with one's parents," he said.

I touched the broken white pottery edge of the cup. "I don't think there's peace for me with her."

"Yet, you keep the shard. Why?"

I set the fragment aside, but kept my gaze on it. "I think to remind me, of her, of my failings, of the simple things that were important. We had jelly jars, old canning jars, and a conglomeration of plastic containers we used to drink out of--but only one real cup. Hers. I took it with me because it was as shattered as my life."

My grandfather nodded. Somewhere inside of me, I felt a small burden lift. The cup stood as a reminder of things broken. It was also a commemoration of the way things once were and could be again.

I took out a small bit of twine. A smile tugged at my mouth.

"Shane, come on. I know just where to set the traps." Sam, my younger brother by almost five years, ran ahead of me. Sam wanted so badly to be a hunter--in the traditional sense. He thought if we could, if he could, catch a rabbit in one of his snares, he would be a man. I already hunted deer beside my father and the other men. Sam's idea was to snare the rabbit and shoot it.

"Sam, wait. This isn't a good idea," I called.

"You don't want me to go with you and Dad," he taunted and pouted.

I remembered rolling my eyes and thinking he sure was proving himself a man, next he'd be crying.

"All right, all right," I'd said and climbed up the rocky trail where we'd been leaving grain to attract the rabbits.

I stood next to Sam as he boldly displayed the small brown rabbit, with his arrow through it, to our father.

"I see," our father said. He peered at the rabbit. "This rabbit will make a fine stew. A brave boy's first hunt."

It took all my control to keep from bursting into laughter. Fine hunt, fine stew, a boy's first hunt. What a joke. But as I'd stood there watching Sam, I'd come to the realization Sam felt shadowed by me. The boarding school had reluctantly skipped me ahead a total of three grades in school. At only fourteen, I stood taller than almost every adult on the reservation. I also went with the men, while he had to stay behind with our mother. At nine, I had gone with the men for the first time.

My father held out his hand. Sam gave him the rabbit. That's when I saw it. Sam had been in such a hurry to get the rabbit back home that he'd sliced off the twine from the snare. A bit still ringed the rabbit's back leg.

"Father, I can clean it," I'd said.

"Your mother can clean a rabbit," my dad said in the tone he used when he wouldn't listen to arguments of any sort.

"Son?" I turned from the steps leading to the loft where Sam and I slept. "It was a good stew."

"Yes," I answered carefully. How could he have missed seeing the twine? How could our mother have missed seeing it?

"It is said that the mark of a true man is in realizing what it is that makes a man."

I frowned.

"Every man has pride," my father continued. "A true man realizes to wound another's pride is to wound the spirit."

"Yes, Father."

"Sam didn't eat much of his first kill," my father stated.

What did he want me to say? He knew what we'd done. Did he want me to confess? Was I supposed to take the blame, being the oldest?

"Maybe he was too excited," I chanced.

"Perhaps. But lost integrity is a hard lesson to swallow." He got out of his chair and walked over to me. "There is great Power in the things that make a man." He held out his hand. The piece of twine lay in it.

I looked down at the twine in my hand.

"If I recall," my grandfather said from across the fire, "you took Sam with you every day for many weeks, until he could shoot as well as you could."

"Yes," I said.

"And you never told him your father knew about his trick."

"I didn't have to. Sam knew."

"You learned an important lesson that day," my grandfather

stated.

I nodded. I'd learned sometimes others were more important than me. I set aside the twine. I would miss Sam, greatly.

I took out an ancient tin of chewing tobacco. I pried open the lid to find the contents as dry as old saw dust. I had another of corn pollen. I opened it as well and set both before me.

"You took those with you on your first vision quest."

"Yes." I thought of that vision, now skewed by the strange dream I'd had in Morning Dove's hospital room. An elk had run over me. No strange creature had shot me, and I'd not seen Morning Dove. My grandfather watched me with his head tilted to the side. Or had it happened that way? Could it be even then a dark side of myself haunted me? I looked at the mostly full tins. I'd wanted to have a visit from a spirit creature so badly I'd neglected to honor the spirits and the sacred directions as often as I should have in those three days. I should have used all the tobacco and pollen my grandfather had given me.

I got to my feet. Though the offerings were dry and old, I offered them to the four directions, alternating them until both tins were empty.

"A thing finished," my grandfather said when I sat back down.

"A thing finished," I echoed.

The next thing was an eagle-bone whistle.

"You must put the notch here." My grandfather leaned over a younger me and touched the wing-bone in my hand.

My hands shook as I notched the bone where he said. I started on the sacred circles that went around it. Its only adornment would be a single eagle feather. I put it to my lips, testing the sound. It made a sharp shrill note, like the screech of the bird it came from.

With a gasp, I hung from skewers through the pectoral flesh of my chest. I blew through the whistle and bit down on it. If the thing cracked apart, I would make a fool out of myself and scream like an idiot. Why had I done this?

The pain slapped across my chest and rammed under my arms. I wasn't just going to have scars. I was going to have whole pieces ripped out of my chest--like some sort of self-inflicted mastectomy.

I blew through my whistle.

I wriggled and bit down on the whistle. Pain lanced up my neck and dark floating specks danced before my eyes. The heat of the sun meant nothing. I dangled in a furnace of agony. The fires of hell were eating me and roasting me from my chest outward. I couldn't bring my arms up at all. They felt dead behind me.

I blew through the whistle.

The drum beat went on and on. The man next to me dropped to the ground. He crawled a short distance and staggered to his feet. He blew through his whistle before he wrenched it from his mouth to let out a triumphant shout. I pumped my legs, wanting to be free.

I blew through my whistle.

Raising my legs as far as I could, I jerked them downward. Someone was cutting through my flesh with a dull blade. It had to stop. The only way was to get free. Where was Sam? Where was my mother? Where was my grandfather? Where was my uncle? Where were my aunts? They were supposed to help me break free. I jerked my legs down.

I blew through my whistle.

The ground hit me, leaving me stunned and trembling. It took a monumental amount of effort to get to my hands and knees. Bright scarlet blood splattered across the backs of my hands. My arms gave out. I landed on my face in the dusty ochre sand. I had to get to my feet. I managed to get to my hands and knees again. I stayed that way, swaying like a cow that is almost asleep on its feet. One foot and then the other. I stood. My muscles screamed, my arms were hot and heavy, my hands felt dead. I raised my arms. They slapped back down to my sides, and I staggered out of the sacred circle.

When I collapsed on the sacred bed of sage, one of the medicine men came to me. He began dabbing at the deep rips in my chest. His role now was to ask me about the visions I'd had. Someone offered me water. I spit out the whistle and met the eyes of the person holding the water bag to my lips.

"Morning Dove," I gasped.

The red dust vanished. I sat in my grandfather's lodge with the whistle in my hands.

"You did not remember her?" my grandfather asked.

I shook my head. When I'd met her on the lakeshore, I would have sworn it was the first time I'd ever seen her. Now that I thought about it, she had been there at the Sun Dance.

"All this time," I whispered.

My grandfather said nothing.

I remembered more of her. She'd been everywhere: at the trading post, outside my parent's house when my father lay dying, at the burial--and all the time she'd kept watching me. But how could that be? She'd been exactly the same as she was now.

"All this time, I could have been with her." I looked to my grandfather for confirmation.

"Perhaps. But without the harmony you are finding now. . . "

"I should have found the harmony then." I held the whistle and touched the tooth marks in the stem. "I did this for the wrong reason. I didn't believe anymore. All I gained from it was pain. Morning Dove wouldn't have chosen me then." I set the whistle aside.

"Grandfather," I began, "I don't understand how it is I'm here. I don't understand how Morning Dove could have been there in my past--the same as she is now."

My grandfather sat in silence. I wondered if he would now dismiss me--no longer willing to help me or listen to me.

"There have been others who had the Power to walk through time. It is a curious Power to have." He looked at me with his head tilted to the side. I got the feeling he wanted me to interrupt him as I had so often in the past. Was he telling me something I wasn't supposed to know?

"Who knows why the Great Spirit gives such a thing to humans who still live. The dead have this Power. The Great Spirit would have reason to give this to those he considers his true children."

I started to ask him what a true child of the Great Spirit was and changed my mind. I would get more information from him if I stayed silent.

"I do not have parents," he told me. "I am a creation of the Great Spirit--not born of men," he answered to my unasked question.

Did that mean Morning Dove was also *not born of men?* I remembered her saying Napi had made her from clay--as he had the First People. Was that why she had been so ill her first years?

"Some with this Power master it and can do much good. But most don't even know they have it. They live in their spirit--not able to cope with any of the places they visit and often die young, thought touched by the spirits." He meant thought insane by others. "There are those who don't quite know how to use the Power the Great Spirit gives them. They must have help--a spirit guide. Those humans who master the Power, who truly know what the Great Spirit has given them, they are the most dangerous--or the most helpful."

He made a gesture towards my bundle. His lips pressed into a thin line. I abandoned the questions I wanted to ask and reached into the hide bag.

The last thing inside was a faded carving of an elk. It was so old that many hands had worn it smooth in places. My father had given it to me.

"It's ivory," my father said.

"Ivory?" I'd questioned. I was sixteen. A man. I had completed high school and a full year at a local college. I already had the offer of a scholarship from two different universities.

"It belonged to my father," my father said. "He gave it to me when I left home. His father gave it to him before that. It goes back farther than any can remember--father to son, since its creation. Perhaps since our creation."

I'd touched the sore lumpy mess left on me by the elk on my vision quest.

"Son, I will tell you the story my father told me." Even as an adult I loved hearing his stories. He held the carving in his hands. "Once there was great good and great evil--like there is now. In that time, the Power to trap evil rested in the hands of a great medicine man. He could fashion any image and see the true Power of a man in it."

He held the carving out to me. I took it. It felt warm in my palm, as if it were alive. I looked up at my father in surprise.

"You see, for you it is warm. It has always been a thing of ice in my hand. This medicine man of old trapped the Power of a Great Elk in the carving. He told all that one day a man would walk who would be part of the Power. But men could misuse the Power of the elk as well. He foretold of those who would pervert it and their evil would linger in the land. So we have kept this, father to son, always protecting the good in it and keeping the evil from escaping. It is your turn now. You must honor it and protect it. If you don't nourish the good in it, the evil will consume your soul."

I looked down at the yellowed carving.

My grandfather added wood to the fire.

I'd thought my father was giving me a lesson on keeping myself spiritually pure. Was this a connection to the past? I thought of the elk-man. Had I let some ancient evil loose?

"Fill your tins from my supply," my grandfather said. He pulled the furs over his head, and, in moments, he snored deeply. My hands felt wooden and heavy as I placed my things one at a time back in their hide bundle. The elk carving sat on a stone near the fire and appeared to prance about in the fluttering firelight. My hands shook when I touched it. The carving felt cold in my hand. Temptation to leave it grasped my soul. Somehow, I was at fault for the creature following me. I carefully tucked the carving into the pouch I wore around my neck.

Outside, it had stopped raining. I would go down to the paddock, check on the horses, and see about getting some sleep before the sun came up. Which couldn't be too far away. I stopped at the rock where Kills Many and I had talked. I set my bundle on it and watched the horses. If only I'd had a few more horses to bring.

The few I had would multiply, but not quick enough to really demonstrate their use. I could have bought more with me, but I hadn't had the time.

Behind me, a dog barked. I turned around to find myself face to face with the gray wolf. I stumbled backwards and fell on the ground. The wolf leapt after me.

Chapter Eighteen
Horse Thief

I felt stone cold, but seemed in one piece. Apparently, the wolf hadn't attacked me. I got to my feet and stumbled. I stood under a bright outdoor lamp. The soft whicker of a horse came to me followed by others. Looking around, I knew where I'd ended up. Midwest Stock Yards, near Lomita, Wisconsin. Lit by an overhead mercury-vapor light, a banner strung across the side of the tin pole-building announced: *Saturday horse sale. More than one-hundred fine animals offered.* My heart raced. I flattened myself against the metal building. How in the hell would I explain my presence here, dressed like this, with no car, and no ID at all?

How had I gotten here? The wolf had leapt at me. What had I done? While I'd stood at the rock, I'd thought of the horses I'd brought and how long it would take to have any sort of herd. My heart pounded against my ribs loud enough I could hear it.

I touched the elk mark on my shoulder. I'd always thought the elk was my spirit helper--not some form of ancient evil that had marked me. Perhaps I'd never had a spirit helper at all, not one a man wanted anyway. Now it seemed the gray wolf had become my benefactor.

A person's spirit helper always knew what lived in your heart. I'd wanted horses. The wolf had brought me to them. The scientific part of me tried to understand how a wolf could travel in time. I shook my head. The wolf wasn't a true wolf. Spirit animals were given special Powers to aid those worthy.

Was I worthy? I doubted it. But I didn't doubt Morning Dove's worthiness--the wolf helped me because Morning Dove wished it. That meant she still wanted me around--or at least wanted my knowledge to help save us.

I crept around the side of the building. A light shone out of a small window. Did this place have guards? I looked in the window. A guard sat at a desk in a chair tilted so far back, it leaned against the wall. A half-full glass of water and a bottle of pills lay next to the phone on the desk in front of him. I banged my elbow on the side of the building when a huge black dog barked at me from inside the small office.

The man grunted once and straightened in his chair. He scratched the back of his head and yelled at the dog to shut up and quit barking at shadows. He moved to the side of the small room and stretched out on a cot. Shouting one more time at the dog to shut up.

The dog raced out the open room door and in moments stood across from me with hackles up and teeth bared.

Several more dogs jumped over the half-door closing off the building. They stood, wagging tails and looking at me. They weren't dogs. They were wolves. More of them came over the door, until I stood surrounded by them, maybe twenty or thirty, it was hard to tell. The largest of them, a huge gray male, yapped at me before it leapt over the half-door. The black dog scuttled off somewhere.

The other wolves let themselves into the auction barn one or two at a time over the half-door. Was the annoyed guard the only one? I glanced back into the office, at the clock above the door-- just past midnight. I doubted anyone else would be here. The spirits were giving me a chance to bring more horses, but did I want to risk someone catching me? I went to the side of the building, vaulted over a fence, and made it easily inside. The gray wolf stood waiting for me. He barked at me again, turned, and moved down a narrow aisle lined on both sides by burlap feed sacks until we stood near the doorway of the small room. The door itself swung outward and was held there by a sand-filled cigarette butt can. Slowly, I walked over to the door. The wolf barked.

"Damn, dog. Shut the hell up." I used that moment to quickly slam the door. Luckily, there was a latch on the outside of it--not a very smart arrangement. I slid the latch home just as the man inside banged on the door.

"Who's out there? Let me outa here," he bellowed. For good measure, I moved several of the feed sacks in front of the door. I shook my head when I saw the black phone cord going through a small hole in the wall--into the room. The phone inside crashed to the floor when I yanked the line. Once I pulled the cord out of the wall jack in the hall, I turned my attention back to the wolf.

The wolf yipped, wagged his tail, and took off back down the narrow hallway. It opened up into an indoor stockyard filled with pens. He padded across the aisle and stood by the first horse pen. If the wolves were here to help me, I wouldn't question how or why.

Acting quickly, I slid latches to the side and let the horses out. The wolves worked with me, gathering the horses in the huge indoor arena. I'd only let out about twenty-five when the gray wolf came to me and let out a single bark. In the arena, the horses stood shoulder to shoulder, packed in.

"All right, boy. Lead the way." I chose a mare with a halter and leapt on her back. She startled, but allowed me to ride. There would be a lot of sorting to do after this. I sincerely hoped I wouldn't find another month had passed. Just for a moment, I felt a twang of guilt. I was stealing horses. A sliver of light opened up. The gray wolf leapt into it. The other wolves ran around the horses funneling them through. Too late now. If we succeeded in keeping our land, this place no longer existed.

We came through the sliver of light directly into the recently built corral. One hundred horses were going to push this pen to the limits. It didn't matter. We would hobble them and round them up later if we had to. I got off the mare and nodded my head at the gray wolf. He gave a little yelp and leapt back into the splinter of light. I followed, aware of voices at the edges of the corral. Someone had seen me come through with the horses. I had no way of knowing if that was good or bad.

After four more trips, there were actually one hundred and thirty horses, I stood near the rock. My hands and feet were numb. My eyes felt filled with grit. Had it gotten that cold? I squeezed my eyes shut and rubbed at them. When I opened my eyes, I was startled to find myself face to face with the gray wolf. My medicine bundle rested on the rock between his paws. Rays of light shot up in pink brilliance above the western horizon as dawn approached. I felt damp from the morning dew. My legs were insensitive, and I began to tremble. The ground in front of the rock was worn free of the grass that had covered it the night before. Dancing all night in a small circle was the only explanation I could see for it. I'd never left this spot, not physically anyway.

The gray wolf gave a small bark. His ears came all the way forward, and he stared beyond me. With a low growl and a snort, he bounded off into the woods. My legs didn't want to support my weight. I stumbled back into the rock when I turned to see who was behind me. I reached around and retrieved my bundle.

"Kills Many is with the youth and the horses you called," Jumper told me. His voice was whisper soft and filled with awe. He extended his hand and drew it back, clinching his fingers against his palm. "I don't mean insult."

I tried to smile at him, but my chattering teeth wouldn't let me.

He thought his offer of help insulted me; perhaps I wanted to be this weak. Medicine men fasted themselves silly. And, in this time, before the white-man, I could imagine it was done with great regularity.

Jumper stepped forward and grasped my arm. He let out a hiss of surprise, almost let go, then tightened his grip. "I don't think the wolf spirits left much of you in this world. You need to get warm," he told me as if I would argue the fact.

"A fire would be nice," I managed through my clacking teeth, hoping he understood.

He pulled off the buffalo robe he wore and tossed it around my shoulders. "I want you to know," he started as we walked like drunken lovers toward my lodge, "if the council chooses me, I will name you, Medicine Elk, my brother."

I stopped. With great effort, I straightened my back. Jumper stepped back from me, looking watchful. Did he mean what I thought? A married brother often shared his wife with an unmarried one among some tribes--if the woman agreed. I didn't know if I could accept his sharing Morning Dove with me. I couldn't see Morning Dove agreeing to it either. If I declined, I would gravely offend him.

"If it is Morning Dove's wish, I accept," I told him. I could manage the problem later if it came to that. At the moment, all I wanted was to get warm.

Inside my lodge, it was comfortably warm. Jumper had taken the time to build the fire pit. I sat as close to it as I could with Jumper's robe still around me. He'd also gotten many things off the floor. I pulled the robe tighter around me and lay down.

"The horses," I croaked.

"Kills Many is strutting as if he were the one to bring them. There are others with him who know horses. They will care for them."

I moved a bit closer to the fire. The shivers stopped, and my teeth were no longer trying to cut out my tongue. I still felt as if I had an obligation to be out there with the horses.

"I should be with the horses," I said.

Jumper looked into the flames and spoke softly. "One of the youth came to get me last night. He said he saw you become two men."

I glanced up at Jumper, but stayed silent.

"I," he paused perhaps gauging what my reaction would be, "I saw you dancing at the rock--and then a bright flash in the darkness. A flash like a falling star."

He stared at me again. My eyes started to close. I forced them open.

"You were at the rock dancing and you were on the back of a horse who had not been there before." The last of his words rushed out as if pushed by his fear. "The you who rode the horse vanished, and then you were dancing around the rock again--I don't know how to explain it, but you were there and yet you were not..."

Jumper seemed to be saying I had been in two places at once. I couldn't ask the wolf how that could be--even if he could tell me, I doubted I would understand.

"I wanted more horses. The spirits let me get them."

Jumper frowned. "I think I will be careful what I ask the spirits for."

The soft thudding of my medicine bundle lulled me further toward sleep. I tucked it into the hollow of my stomach where I lay on my side. A better choice would have been to put it away, but I didn't want Jumper to see the change in it. The soft hide covering was no longer cracked with ancient age. It even smelled like freshly tanner leather.

Jumper added wood to the fire all the way around the outside, like the spokes of a wagon wheel, so they would feed the flames for whatever amount of time I slept. Exhausted as I was, I sat straight up. How long was I gone this time?

"Has it snowed yet?"

Jumper shook his head. "Not yet. But Kills Many has convinced the council the spirits will be angry if they do not make the choice soon. Winter is in the air this day. Over the horizon the clouds look heavy with snow."

I struggled to throw off the robe.

"There is much of the day left. The snow won't reach us for a day or two yet, I think."

I flopped back down. I could barely move, much less hold the attention of anyone while speaking in this condition. "I must speak this day," I told him. I also had to address the problem of so many horses. I would take care of the horses before I spoke, and they would listen to me.

"I don't care about the choice. But I must speak," I said, already groggy beyond control. The words were out of me before I even thought about them. I didn't care about the choice? Who was I trying to fool? I wanted Morning Dove. Her words to me had been about the greater good of our Nation over the good of one life. In this case it was my life and happiness.

How was I going to convince them I should lead--that I was the one to have Morning Dove? I had the books and little else, other than my words. In a panic, I tried to think of where I had put the other things I brought with me. I sat up again. Everything was off the floor except the wicker chest. That was right. What I needed was in there.

I collapsed back down.

"Promise me," I said, "you won't let me sleep the day away. There is something I must do before I speak--and it is time for me to speak."

"Yes, I think it is. You have made a good demonstration of your Power with the horses," Jumper said. "I will wake you before the sun has finished its journey halfway across the sky." Why did Jumper support me when I thought he wanted to rule? I would ask him later.

"Morning Dove." Her name came to me with the desire to hold her.

Jumper stayed silent. I shouldn't have brought her up. In the flickering of the firelight against my closed eyes, he spoke. "She hasn't gone to the women's moon place, not since you left us the first time."

I would have sat straight up again, but the lull of my bundle dragged me down. I felt for an instant as if I had fallen into a dark abyss where there was only the sound of the pounding heart and the figure of the gray wolf, as if he were watching me--judging me. Was I man enough? Was I Powerful enough? Did I care enough? Was I generous enough? Once I woke up, I would have to prove I was all those things.

Chapter Nineteen
Questionable Answers

I thrashed in my blankets and sat straight up. My head connected with a lodge pole. I let out a gasp. The dream had been one of the rare ones where you woke up feeling as if the real world was the dream. I could still hear the elk-man's laughter as he taunted me. In the dream, I had been running away from him. In his hand, he'd held the elk carving. He kept laughing and telling me he would capture my spirit inside the ivory. It was my turn to suffer eternity at the mercy of someone else.

My tongue stuck to the roof of my mouth with insistent thirst. When I tried to swallow, I gagged. I'd brought a leather water bag with me, lined with plastic, but I'd not had the chance to fill it. Jumper wouldn't have done it either, not wanting to assume a female role. With a grunt, I shoved the buffalo robe aside and stumbled to my feet. My head roared as if I suffered from a hangover. Before I could go to get a drink, I dug out the small protective frame for my bundle and set it up. A sling went under the tripod, and, in the sling, I put the bundle. Over the top of the frame I arranged a thin hairless deerskin. No one would touch it. I thought Jumper would consider it safe to be near with the cover over it. I took out a bit of tobacco and sprinkled it over the hide. I offered some to each of the four directions, repeating in my mind the morning words of honor, though I didn't have a clue if it was still morning.

Outside, I stretched, feeling joints pop into place and wishing I could arch my back like a cat to get the kinks out. I was too old to dance all night and to sleep on the hard ground afterwards. The complete silence of the camp made it feel like I was the only one in it. More than likely they were all down by the corral. A glance at the sun made me groan. It hung just above the eastern horizon. I'd only slept an hour or so--the dream had seemed days long.

At the river, I squatted down and splashed cool water on my face. Cupping my hands, I took note of the smooth clean rocks in the bottom of the swift water. The water supply should have been potable. My body needed the fluid. I didn't have time to boil it first. I drank deeply of the cool fresh water and sighed with relief. I should have dug out one of my tin cups because it was hard to get enough by the palm-full. I was tempted to shove my face in the water and suck it in. After two more handfuls, I did just that. On my knees, I plunged my face into the water and sucked in as much as I could before I needed to take a breath. I came up sputtering from the water that went up my nose. Female laughter filled my ears.

A young woman, perhaps only thirteen years old, stood with a full water bag. She giggled again, and I revised my thoughts of how old she was by the speculative look she gave me with her laughs. When I got to my feet, she ran down the path back to the camp. I felt much better. The pounding in my head eased and some of the aches began to vanish.

I took the trail that skirted the camp and headed to the horse meadow. At first, I thought I had taken the wrong path. I didn't hear anyone. The woods around me danced in dappled sunshine in complete silence. I glanced into the trees when a sharp crack made me startle. The gray wolf sat in the undergrowth looking at me. He opened his mouth and yawned before a long sigh escaped him and his jaw snapped shut. He vanished--one moment he sat in front of me and the next the spot stood empty.

I hurried along the path. I didn't end up at the horse corral. I found myself on a steep trail leading up to a series of caves. The openings grinned down at me, sinister--beckoning.

"Wolf?" I said, feeling foolish under my fear. "Where am I? I don't think I want to be here."

Only silence answered me. Half way up the trail to the caves, a man walked stooped over by the bundle of wood he carried on his back. I quickly moved to catch up with him. When I reached him, he stopped and slowly turned to look at me. The bundle of wood got set on the trail between us. He'd coated his entire body with white ash and drawn black and red symbols on his torso and arms. A swirl on one shoulder. A keyhole design on another--a medicine mark long before keyholes were commonplace. On his stomach, he wore the concentric circles with the figure of a man in the middle--a symbol representing the circle of life and man's small place in it. He was a medicine man of some sort.

"It is good the spirits have answered me," he said in a rough voice. "Bring the wood. It is time we finished this."

I had no idea what "this" he expected me to finish, but I picked up the wood. Unable to figure out how to carry it as he had been, I ended up hugging it awkwardly as I climbed the almost vertical path. Smaller twigs twisted in my hair and scraped my face. I couldn't see the path at all and several times I stumbled.

Inside the first cave, a small fire blazed. The medicine man went directly to the fire and gestured for me to put the wood nearby. I untied the woven fiber matt from around it and fed the fire.

"I have waited many years for the spirits to see my worth. I am glad they didn't send me a child in need of teaching. The battle has not treated me well."

I stayed silent. What did he expect from me? Who did he think I was--a spirit-sent helper, I assumed.

He seated himself across the fire from me. Carefully, he unrolled a bit of hide. Inside were several bone tools and two small, pointed rock tools. A sharp chunk of obsidian that looked eerily like my grandfather's obsidian scalpel lay in the middle of it. From another bit of hide, he took a small round disk of ivory.

I could already see the figure of an elk emerging. Automatically, I grasped the medicine pouch I wore. The carving wasn't inside. Panic almost seized me. I pushed it away, deciding whatever the wolf wanted of me here--once I returned, the talisman would be back in place--once the medicine man finished it.

A clay jug sat near his feet. A single band of black encircled it. A thick cork blocked the mouth of the bottle. He used the obsidian blade to work at the exquisite designs. The elk's upraised head with open mouth came to life as I watched. The carving, once it got to me, had lost much of this detail.

I glanced around. Black soot marred the ceiling above me. On the walls, primitive pictographs danced in the flickering light. A man, a woman--she held a string of beads, a medicine man--near his feet a conch shell and an elk skeleton--bigger than a normal elk, with a tremendous set of antlers, graced the walls directly behind the medicine man. Across the top of the wall, a male stick figure held a spear to a female figure's body. The red smear over her figure seemed to indicate the male figure had killed her. An entire trail of this male figure killing female figures lined the wall in a terpsichore of gruesome death. Behind the figure of the man, other deformed depictions of men devoured the corpses left behind by the killer. In one drawing, the killer held his hands up over the smaller ones as they knelt before him. Clearly, he ruled them. Killed at his command or cleaned up after his gruesome work.

I shifted my position and tried to ease away from the pebbles digging into my thigh. The medicine man turned a sharp glance on me. I wanted to shrink into myself. The air felt thick. I could barely breathe and wondered if I were suffering from oxygen deprivation. Time travel, or vision--I had no idea.

"I had begun to think I had to do this alone." He held up the now finished carving. "We will trap the soul of the evil one inside this."

"What did the evil one do?" I chanced asking.

He gave me a startled glance. His shoulders slumped. He shook his head. "I had thought. . . " he began, "I shouldn't have thought my punishment would end. They have given me what I asked for, an adult helper--but without the learned Power I need."

I searched for an explanation. "I know the paths of Power well. The spirits can be elusive in their reasons for sending one where they do. I must know every detail so I don't make a mistake that will let this evil one run free yet." Power stories lost their effectiveness if the storyteller didn't repeat them perfectly. I took the chance this medicine man would agree.

"I did as the Great Elk directed. I trapped the evil one in this jar--but not before he. . . " The medicine man glanced at the wall behind him. I understood. The man, whose soul the medicine man captured, had been a serial killer.

"This evil one," he touched the jar, "Dancing Elk, he tricked me and killed the last of the Great Elk. He took his father's wife. When she would not be his wife and he found she carried his sibling inside her, he killed her. But it was not enough for him--he killed many. Women in villages as far as a man can walk in ten days time died--they all carried children within them. This evil one caused their children to die. He caused the unborn to make their mothers bleed to death. And those he could not kill that way, he murdered in the night. It is said, and I know this to be true, that he drank their souls to become stronger. Those he couldn't get to, he commanded his minions to devour. I helped this evil one, so it is right I have to stop him."

A few small shavings of ivory peeled away from the carving. A trace of tears appeared on his face. "The Great Elk forgave me. But he did not know Dancing Elk. He did not know he was evil, did not know he could command others to help him, or that he possessed the Power of time."

"What if his spirit gets free?" I asked. Dread clasped my heart and made my soul shrink back from hearing any more of the story. The Power of time. Had Dancing Elk mastered it? Obviously, he was the creature who followed me. A man taken by evil could take many forms.

"It can't get free as long as we take care of its prison, as the Great Elk instructed us. I am old. I have no children. You must have a son--or a daughter to pass this to. They must know the importance of the story." He gave me a satisfied and solemn nod. "I trust you. The spirits sent you to me. You will care for this carving--your son will and his son will--they will never neglect it."

He pulled the jar into his lap. "It is time to do this. I fear the spirit inside will break the jar soon. I see him dancing in the form he took from the Great Elk. He will call the dark things here to break the jar and set him free." He tilted his head towards a spot behind me. I picked up the rattles laying there and got to my feet.

What chant did a person sing when trying to defeat evil? I chose a chant designed to protect one in battle. It proclaimed the Power of the singer. It asked the spirits to protect the warrior, or the hunter. I watched the medicine man while I stepped back and forth near his small fire.

He held the jar in his lap. The jar jerked in his hands. When he placed the carving near the cork, a small crack began to open on its side. The medicine man jammed a stone knife into the lid. The crack in the side of the jar widened. A howling wind swooped around the cavern. Dust, small stones, and bits of ivory flew around the small space--flying bits of shrapnel cutting into me.

The jar rattled and jumped.

It fell from the medicine man's hands and rolled across the floor until it stopped against my feet. The medicine man fell over dead with a look of terror frozen on his face.

I sprang forward and grabbed the carving from his hands. The elk-man's laughter began filling the cave. The jar's jumps and shakes slowed down. The fracture now ran almost fully around it. I grasped the pot, trying to hold it together. I didn't have any idea what to do.

"Trap me and all your People will die. I will kill them all. I will hunt you. You will not escape me. No one will escape from those who help me."

I did my best to ignore the shrieking voice. Despite the electrical current dancing through my insides, I shoved the carving into the crack in the side of the jar.

Everything went still.

"I will find you, Running Deer. We are one now. Your People will die. You will die."

The cave vanished along with the echoing voice--the echoing voice of the elk-man. When my father told me the story of the carving, details had been lost and changed. If he had known the true story of Dancing Elk--would it have affected my decisions? Sadly, I doubted it would have.

The things that had happened to me recently had woken me up and filled me with regret. But now I accepted who and what I was. I had the Power to travel time--I was a descendent of those who had trapped the ancient evil--a serial killer, maybe a self-proclaimed witch, one who had the Power to travel time--and I had abandon my past. I had neglected the carving and the story.

I, Shannon Running Deer, with my neglect and disdain had set the evil free. Clasping the pouch I wore, I was relieved to find the carving rested inside.

I came out of the vision at the edge of the forest near the horse corral. There were many people there. Much to my surprise, they were working on enlarging the fence. It extended into the woods as far as I could see and used trees wherever it could to hold the horses. They'd built the fence into the middle of the stream where a strong oak grew on a small clump of land. It snaked back to the shore, thus eliminating the need to carry water to the horses. No one even looked at me.

Quietly, I stepped back into the woods. I had to find my grandfather. I moved along the trail and came out on a side of the village I hadn't seen before. Gathered around a small fire, a group of preteens watched an adult doing something. Several other adult men stood off in the trees observing, but in such a way the children wouldn't feel the need to perform for a parent. I almost walked past when I recognized Kills Many's voice.

I moved as close as I could get without being seen by Kills Many and stood against a tree. One of the other men glanced at me and nodded. I returned his acknowledgment. Kills Many sat with his back against a tree. He held a thin wood stick in his hands.

"You must choose only a true and straight piece of the peeling bark tree." He held the stick against his arm. It extended past his shoulder by a small amount.

Most of the youth watched him with rapt attention. A few held out their own arms as if questioning the length of their arms compared to the considerable reach of Kills Many.

Kills Many smiled and said, "The blood of the tree must be flow-ing when you cut your arrows. Make sure the shafts are as long as *your* whole arm. As you grow and your Power of the hunt grows, so will your arrows."

Kills Many spoke in a soft low tone. It surprised me the man had the patience or the desire to sit with these youth and teach a skill.

One of the older boys doodled in the dirt with a stick. Kills Many's gaze fell on him.

"What do we do next?"

The boy looked up from his idle drawings when he realized all the other boys were watching him. "Peel the stick," he said smartly.

Kills Many made a sound of understanding and for a moment I doubted his skill. Did he use arrows the same length as his entire arm? That would require a long bow, not something he should have been familiar with. He picked up his own bow, rested it in his lap, cut a notch in the end of the long stick, stood up and fitted it in his bow. Ridiculously, it stuck out almost half its length even when he drew his bow all the way back.

Kills Many said nothing else. A couple of the other boys tittered with laughter, but the bored boy understood without Kills Many having to point out his error.

"The shaft should only reach from your fingers to your elbow," one of the youngest boys said.

The man nearest me smiled. His son, I assumed. Kills Many used a steel knife to cut the shaft. Where had he gotten it? Easy, he had traveled in time with Morning Dove. What kind of mess would all this make out of time—out of the world?

He passed the notched shaft to the boy who had given the correct answer. He picked up several more sticks, cut them, and passed them around so each boy held a stick.

He peeled the bark from the last shaft in long, thin, green-tinged strips. Each boy did the same. They passed their sticks to Kills Many. He nodded often, but a few he had to scrape off bits of bark they missed. The boys who had been careless looked at the ground. Next time, they would be more careful without anyone telling them they hadn't done a satisfactory job.

Using a section of hide, he laid the now bare sticks in front of him and tied them in a loose bundle. After each boy nodded their understanding, he wrapped the bundle shut. From behind him, he took out another bundle.

"How many days must you please the arrow spirits in the fire smoke?"

Again, it was the youngest boy who answered. "Almost a moon."

Kills Many didn't praise the boy. He simply unwrapped the sticks. Repeating the process of giving each boy a stick, he waited until they had examined their stick. He opened a pouch and began to coat his stick with greasy fat. He passed this bag around the circle, letting each boy grease their own stick.

"Perhaps the Horse Bringer would like to show us what to do next." He looked right at me. Every boy there turned a questioning gaze on me as well. I felt the other adults looking at me.

I hadn't made an arrow in years. I could make a bow and a bow string--I'd done it often, but store-bought arrows were cheap--I moved into the circle.

Kills Many held his stick up to me. I took it and moved to the small fire. Carefully, I held it out over the fire trying to remember how long I needed to heat it. Too late, I realized I had it too close to the flames. The stick started to burn. I quickly shook the fire out. My face heated with embarrassment.

"Hmmm," Kills Many paused, "perhaps Horse Bringer needs to sit in on our lessons as well."

Several boys barely stifled laughs. I heard at least one adult do the same. In my peripheral vision, I saw three of the adults standing together whispering.

"Perhaps the Wise Warrior should have used less grease," I came back with. Kills Many glared at me.

This time, after wiping a great deal of the grease off, I managed to heat the end third of the stick without flames. The shaft would be uniquely marked.

Kills Many didn't have any choice but to hand me his straightening tool. I handled the bone tool carefully. It appeared very old, worn, with several symbols etched into it. The narrow end fit into my hand well, most likely because Kills Many and I were almost of the same stature. At least the hole through the wide end was the right size for the stick or I would have looked even more foolish. I showed the boys the process, repeating the procedure of heating the stick in the fire and threading it, to straighten a small part of it at a time. I explained about the angle of the tool and the stick, telling them it would take practice to learn exactly how much pressure to use.

When I finished, Kills Many snatched the stick out of my hand

and sat back down in his teaching place. I doubted the boys missed our hostility toward each other. He notched the end of the shaft and demonstrated how to split three separate wild turkey feathers so he used the same side of each feather for each section. He repeated the process until he seemed satisfied with them. Next, he quickly trimmed them to about two inches in length. He passed them around, letting each boy see how he had done it. When they got back to him, he held them out to me--as if I needed the same lesson.

I looked them over. "It seems your teacher taught you well and with patience to make such fine fletching."

"Did your teacher show you how to attach the feathers?" he asked me.

He held out the straightened shaft. I snatched it out of his hand, doubting the boys were paying any attention to the arrow making lesson--their focus had to be on our sparring. My father had shown me how to use pine pitch to glue the feathers on. We'd used thin sinew to secure them. Kills Many watched me with narrowed eyes.

For the barest second, I thought I saw a shadow pass behind him. An elk-shaped shadow. I wouldn't doubt myself or waver and give the creature a chance to trouble me this time.

"Perhaps you know of a way to magically attach the flights?" I asked Kills Many.

He looked at the boys before he handed me his small bundle of sinew. I sat on the ground with the fire at my back and held out the shaft so the boys could get a good look at the way I wrapped the thin strips around each end of the feather pieces--crossing them between each one, adding my own signature to the arrow.

"You can use pine sap to hold them in place while you wrap them." Satisfied with my work, I passed the feathered shaft around the circle.

Kills Many took it and climbed to his feet. A moment later, he retook his seat. The bundle he placed at his feet made a clacking sound when he plunked it down. Rocks hitting rocks? He untied the drawstring and smoothed the large hide in front of him. Chunks of flint, agate, slate, and even a lump of obsidian lay in front of him. He unrolled another bundle revealing a deer antler sharpened to a flat tip, a larger piece of stone--this one smoothed and shaped on one end from the chipping of other stones.

"This day, we won't make complete arrows," he said. "Another day, I will see if you have learned to make the shafts--but perhaps this day Horse Bringer could show us his skill at arrowhead making."

Kills Many held the chunk of obsidian in his hand. He chose the antler tool and held both out to me.

I stood. "It is a skill I do not have," I told him. What was I going to do? Lie? I couldn't make a stone arrowhead.

"And you think to lead us?" Kills Many said. He didn't glance at the adults, but I knew his thoughts were on them just as mine were. "How can a man lead when he does not even have the Power to get his own food?"

His reasoning was absurd. I doubted if very many in the village could make an arrowhead.

"Do you have the skills of a medicine man?" I asked him.

"I have Power enough to make my own medicine. The spirits have favored me and will favor those who follow me--I have never needed the *skill* of a medicine man."

"A man cannot have some of every Power," I countered.

"A man who would lead has to understand and have some of every skill," Kills Many came back with.

I glanced at the adults. They had moved into the small clearing.

"Or be smart enough to realize he needs others to help him lead."

The shadow moved behind Kills Many. I was the only one who saw it--no one else even frowned. It gathered behind him and solidified into the elk-man. My hand went to the carving. The woods stilled. For a brief moment, the elk-man and I glared at each other on some metaphysical plane.

Kills Many broke the silence. "One man will lead. One man will be the Chief of All Time. One man will become the Timeless One and have Morning Dove."

The figure of the elk-man melted into the ground--a cloud passing by the sun--except the shadow slid over Kills Many.

The look in his eyes intensified. His fingers grasped the black stone tighter. His arm muscles tightened.

My grandfather chose that moment to stumble into the clearing.

"You would think with as many feet as travel this path, the stones would know to stay out of my way." My grandfather looked at me. He looked at Kills Many. Most of the children scampered off while the adults lingered.

Kills Many began picking up his supplies. His tools got mixed in with the rocks and flint. He just rolled the bundle up, leaving the wrapping his tools had been in lying on the ground when he left. The bored youth grabbed the leather and ran after Kills Many.

Chapter Twenty
A Man's Worth

The adults, now that the show between Kills Many and I was over, left the small clearing. I didn't doubt word of our confrontation would soon spread. My grandfather watched me with his lips pushed together in a thin line.

I looked at the ground. I hadn't wanted to argue with Kills Many again. I wanted him out of my way, but fighting with him wasn't going to accomplish my goal. Lying on the ground, near where he had been sitting, I saw his arrow straightening tool. Frowning, I picked it up. Kills Many didn't strike me as a man so careless with his tools he would leave it behind. Why had he been in such a hurry?

"Hmmm, odd," my grandfather said.

I picked up the tool and held it out to my grandfather. "If I return it to him, he will probably accuse me of stealing it."

"Every child knows if you leave something, it means you no longer want it. You cannot expect a good tool, such as this one, to be left behind."

I didn't much care about the tool. But I didn't need to give Kills Many another reason to make me into someone scornful. They wouldn't look upon a thief favorably.

"I don't have a use for it." My grandfather took it from my hand.

"You have use for a hundred horses? I do not think that will persuade the council--most of those who have sway with the council have never seen a horse before."

"I need to talk to you. . ."

"I can't tell them to choose you."

I clasped the carving inside the pouch. "Not about the council or their choice."

"You don't want Morning Dove any longer?" He shook his head.

"Please. Don't do this with my words today."

His back straightened. His gaze locked with mine. "Often, I told you that you were leaving yourself open to the evil in your soul. You have never listened to me, and now you wish me to fix what you have done?"

"Grandfather," I started.

"There will be fights over the horses soon. There are many who are already calling you a greedy man." He looked down at the tool in his hand. Kills Many, no doubt, would have started that rumor.

"How do I drive this thing away from me?" I said, holding onto the carving.

"You think I know? I was not there when your ancestor--the Great Medicine Man--helped kill the last of the Great Elks. I was not there when the Great One trapped the One Who Enjoyed Taking Life--were you?" He looked at me with his head tilted to the side.

"I. . . " Had I been there or had the wolf merely shown me a vision I thought I had been part of? Even if I had been there--it gave me no clear idea on how to trap the elk-man.

"You?" my grandfather prompted.

"Nothing," I snapped. He wasn't going to help me.

He shook his head. "One day, I hope you will be ready for the answers needed. This day is not the one." He turned his back on me and stalked away. When he reached the edge of the clearing he said, "A man's worth is not measured in how much he owns, but in how much he can give away. A greedy man is more open to the evil in the world."

"I am aware of that," I said. I doubted he heard me. He had already vanished down the path. I didn't even get a chance to tell him what I planned on doing with the horses.

At the horse corral, I could pick out my own horses. Some of the other horses must have come from the slaughter pen. One mare stood hunchbacked, near the far edge of the original pen, with her backbone visible and her ribs showing. The other horses stood far away from her. Jumper came and stood by my side.

"We should destroy her before she makes the others ill," I said to Jumper without looking at him. How would I fix what I had done? I needed to start with winning the trust of The People. Once I was done with the horses, I could speak to my grandfather again--maybe he would share with me then.

Jumper stared at me.

"What?" I said. He'd said something to me, but I'd been so lost in my thoughts I hadn't understood him.

"I didn't want to tell a warrior to get rid of her without your permission," Jumper repeated. In Jumper's time, a man with this many horses would have been very wealthy--and my grandfather was right--very greedy when no one else had even a single horse. I had to concentrate on the horses and my plan for them.

"Her hide will still be of use. They should drag the rest of her away," I said reluctantly. I couldn't throw the hide away. But I hated giving those gathered any idea of the horses' use except as a helpmate.

Jumper nodded and started toward the far end of the unfinished new fence where some young warriors, a mix of tribes represented, worked. With a nod, one of them ducked under the fence and approached the mare with confidence. He appeared very sure of himself around the mare. He made a wide circle around her back end; he must have come from a time with horses. With a gentle hand, he led her out of the open pen and down the trail away from the healthy horses. I wondered how far she would make it before she collapsed. At least she would be away from the others.

I sought out the Cherokee man who could write and asked him to come back to the camp with me. I ducked inside my lodge and came out with a pad of precious paper and several equally precious pencils. This had to be. I held them out to him.

"Can you draw as well as write?" I asked him.

He took the paper and the pencils. "Yes. I am Spins Much, 1884."

I looked at him and understood much about him by the date he had given me. The Trail of Tears was part of his life.

"Spins Much?" I asked him. I couldn't think of why he would have such a name.

"When I was small, I loved to spin around until I got dizzy. I would lie on the ground and stare at the trees reeling above me. I asked my grandfather why the world spun around that way." He shook his head, laughing slightly. "He declared I was Spins Much since I could make much in the world spin. Once I understood the reason, it was too late, and the name stuck."

He didn't look as though he minded the name at all. My parents had simply given me my name at birth. No one had waited to see what sort of personality lurked inside me. Though my grandfather had called me Helpful Boy until my medicine vision; a name I wouldn't have cared for now.

"I'm going to give the horses away today. For each, if you could write the name of the new owner and perhaps do a sketch of the horse's markings. I don't want fights over them."

"Yes, the horse brought us many benefits, but it also brought many problems."

"Do you think I should have left them behind?"

"No. But others think they are useless and too much work. They didn't see you come in with the first thirteen. Many of them speak as if they are worth more as a food source."

"There isn't much I can do to stop them from eating the animal if I give them one." I loathed the thought. I didn't even like the idea of putting down the old mare and the others that were beyond hope of healing.

Spins Much's grin exposed a missing front tooth. "One thing they don't doubt is your Power. The youth say you danced at the rock and your spirit brought the horses with the help of many wolves. If you tell them the horse flesh will make their spirit sick-- they won't eat it."

What did Spins Much think of my "Power?" I didn't really understand how I had gone back and gotten the horses, let alone earned the help of a wolf pack in the process. I'd seen the way people watched me, though. Their respect was won by their fear of me. A thing I hoped would change soon.

"Perhaps it will be enough." I started toward the horses, and he followed.

At the fence, I stood with my arms resting on the rail. Wolf immediately came to me along with Summer. I ducked under the rail and rubbed his snout while Summer snuffled my arm, wanting her share of the attention. Near the river, downstream from the camp and the horses, a ragged lodge stood. A thin woman leaned on a thick wooden stick in front of the lodge. The hide lodge covering looked as if she had poorly patched it many times. A toddler sat on the ground near her, and another boy stood behind her. I wondered why he wasn't helping with the horses. He looked old enough. A young girl, perhaps nine or ten years of age, came from the river's edge with a water bag. I would have to make sure she went up the river in the future, beyond the camp and the horses.

Jumper joined me at the corral. "She suffers from the sharing blanket's sickness. In my time, a white-priest told me it comes from sharing the blankets of one who is unclean. It killed her husband last summer, after the spirits took his mind."

Syphilis. I'd forgotten about that. If I had a few modern drugs, I could have helped her. It made me angry she was left to live as she was, though, illness or not. All three of her children appeared half-starved. The toddler got to his feet by clinging to his mother. He wore only a thin woven shirt that did nothing to hide his protruding belly. I felt sick. Somehow, I had believed the writing that talked of charity to all those in need. I realized the woman and her children would be dead if no one hunted for her--so some form of charity was being given--just not enough.

"When they are done skinning the mare--give her the hide."

Jumper gave me a surprised look. Many of those around me stared, and looked to the woman. It was as if they thought I suffered from the same disease and it was eating my brain. They may have shared some food with her, but I understood now. They thought evil spirits infected her.

"You can't get her sickness from touching her. And it is unlikely her children suffer from it," I snapped out at those staring at me. I stalked away from Jumper. Those who came from a time with the knowledge of how the disease spread, annoyed me the most. How could they let her endure as if it were her fault? I was even more irritated that they would let her children suffer.

At the paddock, I chose a sturdy-looking pinto. I grabbed her halter and led her to the front.

"This day, I give away my horses." I would give them away even if I felt they didn't deserve them at the moment. Everyone within the sound of my voice stopped their work. It took only moments before word spread, and I had the attention of all of them. Kills Many stood against a tree, with his arms crossed over his chest, and a look of envious fury on his face. Yes, giving away the horses before I spoke to the council was the right thing to do.

"There are those here who understand the Power to control them," I began, using my loudest voice, but not shouting. "All of you must learn the Power as well. Part of the Power rests with how you treat them. Abuse them, and they *will* abuse you." I went on to explain about watering and feeding them. I talked of gathering grasses for them to get through the winter. At this point, a man stepped forward. He must have been a good hunter. He was one of the few who were overweight.

"We must gather food for these *sunka wakan*?" He used the Sioux words for horse--*mysterious dogs*. But his speech didn't sound like he had seen them before. "The hunger moon leaves many dead--too many. I say during the hunger moon, if they cannot find their own food, we eat them."

"This is so," a woman said after she pushed her way to the front. She leaned on a cane, and those around her stepped back. Around her neck, she wore a necklace of bear claws and twists of human hair. "Even now we have wasted days when we should have been hunting, and collecting the last of the wild fruits."

"I saw them dragging lodge poles." This man walked with a limp. Near him, a woman balancing a baby on her hip and holding the hand of a toddler, nodded in agreement.

"If we run out of food here--it will be easy to move to a new place," she added.

"You would starve for the ease of moving your lodge? My dogs carry my things well enough. And they don't eat what an animal this size will," the medicine man woman said.

"I must share my winter meat with my dogs. I don't eat grass," the woman with the baby said back to her.

At the edge of the forest, the gray wolf appeared, standing behind him were several deer. It seemed impossible for them to be suddenly there, but when the soft thud of a drumbeat sounded in my ears, I saw what the wolf wanted. I turned to Jumper.

"Get me a bow, and keep track of those who wish to eat the horses." I hoped someone would let me use their bow--I would have to make one soon.

Jumper gave me a quick nod and dashed across the pen. He talked briefly to Kills Many. Kills Many gave him the bow and quiver from his back with a grin. More than likely Kills Many thought I had no idea how to use it and would look foolish. He must have thought his own Power was very much stronger than mine. Otherwise, he wouldn't have allowed me the use of his weapons.

I whistled, and Summer came trotting to me. With my hand on her shoulder, I leapt on her back. We had done this at the Pow Wows I once attended. I didn't need a bridle. She knew the commands of my knees. Clipping up to the fence, they let me out. Those gathered surged back, many of them clearly afraid of me mounted on Summer, or afraid of her alone. Jumper handed the bow up to me. A man stood nearby holding a spear. I asked to use his spear as well. I anchored the quiver to my back and slung the bow over my shoulder. If I fell off, I would look like a chump. I wouldn't fall off.

The gray wolf howled. Every person turned to look. The herd of deer sprang over the fence and bounded across the pen. With a grunt, I turned Summer. She leapt over the fence rail. Barely keeping my seat, I squeezed her flanks to urge her to go faster. A buck-deer turned his antlers toward us. Summer skidded around him and as she spun, I plunged the spear into his chest. Summer knew these moves even though it was a calf and rope used at the Pow Wows or a stationary straw deer.

Surging after the herd, she ran flat out. I sat as straight as I could, reached behind me for the bow, and nocked an arrow. Letting it fly, I brought down a doe, then another, and one more before the deer were gone out of sight. Summer pranced around the interior of the corral. Like an over-proud teenager, I held the bow over my head and let out a triumphant shout. How could I have forgotten the exhilaration of a successful hunt?

Summer stopped with her sides heaving. Two other hunters had brought down one deer each. That was fine. It fit with what I needed.

"You see," I told the doubters between hard breaths, "on a horse a hunter can bring down many animals."

"And with less danger to the hunter," Kills Many added. He no longer looked at the horses with fear or trepidation. His look was now one of speculation. I supposed he thought he could be much more impressive as a hunter and warrior mounted on a horse. He still looked at me with a gleam of hatred in his eyes.

I leapt off Summer and pulled up a handful of grass. Using the grass like a sweat comb, I began wiping her down. A youth came forward, holding out his hand. I let him rub her down.

I sought out the pinto and led it over to the deer. It pulled back with its nostrils flared. "You will learn to tolerate the smell, my friend," I said. I turned to the crowd. "You see how it knows the scent of death? Any of you who eat one of the horse-people will suffer a spirit sickness that will not go away." In times of starvation, was it right to tell people they had to die rather than eat a ready source of meat? I wouldn't be much of a leader if I expected that. "Only in times of dire need will the horse-people let you have some of their flesh without the sickness."

A ripple of discontent ran through the crowd. A second wave of nodding and understanding replaced it. All the tribes had respect for an animal's spirit. No one would risk spirit sickness for a taste of an animal they didn't desperately need for food.

I used a woven fiber rope to tie one of the deer's front legs together. I looped the rope around the pinto's neck. Easily, I dragged the deer out of the pen and straight to the sick woman. Her eyes met mine in a stunned gaze. She had sores up and down the exposed areas of her hands and arms. They covered her legs as well.

"This horse and this meat are yours, mother. Feed your children well. With the horse, you can move easily when it is time to do so,"

I told her.

"I will be dead soon. A warrior will have to put an arrow in my head when the spirits steal my soul."

I spoke to her older son, a boy of perhaps twelve. "You *will* help your mother skin the deer and take care of the meat." I glanced at the boy's mother. The woman stared back at me. If I could find a natural source of arsenic to use--smelting some copper would work--and I would have to figure out the dose.

"When all is done as it should be," I paused in the silence of everyone listening, and then said, "I will cure her sickness."

Chapter Twenty-One
Some to Keep

No one spoke as I made my way back to the pen. The grass under my feet was already brown from the killing frosts that had come. The sky arched overhead, a solid cap of ash-gray clouds. The air felt charged with the smell of coming snow. I needed to win the trust of these people. But now they watched me warily. They feared me and the Power they thought I controlled even more than before. My grandfather always put people at ease. His words often stung me, but, with others, his words left them to discover within themselves the answers they needed. I had to be able to do the same thing.

When I led the first of the "giveaway" horses out, I heard some of them whispering that I talked of things that couldn't be.

I had a swollen ego because I could call the animals. Had I summoned the deer? I didn't think so.

I was perhaps insane. Maybe so. Would a sane man give up everything to live in very primitive conditions for the rest of his life?

I wanted the place as Chief of All Time. To have Morning Dove, I had to win and accept the place as their chief, so yes, I wanted it.

I only desired Morning Dove. I only wanted Morning Dove. I only wanted Morning Dove--those who said that were more than right. I didn't just want her. I had to have her.

I wished to have the Power of the Timeless One. When I heard those words, I stopped walking and scanned the crowd. I expected to see the elk-man. Kills Many repeated the words. I didn't have any idea what the Power of the Timeless One was--how could I want it? I rubbed the head of the black horse standing silently next to me. Very few talked in support of me.

"You are going to help me change that," I whispered to the horse and began the chore of distributing the animals.

I chose mostly mothers with many children to give the first horses to. I made it clear the woman owned the horse. The men grumbled, but I wanted it this way. I told them the horse-people preferred to belong to a woman. A single man could be their companion, but if he married the horse belonged to his wife. I took care to spread them evenly to all the different bands represented. As the number of horses dwindled, the talk against me slowed, but it still hadn't turned in my favor. Yes, the hunt impressed them, but they doubted the Power I had over the horses--who knew if others possessed it as well.

I gave draft horses to those from tribes made up of farmers. I gave a swift stallion to a woman whose husband was a new runner between tribes. I gave Jumper a sturdy mule. He didn't need the explanation that the animal could carry much, but I gave it anyway. I made sure each person, who received a horse, knew how to care for it. When I was left with just my thirteen, I stood looking at them. A strong man would give away all his horses, my grandfather would say. His wealth would be in his ability to have nothing.

I led Wolf to Kills Many. I still doubted there would ever be trust between us. It was clear he hated me as much as I despised him. I also knew nothing about warfare and would need his help if I managed to convince the council I had the answers. "For you, he is my favorite stallion, in the hopes we will find some sort of peace between us."

Kills Many grasped Wolf's halter with a shaking hand. I had already given him a horse, a sturdy palomino. With two horses, and one of the few single men to have more than one horse, he would be considered well off--once those on the receiving end realized the value of the animals.

Kills Many touched Wolf's forehead and scratched him behind an ear. Wolf pulled back, showing the whites of his eyes. The reaction wasn't what I expected. Wolf liked everyone.

"I thank you," Kills Many told me. Much lower, he added, "Once Morning Dove is mine--if you ever come near her, I do not care what you have given us--I will split your skull in two."

So much for winning his trust. I led another of my horses to Spins Much. With great difficulty and pain, I gave each horse away. Summer stood all alone. I wanted to keep her. I knew I couldn't. I led her to Jumper.

"She will serve you well," I said, and walked away from all of them.

"Medicine Elk," Jumper called from behind me. I stopped, waiting for him to thank me for a second animal. Instead, he walked up behind me and handed me the rope tied to Summer's halter. "A man shouldn't be without at least one horse."

I accepted her return, grateful. Kills Many followed with Wolf. I think he gave him back more out of fear of the stallion than out of any feelings of warmth for me. Three others returned horses as well. People shifted their feet and looked at those standing next to them. Before everyone felt obligated to return my gift, I spoke.

"I am wealthy this day, not because I have more horses than a man needs, but because I have more friends than a man could expect to have."

A collective breath of relief went up from the crowd. People surged around me, thanking me and asking questions. I tried to answer, but when I saw Morning Dove standing off to the side watching me, I couldn't speak at all. She stood with her hair fanned around her and her hand over her stomach. I thought of her words--if she carried my child it would be a bond between us no one could come between. I wanted to run to her and gather her in my arms, proclaiming my love for her as I promised to forever be at her side. I knew it couldn't be--not right now.

The people around me moved back. I stood there staring at her and listening to the hushed whispers of those walking away. The stream murmured. The trees rustled in time to the wind. Summer came up behind me and rubbed her head against my back, pushing me forward, urging me to use the human-lined corridor to go to Morning Dove.

I led Summer to Morning Dove. She met my gaze with a haunted look. I held out the rope. Morning Dove took it.

"Let the gift of this horse show my promise to support the child you carry, no matter who shall be your husband." I almost choked on the words. I knew tears stood in my eyes.

Morning Dove grasped the rope and twisted it between her hands. She met my gaze with her own tear-filled ones. "A thing between us no other can come between," she whispered.

I didn't know what to do. People were purposely not looking at us. They went back to work on the fence with renewed vigor. Others climbed on their horse's back, trying out the strength of their Power over the animal.

"I can put her in the corral for you," I said lamely.

Morning Dove looked briefly at the ground. She tugged on Summer's halter and walked towards the fence. I ended up walking next to her as she led Summer to the gate and let her loose inside the enclosure.

"You will need to brush her every day and. . ."

"I have seen horses before. I will take care of her."

"I'll take care of her. You--I--if you got thrown or kicked. . . Shit." I walked stiffly away from her. This wasn't how it was supposed to be. Intellectually, I knew the Elders would choose a husband for her. But in my own vain and lust-filled soul, I hadn't felt the reality of it. Now that she carried my child--she was mine. In any time, I think I could have made an argument for a valid claim on her. If history was like the books told us, and women were little more than property, she would be mine. I would kill any man who even thought of having her. Much like Kills Many's rage when he'd discovered she carried Jumper's child.

History often got things wrong. There were books out there professing the old texts were skewed by the view of the person writing the history. More accurate portrayals were coming out all the time. But those books had arguments against them as well. Modern people were skewing the view with their ideas. And this bizarre mixture was no place to make any kind of judgment. One thing was for sure: our women had always had a place in the governing of The People, no matter what the "experts" said.

Many times marriages were arranged, an older man to a younger woman or an older woman to a younger man. It assured knowledge got passed on and that The People followed traditions. I was certainly older than Morning Dove.

What knowledge did I have to pass on to her to help us survive? I had ideas, but I doubted I could implement them to any sort of effective end. Once I died, with so long before the white-man came, what would happen? The only thing I could do would be to make sure everything got written down and there were enough people able to read. Oral traditions worked well, but there couldn't be any room for error in our future.

The sun was more than halfway across the sky. The Elders already gathered in the common area of the camp. The clouds were turning steel-gray--heavy with snow, and loomed closer to the earth. It would snow soon. It was time for me to speak, if I wanted any time at all. I still wasn't sure what I would say. A plan had spun itself around in my head during what little time I had slept.

Now, nothing seemed adequate. I had to have Morning Dove as my wife, and, at the same time, I didn't believe they would choose me, no matter what I said. It was like taking the final board exams in college; no matter what you thought you knew--you were sure you would fail. I couldn't fail at this.

The Elders appeared to be from this time--even my grandfather looked as if he belonged here. I didn't have a clue how I would live in a time without even basic sanitation. How would I perform surgery? The simplest procedure could result in massive infections and without even basic sedation--I didn't even want to think about the lack of that.

Before I realized where I was going, I'd walked through the camp and stood at the outcropping of rock where I'd danced. No gray wolf greeted me this day. I stood watching the sun as if by sheer willpower I could slow it down to give me more time.

A branch snapped in the woods. I looked up to see a large animal, a dog--the wolf maybe, disappear into the undergrowth. Slightly in front of the animal, a man walked quickly through the woods. The birds, that moments before had been busy chattering, went silent. How could he be moving so fast? Then I saw the trail. Why hadn't I seen it before?

I needed to speak to the council, but the path attracted me in such a way I couldn't stop myself from following it.

Chapter Twenty-Two
Paths Chosen

Branches snapped back and almost hid the man walking in front of me. Sunlight streaked through the trees. Stark silence blanketed me in a cocoon of humid hot air--only moments before the air had been chill with impending snow. I glanced behind me and stopped walking. The path had vanished. I took a few backwards steps and watched a clump of dark green ferns appear. One moment, I could see the path, and, the next, green life hid it.

I turned to continue following the path. The man ahead of me stood in the same spot. When I looked at him, he spun around and picked up his pace. Now I could see the dog--the gray wolf. A chill came over me. The trail took on the quality of the path I had followed in the spirit world to save Morning Dove. Mist crept at the edges of it and snaked out around my feet. Several times, I lost sight of the man I pursued.

He would stop and wait for me to get the same distance away from him, before he moved quickly ahead again. Time lost meaning. I focused on following. The woods opened up before me, and I stepped out into a clearing.

The first thing I saw was a black Jeep parked with the front bumper against a tree. What in the world was it doing here? I started towards it, stopping when I saw the man. He turned to face me.

"Sam, my god. I didn't think I would ever see you again." I hurried across the clearing to embrace my brother.

My arms closed around empty space. Sam never moved. I stepped back, more than puzzled. The Jeep no longer stood whole. What was left of the front windshield rested against the tree. The side of the Jeep was now twisted and caved in, made worse by the jagged cuts of the Jaws-of-Life equipment.

"No," I whispered. "Sam?" I said without turning to look at him. The wolf started panting. The birds fluttered up out of the trees. Everything went silent again.

"I need you to do something for me." The voice belonged to my brother and yet it didn't. His words sounded as if they were coming to me from the bottom of a canyon--they echoed right next to me and around the small clearing.

I sat down on the ground right where I stood. Tears came. I couldn't stop my shoulders from shaking.

"Damn it. Damn it--you were drunk, weren't you?" Anger came to me along with the mist. It filled the clearing now.

"It's not so bad--this being dead. I see things clearly now."

I jumped to my feet.

"Clearly? It took dying to see clearly? How many times have I told you not to drive tanked-up?" I glanced back at the Jeep. "Fucking hell. How many people did you take with you?"

Sam looked almost sheepish. I suddenly felt more than a little strange talking to my brother. A brother, who if I believed this odd vision, no longer lived.

"Remember that big curve, the one right before the town of Lake Butte de Mort? Hit the big tree that stands right in the fork between the two roads. No one else on the road."

I didn't know what to say to him. Voices made me glance at the Jeep. Red lights flashed and people milled about. I sucked in a breath.

"Are you. . ."

"Yeah, I'm still in there."

I raced across the clearing to find myself staring at the mist-filled woods.

"There is nothing to be done. Not even you can save me."

"Why are you here?" Better yet, why was I here in the land of the spirits?

"I need you to do something for me. I should have done it, but I ran out of time--I doubted. Now, it's too late. In three days, I will be gone--perhaps sooner."

I didn't have anything with me to sing my brother to the other side. If I had to, I would sing. . .

"No." He looked toward the Jeep.

Sam lay inside a lodge where the Jeep had been. Our mother's brother danced around him in full medicine man regalia. He added cedar to the fire and shook his rattle over Sam's physical remains.

Sam's spirit still stood near the edge of the clearing. He grew more insubstantial with each verse of my uncle's chant. He started to speak. I couldn't understand him any longer. He turned and vanished into the mist.

"Sam. Sam, wait. What do you need me to do?"

The wolf barked.

The ground under my feet became a bricked walk. I now stood at the back bumper of the Jag outside my house.

The pavement of the driveway glistened in the moonlight. The Jag sat as I had left it. The right taillight shattered, the front wheels up on the walk, with the skirt under the front end smashed into the brick planter boxes.

When had Sam's accident happened? On the last night I'd seen him, he wouldn't have had any reason to be where he smashed the Jeep. I tried the door and found it open. Inside, the room remained as I'd left it. My spirit wept for my brother. I thought of all the times we'd sat together and ended up arguing the old ways verses the new ways--or the white-way. Now, I wished I'd listened to him--I wished he'd listened to me and gotten help for his drinking.

What had he wanted me to do? I tried to think of the words we'd exchanged the last time we'd seen each other. He'd been drunk and telling me I needed to join him on some sort of spirit quest. He'd given me a book; a Coptic bound volume only an inch thick.

Seated on the top step leading into the living room, I held the book. Tooled into the leather cover the designs made no sense to me--I hadn't seen them before. I opened the cover to see pages covered with small pictograph writing. It resembled the writing on Morning Dove's history wall.

I didn't understand where Sam had gotten the book, or what he wanted me to have it for. Frustrated, I tossed it on the floor. A slip of paper fell out of it and fluttered across the tiles. I snatched it up and unfolded it.

At the top, the business heading said Shilfen Pharmaceuticals. Sam had applied for a job as a guard at their main plant. What in the world? Why had Sam done that--when? I paged back through the book. The symbols still didn't make any sense. I sat staring at the last pages--then I saw it.

People, ill, dying, being buried in mass graves. In the corner, almost too small to make out--a tiny Shilfen logo. This had to be Sam's vision book. The last vision he'd had before he gave me the book, concerned Shilfen.

I had to go to Shilfen, but, first, I had to go to Mercy.

I stared at the open patio door. The wolf sat looking at me.

"This better work, and you better be able to get me out of there if it doesn't."

I took a cab to Mercy. The Jag wouldn't start. Most likely because I had hit the bottom of the radiator on the planters and who knew what else--had I even shut off the headlights that night? In the basement, the same guard sat outside the doors. He leapt to his feet, staring at me. He shook his head and rubbed at his eyes, before he glanced around him.

"Something wrong?" I asked as straight-faced as I could.

"You. . . " His voice trailed off. He shook his head again. His back went straight, and he pulled his shoulders up. "Doc Martins left for the day," he told me.

I had no idea what time it was. After five? The sun had just been setting, so it was after eight. The last van from Shilfen came in around eight-thirty--dropping off the supplies for the early morning.

If I took the elevator I ran the risk of running into other people--and dressed like I was--it wouldn't be a good idea. The burr-haired guard just stood there watching me as I opened the door to the steps. Did he think I was some sort of vision? Maybe I was.

Near the supply docks, the Shilfen van sat with its side door open. A large man, with a long, black ponytail hanging down his back, pulled boxes out of the van and stacked them on a dolly. I crept up beside him. He didn't hear me due to the headphones he wore--with the volume turned up so loud, I could hear the rap music he listened to.

The wolf melted around the back of the van. The driver stood up very slowly. His hand went to the holstered gun he wore. The wolf moved toward him, growling low in his throat. When the guard had the gun strap unsnapped, he slowly began to pull the gun out. I jumped forward and grabbed his elbow, twisting his arm and jerking it back. Reflexes made him hold the gun tighter.

I managed to grab it away from him by twisting his wrist. He stared at me with his hand flexing. I hated pointing the gun at him, but it was the only way.

"Who are you?" he demanded.

"Doesn't matter," I said. The wolf came to stand by my side. "Look. I don't have anything--vaccines. You can't get high off those. Just give me my gun. It's not worth jail time."

"I want your Shilfen pass and your handcuffs," I told him. He stood a great deal shorter than me. His uniform wouldn't fit me.

"What? You can't get into the plant," he said and laughed. Sweat stood out on his upper lip--his laugh nervous.

Now what? I wouldn't--couldn't shoot him. "Wolf," I said and thought very hard about having the man's handcuffs. The wolf moved toward the man. The driver tossed his cuffs at me. I almost made a grab for them. The wolf leapt into the air, grabbing the cuffs, and stopping the man's lunge after me. He lay on the concrete holding his elbow and rocking back and forth. I suspected he'd done some damage to his arm--landed on it.

"My intention wasn't to hurt you," I told him. "All I want is your pass."

He shook his head.

I moved behind him and pulled his arm back. He screamed. I swallowed hard. He had done nothing to me--how could I leave him here hurt, in pain, and having seen me? I reached in front of him and yanked his pass off his shirt. I grabbed his other arm and cuffed his hands together. Seeing his key chain, I took it as well. How long did I have if I left him here before someone found him? It had to be close to nine. Shilfen was the only company that delivered at night. He could be here until morning. I glanced at the steel door that came out of the stairway.

The nurses and other staff often came out there to smoke. I stood and yanked on his good arm. "Get up."

He sprawled on the ground almost knocking me down.

"You can get up, or I'll leave you here. I hope whoever drives in here next sees you."

He spat at me.

"Wolf," I yelled. The gray wolf leapt into the van. I pushed the boxes out of my way and in front of him. He'd get to his feet when we left. He'd tell someone I was here and that I was heading for Shilfen.

I held the muzzle of the gun to his head. My hand shook--hell, I couldn't kill him. With a deep breath, I knocked him in the side of the head. It didn't work. He kicked at me and knocked me down. The gun went flying. He struggled to his feet and tried to ram me with his head. I brought my knee up. It connected with his chin, and he went sprawling. Knocked out from his own headlong collision with me.

I dragged him over to the dumpster area and left him lying next to the gate--inside, where eventually someone would see him, but not too soon.

I parked the van a few blocks from Shilfen and walked down the street to the plant. Only one guard stood in the guard shack. I watched him from across the street. People came and went out of the paper mill behind me. None of them gave me more than a quick glance despite my out of place clothing.

How would I get inside? They changed the guards at the drug plant often to prevent word getting out about their government projects. Chances were the guard wouldn't recognize me--if I had a uniform. In the small picture on the pass--the driver and I looked much the same.

The wolf sat at my side. He'd ridden in the van without making a sound. Now, he whined like a dog that needed to go out. He sped across the street and down the alley next to the plant. I followed.

About halfway around the north side of the plant, a single bright bulb illuminated a gate in the fence. On top of the fence, a security camera panned the area. If they recorded me, it wouldn't matter. But if there were guards monitoring--I would be in trouble.

I edged along the cold chain link of the fence. The razor wire on top of it sung in the dark. It sparkled, reflecting the outside lights in a parody of Christmas tinsel--mesmerizing.

The light on the pass-card box blinked red, red, red. I kept from glancing up at the camera and slipped the pass card through the slot.

The lock beeped, followed by the light changing to green, green, and green. I quickly pushed against the gate. The light turned red again. The gate didn't open. This time I put my foot against the gate, and when the light turned green, I gave it a shove. It sprung open, and I slipped inside. The distance between the gate and the side door of the plant felt like sprinting the length of three football fields while a Gatling-gun tracked me.

I stood pressed against the building, straining to hear if anyone had seen me or been alerted. All I heard was my own heart pounding in my ears. The lock on the door operated the same way as the gate. I tried the pass card and the light changed to green. Once I got inside, I couldn't change my mind. The wolf nudged me.

I slunk inside.

The only lights in the hallway were on top of the emergency boxes placed at each room door. The keys were engraved with lab numbers and designations in a code that meant nothing to me. L-001, RB 13. L-002, RT 12. What did they mean? I looked at every key. One key stood out. It was red steel and the designation of it read L-209, US-P1. Why red? I'd try it first. I guessed the L referred to Lab, the next number the floor and room number.

The doors on the second floor were all the same uniform tan. None of them had windows, and, next to the door, a small sign announced the lab's purpose--in the same ambiguous code as what was printed on the key. I located US-P1 and tried the key. It clunked in the lock as loud as a firecracker in the still hallway.

Inside, row after row of lab tables filled the room. A strong antiseptic smell permeated the air. Against one wall, several cabinets sat--locked most likely. It struck me as odd that there were no refrigeration units in the room. On one table, a folder sat open. I looked at the pages inside.

"Oh my god," I said. Some careless lab worker, or someone working late, had left their work folder open. This lab and those connected to it were working on several things. One of them, what I had originally come after, had produced a combo vaccine. One that could be added to water. All it took was two drops in fifty gallons of water to produce the desired protection--for eight-hundred people. I looked through the pages and found a list of the things it protected against. Smallpox, diphtheria, anthrax--an entire list of bad boys, including the common cold.

Amazed, I continued to page through notes. I found another item Shilfen had been working on for the US Armed Forces, self-replicating, strain-variant penicillin. I glanced around at the cabinets and storage lockers. It would have been nice if the careless person had left numbers to tell me where the things were.

The doorknob clicked.

I ducked behind the lab table and made my way to the far side of the room. I crouched behind the drawer unit of the farthest table. The wolf didn't follow me. I couldn't chance looking around the corner of the table to see where he was.

The soft sounds of someone walking across the floor made my nerves stretch tight and sing with fear.

"I've got everything put together," a woman said. Doctor Martins?

The second person made a small sound of agreement, but didn't speak. Pages rattled, and a drawer opened.

"The instructions are in here. I included a set in the shell itself--just in case you need them."

Another sound of agreement from the second person.

"It would have been a lot easier to put this stuff on a disk."

"No disks. I already told you--no trail of any sort." He sounded angry and annoyed.

A key turned in a lock, and a hinge squeaked. Something heavy got set down on the lab table I had been at earlier. What was going on?

The room door swung open.

"You aren't supposed to be in here," Doctor Martins said. Her voice had risen in tone--someone caught doing something they shouldn't have been.

"I have to check all the doors. Once every hour on this floor. Who are you?" I assumed it was a guard asking.

"Doctor Martins," she answered. "This is my lab."

"And him?"

"My assistant," Doctor Martins said too quickly.

The guard's shoes made a sound on the floor. "Well, you need to lock the door, even when you're inside." The door opened again before it shut with a click. The guard had locked the door from the outside. I wondered briefly if I needed a key from the inside.

"You told me there wouldn't be a guard," the man said. He sounded threatening.

"I don't even know who that guy is. The other guard was a lazy fool. He spent most his shifts on the phone with his girlfriend."

"And if this new guard reports you were here?"

"He won't," Doctor Martins said.

The man stayed silent. His lack of continued protests seemed wrong.

Another cabinet opened, and something else got set on the lab table.

"How much is here?" the man asked.

"What we agreed on--you could vaccinate everyone in China," Doctor Martins answered. She let out a nervous little laugh.

"And the other?"

"Everything I promised. It self-replicates, so you can use it in the field--and each time it replicates the structure mutates so it can fight bigger and better bugs." She laughed again.

"Very good," the man said.

There was a slight sound, like the brushing of fabric over something hard. One of the two gasped followed by a loud thump that made me startle. I barely kept from smacking my head on the metal drawers behind me. A sulfurous smell drifted across the room.

Latches snapped shut, and papers got shuffled. What had happened? I carefully peered around the edge of the drawer unit. Doctor Martins lay on her back on the floor. Blood seeped from beneath her.

Very slowly, I grasped the leg of the stool nearest me. I glanced around the corner again. I could see the man's feet as he shifted his weight.

Where was the wolf? I needed to get out of this lab. I concentrated on the place I had last seen the wolf. He had been sitting right about where the man stood. I took another look around the corner. The wolf sat right next to the man. He didn't pay any attention to him. I blinked. At the same time, I saw the lab around the wolf I also saw trees. Was he holding open a gate of some sort? If so, he had chosen a bad place to do it.

"What the hell?" the man yelled. He stumbled backwards. He must have finally seen the wolf.

I leapt to my feet. If he shot the wolf, I'd be trapped. I raised the stool above my head and threw it. The man's arm came up. The stool connected with his shoulder. The gun skidded across the floor.

On the table, two aluminum-sided cases rested. On top of each, he had stacked files. Next to them, a leather briefcase sat open. The man began to get to his feet. I shoved the files into the soft leather case and slung the strap over my shoulder. The wolf growled. The man glanced back briefly. It gave me enough time to grab up the two aluminum cases. The wolf leapt at the man, knocking him on his back. In one quick move, the wolf ran over the top of the man. He jumped into the sliver of light that opened up. I followed, hoping what I had in my hands was as good as Doctor Martins said.

Chapter Twenty-Three
We the People

I made my way through the trees, skipping any public areas. The air felt crisp. The sky above me shimmered an even sheet of slate gray. I wouldn't have time to investigate what I'd taken from the lab. I tucked the cases away under my bedding before I hurried to the village common area.

Kills Many stood in the center of a ring of men and women who had gathered with the Elders. Standing straight and tall, with red rectangles across his cheeks, he looked every part the savage warrior. I sat down near Jumper.

"He hopes to speak until the snow comes--or until he bores us to death," Jumper whispered to me.

Spins Much leaned forward from his place behind me. "All knew the Elders favored him. His warriors always won when we fought amongst ourselves, and there are many who know firsthand of his generosity. But, now, they are not sure."

How did they see my generosity? Had I only handed them a curiosity, or did they see what the horse could do for them? A persuasive air surrounded Kills Many. He had an unnatural assurance in his posture. Something about it bothered me, and it wasn't only the fact, if he won, he would have Morning Dove. When I looked at Kills Many, I saw a parallel of the elk-man.

"These white-men will land on our shores," Kills Many said. "There are those among us who have seen where they will land. We will greet them with our arrows and send them scuttling on slashed bellies back to their boats. They will know we are people to be reckoned with." He accentuated his words by raising his fist in the air and smacking it into his other palm.

There were many whoops of agreement. Several young men, with red rectangles on their faces, stood and danced in a circle, brandishing weapons and shouting. Most of those gathered here had no concept of what the armaments of the Europeans would be like. In my mind, I saw their great galleons crossing oceans of a vaster distance than most here could imagine. I saw us fighting them before they even set foot on our shores. There would be no welcoming help from any of the native people. I also saw the many paintings that existed of those same wooden ships ringed with smoke from the cannons they carried. They would simply blast our shores until they could move onto our land.

I got to my feet.

"We will gather all our warriors along the coast, and no white-man shall land," Kills Many said quickly. Clearly, he didn't want me to get a word in.

"And will you gather on all the shores of our country?" I asked, "Will every warrior be willing to leave the plains? Will those who live near the great lakes be willing to give up their homes, to spend their lives on the coasts, waiting for the white-man to come? Will those who hunt the great whales be willing to leave their life behind in favor of waiting for war on the shores of our land?" I asked him.

Kills Many glared at me. He crossed his arms over his bulging chest. Those around us stopped their debates. A few nodded in understanding of what I said.

"And you think we should simply continue our way of life, as if we have not seen the vision of the white-man? Do you think this mighty horse will save us?" He strutted back and forth near the fire with his hands at his sides. He flexed his fingers, into a fist and out, into a fist and out-- "A man cannot ride the beast without landing on the ground. A hunter risks his life each time he hunts. No man should risk injury by a creature you have told us is to help us hunt." With those words, he crossed his arms back over his well-defined chest, looking smug.

"Are you saying you don't have enough Power to stay mounted on the gift I gave you?" I asked him, mirroring his posture.

Laughter rang out. Kills Many scowled. "It is you with your trickery who has no true Power."

"I have seen others ride. Jumper, Spins Much, and several women ride well." I smiled at him and swept my hand out, indicating several frail-looking elderly women.

"You called the beasts and handed them out. Perhaps it is only you who holds Power over them. You seek to dishonor me with your ... witchcraft."

A gasp went through the crowd, and before I could speak, Kills Many continued. "Perhaps you have woven a spell over Morning Dove as well. We have all seen the Power of a witch make a woman's belly swell as if she carried a child, when she carried the making of her death--a child who can never be born or be felt to move, yet grows."

My insides clinched. My hands wanted to tremble. There really wasn't any defense against witchcraft. Kills Many knew this. He had provoked a great deal of suspicion about me that would be hard to put down. The more modern of the gathered men scowled, but even some of them watched me carefully. The Navaho believed in witches even in my time. I would be hard pressed to explain how I had brought the horses and danced at the rock simultaneously.

Morning Dove got to her feet. She stood silently for a few seconds. I hadn't noticed it before, but now I saw one of the Elders nod his head at her.

"Do not be a fool," she said. "I have carried a child before, or have you forgotten? I know the sickness that comes with it, and I have seen the way the false child of a witch grows in the womb. There is no woman's sickness, the moon cycles often do not stop, and the belly grows very quickly."

Cancer? It could be. Yet another thing I would have to sit by and watch destroy someone. How did a person defend against being accused of serving evil?

Kills Many's gaze went to the ground. Just before he looked back up at Morning Dove, a chilling smile twisted his mouth.

"I have not forgotten your lost child," he said with apparent remorse coloring his words. "He wishes you for himself. A witch could give you a child. He could keep another from doing so."

Morning Dove raised her chin. Her eyes danced with humor that anger quickly replaced. "He gave me my child in the normal manner. I am sure of this." There were several snickers and outright laughs from those gathered. "And I have never ridden a horse before, yet I rode this day to the hot springs and back. Even when the beast ran, I did not fall off."

Morning Dove's voice fell into the cadence of a storyteller. She used her hands to make sweeping motions while she talked. Her descriptions brought the tale alive. "A big cat stalked the woods in search of an easy meal; a child wandered out of the camp of man, a young couple courting where they would not be seen, a foolish woman on a horse in the woods. The cat came upon me with silent feet. She stood on the trail before me, hungry to feed herself and her cubs. I should have found myself in the jaws of this big hunter. . . " Morning Dove paused and looked around the circle of rapt faces. "The horse knew the danger. It turned without instruction from me and ran back to the camp." Her audience sat back and let out held breaths.

Morning Dove pitched her voice a bit higher and tilted her head to the side. "Perhaps you do not sit well on their back because the horse-people sense the danger in your words to us."

Kills Many looked hurt and surprised by her words. Under the pain and anger, though, I saw something dangerous. Why had I thought Morning Dove cared anything for Kills Many? She'd seemed to be his friend that first day, but thinking back to her words, I could see it was only my assumption she felt warm-hearted toward him.

For several moments, no one spoke. Jumper got to his feet and moved to the center of the circle while Kills Many and I glowered at each other. If Kills Many took out his anger on Morning Dove, I would show him just how protective I felt towards her.

"All here have heard my words," Jumper began. "As a trader, I have often seen that to get along something must be given. We know the white-men will lie and how they will lie to us--using their false words and their false marks. They must not catch us in their untruths. We must learn to read a person in his lies."

I moved out of the center area and leaned against a tree behind those seated. How long would Jumper speak? The temperature continued to drop rapidly. I glanced skyward. Were those small flakes of snow already, or ash from the fire? I had to get back into the circle before Kills Many got a chance to again, or he would keep up the arguments until the snow came down. Kills Many gave me a final enraged look after he moved out of the circle.

Morning Dove moved to sit near my grandfather's wife. I longed to go and sit next to her. She had a blanket around her shoulders. I wanted to share it with her.

Jumper continued to speak on the ways of a trader. He spoke of his ability to read faces and postures, to know when a person exaggerated the value of what they had to trade. He did have a point, as did Kills Many with his war ideas.

War might be the only way to save us. Ultimately, though, I simply couldn't see us winning a war against a superior force. Over everything else, I needed them to understand that they must stay united. Others in my time often debated about whether the Europeans would have won if all the nations of The People had gathered together and united in the fight against them. We had a great deal of time before they came, enough time to catch up and surpass them, but it also left a great deal of time to minimize the threat. Five hundred years from now would anyone remember what we said here, or care? Would they care in a thousand years? Once they embraced modern things and science began to explain away the mysteries, would those around me still believe in visions?

I glanced at my grandfather--he traveled the time stream. I didn't know if his *birth* had occurred here, or if the Great Spirit had placed him on the earth to live on a world devoid of life he needed to create. He'd lived in the modern world since I could remember. And he never embraced modern science to explain much of anything.

Everyone has their way of explaining things. Is the white-man's way better than ours? Who can say? If I say we came to be from the clay of the earth--is that any different than when the white-men say we crawled up out of the muck? Who is to say? Are they not the same thing?

For once, I could see they were the same. What difference did it make whether you said we were single-celled creatures that evolved into upright walking ones, or if you said we were created from it and walked across the land? Both did mean the same thing. Many people believed in the Bible and expressed it as--*Well, we don't know what form God gave the first creatures--the seven days are not literally seven days.* They could say the same of our stories.

Yes, I believed in five hundred years people would still believe in the old ways--even a thousand or more years from now they would. They had to, if we had any hope at all of defeating the Europeans. But those who came would look at all of us as Kills Many wanted others to see me. We would be witches, and evil creatures who served Satan, if we had technology they didn't understand. Somewhere there had to be a balance. I could expect to live another thirty to forty years--maybe longer, was it enough time to see our United Peoples far enough ahead, and on the right track, for things to work out?

"Medicine Elk, if you would come here for a moment? I would like to show them what I mean," Jumper asked.

I put my thoughts aside and moved through the seated people to join Jumper in the circle. At least closer to the fire it was warmer.

"What do you want me to do?" My voice carried a hint of annoyance, but Jumper only smiled.

"You see, when a man lies, it can be with his words, his voice, or his body. Medicine Elk is annoyed, but he didn't want me to know. I know by his voice and by how stiff his shoulders are. You see, he has crossed his arms over his chest, and he avoids looking me in the eye."

Immediately, I uncrossed my arms and met his gaze. He laughed. "You see, now he does the opposite and does it too well. We must all learn to see through the deceptions." With a grin, he left the circle and sat in the dirt close to Spins Much.

Kills Many jumped to his feet. I gave Jumper a quick nod to acknowledge what he had done for me. In the dirt, I drew stick figures until I had drawn a huge crowd of them--so many they overlapped, indistinguishable from one another. Next to them, I sketched a rough outline of the North American continent. I divided it into sections based on how the modern anthropologists grouped the tribes. Eleven different groups. There were some I didn't put in, the Mesoamerican groups, and those exclusive to the arctic and Alaska, as I hadn't seen any representatives of them here.

"So you know where we are from. How will that help us defeat the white-man?" Kills Many stood at the edge of the circle, with the muscles in his jaw tight. I chose to ignore him. One of the Elders made a slight sound and waved him back. Kills Many took a single step back.

I made circles around the stick people until they were separated into eleven groups. From each group, I drew a line and linked that group to an area on the map. So far, it seemed everyone understood what I was doing. At least no one seemed baffled by it.

"So, your solution is for each of us to go back home and await our destruction." Kills Many was definitely getting on my nerves.

I added a circle out in the ocean area with a line above it. I drew lines to attach that circle to each of the eleven areas.

"Each area of our nation has many tribes, but they are of similar beliefs and have common ancestors," I started with.

"Do you think we do not know that?" This came from a man who sat off to the side. He glanced at Kills Many before he continued. "We are one People now, the visions of our medicine men have agreed, and we have held the peace."

"Yes. But it is a long way from here," I pointed to a place in central California, "to here." I touched the map near what would be New York.

"It has taken three years for many of us to reach this gathering place," Spins Much said with an agreeing nod.

"So to start, I propose we organize things to make communication easier between our homelands." I smudged out three figures from each of the eleven groups. Around the large circle in the water area, I drew eleven circles with three figures in each and attached them with lines to the large empty circle.

"Each tribe must select three from their group. A warrior to lead them, if fighting is needed. He must be wise and favor the wishes of his tribe. A trader, who knows enough to learn languages and knows how to read the lies in a person's face. A medicine man, to travel the spirit roads and know the spirits' wishes."

People murmured and nodded their heads. Even Kills Many studied my drawings and gave me a puzzled look. Almost in support of what he proposed, I had suggested we might need fighting.

"These three people must choose a leader from their tribe." I drew a line over the heads of the three stick figures representing each tribe. "Each tribe must do this until," I drew a group of eleven figures inside the big circle, "there is a council of representatives, one from each area." I deepened the line around the large circle.

"Each area would have its own council of three--with one to lead and carry the group's wishes to the big council?" Spins Much asked me.

"Yes," I told him, reluctant to let go of the head-speaking role, even for a question. "We will have eleven people to speak the wishes of our entire nation. A voice for all."

"A ruling council of eleven? How do you expect to accomplish anything that way?" Kills Many questioned me in a voice not filled with the same anger as before. That frightened me. I had no way of knowing what trap he would spring next. Many present wouldn't forget his accusation of witchcraft.

"No. These eleven must choose in the same manner as each tribe and each area. They must choose a Warrior, a Trader, and a Medicine Man. Three or perhaps four men who. . . "

"No," Kills Many said. He brushed his foot over a small section of my map. "Have you not shared the same vision as the rest of the medicine men? They have all spoken clearly--it will be one man who will lead us--one man will be the Chief of All Time. One with much knowledge, and Power--with the gift Morning Dove offers, he will have the Power of the Great Spirit to guide him. Are you saying your vision is different?" His sarcasm rasped across my nerves.

"I won't tell you my vision is different." Visions could be considered an idea of the future, and I certainly had that. I doubted my future was anything like the other medicine men saw, though.

"Clearly, it is, if you expect us to. . ." Kills Many began.

"Let him finish speaking." The entire group went silent. A man who looked older than my grandfather leaned on a walking stick and gazed at Kills Many.

"Yes, Honored Elder," Kills Many said quickly. He stepped back a bit.

In the center of the North American map, I drew three large stick figures and over them I drew a line with one figure on top of it. "Once the eleven have chosen three, these three must choose one to be the headman of all the nations. He will be the one who goes to speak to the white-men's leaders. If we make the choices in good faith, they will choose a leader who reflects the true wishes of The People. One who holds much honor, much knowledge, and has lived enough of life to be rid of the foolishness of youth."

"So, you propose an Elder lead us?" my grandfather asked.

I stared down at the map. I turned to face my grandfather. I had as much said Morning Dove should be given to an Elder. While I had explained and expanded upon my plan, it became clear to me that the Headman of our nation must be someone who had lived many years and was past the hotheadedness of youth. Even Kills Many, whom I thought in his thirties, was too hotheaded for the job.

"Yes, Grandfather," I whispered. I held my head up and didn't look at Morning Dove.

The questions started in an explosion of chatter. People from all the tribes wanted to know how I proposed each tribe choose those who would sit on the many councils. Would a man serve his entire life? What if a man was a poor leader? Could they get rid of him? What if he died? Did he hold the responsibility for teaching his replacement before his time was up? I answered as best I could, redrawing and refining the surface plan I had put before them, until it had many levels of people.

All present agreed that every person must learn the white-man's tongue.

I suggested many women serve and was met with blank stares. Of course women would serve. Morning Dove would be the wife of the Headman of our nation, so it only stood to reason--wives would rule in partnership with husbands and vice versa.

"And what of the sickness the white-man will bring?" This demand from Kills Many brought all the other debates to a halt.

"I have seen in a vision the way to stop this sickness." I sincerely hoped the things I had would work.

"As you will cure the spirit sick woman," Kills Many scoffed and laughed. Many others echoed his sentiment.

"I will cure the woman. It will take many days, as the cure for the white-man's sickness will take many moons and seasons. But it can be done."

"Even if you can cure the sickness they bring, I have seen in my visions that they will be greedy and call us savages. They will kill us anyway." It surprised me to hear the strength in the young medicine man's voice. He was the same one who had beaten the drum for Morning Dove's sing.

"That's why I have proposed a strong warrior be part of each council. A warrior who will know what to do to protect his area, and the rest of us will back him, without question if we must. And if retreat is needed, we as a nation will move his People before many have to die. There must be those who trade, to know of their lies as well."

"I have seen that this white-man is avaricious beyond thought," Spins Much said. "They will not stop at one piece of land to call their own. They will not stop at words. They will demand all of our land." Spins Much stepped forward and drew a line around all of North America. He drew it again until it was heavy and deep.

"He *will* demand all of it."

In silence, I saw the looks of horror on the faces around me. "First, we must escape their sickness, second, we must try to reason with them, and, last, if they will not listen to reason--we will fight them. I have seen it will take many generations for them to arrive on our land. In that time, we could build a great wall, a line we will tell them they cannot pass. It would perhaps leave them enough land to claim, and we would preserve our way of life." My own words sounded like madness--Shannon Running Deer and his *Great Wall*. Would it be any more effective than the Great Wall of China? How would we protect the west coast? The idea of a wall, though, would keep us united in a cause.

"Where would you put this wall? Would you give half our nation to these men? A quarter of it? How much land?" Kills Many's voice held a desperate edge.

At some time, someone must have told him of the white-man's beliefs in land ownership. Or it was a misconception of the modern white who thought the Indian didn't understand such a thing. Land was like the wind; you couldn't pick it up and take it with you, so it couldn't be owned. I shook my head. It was no misconception. The time travelers had exposed those around me to modern concepts. They understood what the white-man believed.

"I wouldn't give them any land to live on," I said quietly, "but it may be our only choice."

Kills Many stared at me for a long time. No one spoke. Spins Much moved up to the map again and made an X about where the first colony of Europeans would be--James Town. "It is here that they will first try to settle our nation."

Kills Many drew his knife. He stood over the map and made a line down it. "Here is the great river dividing our nation. It is our river." Starting at Hudson Bay, he drew a line downward. He bisected Michigan, dividing the great lakes from each other, Lake Superior and Lake Michigan on one side, and the others on the eastern side. He continued down until he reached the Gulf of Mexico. The line represented the shortest distance dividing the North American continent from body of water to body of water.

"If we build a wall, it should go here. All the rest is ours," Kills Many said.

I expected those of the eastern bands to protest. Instead, they looked at each other. An Elder stepped forward. He pointed to a spot in Florida. "My people are here. Our ancestors are buried there. My mother birthed me there. I have seen a vision of the white man moving us from our land. Many die and some bands vanish completely. When faced with the choice of being wiped from the face of the earth or moving--it is always better to choose life."

Arguments broke out. I had nothing else to say. I felt stricken. Anguished, that I'd spoken without enough thought, putting myself out of the running for Morning Dove. Darkness enveloped the camp in a close blanket. Wind whipped through the trees and made lodge flaps snap like the clout of a whip. Dust and leaves swirled across the ground, whirling until they came up against something. Then they stopped, their journey at an end. In the light of the central fire--snow began to descend.

Chapter Twenty-Four
Time Again

I stood at what I thought of as my boulder and watched wispy flakes of snow dance their way to the ground. The horses stood in small groups, rump to rump, already covered with a fine dusting that shone in the thin light of the moon. The gray wolf leapt up onto the rock and pushed his nose against me. I scratched him behind an ear.

"What have I done, my friend?"

"I think, Shannon Running Deer, has learned to care for The People as one."

I moved away from the stone and faced Morning Dove. "Have they chosen?"

"Obviously not, or I would be with my new husband, not out here in the cold with a medicine man who talks to wolves." She smiled. I didn't see any humor in the situation.

"I didn't think when I spoke."

She moved around me. With her hands braced against the rock, she vaulted up onto it. The gray wolf sighed and put his head in her lap. "All there knew the spirits spoke through you. Kills Many is shamed and angry because he knows he did not let the spirits use him." The gray wolf looked very contented to have her attention. I wanted to trade places with him. She continued to run her fingers through the wolf's fur. "Your grandfather is pleased."

"Are you?" As soon as I spoke, I wanted to take the words back.

"When we awoke in your time, I knew I carried your child. The spirits were whispering it to you as well, had you listened to them. When you left, I had to return, or I would have been stuck there until the birth of our daughter. I stood outside the hospital for a long time, wanting to go in and find you. I thought if I told you I had your daughter inside me, you would come with me."

"I wish you had." If only she had come into the hospital. I would have had a full month with her. I shook my head. I needed what happened to me at the trauma center. I had to awaken to the falseness of what my world was to be able to leave it behind. I doubted I would have believed her had she told me she was pregnant.

She sat on the rock with the wolf resting his head in her lap and a look of serenity on her face. Mine. She was mine. Each time I looked at her, I felt an overwhelming sense of possessiveness toward her. *She was mine.* The gray looked up at me with half open yellow eyes. Was he smiling? He yawned and resettled his head in Morning Dove's lap. I didn't want any other man to touch her. Never again. I didn't even want another man to look at her. My stomach twisted, and anger ricocheted off my bones--shredding my heart. How could she be so calm when this night they might very well choose another to be her husband?

I looked away from her. The snow came down in huge flakes now. By morning, it would cover the ground.

The wolf lifted his snout in the air, watching the edge of the forest. I saw the same deer he did. I needed to hunt. No matter what choices the Elders made, I had to eat, and more importantly, Morning Dove did. Kills Many may have promised to take care of her, but I didn't think he would once she was married. I wouldn't consider he had a chance of winning her. I wouldn't fail in my responsibility to her, if he did.

"If I had come and told you I carried our child," Morning Dove said, "even if you believed me, you may have come out of obligation to me. But you would not have found harmony in yourself."

"If this is what harmony feels like--I don't want it."

"The man I met by the lake could not have come here and spoken to the others as you did. That man would have scoffed at our ideas and way of life. He was out of harmony with himself and in denial of what lived inside him. Medicine Elk is no longer at war with himself."

"No, I'm just a damned fool. Why did the spirits make me as I am? Why couldn't I have been content to live as I was?"

She smiled again and ruffled the gray's fur. "I do not know. It seems no matter what they decide, you are a man of great Power."

"Yes, a man who has gotten you an Elder for a husband."

Her hand went to my shoulder. Her light touch followed by a firm squeeze made me want her even more--now. Forever.

"We knew when we shared each other it was possible we would have only one night," she said softly.

"I want more," I said in a raised tone of voice. The gray sighed and got to his feet. He leapt off the rock and vanished into the woods. Home to a mate, no doubt, and warmth.

"I as well." Her voice held a sad note. She got down off the rock, took my hand, and led me into the woods. We circled the camp and came up to the back of her lodge. I stood with her in my arms for a long time, simply holding her against me. She had been encouraged to share herself with men before in the hope she would have a child who would replace her if needed. Since she carried my child, she was now to remain celibate until her marriage to the one the Elders chose.

"No one will see us," she whispered to me.

If the white-man's ways had stopped me before, I felt a burden twice as heavy at the breaking of the laws of my true heritage. A spark of anger flared in me that she would toss aside the law with so little concern. My anger didn't last. My words, my plan, if accepted, wouldn't even allow her Jumper as a mate.

With her face cupped in my hands, I touched my lips to her forehead.

"I can't. Now that I have accepted this, I can no longer choose what I will follow and what I won't. I am a medicine man of The People. I must act like it."

She caught my hand, kissed my palm, and ducked around her lodge. Off to the side, branches rustled in the woods. I caught a brief glimpse of a young warrior. So, someone would have seen us. I made my way around the edges of the camp and slipped past the outer circle of the men who still discussed and argued over the plan I'd presented. No one took notice of me. Anything I could have added would have lacked conviction--all there would know of my pain.

Inside my lodge, I opened the field kit I'd taken from the Shilfen labs. I read through the instruction sheet twice. By adding water to the trays that fit inside, I could manufacture penicillin. After that, I needed to dry a small batch and let it become powder--do the same thing again as needed. This genetically altered version of the drug would continue propagating itself forever, if I didn't use all of it. My first thought was to make several batches so I would have a good supply of it. Once I had those batches started, and placed in their cases, I shut the large case in the wicker trunk.

I'd brought along several old-fashioned syringes, steel and glass affairs with screw off needles I could re-sterilize. I filled one with the ready made penicillin included in the kit. After I sheathed the needle, I put it in my medicine pouch before making my way back around the perimeter of the camp to the area near the horse pen where the woman I had promised to cure lived.

The woman sat, wrapped in a thin blanket, close to a tiny fire outside her tepee. When I stepped into the firelight, she gave me a weary look.

"I thought perhaps your words were only for the benefit of those who would choose our chief."

I sat across from her and pushed a few sticks into the fire, making it flare brighter. "Why are you out here in the cold?"

She shrugged. "I don't sleep well. I get up and down many times each night. It wakes my children."

I moved around the fire and set my medicine bag near her. When I reached to touch her, she jerked back from me with her eyes wide. "I'm not going to hurt you. To help you, I need to touch you."

"You're not afraid of my spirit sickness?"

"No," I said. I should have admitted to some sort of fear, or asserted I could fight the spirit sickness. If she told anyone I didn't have any fear of her, it would reinforce Kills Many's accusation of witchcraft.

"Your Power must be strong," she whispered.

"Will you let me help you?"

She nodded.

"I would like the Power of your name."

"Little Flower," she whispered without hesitation. "I am only Ugly Flower now."

"You must believe I can help you. Your children have lost their father--they must not lose you as well."

She looked away from me. "My youngest son is blind. It may be best for him to follow me into the grave."

"Then there is even more reason for you to continue. He needs you."

She didn't acknowledge my words.

I dug in my bag and took out the things I needed to do a sing for her. I held her wrist, counting to myself--I didn't want to look at my watch, another modern thing that would require an explanation. In place of a stethoscope to listen to her respirations, I held my hand to her back. She sat very still letting me touch her.

Holding the fan from my bag in my hand, I thought of what I needed to say. There should have been preparations for this. I couldn't keep doing things in a way contrary to current beliefs. Those around the fire in the camp were deciding right now who would lead them. Even if they accepted my plan, I'd lost Morning Dove, but I still had a chance to be on the council of three.

If I cured this woman, Kills Many would see I wasn't a witch--or he would condemn me once and for all. I had to help this woman--I wasn't a witch, but I wouldn't be any sort of healer if I turned away from her.

I slipped the syringe into the belt pouch I wore and began a low chant. I used the spirit healing words my grandfather had taught me so long ago. Once they had meant everything to me, then they had turned meaningless and now--now I felt the Power within them. I knew first hand that those who believed they would heal often beat the odds. If this chant gave them hope, then it made sense. But I would combine the modern world of antibiotics with it.

I danced and sang, watching as the woman relaxed. Before long, she curled on her side near the fire and pulled the ratty blanket over her shoulder. I continued to sing until the moon shone high overhead and snow started to cover the ground. She needed to move inside her lodge. I stopped my chant. She didn't move; sound asleep despite the cold and hard ground. I went to her lodge and opened the flap.

I was met by her twelve-year-old son--and the large axe he held in my face. "Get out," he warned.

"Your mother is lying outside, freezing, while you sit in here like a baby instead of a man," I told him and stood up to my full height.

He glared at me. "I am not a baby."

"Your father is dead. That makes you the man of this lodge. That makes you responsible for your mother."

"I am not responsible for her spirit sickness." His sister sat up and held her blind brother against her.

"A man would hunt for his sister and his brother--even if he believed his mother had turned the spirits against her. Your lodge is falling to ruin." I sniffed the air. "It smells of dirt and rotten food. Do you not even know enough to go outside to the toilet?"

His hands tightened on his axe. I was making him mad. I took out a packet of powdered aspen bark. I held it out to the girl. "You must mix this with a bit of water and apply it to the sores covering your mother." She looked at her brother.

"Don't look at him. I saw you getting water. You take care of your younger brother. He has abandoned his duties as one of The People. He is not a man. He is not human."

With a hard yell, the boy swung the axe. I caught his skinny arm and twisted it. He landed on the floor with a grunt. "If you want to be a man, at least act like you're human." I kicked his axe away from him and let him up. "A man doesn't feel sorry for himself. He doesn't blame others for his troubles--he does what he knows is right."

The girl picked up the packet. "I'm not a medicine woman."

"Every woman must know some medicine if she is to care for her children--and for her parents and in-laws as they age. You can do this for your mother." I turned back to the boy. "I am going to wake your mother. You will make sure she comes in here, and that she has a warm bed, this night and every night, until her death. And I will see you hunting to feed those under your care."

He glared at me, but gave me a tight nod.

I ducked outside and watched their mother for a few moments before I took out the syringe. With a quick motion, I injected her in the thigh.

With a startled yelp, she came awake, sat up, and looked around her. I moved back into the trees as silently as I could. I stood in the darkness long enough to see the girl come out of the lodge and convince her mother to come inside. It would take several doses to cure her. It worked this time to trick her, but I doubted it would after this.

The sun already lit the edges of the horizon, yet those around the fire still argued. I avoided the center of the camp and made my way to my home. Inside, I took out my bundle. I would greet the sun before I crawled into my blankets for some much needed sleep.

At my rock, I set the bundle on the surface and began the sun greeting chant. Whenever I chanted now, I heard the drums. Were they a new occurrence, or did I finally see and hear the world as my grandfather did?

I danced back and forth with my eyes closed, breaking out in a sweat that made me pull off my shirt. I knew when the gray wolf came and leapt up onto the boulder. When the sun burst over the horizon, it flashed bright against my eyelids. I couldn't stop, on and on I danced. There were so many things I should have brought with me. I had a mobile surgical kit that would have been useful. I hadn't tanned a hide in a long time, and I wasn't sure even with the help of my survival books I could do it. I had no desire to freeze this winter. There were other books I should have brought as well.

The gray wolf gave a slight bark, and I tripped. Feeling foolish, I sat up. My vision was blurry. I didn't doubt I suffered from dehydration again. When everything around me came into sharp focus--I jumped to my feet.

Chapter Twenty-Five
Much Needed Things

I stood in the great room of my modern day house. My medicine bundle rested on the coffee table on a blanket of dust. All around the room there was a great deal of dust. The wind rattling through the room startled me. The patio doors stood open just as I'd left them. Papers lay on the floor, blown off the table by the wind, several magazines lay with their pages flipped back. Obviously, in the time I'd been gone, it had rained, and the rain had come in. I sat on the couch, picked up my bundle, and held it close. I thought of Morning Dove and of my last conversation with her. I needed to return to the same day. The wolf hadn't come with me this time--he must have sent me, but--how was I supposed to get back?

My grandfather's words came to me: *"There are those who don't quite know how to use the gift they are given, they must have help--a spirit guide."*

Time lost meaning while I sat there and tried to will myself back. It grew dark outside. The wind picked up, rustling the curtains and chasing more papers across the floor. Perhaps I needed to be outside. I got to my feet, picked up a blanket from the back of the couch, and started across the room. Someone pounded on the front door. I wasn't about to open it.

The oak door crashed open, the jam in pieces. John stood in the doorway peering around him as if he'd never been in my house before.

"My god, Shane," he said when he saw me.

"Go away," I told him.

"Christ. I'm not going anywhere. What the hell is going on with you? It's been ten days since anyone saw you. I forced your gate. When I saw the Jag like that, I thought someone rear ended you and you were hurt."

I glared at him. I owed him some sort of explanation--we'd been friends and colleagues for several years. "I smashed the Jag into a pole. Now get out of my house."

"Shane, come on. You need to talk to someone."

From behind me came the click click sound of a dog's nails as it crossed the tiles. The gray wolf stood at my side. John took a step back.

"Leave," I repeated.

"Shane, I'm not leaving you. Admin is having a fit over the Indian ceremony you did in that epileptic's room, more so since they can't get a hold of you. Shilfen is having fits--someone broke into their labs. Killed the head of the vaccine research project they have going. The guard said you were at their Mercy lab the same night--dressed, well, like you are now. That idiot van driver--he says someone broke his arm and stole the Shilfen truck, dressed the same way." John moved across the room toward where the phone sat. "Let me call someone. Jamie's on duty, I think. Let her come and talk to you."

I lunged, caught the phone cord, and yanked it out of the wall, sending the phone crashing to the floor halfway across the room. "You're not going to call anyone."

He backed up, holding his hands out in front of him. He thought I was insane. I very well could be. The wolf nudged my leg. Absently, I rubbed the top of his head.

"When did you get the dog?" John asked in a forced normal tone of voice.

If John saw the gray, then that meant I wasn't crazy, unless I just imagined he saw the wolf. No, I wouldn't fall back into thinking everything happening to me was the fault of some sort of insanity.

"He's a wolf." I moved to the couch and sat down. I had to settle John down--convince him everything was fine. He would go away then--I hoped. "Tell me something. If you could go back into the past and change things--what would you change?"

"Shane, you left the reservation for good reasons. If you'd stayed, you would never be where you are today."

"Where I am today? Just where am I?" My gaze settled on the clock I'd built years ago--one of those spinning ball affairs with the workings visible. I would take the clock back with me. I stood.

John took a quick step away from me. That van driver from Shilfen would have described me as well--not many seven-foot-tall American Indians running around.

I took the clock down from the mantle and set it on the table. With my hands around the dome, I watched the gold balls as they spun. Time raced onward. How much of it had already gone by? Had they already chosen? And Morning Dove, would she think I'd abandoned her yet again? I'd promised to cure the woman--what if I was gone so long she died? I'd managed to get back to the same time twice--I could do it again.

"Christ, man, folks would kill for less than you have." He looked around the house. "Hell, you've done better than anyone I know. You have magic in your touch I've never understood. When you're called in, patients who should be dead, live. Lord knows, if I ever became one with a car, I'd want you in the arena."

"In the spectrum of the world? What have I done to make it a better place? For my People, for anyone?"

"My own people call me an Oreo," John said. "It doesn't do any good. I thought if I got a good education, I would be a role model--no one wants a role model anymore, they want an easy hand out."

"One thing, if you could, what would you change?" I moved to the hall closet seeking out the wool blankets I kept there. I set them next to the clock. John thought I'd exited into the world of the mad. Wild idiot one moment and now calm debater--it did reinforce the over-the-edge persona.

"I suppose I would make slavery never happen."

"So you would choose to change things to keep your heritage, despite the consequences? Regardless if you ended up in Africa and starved to death?"

I moved into the den and began to pull books off the shelves. A good one on *do it yourself* alternative energy forms. Gray's Anatomy. All four thick volumes of the Physician's Desk Reference. A North American atlas. A world atlas. A pharmacy formulary. John followed me from room to room as I sought out what I wanted. In the guest room, a huge buffalo hide, stretched in a frame, covered one wall. I pulled it down and began undoing the thongs holding it in the frame. I had to get back and it had to be close to when I'd left or everything would be for nothing. If I didn't cure the woman--they would discount all I said. The wolf would help me--and if he didn't? I needed to be able to control the time Power the Great Spirit had for some reason given me.

"Shane, you can't go back--"

I landed on my hands and knees in icy muck. The gray wolf licked my face and pawed at me. I used the rock to get to my feet. My shirt lay on the rock, covered with snow, and I felt frozen. I shook it out and pulled it over my head. The sun brightened the gray clouds straight overhead. What day was it? How long had I been gone? I tramped through the slushy-snow and made my way to the camp.

"I thought you would dance all day again," Jumper said when I ducked inside my lodge.

I filled a cup from the full water bag hanging on a pole. "How long have I been out there?" I asked him.

"You don't remember?" He gave me a guarded look.

"The spirits--they had much to tell me," I said to cover my confusion.

"Your grandfather told us you were communing with the spirits. He said Little Flower's illness would require a great deal from you and you would find out. . . "

"Little Flower?" I asked, and then remembered. She was the woman with syphilis. "Sorry. Never mind. My spirit still wants to wander." I looked around and tried to focus. My god. I had been *here* for the past three days. I had gone to Little Flower every evening and sung over her. I'd shown her the syringe and told her I had to sting her with it each day or she wouldn't get well. The Elders were still engaged in debates over who would be on the council. The snow had come down every night before it melted in the mild temperatures of the day, and there had been a problem. Some sort of trouble Kills Many blamed on me. But I couldn't remember what it was. I wanted the books that were back in my modern home--I needed them. Jumper was talking to me.

"Kills Many says we can't go back--"

"--and change the past," John said. I blinked and sat up straight. I sat across from John again. "Burn out happens. Look, all I want is to call Jamie." His voice trailed off, and he frowned. "What the hell?" he whispered.

"I'm not suffering from burn out," I told him.

"When did you put a shirt on?" he asked.

"What shirt?" I said back, as if I didn't know what he meant. I thought back to the lab at Shilfen. I'd rested my back against the file drawers and simultaneously I'd been sitting in that clearing. The difference this time was people in both places had seen me. In the past--three days had elapsed, in modern time only a few hours.

He shook his head. When presented with the unexplainable, it always amazed me how people just blotted it out. John shook his head again and continued as if I hadn't suddenly been wearing a shirt.

"Jamie will come over here. You're fried. You've worked trauma longer than you should have without a break."

"I'm not suffering from burn out," I repeated. "If you must call it something, call it enlightenment."

"Let me go get a knife and help," John said with a nod in the direction of the hide. He backed out of the room and shut the bedroom door.

I worked at the ties for a few moments before the wolf walked over the hide almost on top of my fingers. I bolted to my feet and shoved open the door. John stumbled away and his cell phone skidded across the floor. Without thinking, I grabbed his arm, jerked him toward me, and punched him in the stomach. He doubled over, not even trying to defend himself. When I hit him in the face, he crumpled to the floor. Straddling him, I clutched his shirt and jerked his torso off the floor.

"I told you not to use the phone, any phone," I warned from between clenched teeth. I couldn't let him leave until I was ready to depart. John didn't catch himself when I let go of him. On the other side of the room, I stomped on his cell phone until it broke into chunks.

"All right, Shane, anything you want, Shane," John said, using the standard spiel when dealing with the insane--keep using their name. Agree to whatever they want. It fit my needs. His nose continued to stream blood. From the coffee table, I snatched up a box of tissues and shoved it into his hands.

"I wish I could explain what's going on with me. I can't. Right now, I need to get that hide off the frame."

After John gave me a tight nod, I went into the kitchen and came back with two knives. John followed me into the guest room and knelt near the hide. With one hand, he held a wad of tissue to his face, with the other he sliced at the laces holding the pelt.

The wolf sat near him, yellow eyes intent upon each of his moves. The wolf was my spirit helper--not Morning Dove's. He'd been there when I'd taken the horses. He'd been at my side when I jumped back to Morning Dove's time and when I'd jumped back here--moments before I'd heard him outside my lodge. One day, maybe, I would be able to control my own leaps in time, but, for now, I needed the wolf. I doubted the wolf would let John go anywhere.

In the attic, I dug out my surgical field kit--left from when I did Peace Corps work. The scalpels would be invaluable. I possessed some IV tubing, but it wouldn't do much good unless I could type blood. From another trunk, I came up with an old mirror-operated microscope and a box of slides. As far as witchcraft went, I was raising the hangman's scaffolding. Displayed along the wall going down the steps were several antique surgical instruments. I shuddered. It was a good thing I hadn't needed anything like them, yet. But I couldn't count on no one ever getting seriously hurt. And with the horses, there would be broken bones.

I took down a set of *spoons* designed to remove arrowheads. There were more of the antique syringes and a small surgical saw that would go into my growing collection of medical instruments. A set of forceps was the last thing I took down--so many women died in childbirth. I would see what I could do about improving the odds. When I touched them, I knew I'd skipped back in time again and forwards at almost the same instant.

I now wore a blanket over my head and around my shoulders, poncho style. It was one of the wool ones--that should have been downstairs next to the clock. The wolf hadn't been with me this time. I'd just spent three days in the past. What had happened in that time? There had been a clear scream in the night. I'd run from my lodge. Kills Many stopped me, shouting accusations immediately.

I sank to the steps. A woman had suffered a miscarriage. It couldn't have been Morning Dove. Surely, I would remember that. The Elders had made their choice as well. I had to think. I was on the council--the Elders chose four of us--and we were to choose from amongst ourselves who would lead. Who else had they chosen? I couldn't remember.

Downstairs in the kitchen, I opened a can of peaches and shoved them into my mouth with my fingers. Juice ran down my chin. I licked it from my fingers and tilted the can up to drink the rest. I felt starved. I opened a second can and devoured those as well. I had a stitched-shut cut on my forearm that stung. How had I done that?

Summer had run full out. I'd pulled back the bowstring--I'd gotten the deer. I'd sliced myself, with my own knife, when I gutted the buck deer. When I'd given it to Morning Dove, she'd stitched the wound for me--outside her lodge, because the Elders watched us whenever we were together. No, not the Elders--Kills Many had some of his warriors watching us--for almost six days now. No wonder I felt so hungry--I couldn't remember eating at all.

I emptied every vitamin container I owned into a plastic zip bag. I would dole them out to Morning Dove, at least over the winter, to try to keep her strong to deliver our child.

When I got back to the great room, John sat in a wing chair with the gray directly in front of him. The folded up buffalo hide lay on the couch. I had almost too much for me to carry. Odd, I wore one of the blankets--but it still sat there neatly folded. I felt completely confused.

The wolf let John follow me when I went out to the Jag. I stood for a long moment considering the smashed tail light and rear fender.

I wavered.

It seemed so easy. I would go back and tell them of all the modern wonders and they would follow what I said. When I'd run from the hospital, determined to go back to Morning Dove, it hadn't even occurred to me that they might accuse me of witchcraft.

Witchcraft.

That was it. Kills Many took every chance he had to bring more evidence against me as a witch. Was he actually blaming me for the woman's miscarriage? Why hadn't I thought about the possibility they would see me as some sort of witch? I snorted.

The only thing I'd thought about was Morning Dove, with crazed hormones worse than an impotent man who'd just discovered little blue pills. I stood with my hand on the trunk for a long moment--this was it. Was I of *The Niitsitapii,* or was I white? With a grunt, I pried the Jaguar emblem off the back of the car. This made John take a step toward me.

"We could call someone to pick it up. They could have it fixed in a week," John said, still trying to bring me back to the *real world*. After I shoved the emblem into my belt pouch, I opened the passenger's door. Inside the glove box, I located the title and a pen. I signed the paper and held it out to John.

"You've always liked this thing. It's yours now—before you get it in your name, call my insurance get it fixed."

I pushed the trunk release and went around to the back of the car while John stared, gape-mouthed, at the title in his hands. From the trunk, I took out two old army blankets and the strapped army duffle I always kept filled with extra clothes and aspirin. I dumped out the clothes and went back into the house.

"Shane, please. As your friend, at least come with me, call your grandfather, someone." He watched me as I packed things into the backpack. With one of the kitchen knives, I cut slits in the wool army blankets, making ponchos of sorts. I slid them over my head. Well, at least I understood how the blanket had gotten the way it was. The duffle went under them. That left the buffalo hide, the other two blankets, and the clock. I could manage if I didn't have to go far. The wolf gave me what I took for an agreeing yelp.

"Shane, you can't make a time machine." John sounded frustrated.

"No, I can't, but it isn't going to stop me." It didn't matter what I said to him. He would agree if I told him I could turn inside out and unfold female. Anything to get me to go with him, and to the help he thought I needed.

"Let me help you," he said with an effort to sound as if he believed I could disappear into the past.

I sat at the table and held the clock in my hands. "If you could help me, I'd let you. I've been back. I'm going to change things."

"That's good, Shane," he said. He settled farther back in the wing chair. He was waiting for me to go into a cationic state--which would happen, if I were insane, as he believed.

The wolf came to stand near me. I let calmness overcome me, and I knew the wolf's thoughts. We should go soon.

"John?" He gave me a pain- and fright-filled look. "I'm sorry I hit you."

"I'm not leaving you here--like this," he said.

"The cell phone--did your call go through?"

"No," he said too quickly.

"Is Jamie coming?" The wolf rubbed his head against me.

"Yeah. She should be here soon. Shane, don't be angry with her." Jamie was a small woman, not much larger than Morning Dove. I'd panicked when I'd seen John on the phone. The last thing I'd needed was for someone to cart me off to an institution.

"I wouldn't hurt her. I shouldn't have hit you. I know you don't believe me--but I can't let anyone interfere."

"I'm in one piece," he murmured.

"Goodbye," I said. The wind came up. John turned to look at the sound of the magazine pages shuffling.

The gray wolf jerked his head and turned.

A shaft of light opened up.

John leapt to his feet with his eyes wide. I staggered through on the wolf's heels, leaving John to figure out how I'd gotten away from him.

Chapter Twenty-Six
Forgotten Time

The wolf vanished into the darkness as soon as my feet touched the mushy ground. I stumbled and landed on my knees. When I tried to stand, I couldn't. Feeling along the ground in the dark, I searched for the clock. I didn't have the duffle, and I only wore one of the blankets. My insides clinched and nausea swept over me. I gagged and retched, bringing up nothing but bile. I was back, but I'd skipped enough time for the peaches to be digested.

Normally, a person feels somewhat better after they vomit. I didn't, the world spun, and I fell to the ground. How long had I been gone this time? Had it been as last time and I'd been dancing around the rock the entire time? That couldn't be, because at some point I'd put my shirt back on. I'd gone back to my own time, or I wouldn't have the blanket.

"Medicine Elk?"

Before I could try to speak, Morning Dove knelt at my side. Her hand went to the back of my neck. I raised my head a tiny bit and met her gaze.

"Drink," she told me before she pressed a bladder skin against my lips.

I drank, expecting it to come back up. Some of the nausea passed, and, with her help, I could sit up. I closed my hands around hers and drank down all the water in the skin. A chill came over me, and I started to shiver. The blanket she wore around her shoulders went around mine.

"I can't stay. Those in Kills Many's Society watch every move I make. Falls in the River tells him everywhere I go." She touched my face. "You must stand up to what he is saying against you. It is good you have healed Little Flower, but others wonder why you say nothing in defense of Kills Many's words." She clasped my hands tightly in her own.

I looked down at our entwined fingers. This woman was mine. Our souls had found a path to each other--entwined as our fingers were. I clasped her hands tighter.

"You must fight the spirits who wish to drag you with them. You must stay in this world long enough to fight and beat Kills Many. He will break the peace and destroy us soon."

She jumped to her feet and disappeared into the woods. I sat on the wet ground. I had no idea what else Kills Many could be saying against me, other than further accusations of witchcraft. I remembered being with John for a day--maybe a day and a half. I glanced skyward. I had been here for fifteen days. I'd returned with the clock and my belongings four days before this one. I'd skipped across time like a leaf across the bricks of a patio. Picked up and dropped by the wind, willy-nilly across the cracks, skittering and going airborne once more. Except the winds of time had dropped me on top of my previous place each time. To those who watched me, I'd never left-- in both the eras. I drew the blanket tighter around me and made my way back toward the camp.

I stood in the tree line, grateful for the huge oak tree holding me up, and watched those gathered at the camp's center. Kills Many stood with his back toward me and waved one hand as he spoke.

"The Elders must appoint another to the council in his place. He communes with the evil spirits so much he has not participated in a single discussion."

"He is the Elder' choice. Do you question the Elders as well?" The woman spoke in a loud clear voice--I didn't know her.

"I question any who support him and the evil he has brought among us. Already there have been fights over the horses. He has seduced Morning Dove into breaking her vow to the Elders. . ." Had I done that? The last fifteen days were a muddled mess. If I thought very hard, bits and pieces came to me--but the days seemed more like a dream than reality.

Morning Dove stood and faced Kills Many. Her gaze went to me and moved away. "It is only you who says I broke that vow."

"Falls in the River saw you with him on the very night he presented his evil plan to us."

"We spoke. Nothing more," Morning Dove said. Her voice stayed strong.

"So you accuse Falls in the River of lying? It is a serious charge."

"You accuse me of lying," Morning Dove spat back at him.

Kills Many shook his head. Slow. Calculated. "No, I do not accuse you of lying. He used his Power to seduce you and left you thinking you only *spoke* to him."

A slight smile tugged at Morning Dove's lips. It seemed quite a few took Kills Many's accusations seriously. I wished I possessed Morning Dove's knack for finding humor in every situation.

"I remember well being with him, unlike some who have shared my bed." Peals of laughter rang out. The muscle along the back of Kills Many's arm tensed. I moved away from the tree. If he dared swing on her, I would rip him limb from limb.

"It is only you who says Falls in the River saw Running Deer go into her lodge." Jumper stood with his hand on the hilt of his belt knife.

Kills Many barked out the boy's name in a sharp command. A skinny boy, Falls in the River, couldn't have been more than eleven or twelve years old. Was he the one I saw that night? If so, he was lying.

"Tell them what you saw," Kills Many ordered.

Falls in the River's fearful gaze darted around the circle. He wore the same paint Kills Many did. I couldn't imagine this gaunt preteen being a member of the same Warrior's society as Kills Many--especially since he seemed to lack knowledge and skill. Falls in the River was the same boy who hadn't known the correct way to make arrows. Therein lived the answer to his lie. Kills Many had sponsored him for membership. It was easy to see why. The boy belonged to a society he would have had no hopes of becoming part of anytime soon and all he had to do was lie.

"On the night the witch told us his plan, I followed him. He took Morning Dove through the woods. They stood behind her lodge. . ."

"And?" Kills Many prompted him.

Falls in the River fingered the knife on his belt--a bone-handled knife with a long, well-made obsidian blade. He looked from side to side and finally his gaze settled on Morning Dove. "I saw Morning Dove go into her lodge."

Some made sounds of anguish. Others shook their heads.

"You see. He is no medicine man guided by helpful spirits. He has brought their vengeance down on us. Have not four women already lost their unborn children? This has not happened before--not like this. We all heard their screams of agony when their child fought to keep its life while he danced with the evil spirits to steal it away."

"He cured me!" Little Flower stood on frail thin legs, now free of sores, with her hands balled into fists.

"At what cost?" Kills Many asked her. "Your spirit sickness was far progressed. Are you willing to accept his need of four unborn ones to save your cursed life?"

Four women. I did remember. Each time I'd been at the rock

dancing around it like a man possessed. I'd been a man caught in some sort of time loop. Why had the time stream caught me that way? When I'd ended up back in my own time, I *had* wavered. I'd finally accepted--if I left my own time, I might never be able to return. I'd suddenly doubted my ability to live the rest of my life as if I were on some sort of primitive campout, with no modern help in sight. I'd thought of Morning Dove and of The People--if I had the chance to make things right--I had to take it. So, I'd bounced back and forth between times and ended up being in two places at once.

"You saw him go into the lodge with Morning Dove?" my grandfather asked Falls in the River. His voice sounded strained, ancient--worn out.

Falls in the River took a step back from my grandfather. He looked at Kills Many, and then back at my grandfather. He touched his knife. As soon as he pulled his shoulders straight, I knew what he would say.

"Yes," he said.

This time, all those present began talking at once. I saw only my grandfather with his head bowed as if in shame. He held his hand up. After a bit, those around him noticed. Silence settled. I could only stand by the oak with the wolf at my side and wait for my condemnation to come. The Elders gathered around my grandfather. It took only moments before my grandfather moved away from them and entered the circle.

"Four were chosen to lead us--each trustworthy and honorable. We of the Elder's Council asked those gathered here to choose from these four the one who would become Chief of All Time and receive the Power of the Timeless One from Morning Dove." He shook his head before he continued. In the firelight, I thought I saw tears standing on his cheeks. "I am ashamed of Medicine Elk. I know he is not a witch, but he should not have broken the law of the peace. We must release him from his place on the council and choose another."

I moved back into the dark and vomited again. Out of sight of the camp, I squatted on the backside of the tree. For so long I'd flouted the ways of tradition. My grandfather had no choice but to think I'd seduced Morning Dove--even in my healing of Little Flower I had neglected to follow the correct guidelines. I turned back to face the camp.

Morning Dove got to her feet. "Honored Grandfather, it is not true. We were not in my lodge that night or any night since. You asked me to test him. He refused me."

The anger I'd felt that night at Morning Dove vanished. I shouldn't have doubted her conviction in the beliefs of The People. I understood the importance of the decision, and my grandfather had good reason to doubt me. All too often I rejected every tradition and rule The People had--and I still did.

My grandfather met Morning Dove's gaze. "The one I sent to watch has not come forward. I have not spoken to Beetle Boy since I sent him."

"Further proof he is a witch. Where is Beetle Boy?" Kills Many turned in a circle, watching the faces of those around him. "Falls in the River says the witch went into Morning Dove's lodge. Beetle Boy saw this as well. And now Beetle Boy has vanished." He paused for a dramatic moment. "I have seen Beetle Boy in a Vision. His soul calls out for vengeance. The witch murdered him to keep him silent. It is only by the Power given by the helpful spirits that Falls in the River has not died as well."

There was a sharp cry. A woman pulled at her hair and screamed again. A young woman got to her feet and walked to the center of the circle. "It is not true."

"You call me a liar?" Kills Many bellowed.

"Yes," she said in a whisper soft voice.

"Get this girl out of here. She is barely a woman and thinks to speak..."

"All are allowed to speak," Spins Much said. He stood with his arms locked across his chest, staring with defiance at Kills Many. "Tell us what you wish to," he said with more calm to the young woman.

"On the night Medicine Elk gave his plan, Beetle Boy came to me. He was frightened..."

"You see. He had good reason to be frightened. He knew the witch would kill him."

"He was frightened of you." The young woman shrank back a bit from Kills Many's threatening glare. "He gave me this." She held up a leather thong with a small medicine pouch attached to it. "He said you stopped him in the woods and told him he would die if he spoke of what he saw. I gave him food and blankets to make a journey back to his tribal home lands."

"You misunderstood his words. I did warn him. I knew if the

witch lived and continued to dwell among us, we would suffer, but if we angered the witch it would be worse." He lowered his head as if in sorrow. The man was a good actor. Any could claim the spirits had spoken to them--how convenient for Kills Many they chose now to do so. "I did not want to have to tell of what he did to Morning Dove."

My grandfather stood off to the side speaking to three other Elders. People continued to argue. No one looked at me. My grandfather moved into the circle. He stood with his fingers clasping his walking stick, and his chin almost touching his chest. The mouse on the top of his staff mirrored his position. It took some time before voices went silent.

He moved his gaze around the circle. For a moment, he looked directly at me. Sorrow stood like a silent accusation in his eyes. I had let him down once again. I had let not only my grandfather down--but I had let Napi down, let the Great Spirit down.

"We cannot make a decision this night. I will send a runner to Beetle Boy's People to bring him back--with the horses it will not take long. If Medicine Elk has broken the code of the peace, then there is no choice in what must be done. If Beetle Boy tells me Falls in the River is not speaking the truth, then we will choose."

With those words, he moved away and disappeared into his lodge. I should have moved to defend myself. But when I took a step forward, the wolf tugged on my shirtsleeve and urged me toward my own home. I took one last glance at those gathered to see Kills Many glaring at me. I drew in a sharp breath and yanked my arm away from the wolf. Kills Many no longer stood near the fire. The elk-man stood in his place--his visage faded into the face of Kills Many. What the hell did that mean? Was the elk-man now advising Kills Many directly--the thought didn't rest well with me. Kills Many had enough hate in him already without being influenced by some ancient evil.

My grandfather's lodge door opened, and he stepped out into the night. If only I knew of some way to discount Kills Many's accusations.

Jumper's belongings were still in my lodge, so it seemed he at least supported me with more than words. The buffalo hide covered my bed. On top of the chest, the clock sat, the balls continued to spin one way and then the next. I felt exactly like that clock. Temptation to go to Morning Dove and demand she leave with me soared through my soul. If Beetle Boy didn't return, I didn't have any defense against Falls in the River's lies. If he were alive, and if he came back, he might be too frightened of Kills Many to tell the truth. His return would only settle the question of my honor. There was still the accusation of witchcraft.

A very slight tapping came on the door flap. I didn't want to see anyone. The tapping came again, more insistent this time. Going to the flap, I held it aside. No one had accused me of rudeness--not yet anyway.

A gray-haired woman stepped into my home. I recognized the bear claw necklace she wore with its twists of human hair. No one had told me her name, and she hadn't offered it the day she had challenged me over the horses.

She took a quick glance around her. Her gaze settled on the clock. I thought she would bolt right back out the door. Instead, she squared her shoulders and met my gaze.

"I must speak with you about the women who have lost children."

"No matter what they say about me, I had nothing to do with them losing their children." The very thought made bile rise in the back of my throat.

From under her cloak, she brought out a skin bag. Unexpectedly, my small home filled with enticing smells.

"This is from Morning Dove. She couldn't bring it to you, or there would be greater suspicion."

Grateful, I took the skin from her. I hung it over the fire and dug out two tin plates. The bag was made from an animal intestine and designed to let a person squeeze some of the mashed together contents out. I divided it equally between the two plates and held one out to the woman. With a nod, she accepted it and sat down near my fire.

We ate in silence. The richly spiced food went down so fast I barely tasted it. How long had it been since I'd eaten anything? Four days since I'd had the peaches and before that--I couldn't remember.

"Kills Many talks against you at every turn," she began. "Each day when you went to Little Flower, Kills Many told the tribe you were using witchery to cure her. Each day when you brought meat to Morning Dove, he said you used evil spirits to bring the deer to you. When Cries a Lot lost her child, he said the dance you did with the evil spirits caused it." The woman shook her head.

"I promise you, I wouldn't do such a thing," I said, but how could I prove it?

Her stare rested on the clock. "I have been a midwife for many summers." She took a deep breath and said, "I am Pale Woman."

By telling me her name, she expressed her trust in me and also her disbelief in Kills Many's witch accusation--a witch could use a person's name to curse them.

"I am old," she continued, "forty-nine summers, and have seen many seasons of hunger, when it is best for a woman to leave behind an unborn one in favor of feeding the ones she already has. There are plants the spirits have provided for us that if eaten in the first moon or two after the blood stops, makes the blood start again."

"I know of the plants," I told her carefully.

She smacked her lips together and drew her lip between toothless gums. "Cries a Lot had only stopped bleeding for three moons. Still time, if she took the plants, that she would have just bled. She didn't. Her child came forth in great cramps of the womb and gushes of blood--she is lucky to live still. The others who lost their children happened in the same way." Her gaze met mine in an intense stare. "I know of the plants to make such a thing happen as well. When a child is dead in the womb and must come. . . "

"I don't even know the women. Are you telling me I fed them King of the Meadow?" The use of the tall flowering plant was tantamount to suicide. But in a case where death was sure to come--a fetus dead in the womb--it would be the only chance the mother had.

Pale Woman shook her head. "Each day, my granddaughter watched you. She is Giggling Girl. Only a woman by one season. She told me you have not gone near any of the women who have babies in them. I believe her." The woman got to her feet. "There is danger among us from the harmful ones, but you are not their helper. Someone on the new council of four is. I don't know who, but if the one who fed the women this poison is found, we will know the truth. This person must be found before the Elders choose which of you will be Morning Dove's husband."

She took one final look at the clock before she bolted out the door flap.

Chapter Twenty-Seven
Those Who Trust

I lay curled up in my buffalo hide. Outside, the arguments still went on. One of us on the council was to be Chief of All Time, by tribal vote, not a council vote. That same man would be Morning Dove's husband. It seemed they thought the one who became her husband would also share in her ability to heal--the Power of Being Timeless.

Even if they did nothing to me for what Kills Many said, there would be many who would still think me a witch. It would be enough for them to vote against me, despite the fact the Elders accepted my plan. With my exhausted body protesting, I crawled out of the hide.

My trays of penicillin were full. I sat and emptied each one into the flasks in the case--at least I knew the stuff worked. They didn't require refrigeration. I would need to find a replacement for the glass flasks, if I made more. I would use it sparingly and only in cases of true need.

The bottles of combination vaccine sat in their case, reminding me I needed to find a way to get The People to accept the cure I offered.

Sam. I thought of the night before I'd left the first time--on my doorstep when I'd seen him in a vision state--seen across the veil of living and dead. Sam was supposed to get the vaccine and the penicillin--I was sure of it, and he'd wanted my help. The damned bottle had taken his life before he could. He'd managed to come to me and let me know I needed to do it for him--but he'd waited almost too long.

In my brother's frequent visions, he'd learned there would be a chance to save us. He hadn't doubted. That was why he'd applied for the job at Shilfen.

Shilfen had been preparing this for the military to protect against germ warfare. Anthrax was on the list as well. The note left with the vaccine explained that only one generation needed to receive it, and the immunity would be passed on. I could easily have slipped it into a water supply--if a common one were in use. But each day the women went and filled their water skins at the river.

Inside the lid of the large case, I found a smaller case. It surprised me to find several scratch tubes of smallpox vaccine. My fingers automatically went to the deep vaccination scar on my arm.

The Bureau of Indian Affairs people marched us through the BIA Health Clinic, so a nurse in a white uniform could scratch our arms. My grandfather had taken me fishing in the morning. My clothes were torn and dirty from a fight I'd had with a bramble bush--I still felt a flush of embarrassment over the sound of disgust the woman made. The doctor sitting near her had said, *"Get used to it, Joan. They're all that way."*

I'd realized for the first time that some people didn't like us because we were *Indians*. When the pox pustule developed, I ran to my grandfather--terrified the white-woman had cursed me. My grandfather took it as a chance to teach me some of our history. Once it went away, I walked around with the deep pox scar as if it were evidence of a great battle fought and won. I pondered that a moment.

I took out one of the vaccine tubes. I also measured out a cup of water and added the tiniest drop, at the gallon marking on the dropper included, of the combo-vaccine--I poured this into a gallon-sized clay jar. Jumper used it for water instead of a skin. I tucked the tube into my medicine bag and went out to join the others in the central gathering area.

Kills Many sat on the ground, a small distance away from the central fire, along with Jumper and Spins Much. I should have been with them--a part of the chosen council. Most everyone else, done with debating for the night, sat around the central fire listening to an Elder tell a story. Falls in the River caught sight of me and tapped Kills Many's shoulder. With a rude gesture, Kills Many shoved the scrawny boy's hand off his shoulder.

I ignored the other members of the council and went to stand in the center near the fire. "I seek three who do not believe I am a witch. I will show you I have the cure for the white-man's sickness."

"And how many babies will die this night for your cure?" Kills Many said.

He wasn't talking to me; his question was a sweeping one aimed at getting those around us stirred up again. His callous and calculated mention of the lost babies stirred a vein of anger in me. He seemed to only care about the women as a way to gain an advantage over me.

"I have not, nor will I ever, kill anyone's unborn child. There are others who do such things."

Kills Many looked stunned. He recovered quickly. "None here

will trust you."

The young medicine man, who'd played the drum for Morning Dove's sing, got to his feet and moved into the circle. "I trust this man. While I cannot speak of the battle he waged with the Great Spirit, I know his Power is great. He saved Morning Dove and harmed no one. Have all of you forgotten that?"

"He was in the medicine lodge. Evil cannot enter there," Kills Many asserted.

"How often have you been in the medicine lodge? How can you, who is not a medicine man, tell us what sort of Power resides there?" The speaker was a large man, stocky, but not fat. I recognized him from my vision at the hospital. He had the strength of the elk as well. Except here in real life, he wore ash on his face and in his hair--a mask he hid his appearance behind.

He continued in my defense. "Great evil exists in the medicine lodge. It is the place where it is wrestled with and overcome. I trust this man. Beetle Boy's spirit cries out to me as well. But in my vision he cries for vengeance against a shadowy one. In this vision, I see the shadowy one as he kills the unborn. . . "

"He is the shadowy one," Kills Many accused, pointing a finger at me.

"We are all shadowy figures, most of us displaced to this time by the Great Spirit to save us," the stocky man said. "It is shadowy evil that walks among us. If our council cannot get along--how will we keep the peace?"

Kills Many stood as if he would challenge me right there. I watched him in silence. Finally, he moved to sit at the front edge of those gathered. "I will listen to his talk, but I won't be responsible for the lives his *cure* will cost."

The stocky man went to stand next to the Medicine Drummer. The young woman who wore Beetle Boy's luck bundle came to stand next to them. I drew in a deep breath. What I was about to do could very well seal my fate as a witch, but I hoped it would convince them of my good intentions.

"We have all seen the terrible sickness that causes the skin to burn and sores to come that cover the body and ooze pus." I set the jar on the ground and poured the vaccine into the wooden cup. I held up the wooden cup as if it were an elegant chalice. "In this cupful of water helpful spirits reside. One sip and the person drinking cannot get the sickness the white-man brings."

Kills Many snorted in disbelief behind me. Others echoed his sentiments.

"It will be a long time before the white-man comes. We have all seen this. I don't see how this will prove you have the cure." Spins Much looked apologetic for talking against me.

"What I ask for is great trust. Once a person has had this sickness they cannot get it again. . . ."

"Obviously. The dead don't get ill." Many people laughed at Kills Many's words.

"I speak of those who live through the sickness." I handed the cup to the young Medicine Drummer with instructions not to spill any of it or to drink yet. I pulled off the blanket I wore and then my shirt. A few people leaned forward, their eyes on my chest. What were they looking at? My Sun Dance scars or the elk mark? I didn't know whether the tattoo looking elk would help or hinder the witch accusation. There were nods, and a few people whispered to each other.

I pointed to the deep pox scar on my left arm. What was I going to say? The drink vaccine wouldn't leave a scar like mine to show they had won the battle with the sickness.

"I have fought the evil spirit who wishes to travel with the white-man and bring his sickness to us. I bore but one sore from that battle and now the evil sickness can never harm me again." I paused to let that sink in--a person needed boosters every five years or so--I didn't need to tell them that, and I would make sure they got the enhanced vaccine as well.

"I ask this day for any medicine men brave enough to fight the spirit as I did. They will fight this great battle so they can protect all others. Each person must take one sip from the cup. Once you have, your spirit will be able to reach the medicine man's spirit. You can use his victory against the white-man's sickness. All your children, yet unborn, can use the same victory. Who will battle the white-man's sickness this night?"

"I will," Medicine Drummer said.

"It's a trick." Kills Many's voice boomed over the camp. "He seeks to destroy all the medicine men, so we have no protection at all."

Several others came into the circle, ignoring Kills Many's outburst. All together, ten medicine men stood before me. Some looked fearful. Others puzzled. The protection of the water vaccine would be instant. The medicine men would not get it, though--I wanted them to have a scar as proof of their *fight.*

"The battle will take many days. Preparation must be made in the sweat lodge. We shall meet in the medicine lodge at sunset, where we will fight the evil together."

The men nodded their heads and stayed silent.

"Next, I must have four who are willing to drink the protection offered by the water. They will come to do the battle as well. All will see that the evil cannot enter them. They won't have the battle scar, but will be forever protected as well."

Spins Much got to his feet. Several others stood as well. I motioned to Medicine Drummer and went to stand before Spins Much. From my medicine bag, I withdrew my eagle feather fan and said words of healing over the cup while I waved the feather over it. I waved my hand at Medicine Drummer. He raised the cup. Spins Much took a sip. I repeated the same thing for each of the twenty who stood. I only wanted and needed four, but I didn't want to deny any of them.

Kills Many stubbornly sat with his arms folded and ignored my offer of the cup.

"Go now and prepare for the fight," I instructed the medicine men. Many of them looked at the cup in my hand. But they left the circle to do their private preparations. Pride could be a wonderful thing. Even if they thought Kills Many right--I hadn't offered them the protection from the cup and we were about to battle this deadly sickness--they wouldn't back down now.

I held the empty cup and turned to those who had drunk from it. "You also must be prepared. The evil will try to jump to you when the medicine men battle it, but because you have the aid of the helpful spirit, it will not harm you." I turned and headed for the medicine lodge. I hoped Doctor Martins was telling the truth and hadn't lost her mind. I sure felt like I'd lost mine.

"Each of you will receive a small wound where the evil can enter you," I instructed the medicine men who sat around me. All of us had taken a long, sweat bath and inhaled sacred smoke. The small central fire burned brightly. A young apprentice would keep it going and add sweet grass and cedar to it as we went through our *battle.*

For three days, we'd fasted.

I added a small amount of hallucinogenic mushrooms to the tea I would pass. My grandfather oversaw my preparations in silence. As I finished each step, he gave me a small nod to let me know I had done the things correctly.

I moved to the first man. He sat in stony silence when I scratched his arm with the vaccine. I gave him the cup containing the mushroom tea. He took his sip. All the way around the circle I went. I pretended to take a sip from the cup. The scratch my grandfather put on my arm would do nothing since I'd already had the vaccine and a booster when I'd done some work for the CDC overseas.

Medicine Drummer relinquished his drum to a man who wouldn't take part in our fight. I hated the trickery involved. I longed to be able to tell them it was only a vaccine, and this ritual was unnecessary. Outside, a wolf howled. I shook off a chill.

I needed to lose my doubtful attitude. The man next to me got to his feet and began to dance in a small circle. He knew, they all, as medicine men, knew the tea contained *vision bringer*. Several others joined him, getting their heart pumping to take them to the land of visions much faster.

I looked down at the cup and at the small amount of brown tea in the bottom. I'd made my choice. It was time to make it a true one. I swallowed the rest of the tea and got to my feet.

Chapter Twenty-Eight
Future Visions

At no point did I remember falling down. Yet, I was on the ground when I woke up. I sat up and swept leaves off my clothes. Around me, the medicine men also sat up and brushed at their clothing. We stood at the edge of a village. A board with a skull and cross bones painted on it, along with the black flag meaning plague, hung crooked on a tree. Here, I knew it meant a smallpox epidemic. Some of the medicine men held back when I led the way, but it took only a bit of prompting to get them to follow me. Was I offering guidance to this vision back in the medicine lodge? Perhaps, since I'd drunk the tea, my grandfather offered the direction.

In the village, a pile of bodies waited for a burial that might never come. The US Army had sent soldiers around, who had already been ill, to bury the dead in mass graves. I certainly hoped this vision wouldn't include any of them. The men with me looked around in horror. An ancient medicine man stumbled toward us. He bowed, staggering when he tried to stand straight again. The sickness had covered his arms and face with pox pustulates.

"You have come. I have called for many days, asking for great ones to come and help us beat this sickness."

It made my insides ache that we could do nothing for this man. Without a word, we spread out to the various bark long-houses and tried to make those with the illness comfortable. Each of the medicine men with me applied his own idea of a *cure*. Still, people died. The old medicine man went first. I stood by and watched the futile efforts--at times, I felt frozen to the spot. To read about the epidemic meant little when faced with the reality of it. Finally, I brought out my medicine bag and mixed a cup of the vaccine from it.

"No more can be done here. Come with me," I told those ten with me.

The medicine men followed me to the next village--in the vision state a short walk down a fog-shrouded path. None here were ill yet, but they were fearful the disease would come to them.

"We have been forbidden to leave our villages, so we can't travel away from the path of the illness. We can't go to our winter hunting ground either. I don't know which will be worse, starving or dying of the disease when it gets here," their chief told us.

"Honored Chief, the sickness will not come here." I held up the cup and gave the same explanation I had to those who lived in my village. "One sip, this cup must last for every man, woman, and child here."

He took a single sip, and, soon, almost every person in the village lined up for their part of the Power I offered. The other medicine men watched me this time, some of them turning in their slow shuffling dance. I felt no need to continue my dance. In the next few days, I ate with the villagers, spoke with their medicine man, and watched them go about their daily lives.

Those with me, both the medicine men and those who had chosen to follow as witnesses, did the same. They wandered about the village and whispered about my Power. Most of the medicine men spent a good part of each day dancing in their small circles looking puzzled at times.

Had I lead them on a vision, or had I somehow taken them on a trip in time? I hoped it wasn't the latter--the wolf had not shown up. That would mean I had to guide them back--alone.

I talked often to those who refused the *good spirits*. Nothing I said could convince them a sip of *water* would protect them. One man especially talked against the cure I offered. When I tried to talk to him, he ignored me and went about his life as if we were not among them.

He spent his days making tools for when they were again allowed to hunt--as steadfast in his belief of the white-men simply vanishing as he was in his distrust of my Power over the sickness that could ride the wind.

We'd been in the village for almost five days when the horses came carrying the U. S. soldiers; I stood with the chief as he asked to move his people.

"You isn't go'n nowhere. You don't need to hunt," the sergeant announced. His gaze fixed on me. He encouraged his horse to take a step back. I stood with my hands loose at my sides and stared back at him. "Damn," he muttered.

He motioned to his men, and they brought forth a wagon. He wheeled his horse around, and they galloped away leaving the wagon. I'd seen the pox scars on his face and arms. I looked to the men who had come with me.

"He has fought the sickness," one of them said.

What explanation could I give? "In the land where they come from, there are many sicknesses we have not known. Their spirits know how to fight them."

He looked at the developing mark on his arm. Everyone who had drunk the vaccine developed at least one mark, some two or three, but none of the fever or other symptoms. The mark terrified some of the people, but as soon as they realized they were not getting sick, they went about showing them as a badge of having Power over the sickness.

"It is good that we learn to fight this now."

The residents of this village flocked around the wagon. I knew what to expect, but it still caught me off guard to see the same blankets and furs the sick had died on in the first village.

"The white-man has brought the disease here on purpose," Medicine Drummer said beside me. He shivered, looking pale and bewildered.

"Yes," I whispered. This young drummer would one day make a good healer. He saw and made connections quickly.

One of the medicine men went to the chief and warned him. The chief shook his head.

"My people are cold and hungry. I cannot tell them that they must burn the food and blankets."

We stood off to the side, and time sped up. Days passed. Soon, those who had refused the vaccine became ill. In desperation, they begged me cure them. In my vision, I didn't have anything to help them with. When the soldiers returned, they milled about, not accepting any of the food the villagers offered. Their commander was at first puzzled, and then he became angry. He strode off into the trees. His lower officers followed him. His speech got punctuated with wild hand gestures and the occasional stomp of his foot.

Germ warfare. Practiced since before black plague victims were hacked up and catapulted into cities in the Middle Ages was as ugly as it was in any time. I feared this commander would order the deaths of the villages' inhabitants by a more direct means. Some of the soldiers moved off toward their horses and their guns.

A wolf howled. I found myself on my knees in the medicine lodge, vomiting into a bowl held by one of the apprentice medicine men. He offered me cool water once I finished. The medicine men sat in a circle around me. They looked worn and shaken.

Looking at them, I knew somehow the Power I held over time had taken them with me into the future--or the power of suggestion had led us to the same thing. That didn't explain how the pustulates had developed so quickly. My grandfather met my gaze. He raised his chin.

I looked away. Would doubt plague me forever? Of course, they had seen the same thing. Despite the way the vision started, the mushrooms were only catalysts to take us to some distant place--and with me in the mix, we'd skipped across time. Someday, I would have to test the ability of the mushrooms to let me control the time travel--without the wolf.

One of the medicine men walked about the medicine lodge and scrutinized everyone who had drunk from the cup. He seemed satisfied. "Honored Medicine Elk, you do have the cure to the illness. All must drink from the cup."

"That is my intention. I will teach each of you how to care for the cup and the water. You must travel from village to village, as we did in our vision," I told him.

"This we will do," the other stocky Medicine Elk answered.

"It will take many summers to reach every tribal nation. I believe we must train others to do this as well." This man kept looking at the eruption on his arm while he spoke. "It must be those who have fought the evil who do it. With this mark, all will know they are great men."

I could say nothing against that. I only hoped there was a sufficient amount of the traditional vaccine to mark enough medicine men. At least, it was a start. I felt some relief in having the trust of these men. The twenty who had witnessed our fight gathered around and examined the arms of each of the medicine men. Some of them touched their faces and patted their own arms. Beetle Boy's friend wore a haunted look.

"I have often heard of this sickness," she said to me, "but I didn't think it would be so terrible. These white-men who will come--they have no honor. They gave the spirit-sickness to the new village." She looked at me as if for confirmation she had understood the vision she had shared in.

With a nod, I began to speak. A scream rent the air from outside the medicine lodge. Those gathered inside rushed out the door flap ahead of me. Kills Many stood with tears making streaks in the red paint on his face. In his arms, he held the thin body of Falls in the River.

"Dead, dead," he kept repeating. When he caught sight of me, he dropped the boy on the ground. He drew his war axe and took a step toward me. "He is dead because of you and this medicine of yours. While you deceived the other medicine men, two more women have lost their babies, and this boy has paid with his life."

"If he is so powerful, why doesn't he reach out and get rid of you?" Medicine Drummer asked.

Morning Dove came out of the crowd and stood near me. I wanted to put my arm around her. Kills Many was responsible for the women's miscarriages. I couldn't figure out how he got them to ingest the plants, though.

"You have only words to accuse him. Where is your proof?" one of the witnesses asked.

"While he kept our best medicine men in the medicine lodge, Falls in the River writhed in agony. It is explanation enough for me." Kills Many's eyes took on a feral glow. I heard laughter--Kills Many didn't laugh. The laughter came from the elk-man who stood at his shoulder.

Shouts rose. Most wanted me banished to the wilderness. Others called for my death. Some called for torture, to drive out the evil dwelling within me. All of them wanted a witch out of their midst, no matter what the witch had brought them or could do for them. I couldn't get a word in over them, even if any argument would have helped.

"You didn't kill the boy," the stocky Medicine Elk whispered in my ear. "I have seen Kills Many's look before. The evil lives in him."

"Any idea how to prove that?" I asked him. The image of the elk-man slipped like a specter into Kills Many.

"That is always the problem when dealing with vengeful spirits." He moved away from me. "Stop this! Stop this!" he shouted. "The peace has held for many years. All of us who have seen the vision know--if we don't keep the peace, we will fall to the white-man. Medicine Elk couldn't have killed the boy or taken the babies. In the spirit world, he was with us, never out of someone's sight."

"He has divided himself before. Many saw him dance at the rock and bring the horses," someone in the crowd shouted. They were fast becoming a mob.

"So you will break the peace?" Morning Dove's voice rang out. Angry voices quieted. At least she still held some sway over them. "We have lived by Old-Man's promises for many summers now. All have benefitted. That has not changed.

"You believe Kills Many because he is a strong warrior." She continued. "You do not doubt him because he is a generous man. Is not Medicine Elk also strong? He fought the Great Spirit to keep me in this world; he saved Little Flower from her spirit-sickness. Has he not shown our medicine men that he knows the cure for the white-man's sickness?" She looked toward the medicine men that stood near me. All of them nodded agreement.

"None can say he is not generous," she said. "He brought many horses and gave them all away. He has brought deer into the village and surrounding hills when our hunters have mostly driven the game out."

"He has brought meat to you," someone said.

"And have I not given most of it away? I could not show such generosity if he had not brought it to me. Many of you have benefitted from his calling of the deer as well. No one will go hungry this winter."

"Kills Many brings you food each day," someone pointed out.

With a slight smile, Morning Dove answered, "I always give away what he brings. He is not a very good cook."

I pushed my way to the front.

"Who? Who did you give the cooked food to?" I demanded, gripping both her arms.

Kills Many moved, but two warriors stopped him at a gesture from my grandfather.

Morning Dove looked at me. A look of horror crept into her eyes. She knew as well. She went to her knees and pounded the ground.

"What have you made me do?" she screeched at Kills Many.

The camp exploded into confusion. Kills Many shouted over them. "She gave away the food the witch brought to her as well. I didn't poison my food. He is a medicine man--a witch--he knows the plants to do such a thing." Others heard the desperate edge to his voice.

"I gave the deer Medicine Elk brought me to families where the women were not carrying babies--they could do the work of skinning and cutting easily. The cooked food I gave to those women who were pregnant, to give them a day of rest." Morning Dove sobbed with her hands over her face. "All know Medicine Elk never brought me cooked meat."

Kills Many lunged away from his captors. I thought he intended his axe to connect with me, but Medicine Drummer got in his way. Kills Many's axe came down with a solid final sounding thud against the young man's shoulder. He crumpled to the ground. I saw Spins Much and Jumper standing near Morning Dove. I forgot about Kills Many, trusting those of the camp to go after the real *witch*, and knelt at the young man's side.

I looked up to see my grandfather watching me. "I'll tell you what I'm going to miss--decent conditions to operate under."

My grandfather shrugged. "Still think T. P. would be nice."

Medicine Drummer moaned and tried to move. "Stay still," I ordered. I probed his shoulder and spine with my fingers, longing for a radiology department. The blow had crushed his scapula and broken his collarbone. The rest I wouldn't know until I got inside. A process that wasn't going to be pleasant for the young man or me. The stocky Medicine Elk came to stand near me. The ash he wore had sunk into creases in his face, giving him the visage of a dusty raisin.

"I would appreciate your help," I told him.

He nodded and moved toward the sweat lodge--at least someone would be doing the spiritual part of things. My grandfather directed two strong young men to me, and I gave them instructions for moving the drummer. Despite what must have been great pain, he didn't cry out. I didn't think that would last.

When I finally had the chance to lie down and sleep, I slept without moving. I woke up with my shoulder and neck stiff from the single position I'd lain in. My tongue stuck to the roof of my mouth. I wasn't hungry. I could recall only eating what the midwife brought me in the last fifteen or so days. I knew that was wrong, but I had gone without for long enough my body had given up reminding me.

Medicine Drummer slept soundly. I'd repaired his shoulder as well as I could without pins and steel plates. It had taken three men to hold him still while I put things back together. He'd bit down on the furs in front of him and stayed quiet for the most part, but he couldn't stop the involuntary jerks of his body as it tried to move him away from my probing fingers. When he finally passed out, I don't know which of us felt more relief. Now, it was up to time to see how well he would heal. I'd given him an injection of the penicillin as well. At least he wouldn't have infection to fight.

The lodge flap opened, and Morning Dove came in. She looked

concerned and pleased at the same time. I longed to reach out and take her in my arms. Much to my surprise, she sat right next to me and pulled my arm around her. She snuggled into me. I put my other arm around her. I didn't care if she was testing my resolve or my honor. Her hand traveled over my bare chest, her fingers teasing one of my nipples until I clasped her hand. Holding her was one thing, but if she kept doing that I would make love to her, and I would have another battle on my hands to keep my life.

"They voted last night. Sees Shadows is now a member of the council in Kills Many's place."

I didn't know Sees Shadows, but I hoped he didn't think I was a threat the way Kills Many had.

"What did they do to Kills Many?"

"They voted Heavy Walker to take your place," she told me.

I pushed her back from me, staring into her eyes. They had voted me off the council. "Is that why you're here with me? It doesn't matter anymore?" There was a bitter edge to my voice that I couldn't keep hidden. Morning Dove smiled.

"You are not on the council because they made you my husband last night, and the Chief of All Time--with four to advise you."

I crushed her against me, taking in the scent of her hair and the feel of her slim body. If all else went wrong, I had her. "When will they let us have the ceremony?" I asked her.

"I am already your wife. But they will have a feast to celebrate our joining in a few days--I will choose you, in front of all."

My stomach rumbled.

"I have food ready in my lodge." She got to her feet, and I got to mine still hanging onto her hand--I never wanted to let her go. One of the medicine men, to whom I'd given the smallpox vaccine, sat near the doorway. I'd intended on giving the ones who had taken the oral vaccine a scratch vaccine to prove my cure worked. The proof after the vision was not needed, it seemed.

Outside, several warriors stood with their horses. They looked at me when I came out of the medicine lodge. I hated the chill their stares gave me--they were man hunters. That meant only one thing. I grasped Morning Dove's elbow.

"Where is Kills Many?" I asked her.

"In the confusion, he got away. He took three others with him-- all with horses. No one saw which way he went."

"Fuck."

"They will find him," Morning Dove told me. The warriors moved about with grim purpose. They spoke little and, when they did, only a word or two as they got ready for their manhunt.

"I need packs to travel with. May I take Summer?" I thought for a moment she would argue with me. Her fingers lingered on my face; her gaze searched mine with fear and understanding. This was the reality of life in this time. It wasn't easy to take her hand away from me. I brought her fingers to my lips. "He can't be far. We'll catch him. I'll be home in time for our feast."

"Come back to me, my husband," she said before she ran across the camp to get my packs.

"I'm coming with you," I told the men.

Chapter Twenty-Nine
On the Trail of Evil

We started out late in the day. Kills Many had a full day on us. His quick escape left a clear trail of broken branches and churned-up ground to follow. Late in the evening, we found a spot where he'd made a short stop. He'd tied his horse to a tree, and she'd torn up the grass to eat and pawed the ground, most likely when she'd run out of food. If he kept on not letting the horse get enough food, she'd get hard to handle, a small advantage. The few lingering rays of light wouldn't last.

I decided we would make camp in the same spot. Sees Shadows assigned guards and promptly went to his bed. He was a compactly built, silent man who looked at me with what I took for contempt. He regarded everyone the same way. The most striking thing about him was his eyes--bright blue set in a face darker than mine. He wore his glossy raven-dark hair in two short braids. He didn't look mixed, but the almost aqua color of his eyes spoke of something in his ancestry that wasn't American Indian--perhaps not even human. His gaze cut a swath straight into a person's soul--wisdom, judgment, and sentence--all in one intense look.

I shook off the eerie feeling he gave me and tried to let sleep take me. The ground didn't make a soft bed, or a warm one. When I turned on my side, I realized I should have dug out a spot for my hip. Not wanting to look foolish, I turned on my stomach. Sleep didn't want to come. Where was the gray wolf? On top of that, I kept thinking of Morning Dove.

My wife. I would rather have been in her lodge with her--doing something other than lying in the forest shivering.

A twig snapped in the woods off to my right. I didn't move. More twigs snapped, and leaves crunched. I reached for the bow by my side. Could I shoot someone--even a man like Kills Many? In my mind, I brought up an image of Morning Dove when she'd discovered Kills Many had used her to kill the other women's unborn children. Yes, I could shoot him.

A dark form crashed out of the woods. I brought my already nocked arrow to bear on it. Then lowered it.

A startled deer stopped in the center of the camp, snorted, and took off back into the woods, perhaps more terrified than us. Sees Shadows grunted from his sleeping place.

"I will go check on Rabbit Hunter," he announced and left the sleeping area with considerably less sound than the deer. Rabbit Hunter. Before we left for our journey, Sees Shadows introduced him as One Who Hunts Many Rabbits. Sees Shadows was One Who Sees Shadows Behind Every Rock. People shortened Fish Teeth from Man Who Catches Fish With His Teeth. Names in my time certainly lacked something. I was simply Shannon Running Deer. My father had been James Running Deer. Running Deer was our last name. Names the way they were now was one thing I didn't want to change. A name worded 'Man Who Catches Fish With His Teeth' told you more about the person than Shannon ever told anyone. Nicknames, though, seemed to span time.

"Damn," I exclaimed when Sees Shadows knelt right next to me. He gave me an odd look and one of reproach for my outburst. "You scared me," I admitted by way of explanation.

"Rabbit Hunter is dead. Fish Teeth as well. The evil one took them both with his arrows when Fish Teeth went to relieve Rabbit Hunter." Sees Shadows looked at his clasped hands for a brief moment. "We must move into the trees. I was a fool for thinking this clearing a good place to stop. The full moon outlines us much like a fish in a still pool flashing in the sun."

He left my side. I sat for a silent moment. It was my fault. I'd suggested we camp here--as their leader, they hadn't questioned me. Sees Shadows blamed himself--he was our war leader and hadn't spoken out. I didn't doubt he assigned some blame to me as well. Around me, the other five men quickly gathered our gear. I collected my things as well. I didn't think like the men from this time, or even like the men from before the 1900's. I didn't expect arrows to come flying out of the dark, or about the full moon and the light it cast. Did Rabbit Hunter or Fish Teeth have a wife and children?

As a surgeon, I dealt with life and death on a daily basis. I always made it my job to inform people of a loved one's passing. Afterwards, I often spent a great deal of time wresting with my guilt. My culpability this time would nibble at my soul for a long time to come.

It took only moments before we were in the woods, sitting within sight of each other and our backs to trees. Every sound startled me. Repeatedly, I directed my bow, only to find relief when the lump I aimed at turned out to be a rock or a clump of branches.

In the morning, we tied the two dead warriors to their horses and let the horses go. They would go back to the herd. I longed to write some sort of note to Morning Dove, telling her I still lived and intended to keep it that way. I couldn't do anything to erase the grief of those warriors' families.

All day, we followed Kills Many's path, although he now took care to try to hide it. At noon, I knelt where it looked like he had carelessly crossed some sand. There were clearly four sets of hoof prints. That we knew. I touched each set, measuring depth. One set measured a fraction deeper, but all four were fairly deep.

"All have riders," Sees Shadows said. I thought of Kills Many's warrior society--those who wore the red rectangles across their cheeks--three of them were out here with him. And if they were of the same caliber as Kills Many--we faced a hard fight.

"Yes. Or he's loaded the other's with enough supplies to make it look that way," I added. I doubted with the introduction of the horse being so new he would have thought about the prints they left. But even a man more loaded with packs would leave deeper prints--it was not a huge leap to apply that to the horses.

"His flight from the village happened too suddenly for him to have the time to take much. A man on the run doesn't take the time to hunt either," Sees Shadows said. He scanned the banks around us. "We haven't seen anywhere for the other men to climb out of here. They are still with him."

"Suggestions?" I asked.

"You are our Headman--what do you suggest?" he asked with worry in his blue eyes.

"That's why I wished for a council--to advise me."

"My advice would be to go back to our lodges, eat good food, and share a blanket with someone." He looked down the riverbed. Then up at the sky. His gaze returned to me. "This one, he will spread his evil words and undo the peace." He gave me a haunted look. "1860. I have made many mistakes. I don't know why Morning Dove brought me."

"I made a big one last night," I said quietly.

He shook his head and looked down at his hands, loosely clasped between his knees. "I was a tracker for the U. S. Armies."

"The spirits led Morning Dove to you because you know what we face in the future." I stood up and dusted off my hands. "We must go on." The other five stood with their backs to us and watched the sides of the wash. Trees and brush covered one side in a blanket of bare thicket. On the other side, a towering face of jagged rocks reached into the sky. A horse couldn't make it up there, and if one went up the other side, a clear path would be left. Ahead of us, the wash turned back into the rocks and gravel that had previously hidden Kills Many's tracks.

"Maybe it'll rain, and he'll drown," I said without thought. A flash flood would trap us as well.

"He travels in this riverbed because he knows it makes him hard to follow," Sees Shadows said.

"I know that," I snapped. We looked at each other. "I apologize. I think of the food he gave Morning Dove, and it makes me very angry. He tried to kill my child, and it would have destroyed Morning Dove to lose another."

"I don't think he intended Morning Dove to eat the poisoned food. He knew she gave it away, and he knew her pattern of charity. She has always given to those who were pregnant first."

"He harmed her by making her an instrument of his evil." I tugged my breach clout up and knotted my belt in a tighter loop. I'd lost a lot of weight. Plus, I hadn't worn a breach clout and leggings for more than a day's length before--and I'd cheated then and worn boxers underneath. Whenever I caught a flash of bare hip and buttocks from the other men, I felt exposed myself. Riding bareback was also leaving me chaffed in places that weren't very comfortable.

We mounted the horses, and, on Sees Shadow's advice, we galloped along the riverbed to catch up. As long as the sides remained steep, and we saw no evidence that Kills Many or any of his people had climbed up the tree-lined bank, we would continue to run as far as we could.

The sides began to slope lower and lower until we sat on our horses, looking out over a vast grassy plain. Kills Many's party now went in two different directions. Two went one way and two the other. After studying the hoof prints in the dirt, Sees Shadows stood and pointed to the right.

"The evil one went that way. He is a big man, so I think his horse leaves the deepest prints."

I studied both directions. If I were Kills Many, I would arrange for my people to meet at the other side of this clearing--where I would ambush my followers. We had to catch them before that happened.

"Take two warriors with you and follow the left trail. I will take one man and meet you on the other side," I told Sees Shadows.

He laughed--a tight nervous laugh. "You, medicine man, need to take two warriors with you." He waved to one of the others. They galloped off down the left trail before I could say anything about it.

Summer took up a good ground-eating pace. The two warriors with me didn't ride as well as I did, but this trek was teaching them quickly. The sun rested on the horizon by the time we sighted two horse-mounted warriors ahead of us. My heart sped up. Yes, one of them was large enough to be Kills Many. I wanted to be the one to do away with him.

I kicked Summer's flanks. She took off at a full gallop. I longed for a gun--a long-barreled buffalo gun. I would have stopped right where I was and picked them off, caring later about who they were. They were with Kills Many; therefore, they supported him. Hoof beats sounded from behind me. I hoped neither one of the men would fall off.

The two ahead of us reached the woods and dismounted. I shouted to those behind me to move off. An arrow whizzed past me, followed by the screech of a horse and the sound of a man being thrown. I yanked Summer to a halt. Grabbing her halter, I pulled her down into the tall grass. The other horse didn't know the same trick and wouldn't lie down.

"Let him go," I told the warrior, Swims Like an Otter. Otter reluctantly let the horse go. He crawled over to the thrown warrior. I glanced at him. He shook his head. Either the fall or an arrow had ended his life. I took in a deep breath. Death this way gave no time to mourn those who lost their lives. I would do what I could for the families of these men once I returned.

Otter knelt out of the grass and let two arrows loose before another arrow came back at us. He belly crawled over to me.

"I think I got one of them."

Fear stampeded through my chest. I sat up out of the grass and let an arrow fly. I got silence for an answer. Using great caution, we both scanned the edge of the clearing for any sign of Kills Many or the other warrior. Two horses grazed at the edge of the trees, as if unaware of a battle going on.

"I don't think I hit the other one," I said. It looked like Kills Many had been hit, but something nagged at me in the way he'd grabbed at his chest. I hadn't actually seen an arrow protruding from his flesh.

"I hit the first one. I saw my arrow go into him and the blood."

If one of them lay wounded or dead, he wouldn't be looking for us. If Kills Many only pretended I'd hit him, he had to be in the trees watching us or laying on the ground. I didn't think he was in the trees. On the ground, his position wouldn't allow him to see us very well. I moved back to Summer and let her up. She shook herself and pulled up a clump of grass.

I stood on the other side of her, so her body shielded me from view. "I'm going over there. Cover me with your arrows from here." Before he could protest, I mounted and hung over Summer's side so the horse hid me. My muscles screamed in protest. Like the hunting from horseback--it had been a long time since I'd demonstrated this trick. I kept Summer moving at an angle to the position of the others, letting her grab up snatches of grass. Hopefully, the others would think she was simply coming to join their horses.

The other horses whickered. Summer answered. I dropped to the ground, nocked an arrow, and rolled on my back. No one intercepted me. Feeling foolish, I army-crawled along the ground until I got to the warrior Otter shot--dead. Could I have hit Kills Many? I let out a breath and relaxed a bit.

A foot crashed down on my wrist. I grabbed for Kills Many's ankle. He snatched up my bow and leapt out of the way. He turned and before I could reach him, he fired an arrow.

Not at me.

From the clearing, I heard a yelp and knew Otter had been shot. With Kills Many's aim, I didn't have much hope for the man. Kills Many turned towards me. I scrambled along the ground and caught his leg around the knee. He came down almost on top of me.

I tasted blood when he rammed his head into my face. I reciprocated by slamming the heel of my hand into his jaw. His fist went into my diaphragm with enough force to take my breath away.

We pummeled and beat each other, without either gaining the upper hand. Kills Many was crazy and careless. I was weak from not eating regularly. Together, we stopped. Both of us winded. Watching each other, we tried to catch our breath. With a grin, Kills Many leapt after me. I landed on my back with a hard thump. Kills Many raised his arm. I had just enough time to see the rock grasped in his hand before he hit me with it.

Chapter Thirty
Kills Many's Way

Rain fell on me. Had Kills Many hit me and left? Doubtful. So maybe he'd killed me, and I didn't know it yet. I'd had enough of being almost drowned by the pouring cold rain. I tried to move. Simultaneously, both my arms felt wrenched to the bone. My fingers curled, and my arms wouldn't move from their outstretched position. I turned my head and tried to raise my left arm. A leather thong around my wrist, attached to a stake in the ground, held it in place. I didn't have to turn the other way to know leather straps also held my other hand. At this point, I didn't feel anything. Not pain anyway. It felt like my fingers were permanently curled. When I tried to straighten them, pins and needles danced up and down my arms.

Experimentally, I tried to move my spread-eagle legs together and found they were secured in place. I raised my head, but couldn't see what held them. I assumed ties held them the same way as my arms.

Warm fluid ran over my face, running into my right eye and turning my vision momentarily red. My left arm tingled, and, by lifting my head a bit, I could see a long, jagged slash down my shoulder almost reaching my elbow. The entire biceps looked blackish with bruising. Did I have a broken bone? Despite the icy rainfall, sweat broke out over my body. Why wasn't I shivering? With a jolt, I knew. Shock couldn't be far behind the trauma my body was experiencing.

Where was Kills Many? He wouldn't stake me out this way and leave. Panic began to set in. I struggled to pull one of my hands free. Frustration made me arch my back. I tugged harder--my left arm felt as if it would come off. I longed for the eagle-bone whistle I'd blown my screams through during my one Sun Dance. Someone had told me it was to whistle the hurt away. It wasn't. It was a way you could scream, and no one would know.

I didn't care who heard me. If I got lucky, someone other than Kills Many would come and set me free. I screamed with effort and pulled even harder--desperate to rip the stake out of the ground and get free. It did nothing except make my heart pump and my left arm hurt with a twisting torment I'd never experienced before. It certainly hurt more than the Sun Dance skewers.

Through the suffering, my mind registered a presence near me.

I opened my eyes to see Kills Many standing over me. As I thrashed on the ground, he stomped on one of my shins. I didn't even feel it as pain. I spat at him. It was an asinine thing to do, and I knew it, but it was all I had.

Kills Many laughed. "When you came, I knew I had to get rid of you." He squatted down as if we were having a friendly conversation. "All the others, they had good ideas, but they were nothing new. You came with your true passion for Morning Dove and your ideas the others listened to. You thought to rob me of the Power that is mine."

"Morning Dove doesn't want you. She wants me," I told him. At this point, it didn't matter what I said. Death would come and nothing I did or said would change Kills Many's mind. I hoped Jumper would care for Morning Dove.

Kills Many laughed again. "I don't care if she hates me. It is the Power of the Timeless One I want--I will be Chief of All Time. When I am done with you, only your bones will remain for her to mourn over. I will take her and the Power she offers."

"Do you think if you kill me, she'll welcome you?" The rain turned into sleet. Exposure would do me in before Kills Many did. I struggled again to get free. This time, I managed to keep the screams to myself.

Kills Many straddled me and dropped down. One of his knees smashed into my groin. I howled. When I regained consciousness, I didn't see Kills Many until he stood over me wearing a satisfied grin.

"You scream like a baby," he told me.

At least I can make a baby, I thought. But I couldn't form the words to hurl the insult at him.

He kicked me in the side before stomping on my left arm--if the bone had been in one piece before, it no longer was. I jerked, and new circles of misery tore up and down my arms and legs--my shoulder sockets felt wrenched out of place. My head pounded with a steady thumping. Bile sprang up the back of my throat. I longed to pass out again. I stared at the sky--a hollow void opened in me. The pain went there--leaving me empty and detached.

"Morning Dove," I whispered. We'd had one chance to be with each other. I wanted more. I wanted a lifetime with her. Tears came to my eyes when I thought of our unborn child. If Kills Many went back to the village, there were many there who would protect Morning Dove from him. He would never get near her. But she would raise our child alone.

Kills Many continued to walk around me, kicking me when the mood struck him. All he had to do was touch me lightly, and I jerked, unable to stop myself.

A loud roaring filled my ears, and heat spread through me. I viewed him as he came toward me again. Maybe some of my spirit left me. I bucked and twitched, but it now happened to someone else.

"Before you came, she was mine," Kills Many said. "I took care of her when no one else would. She would have died if I hadn't hunted for her. How dare she share my bed and then toss me away like a worn-out hide?"

I thought of Morning Dove. Why had she gone to Jumper? The spirits had told her she should. But why did she tell Kills Many about it? At first, I'd thought him wounded by her. He had taken care of her. Now, I didn't think life with him was as wonderful as he thought. He kicked me again.

"Fuck you," I screamed at him not caring if he understood the words. "Fuck you to hell." I concentrated and shouted at him in Blackfoot, "You killed her baby."

The reward for my outburst of defiance was a sharp kick to my ribs. Spots danced in a field of darkness before my eyes. Ironically, I felt warmer now.

"Jumper's creature. She flaunted the fact that Jumper gave her what I couldn't. Told me he treated her gentle--said she hoped they chose him as her husband. Gentle does not make a baby. A man must overcome a woman's Power to plant his seed." He paused and studied my face. I tried to stay calm--trying not to think about what he would do to me next. "I found the herbs I used to get rid of the babies in her baskets. Do you know what that means? Do you?"

Had Kills Many actually found the poison among Morning Dove's curing herbs? Of course, she would have them. They were the only method of birth control available in this time. I found it hard to believe she would use them personally, but it didn't mean she wouldn't use them to help someone else in need.

"I asked you a question," Kills Many said. He paced around me, clearly agitated. He stepped over me. When my left arm jerked in anticipation of what he would do, razors etched a path into my chest. He shouted, "Answer me! Do you know what it means?"

I didn't even know what the question was anymore. My ears

filled with a clamor that blurred his words. My vision field narrowed. My peripheral sight vanished.

He stood back from me. I tried to focus on seeing when he would attack me again.

Instead, I saw a dark shape swinging in the trees. Back and forth, back and forth. A body, hanging upside down and partially gutted, dangled from a rope over a sturdy branch of an oak. Could I be hallucinating? A specter manifested into being near the dangling cadaver. The elk-man. He caressed the un-living flesh of the corpse--a lover's touch. Shadows danced around him, like leaping dogs, they sprang into the air nipping bits of meat off the dead.

When Kills Many kicked me again, I had to look away from the elk-man.

"Do you know what that means?" he demanded again.

"I don't know," I managed to shout at him.

Who had Kills Many strung up and sacrificed?

"She killed the babies I put in her. She will pay for every one of them." He stood, blocking my line of sight. Somehow, I knew the elk-man still lurked behind him. "I already took care of Jumper's creature. I sat and watched her drink her morning tea. I knew she would rush to protect him. He is an infant--a woman, like you in a fight. I only needed to hit her once, and all thought the loss of the thing inside her a tragic accident." He circled me, waving a burning stick. "Oh, yes, she will pay. I will have her as I want her, and she will give me the Power I have a right to. I will kill the thing you put into her."

My vision cleared enough for me to see the manic rage come over him. He shook and gritted his teeth. Long shadows filled the small clearing--it looked as if Kills Many's and the elk-man's shadow were one.

Death would come soon.

The burning stick touched me. I couldn't stop the shout of rage and pain that escaped me.

Kills Many laughed.

The elk-man laughed.

They laughed as one.

"I have thought a long time about this," Kills Many said. His words repeated--a whispering soft echo of the elk-man's voice from my vision of the Great Medicine Man. Dancing Elk promising to find me. Promising that we were one--promising I couldn't escape him.

"We are not one," I said.

Kills Many glared at me. "One? Do you think we are brothers because we are of the same tribe?" He squatted near me again. Using the un-burnt end of the stick, he ran it over my ribs. "Those from your time, they are nothing. I have seen how they live--men do not know how to treat an enemy--to put a man in a cage..."

Obviously, Kills Many had seen a jail or spent time in one. Had Morning Dove done so as well? I hoped not.

"I will honor you with many days of life--with many chances to prove you are a man," he said with a feral grin. "I think this day you are cold. Would you like a blanket?"

"I'd like you dead," I told him.

A wolf howled in the distance.

Kills Many turned and scanned the woods. With quick steps, he moved out of the range of my vision and came back with his war axe. My insides clinched at the thought of being hacked to death. If only the wolf would come--even if no help arrived for me, I wanted Kills Many dead. Looking at him, I saw something that made frost run through my veins. Over his shoulders, he wore a fresh wolf skin. Dread filled me.

I knew why the wolf wasn't with me.

I whispered words of thankfulness for the gray's service to me and wished him well on his journey. I told him I would soon walk with him again, if he would have me.

Kills Many held a coil of rope in his hands. He tied a rock to one end and tossed the weighted end up over the branch next to the dead man. The stone hit the ground with a thump. He tied the rope off before he turned to face me again.

"This one," Kills Many said indicating the gutted body, "he did not deserve to be honored. He begged me for his life--he didn't want to be a man in the afterlife. I offered him his male parts--he couldn't swallow them even with my help."

I swallowed the lump of vomit that rose to the back of my throat. The idea that a person needed all their parts in the afterlife had once seemed absurd to me--now I doubted, and wondered if Kills Many cut off my testicles and penis, could I swallow them, if offered--so I was a man in the next life?

He used the stick to trace a line down my stomach, edging toward my groin. I stayed very still and locked my gaze with his.

"No, being a man means nothing to you," Kills Many said. He rose and walked away from me. The elk-man leaned against a tree--he appeared solid. A true fusion of man and beast. Wood smoke floated across the clearing--along with it, the scent of cooking meat. Despite my situation, my stomach rumbled.

"You won't be a medicine man in the next world," Kills Many said when he returned. I lay very still, doing my best to feign disinterest in his words. Nothing happened for several moments. He kicked me in the side. My body jerked with the force of his blow, but I managed to keep myself from reacting.

A small laugh escaped him. He fell on my right arm. I couldn't stop my reaction when he drove his knife through my palm. I tried to roll to the side. My right arm jerked with my desire to get him away from me. My breath came in quick starts. Blood filled my mouth--I realized I hadn't made a sound when he drove the blade into my hand. I'd bitten down on my tongue--a warrior of The People in the face of pain.

Kills Many stood near my feet, regarding me with his arms crossed over his chest.

"This night you shall have a blanket," he said.

"No. He does not deserve warmth--kill him. Kill him now--I must have him as the other."

I strained to hear the voice of the elk-man. Would Kills Many do as he said? Was I imagining things? My arm throbbed--I couldn't feel my hand. I could see it--the knife still sticking up out of my palm. But my body was protecting me from the pain, giving me a chance to escape the *thing* causing the trauma. As if I could do that--at some point, I would feel what he'd done to me--fully.

In one swift motion, Kills Many landed on my chest. His knee drove the air from my lungs. I tugged at my bonds, struggling to speak. Kills Many shook his head and, after giving me a savage blow to the face, he stood.

"Not yet. Not yet," he repeated several times. "I will have his Power as well."

I lay on the wet ground, still not feeling the blade in my hand, but oddly aware of something sharp digging into my back. I opened my mouth and let icy sleet fall on my tongue. I swallowed two mouthfuls before Kills Many returned.

He dropped a hide over me and bound my face so I couldn't drink any more of the rain. Apparently, my ability to endure having my hand impaled, silently, had earned me the right to shelter against the cold--but not to have fluids.

The hide kept a bit of the cold at bay, but I still felt frozen. A bright bit of light shone from Kills Many's fire. I wanted more to drink--needed it. My stomach chewed at my insides with growing hunger, and the dull ache in my hand would soon turn into a conflagration of pain I didn't want to feel. Exhausted beyond endurance, I slipped into sleep, despite my best efforts to stay awake--if Kills Many finished me as I dozed, I would welcome it.

Chapter Thirty-One
How Many Days

I came awake with a jolt. Orbits of pain tore through every part of me. My right hand existed only as a pit of agony. Cruel laughter came with the next splash of water that hit my face. I blinked against the dirt and blood being washed into my eyes, struggling against the barrier preventing much needed moisture from getting in my mouth.

Kills Many leaned over me and sliced the leather from my face. I felt his knife go into my flesh--not as pain. A sharp feeling of skin giving way, much like having a tooth pulled while under the influence of Novocain. Why couldn't my hand feel the same way?

Moments later, Kills Many sat in the grass near me. The aroma of roasted meat caressed and teased me. Uneasy, I glanced at the hanging body. Flies now swirled around it in a black mass. It didn't look like he'd butchered any of the flesh. If I remained silent through his ministrations this day, would he feed me?

When did I last eat? The only water I could remember was the rain from the day before--if it was the day before. I didn't know how long Kills Many had held me captive. It seemed only a day or two, but I felt far too hungry and thirsty.

"Bastard," I muttered. My voice came out scratchy and barely audible.

"Did you say something?" Kills Many asked. He made a show of chewing his food loudly, adding sounds of satisfaction.

"Asshole," I said next.

"You want some of the meat?" He stood over me. Very slowly, he let some of the juice from his meal run over my face. I licked at my lips and turned my head trying to catch some of it. He laughed and shoved a large chunk of meat into his mouth. A second piece hit me in the chest--out of reach. I could smell it. Almost taste it. My stomach rumbled.

Kills Many roared with amusement.

"Kill me," I told him.

"Not yet," he said. He picked at his teeth with a long thin obsidian blade--a fleshing tool.

"I will hunt you from the next life," I whispered--when I wanted to shout.

Kills Many nodded. "A witch could--but I think you are nothing but a weak man." He cleaned his nails with the knife. He inspected his hand while a specter of the elk-man watched over his shoulder. The elk-man spoke--but I didn't know what he said. Kills Many looked at me and yanked the hide away.

Crazy anger made more sense than his apparent calm. It was also less frightening. Completely at his mercy, I couldn't do anything except wait for death to come, and hope it came swiftly. I doubted he would kill me before he had tortured me for as long as he could. Perhaps he was an inept practitioner of the painful arts--women usually had the job of *honoring* an enemy.

"If you kill me," I said with difficulty, "Morning Dove will avenge my death."

He kicked me in the side. "I know how to keep a wife. She will obey me. I will tell her often of your weakness."

I would have spat at him if my mouth hadn't been sand dry. My lips felt swollen, and my throat constricted--stuck to itself, choking me every time I tried to swallow.

"No peace," I told him, "my spirit will haunt you forever."

I started to cough and wheeze, bringing up bile that didn't do anything to wet my throat--it only burned and made me try to swallow with nothing to go down.

I must have dozed or blacked out. When I opened my eyes, I hadn't even realized they'd been shut. Kills Many stood over me holding a blazing stick. Had he been burning me with it? Was that why I had lost time and awareness? He moved closer--pacing back and forth. The elk-man stepped with him--a perfect shadow.

"He cannot follow me; he is weak. He screams like a woman."

His words didn't make sense. Had I said something to him? If so, his answer puzzled me. The elk-man leaned close to me, but the shadow of his man-legs stayed joined to the shadow of Kills Many's.

"He can follow you. Morning Dove, she has already given him part of her Power."

"She has not," Kills Many shouted. He spun as if he would attack the figure of the elk-man. Instead, he dropped the flaming branch and drew his axe. When he swung his axe, the elk-man vanished--into Kills Many. I saw two of Kills Many--but one figure leaned out of the other--with an elk's antlers. The sharp blow of his axe glanced off my side. I tried to suck in a breath, but couldn't.

He snatched up the burning stick--held it above me for a terrorizing moment, as if he would thrust it into the axe wound he had made. Instead, he dropped it on my stomach. I twitched and bucked against my bonds--the branch stayed stuck to me. The smell of my own cooking flesh snaked its way up my nose and seared into my brain.

I saw him as some partly transparent figure coming at me with the fleshing knife. When the blade cut into my foot--a loud scream filled the clearing. Who screamed? Through the haze of my dimming vision, I saw ghostly dancers prancing around the clearing.

Morning Dove.
My mother.
My father.
Sam.
They danced.
Pointed at me.
Laughed.

I called for my father, my grandfather--for anyone who would come and set me free. I tugged at my bonds--heard the ripping sound of the earth, a tent stake being pulled. I jerked my right leg again. My right foot came free. My nerves jumped--I had to stop the scorching anguish of Kills Many's knife. Driven by adrenalin, I smashed my leg into Kills Many's back. He toppled forward with a shout of rage.

He spun towards me and held up a long strip of flesh--mine. Blood dripped from the sole of my foot in his hand. I tried to kick him again. He stood too far away.

"You will not follow me," Kills Many announced. He strode to his fire. In moments the scent of burning skin filled the clearing. Or was it the flaming stick he'd tossed on my chest? I no longer knew.

"Morning Dove," I thought I whispered. Sound didn't escape me; I only said it in my head--again and again.

Bright light woke me. I jerked awake, gasping for breath--afraid I was burning. I'd dreamed I'd been on fire--all of me. The bright light came from the sunrise. Someone cast a shadow over me. Kills Many?

My father stood at my feet, looking down at me. Over his shoulders, he wore a gray wolf skin--the grinning snout resting on the top of his head.

"Dad? Dad, where am I? I can't move--Dad?"

"Son, lie still. Be silent," my father said. "The horses ran away last night. The evil one, he gets ready to try and find them. You must stay calm--close your eyes, my son."

My father faded from sight.

"Dad, don't leave me. Dad?"

Footsteps like thunder rolled across the clearing. Kills Many. Kills Many--holding his bow and quiver. Kills Many looking down at me. I didn't blink. I stared up at the brightening sky. He prodded one of my feet. Barbs flew up my leg--not my leg. I only knew what he did. It wasn't my leg. It couldn't be. I lay staring upward. Unblinking. Dead?

A wolf howled.

Kills Many cursed. "You, you with your trickery chased the horses." He gave my left foot a ferocious kick.

Spots danced in the air before me--bright pinpoints of light followed by red-tinged blackness overcame my senses. I saw him move away from me in a sepia world. He knelt on the ground, touching the forest floor before he strode off out of sight.

"Son. Son. Drink," my father said to me. His hand went to the back of my head. He helped me to drink down cool fresh water. I swallowed eagerly.

I tried to speak--words wouldn't come. He helped me gulp more before he moved to my right hand. He tugged the stake out of the ground and went to my left hand. My muscles refused to obey. I continued to lie and stare.

More water.

He touched my right foot--the sepia world came back.

I lay staring up into the face of the gray wolf. He gave a single yap and vanished into the woods. Kills Many again. Staring down at me. My right leg moved--my left still anchored to the ground. He didn't notice. I lunged.

A cry of surprise escaped him. I rolled away from him--managed to get to my knees. In the grass in front of me lay a bow and several arrows. I grabbed for them with fingers that didn't want to close. I couldn't shoot a bow.

Kills Many yanked on my hair. I toppled backwards. My teeth met the flesh of his arm--blood and pulp filled my mouth. He punched me in the face. I shoved at him with my right arm. The broken knife blade through my hand danced in mockery of my weakness.

With his knees on my hips, he raised his axe. I would only have one chance. Up through his diaphragm, into his lungs, into his heart--into a main artery. I stabbed him in the stomach--pushing the arrow into the soft flesh at the base of his ribs, the end of the shaft jabbed into the palm of my left hand. I kept shoving. Bloody froth came from his mouth. He peered at the arrow sticking out of him.

The flights twisted to the right slightly. The ties holding them, crossed between each feather--my pattern. The shaft with its burn marks from my error when I'd made it. The obsidian arrowhead, buried in Kills Many's chest cavity, made by him. His life ended by the one thing we had done together.

I tried to scramble backwards, but Kills Many managed to hold me. He raised his axe again--a choking gurgle came from his lips. He sprayed me with his blood. The elk-man howled for him to kill me.

A low growl came from the woods just before a blur of gray fur flew past me. Kills Many toppled backwards, struggling with the weight of the snarling wolf. The wolf yelped once. Kills Many grunted with what I thought was surprise.

A long drawn out scream filled the clearing--the elk-man. His inhuman voice shrieked in a whirlwind of leaves and dirt--sticks and branches flew at me. Around and around. Louder and louder. The elk-man stood up from Kills Many's corpse--a thin specter of his former self--smoke-like--spirit-like. His gaze met mine with fiery hatred blazing in his eyes. Every leaf and twig in the clearing followed the elk-man upward in a roaring cyclone of noise.

Thunder roared overhead--the dangling body flew from the tree--Otter. The elk-man grasped for the corpse's hand. It appeared that Otter danced away from him, preventing him from a physical hold in the solid world.

Otter's body hit the ground, and all went silent. The debris turned into sparkling bits of light and vanished.

Snow began to fall. My side felt on fire. I lay on the ground--too exhausted to move. Like a toddler trying to learn to crawl, I managed to get to my knees, and then, using my right foot, I lurched to my feet.

The ground rushed up and crashed into my face. I rolled on my side, gasping and shaking. My hands clasped my knees, holding them pressed to my chest in the fetal position. Kills Many had striped both my feet of their soles.

Shadows slipped over me and the panting of a dog--of several dogs, filled my ears. I turned on my back, meeting the gaze of several wolves, who looked back at me with slanted golden eyes. So I would be wolf food. It must not have been the gray who came to my rescue. I knew it couldn't have been. The wolves just sat looking at me. Becoming wolf food wasn't any more appealing than Kills Many torturing me to death.

A moment later, or it could have been hours, the gray planted his feet on my chest and looked me in the eye. His wet tongue went over my face. I didn't even mind his drooling on me. He was alive and with me. The sounds of the other wolves as they devoured Kills Many came to me. I shut them out. At least they weren't eating me. The gray licked my face again.

He settled next to me. Soon after, the other wolves crowded around, lying over me and next to me, shielding me from the cold rain and offering warmth. Maybe I had a chance if someone, Sees Shadows perhaps, came to find me. I closed my eyes, wishing I could hold Morning Dove, wishing I could stroke the wolf's head--I couldn't move. And no matter how I tried to think myself elsewhere, I stayed right where I was.

I awoke to patches of clear blue sky through the trees. Only the gray remained near me. He raised his head and gave a short bark before he ran off into the woods. Part of the chill had disappeared from the air, but now with the wolves gone I felt cold again. I lay very still, afraid of the pain, afraid if it overwhelmed me again I would pass out and never wake up.

Somehow, I'd always thought death would be something other than this static wait for it to come. Was this the reason the elderly lay in bed staring out a window or at the ceiling? Were they simply waiting for the reaper to come and take them to the next life?

"Morning Dove," I said, speaking to her even though I knew she couldn't hear me. "Know I love you. You made me realize I was wasting my life. I see now, success can be measured in many ways and no matter what, that measurement must be in the old ways. A man is only worth what he is willing to give up. I would have fought any of them to have you and would have given you up to save us from the Europeans."

Birds came and went in the trees above me. A squirrel stopped in the branches over my head and was kind enough to drop an acorn on me. It promptly scolded me as if I were responsible for the loss of its supper. Wafts of smoke from Kills Many's smoldering fire drifted to me from time to time, making me long for the warmth a hearth offered.

The tree branches creaked. Where had Otter's body landed? Or had he been an apparition, like the elk-man? A seeing of the past and the way Dancing Elk had killed some of his victims? Otter had been dead--Kills Many had not strung him up and gutted him--still living--as he'd claimed. For the time being, I was glad I didn't have to look at him.

When darkness came, the wolves returned. They sat in a circle around me, tongues lolling and faces alert, until the gray came. Instead of lying down, he worried over me, licking my face, nudging me under the chin, and making whimpering sounds. I bunted my head against him to let him know I was grateful for his company. I didn't relish dying alone. I managed to move my left arm--a harpoon of pain thrust up my limb. My screech echoed off the trees.

The gray stepped back, eyeing me for some time before he went to my right hand and began licking at the broken blade piercing it. With a snarl, he grasped the obsidian and yanked on it, twisting his head from side to side--a dog playing tug of war.

The pain came as hot sparks that exploded in my brain. I thought I would pass out. I had never fathomed that anything could feel like it did. The wolf tugged and yanked. I thought of the trauma unit. Pain was secondary.

Stabilize the patient.
Pain.
Was.
Secondary.
Stabilize the patient.
The hell if pain was secondary. I shrieked.

The wolf leapt back. Through my shaking and gasping, I tried to call him back. I needed to stay silent, or I would scare him away--then I would be utterly alone. He came back to me with his head low and lay next to me.

Patients who refused to move after surgery or when injured annoyed me--a simple concept, move so they could be helped. A snort of amusement escaped me--I understood their refusal now. I had to move. Rolling to my side caused blasting white pain to fill my head. I blew air through my lips as if I had my bone whistle.

I couldn't move my left arm. The wolf yanked at my hand--trying to help me up.

"Good boy," I managed and tried to bring my hand onto my chest. My arm felt like someone had dropped a boulder on it. The wolf moved to my other hand and began worrying over it--encouraging me to keep trying. I wasn't going to be able to walk anywhere. I felt hot then frozen, and imagined infection raging through my body in great waves. I didn't have any clothes, and, with the darkness, the icy cold returned. It had been some time since any of the smoke from Kills Many's fire drifted over to me. I could only hope some embers remained. If I got to the fire. If I could crawl. If I didn't die of infection. If I didn't succumb to exposure.

When I succeeded in getting to my hands and knees, radiant splatters cavorted before my eyes. I refused to black out again. Pain bolted through my side. I'd forgotten the axe wound. I collapsed back on the ground. The wolf lapped my face.

"I don't suppose you could take me back to Mercy Trauma Center?"

The wolf contemplated me with his head cocked to the side and his tongue hanging out.

"I didn't think so." I took in several deep breaths. In a quick movement--I sat up.

The wolf yipped and leapt in a circle.

I sat flopped forward, my chin against my chest, with my arms feeling like they belonged to someone else. I managed to raise my left arm and get it into my lap. My entire hand was a swollen, bluish mess. Around my wrist, several rounds of leather thong remained. The circulation diminished--the palm of my hand slashed.

I sat staring at the blade through my right hand. Transfixed impalement--a perfect example. It didn't seem to be a thing attached to my body.

Bloated.

Ugly.

Horrible.

Someone should start an IV, lactated ringers with a bolus of antibiotic; Keflex was a good one--get a start on the infection right away. Blood counts needed to be done. And god-damn-it, morphine was in order. X-rays stat. The sounds of the trauma center grew up around me.

"Shane, my god. Can you hear me? Who the hell did this to you?"

"John?"

"Give that to me."

"John?" I tried to look around, but everything had gone suddenly bright.

"Pull it now. No, I don't want to wait for surgery. Shane? Can you hear me--fuck? Just stay with us."

Someone's hand went to my left shoulder. Hands grasped my right arm. I think I screamed. Something jabbed me in the hip. And then something else. Someone pried at my left hand. It hurt like hell.

The wolf growled.

Choose Running Deer, he seemed to be saying to me. *Choose.*

"Morning Dove," I whispered.

Someone touched my legs--my feet. I kicked at them.

The wolf appeared as a dark shape among the brightness.

Choose.

"Shane, wait. At least let us. . ."

Choose.

"Morning Dove," I said again.

The trauma center sounds vanished. I still sat in the woods with my bloated hands in my lap--the knife blade gone from my right hand. I puzzled over that for a few moments before I accepted it. What remained of Kills Many lay off to the side of me. I looked away. It didn't revolt me--I found too much pleasure in seeing him that way.

The stake my right foot was tethered to only stuck up an inch or two out of the ground. I tried to jerk my right leg up to get my foot free and almost blacked out.

I needed to get free in one quick motion. I clamped my jaw together and lurched into a standing position. I toppled over.

The wolf's tongue going over my face brought me back to awareness. Snow came down in huge wet flakes mixed with rain. I sat up--my foot now free.

I raised my left hand and used my teeth to pull at the thong around my wrist. My jaw started to ache, and it began to snow in a heavy blanket of white before I finally got one end free. I hadn't been able to get the knot undone, but I'd managed to chew through the thin leather. Immediately, my hand began to tingle. The wolf was nowhere in sight.

I brought my right arm up. By staying curled in a fetal position I could contain some body heat and also work at getting my right hand free. I chewed and chewed, feeling nauseated and lightheaded. The leather got thin and slimy. I almost laughed at the thought of my reluctance to drink water from an animal product bag my first day in this time. When the strand finally broke, it did little to relieve the pressure building in my hand. Inches from my face, Kills Many's war axe rested.

I couldn't use it for anything with the way my hands were. A throbbing center of agony took the place of my right hand. I began to try to flex my fingers. My little finger wouldn't move at all. I shook with the effort it took to curl the one next to it. I laughed aloud when my first finger and thumb came together. If only some sense of touch would return.

I grasped the axe with my left hand--I couldn't carry it. It didn't seem my arm was broken, I could move my fingers, and turn it-- with a lot of pain, but when I'd pushed the arrow into Kills Many's gut, I'd punctured my own hand. My left humerus most likely had a deep bone bruise.

I glanced at my feet--normal looking from the top, if blood-coated feet were in fashion. I turned my ankle--so I could examine the bottom of my foot, no bones visible, but the fatty tissue under the sole bled in a steady stream. Gouged in places to expose the musculature of my foot--and decorated with leaves and dirt, healing wasn't going to come soon. I looked away. Skin grafts should have been done, and even if they were successful, I would never be able to walk for any amount of time without wearing it through.

Kills Many's shelter and what was left of his fire stood a short distance away from me. Even if no embers remained, it would be a far better place to be than sitting in the cold wet. Using my right elbow, I dragged myself toward it. By the time I reached it, my breath came in fits matching the rhythm of my pounding heart.

Kills Many, it seemed, had planned to stay here for a bit. The lean-to rested over a rock-lined pit about two feet deep. He had carpeted one end with dry grass and a buffalo hide. In a pie-shaped wedge, lined with smooth river-stones, he'd built his fire pit. Over the fire pit, he'd built a separate lean-to of branches and pine boughs--to protect the fire from the snow and rain. A stack of twigs and other small pieces of wood, mostly covered with a rain-proofed hide, sat ready. Hanging from the branches of the lean-to were several hide bags. I hoped they contained food. When I spotted the bladder skin, I almost sighed with longing. My throat felt dry with urgent thirst.

Attached to the lean-to there were two poles with their ends buried in the ground on the other side of the fire pit lean-to. Over the top of those, another hide had been secured. Smoke could still escape, but the arrangement would funnel heat into the shelter. Knowing it would hurt, I rolled into the pit. Surprisingly, it didn't make the pain any worse and being out of the snow and wind made me feel instantly warmer.

Movement caught my eye, and I saw someone leaning over the fire pit. Sees Shadows? No, it wasn't him, but this person moved in a way that stirred memories.

"Dad?" It couldn't be my father. But he looked and moved like my father--like the man who had set me free.

"Son," the man said, "you shouldn't be out here without a fire to warm you." He held a buffalo horn in his hands. Kneeling by the fire, he emptied the horn into the center of the pit. A coal carrier perhaps?

The wind picked up and rattled the shelter over my head. When I looked back, the gray wolf sat near the fire pit. I stayed still until I knew I had to move or lay in one place and die. Edging over to the fire pit, I took a stick between my teeth and poked at the pile of coals. In the center, I saw a bit of red. It took forever using my teeth, and my now partially functioning left hand, to get small twigs into the glowing center. I tried blowing on the embers and got a face full of ash for my efforts. I crawled into the shelter.

There I discovered a long thin piece of obsidian attached to a bone handle--another fleshing knife or the one he'd used on my feet? I held it between my thumb and the first two fingers of my left hand. My arm shook. I couldn't close my fingers very tightly, but I had no other choice. I sat against the edge of the pit with my ankles in front of me and my knees out to the sides. Under me, I pushed the buffalo rug aside. No use in getting blood on it that the wolf might find objectionable when he returned.

I slashed the bindings around my ankles. The flow of blood from the wounds to my feet increased.

The scent of wood smoke came to me. A small fire danced in the fire pit. Fire. I had water and fire--if the bags and parfleches in the shelter held food, I had the basics for survival. I made my way over to the fire, pushed small sticks into it in a wagon wheel pattern, and placed some larger ones in with them, building up quite a pile to feed the fire. I drew some larger pieces out.

My father had taught me how to make campfires. As a child, I'd always wanted a *big* fire, it would be warmer, and more fun. My father always insisted a small fire gave more heat. I always silently disagreed. On one cold night, as snow came down and I thought I would freeze, he built a big fire. Not a bonfire, but a big one. I couldn't sit close enough to it to really get warm. It toasted one side of me while the other side froze.

I drank a good amount of the stale water from the skin. In a parfleche tucked under one edge of the buffalo hide, I found pemmican and dried meat. I choked some down. With food and water in me, and a fire to keep warm, I allowed myself to relax and consider I might live. I curled up under the hide and let sleep come.

"Morning Dove, wait for me. I will return."

Chapter Thirty-Two
Survival

I had no way of knowing how many days had passed since Kills Many started my ordeal. I ate sparingly of the food in the shelter and collected water from the daily rain showers. So far, the nights brought snow that melted in the warmer temperatures of the day. On this day, I woke up to find the wolf stretched out against my back and a dead rabbit lying near my face. Using the thin knife, I managed to skin and gut it with one hand.

My right hand now throbbed steadily. I could uncurl my thumb and index finger, but I couldn't bring them together. Infection made it pulse with each beat of my heart. My feet were in the same condition. I couldn't stand. I did everything on my knees and with my left hand. Somewhere, I had lost whole periods of time. I didn't remember getting the knife out of my right hand at all. I had vague memories of Kills Many standing over me with his war axe, and positioning the first of the stakes he used to pin me to the ground, but the rest was a blur. The mind did that for you--erased painful trauma.

I propped the rabbit carcass over the fire, using some green sticks and sat down close to the warmth. I wore a war shirt and a set of leggings that once belonged to Kills Many. Forget the breach clout--the thought of wearing one Kills Many might have worn revolted me completely. Around my shoulders, I kept a deerskin blanket to ward off the chill days and frozen nights. Kills Many had several hides and thick warm shirts tucked into waterproof parfleche pouches, so I didn't lack warm clothing.

Using two deer scapula, already scarred from heat, I dug another hot rock out of the fire. I added it to the wooden bowl filled with water at my feet. Steam rose--the water almost boiling. I used the thin knife to dig at the oozing scabs on my feet. Several times a day, I repeated the ritual: get rid of the scabs and soak the wounds. By probing at my feet, I found the bones and tendons whole--it didn't matter. Even if tissue ever regrew over them, they would be far too sensitive for me to walk, much less make the trip back to the camp. Corruption kept them unhealed and soon gangrene would set in. Infection raged in my left hand, but not to the same degree as the right. In my right hand, I couldn't even tell if the bones were in one piece.

When the wind blew in the right direction, I got a good whiff of

Kills Many's rotting corpse. The wolves hadn't eaten him--they'd torn him apart. The daytime temperatures still warmed into what I thought were the fifties and sixties, warm enough flies and mosquitoes still bothered me. Otter's body was nowhere to be seen.

The utensils and dishes Kills Many left behind hung from the framework of his lean-to. On my knees, I used a long stick grasped in my left hand and managed to knock down a wooden cup. Just that small amount of exertion left me lightheaded and swaying. With no alternative, I crawled to what remained of Kills Many. Decomposition had completely exposed parts of his skeleton, while others decayed in the rays of sunshine coming through the trees. More than a few hardy flies buzzed around his remains, most likely the same ones that shared my shelter.

I poked at the corpse until I could turn the rib cage over. Under him, I found what I wanted. A squirming mass of maggots. With only one hand to work with, it proved a difficult task to get a good portion of them into the cup. I glanced down at them.

"Nature's cleaning crew."

The wolf stood inside the shelter and made small whining sounds of inquiry.

"Don't worry, fella; I'm not going to eat them." Holding the cup in my teeth, with the wriggling mass under my nose, I crawled back to the shelter.

The wolf curled around my back when I sat next to the fire. I used the knife to scrape away the scabs on my feet. Despite the daily soaks, the wounds were ugly and black in places--mostly without feeling. With a shudder, I shook maggots into one of the wounds, counting them, and then packed it with dried moss. Using my teeth and my left hand, I wrapped a tight bandage of soft strips cut from the fresh rabbit skin around them. It would tighten around my foot as it dried. I hoped only tight enough to do the job, but not so tight it would cut off my circulation. Slow and tedious, it took a great deal of time to complete the process for both feet.

Doing my right hand proved almost impossible. Even the smallest touch sent barbs pricking up my arm that left me shaking and seeing spots. I finally grasped the edge of one of the largest scabs with my teeth and jerked my hand away. Pus squirted from the wound. I felt faint. When the quaking in my left hand stopped, I was able to work at my right one. I poured some remaining maggots into my palm, packed the wound with dried moss, and enclosed it the same way as my feet. Even after I'd cleaned everything I used, I could still smell the rotten flesh of my hand.

Revulsion and adherence to modern things had led me to wait too long. At this point, I held little hope of saving my hand. Once the poison spread into my wrist, I would lose the whole arm. If I couldn't cut off my own hand, I would die for sure, and, after coming this far, it would be foolish. I'd never perform any kind of delicate surgery again anyway. The wolf pushed his head in my lap and sighed.

I rubbed at his fur with my left hand. I didn't have the strength to do an amputation on anyone, much less of my own hand right now. The rabbit smelled done, and I needed sleep.

"Tell you what," I said, speaking to the wolf, "we'll share the rabbit first and sleep before I do this. How's that sound?"

The wolf raised his head and stared at me unblinking.

"I'll take that for a yes."

That night, snow fell in huge flakes, covering the land in what I thought would be a staying snow--the temperature dropped quickly and a north wind blew steady and strong. Where was I on the North American continent? I'd assumed some place central, but winter came too fast and sudden. The days were suddenly too short. I had to be somewhere in Canada.

I'd had only a brief time to get to know Sees Shadows. It didn't matter--I would miss him greatly. He had to be dead. Otherwise, they should have found me by now. We'd ridden three days out from the camp at a good pace. Kills Many, I thought, took me at least another day beyond.

He'd bonked me on the head at least one other time when he thought I would regain consciousness. He could have taken me any number of days away tied over Summer's back.

I'd smacked the ground hard when he'd pushed me off Summer. And just before he'd hit me again, I'd seen the shelter.

I reached behind me and patted the gray, suspecting that he'd chased the horses. I longed for something of Morning Dove's. Most of all--I longed for her. Would she want a husband with only one hand? Would she want a provider who couldn't stand on his own two feet? How would I hunt that way? Would anyone respect a chief with one hand?

I tossed and turned that night until the wolf bounded out of my shelter. My dreams were about Morning Dove and filled with the visions I'd had of the diseases destined to decimate the Americas. The worst of all of them came near dawn. Morning Dove struggled to give birth to our child. All around the birth lodge horrible maimed creatures danced. Kills Many brandished his axe and laughed in time to the elk-man's lewd suggestions.

Shaken, I watched the sunrise, honoring it with chants and prayers. My feet felt considerably better. My hand still throbbed. I pushed the bandage back a bit, examining the heel of my hand. The flesh appeared puffy and pinkish, but the angry red streaks of spreading blood poison hadn't appeared yet. I'd wait a bit before I amputated my hand.

My days took on a pattern. I checked my hand on waking each day. The wound in my side had been a shallow one, and it healed quickly, luckily with no infection. My feet healed slowly and painfully. The wound in my hand wanted to stay unhealed. While the infection didn't seem to be spreading, the wound wasn't mending either. I'd cleaned the maggots out of my feet already. I replaced them in my right hand for the third time on a morning so cold even the air felt breakable. The flies were gone, and Kills Many's corpse was frozen to the ground.

The gray wolf had been gone twelve days now. I'd started making a notch in a shelter pole for each day. Each dawn, one of the other wolves, a smallish female, brought me something to eat. I could lean on a crutch I'd fashioned and walk some. I used soft rabbit skin next to my feet and a packing of moss under a pair of moccasins to cushion my feet, but standing caused excruciating pain. I used my walking time to gather wood to keep my shelter warm. All the way along the northern side, I'd leaned pine branches. Only the southern side remained open. I needed to cover that side as well with the cold weather deepening.

With each step painful, I hobbled to the place where I gathered pine boughs and wood from a fallen tree. It took a lot of effort and time to gather the branches with my right hand all but useless. The woods were thinner here. I suspected if I could travel any distance I would find a riverbed or a clearing of some sort.

Why was this shelter here? It could have been a hunter's stop over. But when I thought about Kills Many, I suspected he had come here and made this his backup plan. If the council didn't choose him, he would have taken Morning Dove for the mystical Power she was supposed to give her chosen husband.

By spring, I could probably travel that far--in slow increments. I would head south and find my way back to Morning Dove and our child.

Chapter Thirty-Three
New Faces

I felt horribly ill. I couldn't sit up without retching and reeling with dizziness. My hand looked no worse, nor did it look any better. My insides felt on fire. In the last few days, I'd only eaten what the female wolf brought, saving the rations in the shelter for a time when the wolves decided I didn't need their help anymore. I suspected some dirt had remained in the wound to my side and now festered. With my immune system weakened, anything could kill me. I never realized how long natural healing took. With some of my penicillin and little infection to deal with, I would have been up and around by now--metaphorically speaking--my feet would plague me the rest of my life. Instead, I lay in my shelter with the fire burning low and the buffalo rug thrown off me--desperate to soothe the flames raging in my blood.

My body temperature had to be dangerously high. When I heard a horse whinny--I dismissed it as delirium.

Something dragged me across the ground. A sharp bump made me swear. My entire body hurt. I opened my eyes. The sky stretched above me--an arch of clear blue. Where was I? I turned my head and discovered I lay on a travois behind a horse. More delirium? The horse stopped, and a face filled my vision.

"Do you know who I am?"

I shook my head. Was I supposed to know him? His nose crooked to one side and back again. His grin showed two missing front teeth. Skin that looked like old leather covered his deeply wrinkled and tattoo-lined face. He had to be the ugliest man I'd ever seen--not a face I would forget easily.

"Here, have something to drink. It tastes like vomit and shit stew; drink it anyway. I've infused it with willow bark, chuchupate, and dog wood." He held a cup to my lips, and I drank the vile mixture. He nodded his head as if satisfied with a child who has completed a task successfully. After he wiped my lips, he gave me clear water.

"I still don't know you," I told him.

"I am One Who Walks too Heavy to be a Warrior. Do you know who you are?"

"Foolish Man Who is Not a Warrior, But Tried to be," I said.

He roared with laughter, making the horse lurch to one side.

"Well, Foolish Man, as long as you remember who you are, that's good enough."

"I am Medicine Elk," I said quickly, not wanting to be called Foolish Man. I knew who he was now--the medicine man who wore the ash on his face when he joined me in *fighting* the smallpox. "How is my wife?"

"Twenty days ago, a wolf came into the village. Morning Dove has always spoken any language. I didn't know she spoke the language of the beasts, though. Many were for killing the wolf--afraid a beast that would walk in the village of men must have the foaming mouth sickness, but it went straight to your lodge. Scared Jumper into running out in the snow--naked as birth." He laughed at this as well. "Some of us thought the wolf possessed your spirit returned to us. Others said it was the same wolf who was your helper. Morning Dove told us the wolf knew where you were."

He gave me more water and dug in a pack at my side coming up with some jerky. He tore it in half with his large teeth, and offered me some. I accepted with my left hand. My right arm lay anchored to my chest. I suspected I no longer had my right hand. I didn't want to know yet, so I ate the meat.

"Four of us followed the wolf. Sees Shadows and his two warriors are a half-day ahead. They will have a camp ready by the time we catch up."

"I'm glad Sees Shadows lives."

"His horse came back with him. Three arrows sticking out of him, two in his rump." Heavy Walker slapped his thigh and laughed again. I suspected the reason he never became a warrior was because he thought everything was funny and couldn't contain his laughter.

"My horse?"

"She came back three moons ago." His tone turned serious. "Sees Shadows wanted warriors to go after you. Jumper and Spins Much felt the same. I didn't think a search a good idea. No one knew if the evil-one lived yet--or if you did. The Elders agreed it would risk too many men to look for you. Morning Dove, she retreated into silence many took to mean you were dead."

"Our baby?" I asked.

"Making your wife's belly grow," he answered. He stood up and pulled his heavy robes forward and walked back and forth turning his head from side to side. He squatted back down near me and offered me more water.

I drank. I didn't blame them for not wanting to risk more people to come after me. After I swallowed the last of the jerky, I slowly felt under the furs over me and was gratified to find my right hand still attached to my wrist. Three moons?

"How long have I been gone?" I asked him. It couldn't have been three months since Kills Many had tried to kill me.

"Three moons. We came to look for you because Morning Dove said we should. None have ever doubted that the spirits guide her." He paused. "Any would have gone to bring even your bones back to her."

"How bad does my hand look?" I asked him next.

"I've changed the bandages and moss. No maggots to be found. You will have your hand, but I don't think it will be much use--even with Morning Dove's help. Evil spirits inhabited the wound in your side. I opened it up. I think they are gone now." He got to his feet.

"Thank you." What else could I say?

"Nine days I rode here, and we have three to go before we get back to the village. Morning Dove will make you well; it is part of the Power of the Timeless One."

He got back on his horse. I closed my eyes and tried to ignore the jolts of the travois as it traveled along the frozen ground.

I slept erratically that night, alternating between lucid moments and those filled with nightmarish creatures--half one animal and half of another. It wouldn't have been so bad, but most of the animals danced about on legs stripped of hide, some had their bellies slit as if someone had partially butchered them--and let them escape. Blood oozed and dripped. The animals howled as if I were the one responsible for their condition. And Otter--he followed the animals around holding his own guts in while trying to put their insides back into their bodies.

During the periods of lucidness, I was aware of Heavy Walker chanting and singing over me. He forced more vile medicine down my throat along with so much water I begged to get off the travois and piss.

He and another warrior hung onto me. I laughed.

"I'm a grown boy. I can do this myself."

"It is best if we come with you, Medicine Elk. The evil of your enemy stalks these hills this night and wants to take you with him." Heavy Walker sounded tired. I felt guilty for being a bad patient.

With my left hand, I did what they'd brought me into the trees to do. My feet still ached, and, without their help, I would have needed my crutch to walk. We turned to go back to the small camp. I heard a crack in the woods to my right. I turned, peering into the trees.

"Come, Foolish Man. You need to get back into your bed." Heavy Walker's voice sounded urgent and concerned.

I knew why. There standing in the woods was an elk. Not the graceful Great Elk who had marked me. This creature came from my delirium, except I was on my feet and lucid. It lowered its gore-covered antlers and ran at me on legs stripped of flesh. I shoved Heavy Walker and the warrior away from me.

The pain in my feet vanished as I ran from the apparition chasing me. It came crashing through the woods right behind me. I turned back, and now the creature ran on the legs of a man with an elk's head and torso. I couldn't outrun it, so I turned to fight it. It grew arms, and one of those arms punched me with a fist that seemed twice the size of a normal man's.

Morning came with me tied back on the travois and Heavy Walker wrapping my feet in clean skins.

"You have reopened the wounds to your feet," he told me.

"I'm sorry."

"No need to be. The one who did this to you became possessed by a great malicious spirit. His death set it free, but it wants to live in our world again. Your Power is great, but it knows you are weak and seeks to take your body from you." He studied me for a moment. "I think this is what chased you last night until you ran into a tree. The rest of us saw nothing, but I felt its evil Power. Morning Dove will help you fight this evil when we get back."

He studied me for a long moment before he turned away.

"You don't think I'm going to survive, do you?"

"I have not seen a man suffer what you have and live this long. Only a short time before I met you, I returned from my home--a man there had been fighting a long time against the same sort of evil. He lived less than a moon, in pain--before he died."

He glanced away from me. His absence to attend one of his own explained why I'd not seen him sooner--and without his ash paint. He must have held a lot of sway over the council for him to be chosen in absenteeism. He touched my hand and shook his head.

"The evil is trying to take you even now, that's why your wounds have not healed in such a long time. The sun has crossed the sky more than ninety times since you went after the evil one and yet your feet still bleed. Your side doesn't heal. Your other hand struggles to die, yet it doesn't poison you. I don't understand. I only know your Power is great. One who can fight the Great Spirit for a soul can fight the evil wishing to take him." He shook his head. "But a demon can fight forever, a man cannot."

I stayed silent, considering his words. Ninety days. To me it hadn't been so many. I'd only marked twenty-five days on the pole. Who knew how many days I'd spent in delirium, though? He did have a point, why were my wounds still open? With sudden clarity I remembered.

"Shane, can you hear me? What the hell happened? Who did this to you?"

The wolf's voice in my head telling me to choose.

I'd looked right at John and seen some sort of understanding in his eyes. He believed I'd traveled in time. He had to. He'd been right there when I'd vanished. I'd seen him fill a syringe and felt the jab of the needle and the burn of antibiotic going into my flesh. They'd treated my left hand, and that was how the blade had gotten out of my right hand.

The wolf had called me again.

I'd heard John yelling at me to stay, and then I was back in this time. I'd time jumped as I'd done before. For me, twenty-some days had passed. For those in this time, over ninety.

"Heavy Walker, I will win the fight," I said.

"I hope so." He got on his horse, and my day of bumpy agony started again.

I dreaded nightfall. Heavy Walker took me to empty my bladder before the sun went down.

"This night--only the medicine. No water until morning."

"Good idea," I said even though I wanted a drink. And not of water.

Once he tied me down, I tried to sleep. My eyes didn't want to close even though I knew it didn't matter if they were open or not. Whatever waited out there would come for me--asleep or awake. I thought back to the night I'd seen the elk-man follow Kills Many. I'd refused to let the creature possess me. Kills Many, with his manic desire for great power, would have been easy prey. The question remained--how did I fight it? How did I re-trap it in the carving?

The others sat around the fire, talking in low voices. I yearned to join them. Even fifteen days was a long time to be without other human company. The wind whistled through the pines around me. I clearly remembered every detail of the vision or time travel where the medicine man and I had trapped Dancing Elk in the carving--but I didn't have any idea how to catch a soul in a jar.

"Heavy Walker?"

The voices stopped. He moved to sit near me. "I thought you were asleep."

"When Summer returned, were my medicine things still on my saddle?"

"Yes, Morning Dove has them. She will keep them safe."

I groaned out loud.

"Is there some danger in them to her?" he asked suddenly.

"No. I know how I must fight the evil coming for me, but I must be free to do it."

"If I let you free and you run away, Morning Dove will not forgive me if the evil-one kills you now--or a tree."

"The evil can kill me right here. I understand why you want to keep me tied. Will you help to fight it?"

"I am part of the council of four. We have taken an oath to aid you in ruling The People. I cannot do so if you are dead." He paused. Made a sound of frustration. "Your Power is strong. What should I do?"

"Gather branches; pine branches. You must lay them out in the shape of a medicine wheel--large enough for me to sit inside. At each of the four directions, we must start a fire made from pine pitch. I'll need a rattle and a sacred pipe, with tobacco if you have it. I will also need ash paint, and coal as well."

He gave me a skeptical look. "I will do it."

I watched as he constructed a circle in the darkness. He'd sent the warriors ahead to make a camp a distance away from us. He set out four pine pitch lamps they'd brought to give heat to their small shelters. Once he finished, he offered a pinch of tobacco to the four directions and approached me.

He untied me in silence. I moved with his help to the center of the circle and sat down, crossing my legs and resting my useless right hand in my lap.

Heavy Walker set a small wooden bowl in front of me--inside a thick, black, waxy looking paint shone in the moonlight. He moved to the fire and returned with a pouch filled with ash. I watched in silence as he added water to it and mixed it.

"I have to cover my body with the ash."

I saw understanding in Heavy Walker's intense stare. He held the pouch up and chanted over it in words I didn't understand. After he finished his chant, he began covering me with the ash-paint.

It felt warm against the part in my hair. He continued to chant softly as he coated my hair and face. His words didn't stop until he had covered me to the waist. Surprisingly, some of the night's cold left me.

Without instruction from me, he lifted the small bowl of black paint and using one finger he drew symbols on my body--the same ones the medicine man of old had worn to capture Dancing Elk the first time.

How could he know what ones to use? I watched his eyes and knew. The sprits were guiding him.

He drew the concentric circles with the man inside last. He spoke one final word--a hard sounding guttural one, got to his feet, and put away the paint.

"I will help you fight," he announced when he returned to me.

"No. You must go and stay with the others." I held out my left hand for the rattle and pipe he held. When he hesitated, I added, "The evil doesn't want you. It's something I must fight on my own."

He handed me the pipe first and then the rattle. In silence, he lit the pine pitch lamps. He stood for a long moment before he lit the pipe for me as well.

"I have named Jumper my brother. Morning Dove knows this. If I don't win this night--if the evil takes me, you know what must be done--before I make it to the village."

He gave me a stern nod, got on his horse, and galloped off into the dark.

Chapter Thirty-Four
Evil's Fight

I sat in my circle of pine boughs feeling like an imbecile. I began a chant designed to drive evil out of a person and almost yelped when echoing laughter answered me. Had Heavy Walker stayed behind? No, he wouldn't laugh at me--not now. The elk-man came out of the dark. He watched me with his muscular arms crossed over his elk torso.

"You are mine. Don't you see? I marked you all those years ago and took your Power from The People. I drove you off the reservation."

I ignored his words and continued my chant.

"Your words have no Power anymore." He continued, "You will walk with me again. We will have greater Power than you ever thought possible. The other was weak. You are far stronger. Morning Dove will be yours. She will spread herself for you each day and you will take her as a man does. You will make her feel your strength. She will give up the Power of the Timeless One readily. You will live forever. Un-aging. Forever--younger than you are now. But you must take the Power by force. I will give you the strength to take her as you must."

I kept chanting, refusing to falter. Had some form of evil influenced me all those years ago? No. I refused to believe that. My grandfather would have known.

"Go back to your evil lord, whoever he is, and be gone from our world," I told him. "You don't hold sway over me anymore."

He laughed. "Don't I? You have been with Morning Dove only once, and she carries our spawn. Remember how it was? Her hands on your shoulders, our phallus buried inside her while we held her legs so she couldn't get away. She fought us, didn't she? She bit us and scratched us. But we held her tighter, refusing her request to be gentler."

I faltered, remembering the bruises I'd left on Morning Dove. Had she actually fought me when I'd thought we'd gotten carried away in our passions? My momentary lapse was all he needed. He danced into the circle with a war axe in his hand.

Recovering quickly, I raised the pipe, drew in a mouthful of the sacred smoke, and blew it at him. He backed out of the circle.

"She is mine and mine alone," I said. "I have never shared her with you. I never will."

The elk-man began his own dance around the outside of the circle. I heard Morning Dove's cries as I'd made love to her, but now instead of breathless whispers of encouragement, she cried for me to stop. I was too large for her. Why did I need to hurt her? Why wouldn't I stop? Her voice seemed so real and the longer it went on, the fainter the memory of our passion became. The elk-man leapt into the circle and almost knocked me out of it. All around the small camp half-skinned animals danced and shrieked. The same ones that had been depicted on the Great One's cavern walls.

I shoved the elk-man back out of the circle and struggled to my aching, torn feet. "You won't have her. She is mine. Her child is mine."

I danced in a small circle, pressing the fingers of my left hand into the palm of my right hand. Pain lanced through me. I thought of my long ago Sun Dance. I understood the Power in it now. I called the memory back until I relived being raised off the ground by the skewers through my flesh. I dangled, blowing into my whistle and calling for the spirits to help my father. But they hadn't. The very next day, the doctors told him his cancer had spread astronomically. He had only days to live.

"Yes. Yes. Yes." The elk-man chanted along with its gruesome followers. "Had you called me, I would have saved him."

I dangled and spun. My chant began to change to one of welcoming the evil elk.

"Shannon. The spirits came to me. You see. I am well. All is in harmony with me."

I stopped dancing and stared off into the darkness. My father walked toward me. The elk-man tried to block his path, but my father easily walked through the apparition. The elk-man's followers danced around my father, but they couldn't touch him in spirit form. He stepped into the circle and stood before me.

"Let your heart free, my son. Your wife awaits you. I have spoken to her." He held his hand out to me. The elk carving rested in it. How had it gotten out of the pouch I wore?

"Believe in your own Power. It is good and strong, if only you can know that in both worlds."

"Father...," I began. But even as I said the word, he changed and turned into the gray wolf. As the wolf, he dropped the talisman into my hand. His gaze met mine. I began to dance again. This time,

I saw Morning Dove when she came to me--before I'd gone after Kills Many. The love in her eyes and the soft touch of her hand to my face--true memories.

"Come back to me, my husband."

The wolf gave a yip and leapt out of the circle. The creatures fell on him, tearing at him as he fought them. The elk-man began to fade from view with the fervor of my words. I chanted and lived the sun dance simultaneously.

The elk-man howled with frustration. I no longer heard his prompts. When I fell to my knees, I relived the triumph I'd felt all those years ago, and the elk-man vanished.

Silence held the darkness in thrall.

The wolf lay torn to pieces by the elk-man's creatures. His life given to help me.

I crawled out of the circle to what remained of the wolf. I touched his torn and bloody head. Tears fell--tears I had been unable to shed when cancer took my father. I'd been too angry--too far out of harmony. The frozen cold of the night hit me. I shivered.

"Thank you, wolf-father."

Chapter Thirty-Five
Homecoming

I slept for most of the three days it took to get back to the village. Heavy Walker spoke to me and cared for me, but exhaustion left me speechless. I didn't even respond when they moved me into the medicine lodge. Young Medicine Drummer took me from the care of the warriors while Heavy Walker spoke to my grandfather.

"I think his spirit is as wounded as his body," he said.

How could I explain that my spirit was finally, truly healed? I didn't know how to tell them the icy river water had washed away more than ash and paint--it had rinsed away the last of the disharmony in my soul.

"You must give him time to sleep and heal," my grandfather said. I didn't hear Heavy Walker's answer.

My grandfather came and squatted next to me. He studied me for a few moments, took my right hand, and looked at it. "Do you regret your choice?"

"What do you want me to say? I can't say I am glad that I no longer have the use of my hand. I won't say that walking like a crippled drunk will please me--but I couldn't dwell in the white-man's world any longer." I smiled slightly. "Even for T. P. and chocolate."

"Your wife will come to you soon. I saw her going to the women's bathing hut to be fresh for the consummation of your marriage."

"Anyone ever tell you that you're a dirty old man?" My words sounded flat to my own ears.

He grinned. "You have met my wife. She tells me I am spry for my age and smiles about it."

"Morning Dove will be disappointed. I am too ill and too tired."

"Ah, boy, don't be a fool. Have you never let the woman be on top?" The lodge flap opened. He got to his feet.

He stood near the door talking in a low voice to Morning Dove. She laughed softly. The sound of it a subtle tease along my senses. My grandfather went out, leaving us alone.

The soft tinkling of bells came to me when Morning Dove walked across the medicine lodge. She knelt next to me and studied me. Her face looked drawn. There were dark circles under her eyes along with a puffiness I took for lack of sleep.

"Husband," she whispered.

I reached with my left arm and pulled her down to me, holding her, clinging to her while she cried. I couldn't even stroke her hair with the curled useless thing that now masqueraded as my right hand.

"I thought I had lost you," she said into my shoulder. "When Summer came back without you, all believed you were dead. I told them I would know in my heart if you were. They only shook their heads and left your things as they were, to humor me I think. And when so much time passed. . ."

"Morning Dove," I whispered. "I also didn't think I would see you again. I dreamed of you often, and, sometimes, in the darkness I spoke to you. I missed you."

She sat up away from me and pressed my hand to the swollen mound of her stomach. On her thin frame, it seemed she was more than four months gestation. "Inside me, I feel the fluttering of her life already. The midwife laughs at this, but I know she is there."

I curved my right arm around her back and reached up to touch her face with my left hand. I needed to explain to her, and I didn't know what to say.

"I spent many days in pain from what the evil one did to me," I began.

She reached around and pulled my right hand into her lap. "Heavy Walker spoke last night of the camp you made and of all you did for yourself. He said a man who let pain swallow him could not have done what you did." She smiled at me, bright, hopeful, happy--relived. "He terrified the children with the story of the evil you fought. Many mothers will be up long nights settling their fears."

"I suppose that's one way to keep them from wandering away in the woods," I said.

"I will tell our daughter of your bravery, but I think I will not tell her of the evil one too soon," she said with a slightly nervous laugh.

"Perhaps she'll need to hear it to know why her father is crippled." The bitter edge to my voice made me cringe. Self-pity wasn't something I wanted to indulge in.

"The gray wolf came and told me you lived. He appeared as a man to me. At first, I thought he was you." She looked at me expectantly.

"My father," I answered, hearing the catch in my voice.

"I am sorry he died."

"He died some time ago. Only his spirit came to me as the wolf. But I understand what he wanted to tell me."

"He will rest now. His spirit is finally in harmony."

I cringed when she touched my right hand and pried at my fingers. "Your hand still bleeds." Surprise colored her voice, and I saw something in her eyes that looked almost glad.

"So do my feet--they may never heal correctly. Even this hand breaks open if I use it too much." I held out my left hand for her to see.

She drew her knees to her chest and sat that way for a long time. I would forever see her radiant smile the way it was that day on the lake. Now, she sat with her arms around her legs and a thoughtful expression on her face. A smile tugged at my mouth. She liked to sit in that curled together position. In a short time, I didn't think the growth of our child would let her. From all I knew of her, she had suffered a great deal in her life, but since I had last seen her, she seemed to have aged; the look of wild innocence in her eyes now replaced by a shadow of fear. I vowed to do all I could to make her world a safe place once again.

"I'm sorry. I. . . "

She pressed her fingers to my lips. "Shhh. It is said for the Power of the Timeless One to be passed on, I must choose you at the dance--a true choice. I did not think we needed the ceremony. I see what the spirits are telling me. It must be the true gift. You must become as I am, quickly and not over time." She leaned forward and kissed me on the lips in a chaste way. "It is good you are not healed. I will tell the Elders; I will choose a husband this night. We will hold a woman's dance during the hunger moon. We shall have our wedding feast. A good way to break up the boredom."

She leapt to her feet before I could say anything against it. I could only think she spoke of the difference between a consummated marriage and one that wasn't. Did she think I needed the dance to feel like a man again? I flopped onto my back. How angry would she be if I couldn't consummate our marriage--I didn't think I was healed enough to function. *It is good you are not healed.* How could she think it a good thing I wasn't healed?

A great fire burned in the village common area. The night crackled with cold, but people moved about as if it were midsummer. Morning Dove was right about that part of it. People did welcome a break from the norm. I assumed it was January, maybe late December. A time when people would have gathered on glacial nights in the double tepees making up the medicine lodge and listened to stories--trying to forget stores that were growing low. Thankfully, this year, low provisions weren't a worry.

I sat as close to the fire as I could without burning up. My feet were warm, but I could feel they were bleeding again. Jumper sat next to me, and, every time I looked at him, he looked back with concern. Heavy Walker watched me as if I would topple over any moment. Even with the penicillin, my wounds didn't improve. I wondered if I had some sort of unnamed staph infection not allowing me to heal. Heavy Walker would have agreed with me, giving the infection a name: evil.

"When spring comes," Jumper said next to me, "we will hunt the bison--show all here how to do so from horseback."

In the past five days, Jumper never mentioned my ordeal. He talked of the things I had proposed. He often made suggestions or talked of things we would do *once I was well*. I looked down at my aching hands. I laughed for the first time in weeks--all of this seemed absurd.

My torture. Being in the past. Jumper's insistence that I would be as I was before. Morning Dove's apparent pleasure at my inability to heal.

"Shit," I said, trying to stop my laughter.

Jumper looked alarmed at my sudden outburst. Heavy Walker crossed the camp. Both men stood looking at me with dismay. I laughed until I hiccupped and had to wipe tears from my eyes. I held my left hand out to Jumper, showing him the unhealed depression in my palm.

"Don't you see?"

Jumper frowned. Heavy Walker leaned toward me and peered at my hand.

"See? What is it you see?" Heavy Walker asked.

I slowly shook my head. They didn't see. Perhaps I would die--we would fail. It came as an alarming thought. I squeezed my hand closed, not caring if it started bleeding. I wouldn't let us fail.

"Never mind. I'm fine. Go and enjoy the food." Both men looked reluctant to leave me.

Jumper turned to watch the men getting ready to start their drumming. With a deep sigh, he said, "The Elders have informed me I will gain a wife this night."

Heavy Walker sat on the other side of me. He grunted. "I have no objection to a wife. We follow your plan, and you have called for us to have wives. To keep us in line, no doubt. I only hope she is fat enough to keep me warm when the nights get this cold."

Sees Shadows came and sat behind me. "I don't want a wife ... not one The Elders will choose for me anyway." He did sound very unhappy about the fact.

When the drums started, we subsided into silence. The five women who came out to dance moved around the circle to the beat. I had a chill of déjà vu. The voices and the drums sounded the same as they had in my first vision of this time. I almost expected Heavy Walker to whisper that Morning Dove had to choose this night.

Instead, amidst small laughs and bright happy voices, a woman moved to stand in front of us. She raised her head, and I was surprised to see Little Flower. She had gained weight and was actually quite attractive. She held a string of shell beads in both hands. Sees Shadows shrunk back. She giggled like a girl and dropped the strand around Jumper's neck.

"One shouldn't doubt the wisdom of the Elders," he told me. He got to his feet, and, with a smile put the blanket, he wore around her shoulders. They walked off towards her lodge to the encouragement and randy advice of some of the younger men.

The other women continued to dance under the speculation of who would be chosen next. From those seated, another woman got up to dance. She was encouraged just as the others were. I frowned. She was a tall woman, over six feet, I thought. Sees Shadows moved up next to me. His eyes focused on this new woman and followed her as she made her dancing rounds.

"You see," Heavy Walker said to Sees Shadows, "the Elders have been watching us. They know our desire as well as what The People need. Honey Woman will make a good wife. She can see things from both sides."

Honey Woman, I realized, was a 'two spirit'--a man who lived as a woman in all ways. "And you," I said, leaning toward Heavy Walker, "what one have you favored?"

He smiled at me and caught a laugh that tried to escape him. "Any of them who are more than skin and bones."

I shook my head and smiled.

"Hush. You should know better, Medicine Elk. You are an elder," my grandfather said.

I gave him a cross look. I had seen forty-eight summers. I wasn't that old. In this time, though, that did make me an elder.

Among the women dancing, there were two who were heavier than the rest. One of them moved towards us and in a teasing manner she held her strand of nut-shell beads out as if she would put them around Sees Shadow's neck. Moments later, Honey Woman moved to stand in front of Heavy Walker, who looked alarmed. Both women leaned forward and slipped their strand of beads over the men's heads.

They looked at each other. Sees Shadows glared at Heavy Walker.

Both women laughed. Honey Woman touched the other women's shoulder. "We have mixed up our beads."

Smiling, they switched places and both my other councilors gladly went with their new wives. I looked around for Spins Much and didn't see him.

"He is already married," my grandfather said, "to a suitable wife. She will have his son when your daughter is born."

I glanced at my grandfather's staff. The carved mouse twitched--became real. It scampered down the staff and came up to me. I glanced at the others. Everyone still watched the women dancing. The mouse chattered at me around the bone he held. I blinked.

"Yes, I am Mouse. I won the game among the animals to see who would be Chief of All Time. What is mine to keep is mine to give away. I am too small to be your chief. I want to live in peace with my wife and family. I get my living easily. I don't like to have enemies. I am going to give my right to be chief to the one that Old-Man has made like himself. I choose you to lead all of us, for all time."

"I thank you, mouse brother," I said back.

"Humph, I am Sister Mouse," she corrected. She scrambled into my lap where she dropped the bone. After that, she scuttled along the edge of the circle of people and vanished into the frozen darkness.

The bone I held appeared to be a tooth of some sort--huge, a mammoth perhaps. I tucked it into the pouch I wore. I clasped it for a moment to reassure myself of the elk carving's presence.

The other women stopped dancing. The camp went silent. I looked up. Morning Dove moved out into the circle to do her solitary dance exactly as she had in my first vision. She stirred me the same way she had before--knowing and loving her hadn't changed the way I felt. I simply felt worn thin from everything that had happened to me.

When she stopped before me and held out my dog tags, I leaned forward, letting her put them around my neck.

"Shannon Running Deer, Medicine Elk of The People, I choose you." She turned and ran across the camp to disappear into her lodge.

I sat staring after her.

"Glued to the ground?" my grandfather asked.

Getting to my feet was harder than I wanted it to be. I saw several people move as if they would help me and then pull back. Walking, hobbling, and limping across the silent camp seemed to take forever. When I finally stood outside Morning Dove's lodge, my heart thundered in my ears. I couldn't shake off the thought that I would enter and she would be in the condition she had been in after the car ran her over. Everything would vanish. I would be back in my own time trying to save her life with no miraculous recovery in sight.

I opened the flap and stepped inside.

Morning Dove smiled at me. I expected her to be nude--waiting for me. Instead, she wore the thin indoor tunic I had seen before, with a blanket around her shoulders.

"Come, my husband. Have something to eat."

I fell more than sat on the mat near the fire. She handed me a plate of food. I ate while I watched her. She got a plate and some food and sat near me. We ate in silence with our legs crossed and our knees touching. I balanced my plate on my lap and steadied it with my crippled right hand. It took forever for me to eat. Morning Dove paced herself so she put her last bite in her mouth after I ate the last bite of mine.

She stood and took off the blanket she wore. Her lodge was warm, far warmer than the outside air, but cool enough goose flesh made her nipples stand out. Very slowly, she peeled off her tunic. She held her hand out to me and whispered, "Come, share my blankets."

"Morning Dove. . . "

"No more words. In the morning, you will be well."

I followed and let her help me to undress. She said nothing. With gentle hands, she pushed me down onto her bed and began moving oiled hands over me. I found myself relaxing and wanting her. When she indicated I should turn on my back, I did so. She ran her hands up and down my legs, paying prolonged attention to my feet. I tried to keep from flinching, even when I did, she didn't stop her massage. Straddling me, she began rubbing my chest and arms.

I wanted her so much, and my body refused. I began to get angry. Anger, first at myself. Then my anger was at Kills Many. I wanted to shove her hands off me. I squeezed her arm tightly in my left hand.

"She will spread herself for you each day, and you will take her as a man does. You will make her feel your strength. . ." The elk-man's words echoed in my ears. *"Come to me, come to me, and come to me, through her, we will be one, and you shall have all the Power. It is not too late."*

Despite my wish to shut the creature out, I began to react. Morning Dove said nothing. She watched me with anguish in her eyes. Had I taken her this way the first time--out of anger?

I hadn't.

I couldn't.

Very slowly, I let go of her. "Morning Dove, I'm sorry. Maybe we should wait until I heal more."

She touched her lips to mine and reached back guiding me, half limp, into her. The elk-man howled with triumphant laughter.

"We are one now," Morning Dove told me. "No other can come between us."

I met her gaze, reached with my left hand, and touched her swollen belly. My child and mine alone. No creature of darkness had helped me give her the child. The elk-man's laughter became shouts of rage.

Morning Dove leaned over and locked her mouth with mine. I got lost in being with her. My hands no longer hurt--I forgot the pain in my feet. I still heard echoes of the elk-man. Each time I heard it, the voice tried to drive me to be violent with her. I fought the urges, clinging to Morning Dove, whispering her name--driving the creature's voice and form away from us.

I remembered each encounter I'd shared with her--I saw things I thought might be in our future. I saw us surrounded by children. We stood on a wall together, watching the white-man as he tried to invade us. I sat in councils that seemed to span time. And always Morning Dove was there, by my side--part of me.

Abruptly, the elk-man's voice stopped.

I found myself lying on my side with my arms around Morning Dove as she slept. I no longer felt any pain. Reaching up, I touched her hair and jerked my hand back. My right hand. I opened my fingers staring at the scar in my palm. Both my hands were completely healed and worked as they should. I wiggled my toes and ran my foot along Morning Dove's leg--no pain, healed. I hugged Morning Dove tighter.

"How?" I stammered.

She stirred and turned to study me. "You are as I am now." Very gently, she touched my right palm. "You will heal now as I do."

"We are not done yet," the elk-man's voice whispered in my ear.

"I will be ready for you," I whispered back.

-END-

The Chief of All Time
A Blackfoot Why Myth

There was much quarreling among the animals and the birds. Bear wanted to be chief, under Old-man, and so did Beaver. Almost every night they would have a council and quarrel over it. Beside Bear and Beaver, there were other animals, and also birds, that thought they had the right to be chief.

They couldn't agree. Some said the greatest thief should be chosen. Others thought the wisest one should be the leader; while some said the swiftest traveler was the one they wanted. So it went on and on until they were most all enemies instead of friends, and you could hear them quarreling almost every night, until Old-man came along that way.

He heard about the trouble from Rabbit. He listened to what each one had to say. When they finished talking and the quarreling commenced as usual, he said, "I will settle this thing right here and right now, so that there will be no more fights over it, ever."

He opened his paint sack and took from it a polished tooth and he said, "This will settle the quarrel. You all see this bone in my right hand?"

"Yes," they replied.

"Watch the bone and my hands."

Old-man sang the gambling song and slipped the bone from one hand to the other so rapidly and smoothly that they were all puzzled. Finally he stopped singing and held out his hands--both shut tight.

"Which of my hands holds the bone now?" he asked.

Some said it was in the right hand and others claimed that it was in the left. Old-man asked Bear to name the hand that held the bone, and Bear did; but when Old-man opened that hand it was empty. Everybody laughed at Bear. Old-man smiled a little and began to sing and again pass the bone from hand to hand.

"Beaver, you are smart; name the hand that holds the bone this time."

Beaver said, "It's in your right hand."

Old-man opened his right hand, but the bone wasn't there. "Now, you see," said Old-man, "this is not so easy as it looks, but I am going to teach you all to play the game; and when you have all learned it, you must play it until you find out who is the cleverest at the playing. Whoever that is, he shall be the chief of all time under me."

Some said they didn't care much who was chief, but most all of them learned to play pretty well. First Bear and Beaver tried it, but Beaver beat Bear easily and held the bone for a long time. Finally, Buffalo beat Beaver and started to play with Mouse. Of course Mouse had small hands and was quicker than Buffalo--quicker to see the bone. Buffalo tried hard. He didn't want the Mouse to be chief, but it didn't do him any good; Mouse won in the end.

It was a fair game and Mouse was chief under the agreement. He looked quite small among the rest, but he walked right out to the center of the council and said: "Listen, brothers--what is mine to keep is mine to give away. I am too small to be your chief and I know it. I am not warlike. I want to live in peace with my wife and family. I know nothing of war. I get my living easily. I don't like to have enemies. I am going to give my right to be chief to the man that Old-man has made like himself."

CPSIA information can be obtained at www.ICGtesting.com
Printed in the USA
BVOW03s1045220114

342660BV00011B/504/P